But Wisdom ever plays before the Lord,
delighting in the company of men;
and so the music's master, with his hoard
of laughter-tempered learning, took a pen
and wrote this counterpoint — God be adored! —
in which the numbers skip like lambs. Amen.

Mark Amorose,
from "On Listening to Haydn"

Playing Before the Lord

THE LIFE AND WORK OF
JOSEPH HAYDN

Calvin R. Stapert

WILLIAM B. EERDMANS PUBLISHING COMPANY

GRAND RAPIDS, MICHIGAN / CAMBRIDGE, U.K.

Published 2014 by

Wm. B. Eerdmans Publishing Co.

2140 Oak Industrial Drive N.E., Grand Rapids, Michigan 49505 /

P.O. Box 163, Cambridge CB3 9PU U.K.

Printed in the United States of America

20 19 18 17 16 15 14   7 6 5 4 3 2 1

Library of Congress Cataloging-in-Publication Data

Stapert, Calvin, 1942-, author.

Playing before the lord: the life and work of Joseph Haydn / Calvin R. Stapert.

pages   cm

Includes bibliographical references and index.

ISBN 978-0-8028-6852-7 (pbk.: alk. paper)

1. Haydn, Joseph, 1732-1809. 2. Composers — Austria — Biography.

I. Title.

ML410.H4S785   2014

780.92 — dc23

[B]

2013038043

www.eerdmans.com

Dedicated to
my children, their spouses, and my grandchildren
and to the memory of
Jonathan and Elizabeth

Contents

Preface   ix

Illustrations   xv

1. Ancestry and Early Boyhood in Rohrau and Hainburg
   — To 1740   1

2. Choirboy at St. Stephen's Cathedral, Vienna
   — The 1740s   9

3. From the Streets of Vienna to a Pilgrimage,
   and Then to a Wretched Attic
   — The Early 1750s   17

4. From Freelance Musician to Music Director for Count Morzin
   — The Later 1750s   26

5. Vice-Kapellmeister at the Esterházy Court
   — 1761-66   39

6. Symphonies and Baryton Music for Prince Nicolaus
   — 1762-68   53

7. Kapellmeister at Eszterháza Palace and
   Composer of Church Music
   — 1768-72   69

8. *Sturm und Drang:* Symphonies
   — 1768-72   82

Contents

9. From Divertimenti to Sonatas and Quartets
   — The Late 1760s and Early 1770s   99

10. Opera at Eszterháza
    — 1768-83   III

11. Symphonies and Sonatas during the Peak Opera Years
    — 1773-81   124

12. "New and Special" String Quartets and a Special Friendship
    — The 1780s, Part 1   140

13. New, Revived, and Unique Genres
    — The 1780s, Part 2   155

14. Music for London, Vienna, Paris, and the King of Naples
    — The 1780s, Part 3   167

15. From Vienna to London
    — 1790-91   182

16. Life in London and a Return to Vienna
    — 1791-93   196

17. Back in London
    — 1794-95   210

18. Back to Vienna: A Fruitful Final Harvest
    — 1795-1802   228

19. Infirmity and Death
    — 1803-09   244

20. Music for Troubled Times   251

Appendix: Outline of Haydn's *Creation*   259

Glossary   263

Works Cited   268

Index of Names, Places, and Terms   274

Index of Haydn's Works   280

If you know any music by Haydn, you probably know his symphony nick-named "Surprise." At least you know the theme of the second movement. The tune is simple in the extreme. One could be excused for thinking it naïve or childlike (or, more negatively, childish). Be that as it may, that tune defines Haydn in the minds of many. Furthermore, his own nick-name, "Papa," suggests a likeable old man, and the simple tune perhaps suggests a touch of senility — a "second childhood."

You may also know that the symphony got its nickname because in the midst of that tune — which is as soft and gentle as it is simple — at the most unexpected moment, the full orchestra plays a single loud chord. Haydn supposedly said he did it to "wake up the ladies." This has provided the second ingredient that has defined Haydn in the popular imagination — he is humorous or witty (or, more negatively, silly).

So Haydn, if he is known at all, has become viewed as a composer of nice, congenial music that is often humorous and filled with simple, likeable tunes. There is truth in that view, but it is far too narrow for a composer whose music includes *Stabat mater dolorosa* and the *Seven Last Words of Christ on the Cross* as well as comic operas, masses as well as Scottish folksongs, a "Trauer" Symphony as well as a "Surprise" Symphony, and whose greatest work, *The Creation,* celebrates everything from the stars to the lowly worm through music that can be as terrifying as chaos, as glorious as the heavens, as wild as the sea, and as peaceful as a limpid brook. What C. S. Lewis said about the poet Spenser is equally true of Haydn. His work "reaches up to the songs of angels" and down to "the horror of fertile chaos. And between these two extremes comes all the multiplicity of human life."[1] Although Haydn's

---

1. C. S. Lewis, *The Allegory of Love* (New York: Oxford University Press, 1958), p. 359.

music does reach both ends of that gamut, it dwells more often between the extremes, amidst the "multiplicity of human life." And although his view of life favors brightness over gloom and the comic over the tragic, it is neither less profound nor less true for that. Haydn, by all accounts a devout Christian, would have agreed with Jeremy Begbie: "Any music which dares to bear the name 'Christian' will resound with the heartbeat of joy."[2]

You will not have to read very far — in fact you have probably read far enough already — to realize that I love Haydn and think he belongs very near the top of any list of greatest composers. But since at such exalted heights it is pointless to rank, I have no intention of arguing for a specific place for Haydn in the pantheon of composers. If I am bothered that Haydn's stock has slipped since the days when he was widely recognized as Europe's greatest living composer, it is not for his sake. Though at one time it mattered quite a bit to him, he has no such concerns anymore. But it does matter to me. They say "misery loves company." Perhaps. But it is more to the point here that "joy loves company." Seventeenth-century minister and metaphysical poet Thomas Traherne said, "You never enjoy the world aright, till you so love the beauty of enjoying it, that you are covetous and earnest to persuade others to enjoy it."[3] That is how I feel about Haydn's music. I am "covetous and earnest to persuade others to enjoy it," and to that end I have written this book.

To enjoy Haydn's music it is not necessary to know the man who made it, but I think it helps. In nearly four decades of teaching music, I have found that students (and, I suspect, people in general) are interested in people. So it is not surprising that it was often easier to pique students' interest in an unfamiliar piece or repertory of music if they knew something about the person, or people, who made that music. Of course, it works the other way too. Interest in music often leads to curiosity about those who made it — which in turn can lead to better understanding and fuller appreciation of music that is already enjoyed. So this book is a biography. Of course music was at the center of Haydn's life, and it is his music that still "lingers on." But since I am convinced that his music has more to offer us than it can give if it merely lingers around the periphery of our musical lives, this book is also a listener's guide — which implies, of course, that listening needs to go along with reading. Fortunately most of Haydn's vast

2. Jeremy Begbie, *Music in God's Purposes* (Edinburgh: The Handsel Press, Ltd., 1989), p. 18.
3. Thomas Traherne, *Centuries* (Wilton, Conn.: Morehouse Publishing, 1985), The First Century, 31, p. 15.

output has been recorded, and much of it is readily available, if not from your local music store, then online.

The book is a listener's guide on several different levels. At the broadest level, it gives an overview of Haydn's huge and diverse output. At a deeper and more specific level, it gives a wide range of general descriptions or characterizations of pieces or repertories. At the most detailed level, it provides analyses of a few pieces (or of small parts or specific aspects of them). None of these levels, including the survey, is complete. Although the survey is comprehensive, not every piece (or even every genre) gets mentioned. And, of course, in a book of this scope, description and analysis have to be selective — increasingly selective as they get more detailed. So you will encounter, for example, an analysis not of Symphony 6 or even of just one movement of it. Rather, I offer an analysis of part of the first movement, and that is limited mainly to matters of balance and proportion. This should not be taken to mean that balance and proportion are what that music is "all about," or even that they are the most important aspects of that music. Balance and proportion are important aspects in all of Haydn's music, and the exposition of the first movement of Symphony 6 seems to me to be a particularly good example, both in the sense that Haydn does it very well and that it is relatively easy to understand. Other descriptions and analyses will focus on other aspects — such as harmony, rhythm, orchestration, or motivic development. They are all important in varying degrees in all pieces, and I hope that a sampling from a variety of pieces will enable you to listen more perceptively to other pieces. As a listener's guide, then, this book is like a trail guide. Such a guide might give a hiker a general overview of the terrain and point out some things to look for along the way — a broad vista here and a stand of virgin oaks there, here a habitat for a rare species of warbler and there the remains of an early settlement. And just as the trail guide, incomplete though it is, can open a hiker's eyes to more of what there is to see along the trail, so too this book, as a listener's guide, can alert a listener's ears to what there is to hear in Haydn's music.

That being said, I still need to add something about music analysis. Survey and description do not usually present problems for a general reader, but analysis may turn some away. I am fully aware that some are frightened or simply "turned off" by anything that smells of music theory and technical jargon — and with good reason. Much analysis is cold and abstract, and much analytical writing is nearly impenetrable. But they need not be. I will not be so brash as to claim that I have avoided both problems, but I can assure you that I am aware of them and have made a serious effort to avoid them. I do not promise easy reading all the way through, but I have kept parts that might be "rough sledding" relatively short and infrequent. I have avoided technical jargon as much as possible, but — I confess — I have not eliminated it. Sometimes eliminating technical terms makes a description more, not less, complicated. Technical terms, if used judiciously, keep language from becoming overly cumbersome. It is much less cumbersome to say "The recapitulation presents the main theme as a fugal exposition" than it is to write the same thing in a paragraph in which definitions of the terms "recapitulation" and "fugal exposition" are embedded — and without those definitions using other technical terms (for example "sonata" and "tonic key") that would themselves need defining. Such a paragraph would be, if not absolutely impenetrable, at least much more difficult to understand than the original sentence — provided, of course, that the technical terms in the original sentence were understood. Hence I have provided a glossary that includes basic definitions of the musical forms involved.

The glossary (plus my effort to keep the need for it at a minimum) should keep the analytical parts of the book from being far from impenetrable. But won't they still be cold and abstract? To that I can only respond by saying that technical matters of form, texture, harmony, rhythm, phrasing, and the like are not *merely* technical. They usually, if not always, have an effect on the expressive, rhetorical, or dramatic character of the music. The language might seem cold and abstract, but the music it is describing is not. The purpose of the language is to guide the hearing, not to be a substitute for it. And sometimes the best language to guide our hearing is technical.

But technical language is not the only language that can help guide our hearing. Non-technical, affective-expressive terms can provide helpful description and characterization of music. Many listeners, however, think (or were taught to think) that all non-technical, affective language is merely subjective. In *The Abolition of Man,* C. S. Lewis quotes an elementary English textbook as an example of that all-too-common view. The authors of the textbook wrote: "When the man said *That* [a waterfall] *is sublime,* he appeared to be making a remark about the waterfall. Actually he was not making a remark about the waterfall, but a remark about his own feelings."[4] But in spite of what is commonly thought (and taught), non-technical language is not *necessarily* subjective. The waterfall alluded to in the above quotation was being viewed by poet Samuel Taylor Coleridge and another tourist. In her diary, Dorothy Wordsworth, wife of poet William Wordsworth, tells us that

4. C. S. Lewis, *The Abolition of Man* (New York: The Macmillan Company, 1965), p. 14.

Coleridge, who is always good-natured enough to enter into conversation with anybody whom he meets in his way, began to talk with the gentleman, who observed that it was a *majestic* waterfall. Coleridge was delighted with the accuracy of the epithet, particularly as he had been settling in his own mind the precise meaning of the words grand, majestic, sublime, etc., and had discussed the subject with William at some length the day before. "Yes, sir," says Coleridge, "it is a majestic waterfall."[5]

Like waterfalls and all sorts of other things, music, as Aristotle said, has character, and words used to describe or characterize it may be accurate or inaccurate, true or false, in varying degrees depending on the listener's attentiveness and perceptivity. If the affective language comes from a musically perceptive listener, it probably says something true about the music. Technical analysis and affective description both have a role to play in helping us hear music more accurately and fully, with greater understanding and enjoyment.

The Hoboken Catalogue

The standard catalogue of Haydn's vast output was made by Anthony van Hoboken (1887-1983). In it every work is identified by a Roman numeral indicating its genre and an Arabic numeral for the specific work — for example Symphony 64 is Hob. I:64, *The Creation* is Hob. XXI:2, and the Scottish folksong "Lassie wi' the gowden hair" is Hob. XXXIa:272. Most of the time, the complete Hoboken numbers are not necessary for identification. The symphonies, for example, can be simply and unmistakably identified by the Arabic numbers. I will also use just the Hoboken Arabic number to identify keyboard sonatas and trios. Although there are competing (and maybe better) numbering systems in use for those genres, the Hoboken numbers still have wider currency. The Hoboken numbers can be dispensed with entirely for the string quartets. I identify them (as they customarily are) by opus and number (for example Opus 20, No. 6). Vocal works can be identified by their titles (for example *The Seasons*), or if necessary by title and key (for example *Salve Regina* in E), but when confusion is possible (for example there are two *Te Deums* in C) I give the complete Hoboken numbers.

5. Dorothy Wordsworth, *Recollections of a Tour Made in Scotland A.D. 1803,* 3rd ed. (Edinburgh: David Douglas, 1844), p. 37.

Keyboard Instruments

Keyboard instruments were changing during Haydn's time. Harpsichords and clavichords were giving way to fortepianos (also called pianofortes), the immediate ancestor of the modern piano. Even after the fortepiano had become the instrument of choice, much of the music could still be played on any keyboard. Composers and publishers, of course, did not want to turn away potential customers simply because they had not traded in their harpsichords and clavichords for fortepianos. Therefore, they continued to use the generic term "clavier." I will follow suit by consistently using "clavier" or the English equivalent, "keyboard," rather than specific instrument names.

A Note about Sources

Haydn biographies began to be written early. The two most important are by G. A. Griesinger and A. C. Dies. Both men knew Haydn well and had extensive conversations with him late in his life. I quote from them often. Both were translated by Vernon Gotwals in *Haydn: Two Contemporary Portraits* (Madison, Wisc.: University of Wisconsin Press, 1968). Throughout the book I also quote frequently from other sources that are contemporary (or nearly so) with Haydn. Like everyone who has studied Haydn in the last three decades and counting, I am incalculably indebted to the indefatigable H. C. Robbins Landon. His monumental five-volume work, *Haydn: Chronicle and Works* (Bloomington: Indiana University Press, 1976-1980) has brought mountains of relevant eighteenth- and early-nineteenth-century source material within easy reach. Unless otherwise noted I took all quotations from the two biographers from Gotwals's translation, and all other quotations from contemporary sources from Landon's volumes. Rather than overburdening some pages with footnotes, I have cited them parenthetically in the text.

Obviously, my indebtedness extends beyond Landon and Gotwals to the work of scholars identified in the footnotes, and beyond them to many individuals whose work is not acknowledged. I thank them all for making my work sometimes easier, sometimes harder, and (in either case) better — though of course the flaws that remain are mine.

**Portrait of Franz Joseph Haydn in 1791
by Thomas Bush Hardy (1842-1897); Royal College of Music, London.**
(Photo: Erich Lessing / Art Resource, NY.)

Pastel drawing of the birthplace of Haydn in Rohrau, Austria;
Museum der Stadt Wien.

(Photo: Alfredo Dagli Orti / The Art Archive at Art Resource, NY.)

**Pen and ink drawing of the Haydn family making music: Matthias Haydn,
Joseph's father, Anna Maria Koller, Haydn's mother, and Joseph, the second
of twelve children; Haydn Museum, Rohrau, Austria.**

(Photo: Erich Lessing / Art Resource, NY.)

Portrait of Nicolaus Joseph I, Prince Esterházy "the Magnificent" (1714-1790), Austrian Fieldmarshal and Haydn's patron and employer, ca. 1775, by an anonymous 18th-century artist; Hungarian National Gallery, Budapest.
(Photo: Alfredo Dagli Orti / Art Resource, NY.)

A concert hall in Esterházy Castle, where many of Haydn's symphonies were first performed while he was Kapellmeister; Eisenstadt, Austria.

(Photo: Erich Lessing / Art Resource, NY.)

Scale model of the theater in Eszterháza Palace where many of Haydn's operas premiered during his time as Kapellmeister for Prince Nicolaus I (the theater itself no longer exists); Haydn Museum, Rohrau, Austria.

(Photo: Erich Lessing / Art Resource, NY.)

**Portrait of Johann Peter Salomon (1745-1815),
Haydn's concertmaster and impresario in London,
by Thomas Hardy (1757-1804); Royal Academy of Arts, London.**
(Photo: Erich Lessing / Art Resource, NY.)

Haydn, in his last public appearance, at the performance of *The Creation*
celebrating his 76th birthday, in the Great Hall of Vienna University,
March 27, 1808; Museum der Stadt Wien.

(Photo: Alfredo Dagli Orti / The Art Archive at Art Resource, NY.)

CHAPTER I

Ancestry and Early Boyhood in Rohrau and Hainburg

TO 1740

Just see the little house, and such a great man was born in it.

BEETHOVEN

An April Fool?

Franz Joseph Haydn was baptized on April 1, 1732, in St. Vitus's Church in the village of Rohrau near the Austrian-Hungarian border. Some have taken April 1 to be his birth date, but it is more likely that he was born on March 31, the day before his baptism. On at least one occasion, however, Haydn claimed to have been born on April Fool's Day. He told his student Sigismund Neukomm: "I was born on 1 April, and that is the date found in my father's *Hausbuch* — but my brother Michael maintains I was born on the 31st of March because he doesn't want it said that I came into the world as an April Fool" (Landon 1, p. 44). One gets the impression that music's wittiest composer, the composer whose best-known work is called the "Surprise" Symphony — and whose works contain no end of surprises — thought it would be appropriate if he had been born on April Fool's Day. Whatever the date of his birth, Haydn would surprise the world with his rise from humble, unpromising origins to become one of the world's greatest composers.

Ancestors

Haydn's ancestors, at least as far back as his paternal and maternal great-grandparents, earned their living by the work of their hands and the sweat of their brows. They were farmers, skilled workers, artisans, and common laborers. None were lawyers, doctors, clergy, or other educated professionals, and none were musicians. Though generally not impoverished, they could rarely feel financially secure. And for all of them the insecurity of life was increased by the constant threat and frequent outbreak of war.

The greatest danger came from the expansionist ambitions of the Ottoman (Turkish) Empire. During the seventeeth century, it was at the peak of its power. It controlled most of northern Africa along the Mediterranean Sea. Its territory continued down the western side of the Red Sea and up the west coast of the Arabian Peninsula. To the east it continued as far as the Persian Gulf and the Caspian Sea. It surrounded the Black Sea and went along the eastern and northern shores of the Mediterranean and up the Adriatic Sea almost to Venice. It controlled much of southeastern Europe, including Hungary, and it had designs on Austria.

In 1683 an enormous Ottoman army led by grand vizier Kara Mustafa Pascha besieged Vienna for about two months. But on September 11 and 12, 1683, in the Battle of Vienna, an army of Austrians and Poles under the leadership of the Polish king, Jan Sobieski, defeated the Ottoman army, putting an end to Ottoman expansion. In 1686 the Hungarian city Buda was liberated, and with the signing of the Treaty of Karlowitz in 1699, the Ottoman Empire lost control of most of its European territories, including Hungary, which again came under the rule of the Austrian branch of the House of Habsburg. So by the end of the seventeenth century the Turkish threat had been turned back. Had it succeeded, who can tell what the consequences would have been for Austrian culture, in particular the Viennese musical culture that was to flourish so brilliantly during the last half of the eighteenth century — and well beyond — with Haydn at its head? Whatever the consequences might have been, they would have been momentous. No wonder Austrians have celebrated the victory at the Battle of Vienna ever since.

Coincidentally, but appropriately, Haydn's life as a musician was bracketed by involvement in those celebrations. When Joseph (he never went by the name Franz) was six years old and going to school in Hainburg, the town celebrated *Jubilaeum Universale* to commemorate the 1683 victory "over Turk and Heathen" (Landon 1, p. 54). Joseph sang in the choir.

At the other end of his life, the last major composition he completed was the *Harmoniemesse,* first performed in 1802 on the Feast of the Most Holy Name of Mary. In 1683 Pope Innocent XI had made it a universal feast to commemorate Jan Sobieski's victory, a victory believed to be the result of Mary's intercession.

Although the advance of the Ottoman army had been turned back, before it was halted it had laid waste large parts of Hungary, Rumania, and Croatia, as well as the borderland of Austria, homeland of Haydn's ancestors. Hainburg was among the towns that the Turks devastated. They killed so many of its inhabitants that one of its streets came to be named "Blutgasse" ("blood street"). Among its inhabitants were a castle laborer and his wife, Caspar and Elisabeth Haydn, Joseph's great-grandparents. They were probably among the casualties of the slaughter, but their oldest son, Thomas, an assistant wheelwright, survived. In 1687 he married Catharina Blaiminger. The two would become Joseph's paternal grandparents.

In 1699 Catharina gave birth to their sixth child, Mathias Haydn, who would become the father of Joseph. Thomas died two years later, leaving Catharina with Mathias and his five older siblings. Catharina soon remarried another wheelwright from Hainburg with whom she had four more children. So Mathias was brought up by his mother and a cantankerous stepfather in a household of five older siblings and four younger half-siblings. The inevitable tension and insecurity in his boyhood home were exacerbated by the unstable political situation. Although the Turkish threat had been repelled, the years of his boyhood were hardly peaceful. Hainburg and other Austrian towns along the Austrian-Hungarian border were continually threatened by the Hungarian *kuruzzen,* peasant armies under Prince Francis II Rákóczy. Until 1711 when a peace agreement was reached, Hainburg was filled with billeted soldiers and refugees. No doubt Mathias's stepfather, like every adult male, had to take his turn at keeping watch on the town walls and at digging and serving in the trenches around the town.

The situation was similarly precarious for the Koller family. Joseph's mother, Anna Maria Koller, was born in Rohrau in 1707. Her father was Lorenz Koller, a farmer who, as a boy, had witnessed the Ottoman invasion. He became a widower at a young age, remarried in 1702 at age twenty-seven, lost all his possessions in 1704 to marauding *kuruzzen,* rebuilt his house, and then saw it burned in 1706. Anna Maria was born the next year. Meanwhile, Mathias apprenticed as a wheelwright with his stepfather, but left Hainburg at age eighteen. His whereabouts for the next ten years are largely unknown, but in 1727 he settled in Rohrau and married Anna Maria in November of 1728. Four years later, Anna Maria would give birth to their second child, Franz Joseph.

Rohrau

Rohrau is located on the river Leitha about thirty miles southeast of Vienna. A. C. Dies, one of Haydn's first biographers, described it as an unimportant market town consisting of only about sixty-five houses. The house where Joseph was born was typical — a low building of clay with a thatched roof susceptible to fires. Much of the land was low-lying and apt to flood. As Beethoven lay bed-ridden during his final weeks, a friend brought him a picture of Haydn's birthplace. Another friend reported: "The picture caused him great pleasure; when I came at noon, he showed it to me at once: 'Look, I got this today. Just see the little house, and such a great man was born in it. Your father must have a frame made for me; I'm going to hang it up."[1]

The ruling family in Rohrau was the Harrach family. Carl Anton Harrach was the count when Mathias and Anna Maria were married. Prior to their marriage Anna Maria worked as a cook in the Rohrau Castle. At the time no one would have dreamed that, more than sixty years later, Count Harrach's grandson would erect a monument in the castle gardens to the son of his grandfather's cook. The grandson wrote to Dies: "I considered it fitting and proper, as well as an honor for my park, to erect in the castle precincts surrounding his birthplace a stone monument to the laudably celebrated J. Haydn" (Dies, p. 161). He placed the monument at a bend in the river where it was deep and broad so a canal could be dug to form an island. He planted the island with poplars, and along the bank he planted weeping willows, plane trees, tulip trees, and other exotic species. A plaque read:

1. Gerhard von Breuning, *Memories of Beethoven: From the House of the Black-Robed Spaniards,* trans. by Henry Mins and Maynard Solomon (Cambridge: Cambridge University Press, 1992), p. 98.

TO THE MEMORY
OF JOSEPH HAYDN
THE DEATHLESS MASTER
OF MUSIC,
TO WHOM EAR AND HEART
CONTENDING DO HOMAGE

Father and Mother

After his marriage to the elder Count's cook, Mathias continued to work as a wheelwright. He also owned some farmland and a few cattle. He was a hard-working man who provided a decent living for his family. The towns-people respected him and chose him to be *Marktrichter* (village magistrate) as his father-in-law had been before him. As magistrate he was responsible for "the good conduct of the population and had to keep a sharp lookout for adultery or excessive gambling. He had to see that people went to church and did not break the Sunday rest. It was his job to allot among the inhabitants of Rohrau the labor required by the patron, Count Harrach, and he was responsible for keeping the local roads in good repair."[2]

Anna Maria bore twelve children between 1730 and 1745. Joseph was her second child. Of the twelve, only six survived childhood. (Mathias would remarry after her death in 1756 and have five more children, but all of them died in infancy.) She was industrious and orderly in her management of the busy household. Haydn told Dies that she "was accustomed to neatness, industry, and order, which qualities she sternly required of her children from their tenderest years" (p. 80). She was also deeply religious and hoped that Joseph would become a priest. "My parents," said Haydn, "taught me neatness and order in earliest youth, and these two things have become second nature to me." Dies added: "He also owed it to his parents that they had encouraged him in the fear of God and, of necessity because they were poor, in diligence and thrift. Plain virtues that you very seldom meet in our young geniuses" (p. 79).

2. Karl Geiringer, *Haydn: A Creative Life in Music,* 3rd rev. and enlarged ed. (Berkeley: University of California Press, 1982), p. 7.

Music in the Haydn Household

Although neither parent had any musical training, there was music in the Haydn household. Dies wrote that Mathias "learned to play the harp a little and, because he liked to sing, to accompany himself on the harp as well as he could. Afterwards, when he was married, he kept the habit of singing a little to amuse himself" (p. 80). G. A. Griesinger, another of Haydn's early biographers, added that "Anna Marie used to sing to the harp" (p. 9). The children also participated in the music-making. Mathias insisted that the children "join in his concerts, to learn the songs, and to develop their singing voice. When his father sang, Joseph at the age of five used to accompany him as children will by playing with a stick on a piece of wood that his childish powers of imagination transformed into a violin."

Mathias also organized concerts among the neighbors, and Joseph's talent became generally known in Rohrau. "When the talk was of singing, all were unanimous in praise of the cartwright's son and could not commend enough his fine voice." More important than the impression Joseph's singing made on his neighbors was the deep and lasting impression the songs made on him. As Griesinger put it, "The melodies of these songs were so deeply stamped in Joseph Haydn's memory that he could still recall them in advanced old age."

Joseph was not the only one of the siblings to benefit from the informal music-making in their home. His younger brothers also became musicians. Michael became a distinguished composer in his own right — now known mainly for his church music — whose work was much admired by his famous brother, and Johann Evangelist became a singer in the Esterházy Chapel Choir, a position that came to him more because of his brother's and the prince's benevolence than his own talent.

When Joseph was five, the family music-making led to his first formal education. Mathias Franck, a schoolteacher and distant cousin from Hainburg, heard Haydn sing. He noted Joseph's talent for music and urged the parents to send him to school in Hainburg to help him acquire "an art which in time would without fail open to him the prospect 'of becoming a clergyman'" (p. 9). No doubt that was a persuasive selling point with Joseph's pious parents, especially his mother.

School in Hainburg

It was probably in the spring of 1738 that Joseph went to Hainburg, a small town about eight miles northeast of Rohrau. There he lived with the Franck family, attended Franck's school, and sang in the choir of the Church of Saints Philip and James, where Franck served as choir director. In his auto-biographical sketch in a letter of 1776, Haydn referred to his experience in Hainburg: "Almighty God (to Whom alone I owe the most profound grat-itude) endowed me, especially in music, with such proficiency that even in my 6th year I was able to sing some Masses in the choir-loft, and to play a little on the harpsichord and violin" (Landon 2, p. 398).

The school in Hainburg had an enrollment of about seventy to eighty students. The school day began at 7:00 a.m. The students went to mass at 10:00 a.m. and then home for lunch. Their studies began again at noon and continued until 3:00 p.m. Music was taught in the afternoon, after the stu-dents had finished classes. In addition to the basics of reading, writing, and arithmetic, the students learned from the Bible and the catechism. They learned writing by copying from Ecclesiasticus (The Wisdom of Sirach) and *The Imitation of Christ* by Thomas à Kempis. The Hainburg "Instruc-tions for the School Master" give a good picture of the instruction that was expected. Franck, assisted by two precepts, was to "instruct the children in good behaviour and rectitude by giving them good lessons every day, and also in declamation, dictation, and written exercises which are to be corrected, [and] [e]very six weeks there were examinations and reports."[3] And, of course, he was in charge of discipline. The "Instructions" say that "punishments are to be meted out justly (as is appropriate to small children by birching and caning) and not by pulling their hair and other improper forms of hard beatings" (Landon 1, p. 52).

Haydn told Griesinger that he was instructed "in reading and writing, in catechism, in singing, and in almost all wind and string instruments, even in timpani. 'I shall owe it to this man [Franck] even in my grave,' Haydn often said, 'that he set me to so many different things, although I received in the process more thrashings than food.'"

Regarding tympani playing, Haydn told the following incident to Dies.

---

3. H. C. Robbins Landon, *Haydn: Chronicle and Works,* vol. 1 (Bloomington, Ind.: Indi-ana University Press, 1980), p. 52.

> It was Rogation Week, a time of many processions. Franck was in great difficulty because of the death of his drummer. He cast his eyes upon Joseph, who would have to learn the kettledrums in a hurry and thus resolve the difficulty. He showed Joseph the elements of drumming and then left him alone. Joseph took a little basket of the sort country people use to bake bread, covered it with a cloth, set his invention on an upholstered armchair, and drummed away so enthusiastically that he never noticed what a dust was raised by the meal in the basket, ruining the chair. He received a rebuke for it, but his teacher was easily calmed when he observed with astonishment that Joseph was becoming a perfect drummer so quickly. (pp. 81-82)

A portrait of Franck still hung in Haydn's house when he died, a testament to his abiding gratitude. He further showed his gratitude by bequeathing one hundred gulden to Franck's daughter in his will.

Joseph was not in Hainburg for long. In an autobiographical sketch in a 1776 letter, Haydn wrote, "When I was 7 the late *Capellmeister* von Reutter [of St. Stephen's Cathedral in Vienna] passed through Hainburg and quite accidentally heard my weak but pleasant voice" (Landon 2, p. 398). Reutter was on a recruiting trip when he stopped in Hainburg to visit an old friend, the parish priest. He informed Reutter about Joseph, praising his voice and musical talent. Reutter summoned Joseph and Franck to an audition. During the audition the poorly nourished Joseph

> cast longing glances at the cherries that were sitting on the table. Reutter tossed a few handfuls into his hat, and seemed well pleased with the Latin and Italian strophes that Haydn had to sing. "Can you make a trill?" asked Reutter. "No," said Haydn, "for not even my cousin [Franck] can do that." This answer greatly embarrassed the schoolteacher, and Reutter laughed uproariously. He demonstrated the mechanical principles of trilling, Haydn imitated him, and at the third attempt succeeded. "You shall stay with me," said Reutter. (Griesinger, pp. 9-10)

Soon thereafter Haydn left Hainburg for Vienna to be a choir boy at St. Stephen's Cathedral.

CHAPTER 2

Choirboy at St. Stephen's Cathedral, Vienna

THE 1740S

Hey! What are you up to there, boy? Aren't two voices enough for you, you little blockhead?

REUTTER

I was once a choir-boy, Reutter took me from Hainburg to St. Stephen's in Vienna. I was diligent. When my comrades went to play, I took my little Clavier under my arm and went up to the attic, where I could practice undisturbed.

HAYDN

Vienna

The walled Austrian city of Vienna, to which eight-year-old Joseph now moved, was the capital of the Holy Roman Empire. It had been the residence of the Habsburg court since the fifteenth century. During the sixteenth and seventeenth centuries the city had faced serious threats from the Ottoman Empire, but a remarkable resurgence followed the 1683 defeat of the Turks. Population grew rapidly, and rebuilding brought the city to the height of its glory. By 1740, when Joseph came to be a choirboy at St. Stephen's Cathedral, Vienna's population had more than doubled from the eighty thousand it had been around 1700. Politically and culturally it was the most important city in the German-speaking world and a melting pot of many ethnic and linguistic groups.

Located in northeast Austria on the south bank of the Danube, Vienna is surrounded to the west and south by the wooded, rolling foothills of the Alps — the Vienna Woods (memorialized in the waltz by Johann Strauss II) — and to the north and east by the Little Hungarian Plain. Like Rohrau and Hainburg, its neighboring villages near the border of Austria and Hungary, Vienna had a substantial number of Hungarians and Croatians mixed among the predominant Austrians. Johann Pezzl (1756-1823), in his *Sketches of Vienna,* wrote that "you can often meet the Hungarian, striding stiffly, with his fur-lined dolman, his close-fitting trousers almost to his ankles, and his long pigtail."[1] You would also meet significant numbers of Moravians and Bohemians from north of the Danube. Though German was the predominant language, you would also hear the languages of Hungarians and various Slavic people; and since Vienna was the capital of the far-flung Holy Roman Empire, you would hear Italian and French as well. On October 1, 1740, not long after Joseph moved to Vienna (we do not know exactly when he moved), Emperor Charles VI died. Maria Theresa, his twenty-three-year-old daughter, succeeded him. Despite the growth and rebuilding that had been going on in Vienna during Charles's reign, he left the new and inexperienced empress with many problems, in particular a poor economy and looming wars.

During the decade of the 1740s, Austria was involved in the War of the Austrian Succession (1740-1748), which included the First and Second Silesian Wars waged against the Prussian king, Frederick the Great. In the end, with the signing of the treaty of Aix-la-Chapelle, Austria did not fare too badly. She lost parts of Silesia and a few duchies in Italy, but the Pragmatic Sanction of 1713 was accepted. This allowed a woman to inherit the Austrian throne and thus legitimized Maria Theresa's authority. In 1745 her husband, Francis Stephen, was elected Holy Roman Emperor, but Maria Theresa was the *de facto* ruler.

As a young boy from a rural village, Joseph must have been dazzled by what he saw of the splendor and cosmopolitan character of Vienna. Soon after his arrival he probably sang at two services in St. Stephen's related to the change of rulers: the commemorative service on October 20, 1740, for Charles VI, and the ceremonial service at the Oath of Fealty to Maria Theresa on November 22. On other occasions, too, his participation in the St. Stephen's choir gave him glimpses of the larger world around him, mu-

---

1. Quoted from Rebecca Green, "A Letter from the Wilderness: Revisiting Haydn's Esterházy Environments," in *The Cambridge Companion to Haydn* (Cambridge: Cambridge University Press, 2005), p. 26.

sical as well as political. On February 13, 1741, eight-year-old Joseph sang at the requiem service of one of Vienna's leading composers, Johann Joseph Fux, whose important treatise on counterpoint would in a few years play an important role in his development as a composer, and later would be a basis for his own teaching. Another leading musician of the preceding generation, Antonio Vivaldi, died five months later on July 28. He had recently come to Vienna, most likely to stage one or more of his operas, but perhaps also in the hope of obtaining a post from Charles VI. Charles's death, however, ended any such aspirations, and Vivaldi died in Vienna a pauper, having squandered his once substantial fortune. Six choirboys, all that could be afforded, provided the only music at his funeral. It is tempting to think that Joseph was one of them.

Despite being involved in the music making at important occasions, Joseph, at his young age, could hardly have been aware of the political issues facing his homeland and the new empress, and no more than vaguely aware of the place composers like Fux and Vivaldi had in the wider musical world. His initiation into those wider worlds had barely begun. His occasional and tangential contact with the rich and powerful of society afforded no hint that he would one day be able to say to Griesinger, "I have associated with emperors, kings, and many great gentlemen and have heard many flattering things from them" (p. 55). While he remained a choirboy at St. Stephen's, his initiation into the wider musical world would remain relatively narrow, but the depth of his immersion in the music at St. Stephen's made up for whatever it lacked in breadth.

St. Stephen's Cathedral

St. Stephen's Cathedral was first built during the twelfth century. During the ensuing three centuries it was greatly enlarged and transformed in style from Romanesque to Gothic. In 1469 Vienna was established as a separate diocese with St. Stephen's as the seat of its bishop. It became the seat of the archbishop in 1723. An imposing building located in the center of town, its height of 137 meters made it Vienna's (and all of Austria's) largest church building. It was apparently less than inspiring to the music historian Charles Burney (1726-1814), who wrote: "The church is a dark, dirty, and dismal old Gothic building, though richly ornamented; in it are hung all the trophies of war, taken from the Turks and other enemies of the house of Austria, for more than a century past, which gives it very much the appearance of an old wardrobe."[2] But to young Joseph the building must have seemed more like what Karl Geiringer describes — a building that fills an observer "with awe and amazement," whose "Gothic architecture seems to lift one from earth into higher and more spiritual spheres." And when he says that "every step brings new surprises and wonders," and that the building "is so full of power, so imbued with the mystery of life in all its aspects, whether lofty or humorous, that it would be impossible ever to know it completely or to plumb its many profundities,"[3] it seems that he is also describing the musical oeuvre Joseph would grow up to produce.

According to tradition, the imperial court worshiped at St. Stephen's on high feast days of the church year instead of at the court chapel. These and many other special days were celebrated with great pageantry which included elaborate processions. The Viennese, like Austrians in general, were very fond of processions. One such procession was for the celebration of the fiftieth anniversary of the priesthood of Vienna's cardinal archbishop Sigismund von Kollonicz in 1749.

> An enormous procession of clergy and dignitaries marched solemnly into the cathedral, which was lighted with myriads of candles. Archbishops, bishops, and prelates assisted at High Mass, all dressed in the most ornate robes and carrying gorgeous wreaths on their arms. Cardinal Kollonicz' wreath was of pure gold, a present from the Empress Maria Theresa, and the chalice he used was adorned by a magnificent wreath wrought in silver, a gift from the Queen of Portugal. The imperial family was carried to the building in golden sedan chairs and accompanied by the Knights of the Golden Fleece, the ambassadors, and the high nobility, all resplendent in robes of gold and silver encrusted with precious stones.[4]

On another occasion the massed choirs of St. Stephen's, the Jesuit College, and other institutions presented an oratorio by Reutter based on the life of Emperor Constantine in the Jesuit theater. Empress Maria Theresa and other ranking nobility and clergy were in attendance. And at an outdoor celebration in honor of St. John, the choirboys "performed on bril-

2. Quoted from David Wyn Jones, *The Life of Haydn* (Cambridge: Cambridge University Press, 2009), p. 10.

3. Karl Geiringer, *Haydn: A Creative Life in Music,* 3rd revised and enlarged edition (Berkeley: University of California Press, 1982), pp. 18-19.

4. Geiringer, *Haydn,* p. 22.

liantly lighted boats lying in the Danube Canal opposite the saint's statue, and on St. Nepomuk's Day an evening performance of a Reutter oratorio was given on the beautifully decorated Vienna 'High Bridge' in the presence of a distinguished audience."[5]

Musical Training at St. Stephen's

No doubt such occasions made a big impression on a young boy from the country. But it was the day-to-day training and musical experiences that prepared him for the future that was in store for him, a future that neither he nor anyone else could have imagined at the time. The biggest part of the training came in the daily preparation and singing of liturgical music. Twice a day, at High Mass and Vespers, the boys sang the liturgy. They sang music by contemporary composes like Reutter himself, as well as by composers of the preceding generation — Antonio Caldara, the aforementioned Fux, and Reutter's father — and earlier composers such as Alessandro Scarlatti and Gregorio Allegri, and even as far back as Palestrina. Some ten years of daily rehearsing and singing the great liturgical music of the Catholic Church provided invaluable training for the future composer.

But Haydn's musical training at St. Stephen's went beyond singing. "I learnt the art of singing, the harpsichord, and the violin, from very good masters" (Landon 2, p. 398), he wrote in his autobiographical letter of 1776. As a keyboardist, he never achieved great virtuosity, but his work-a-day capability enabled him to accompany singers, play the organ in church, teach, and use it as a tool for composing. As a violinist he became a fine player of chamber music. All this, of course, was invaluable, but his general education suffered. He received a little instruction in the basics — Latin, writing, arithmetic, and religion. The same could be said for music theory and composition. According to Griesinger

> no instruction in music theory was undertaken in the Choir School, and Haydn remembered receiving only two lessons in this from the excellent Reutter. But Reutter did encourage him to make whatever variations he liked on the motets and *Salves* that he had to sing through in the church, and this practice led him to ideas of his own which Reutter corrected. He also came to know Mattheson's *Der vollkommene Kapellmeister,* and

5. Geiringer, *Haydn,* pp. 21-22.

Fux's *Gradus ad Parnassum.* "I did, of course, have talent. With that and with great diligence I progressed." Stimulated by his imagination, he even ventured into composition for eight and sixteen parts. "I used to think then that it was all right if only the paper were pretty full. Reutter laughed at my immature output, at measures that no throat and no instrument could have executed, and he scolded me for composing for sixteen parts before I even understood two-part setting." (p. 10)

No doubt some of this is exaggeration. Dies concurred with Griesinger regarding Joseph's general education: "He did learn a little Latin. Everything else went by the board" (p. 86). But regarding music theory, Dies maintained that he had some basic instruction: "As soon as Joseph had received as much instruction as he needed to fulfill the duties of choirboy, the instruction came to an abrupt standstill" (pp. 85-86). That minimal instruction was probably based on an unpublished primer by Fux titled *Singfundament* ("Foundation of Singing").

Although Griesinger and Dies tell the story a bit differently, they agree that Joseph's early attempts at composition were self-motivated and that the criticism he received from Reutter was off-hand and sporadic at best. As Dies tells it:

Joseph was then already busy with composition in his spare time. Reutter surprised him once just as he had spread out a *Salve regina* in twelve parts on a yard-long sheet of paper. "Hey! What are you up to there, boy?" — Reutter looked over the long paper, laughed heartily at the copious sprinkling of *Salves,* still more at the boy's preposterous notion that he could compose in twelve parts, and added, "Aren't two voices enough for you, you little blockhead?".

Joseph knew how to profit from such lightly tossed off comments. His compositions took on a less monstrous appearance. (p. 87)

None of Joseph's juvenilia has survived, but the image of an eager boy taking on challenges that were beyond his ability and trying to impress his teacher by filling staff paper with lots of notes rings true. However, working through the treatises of Mattheson and Fux on his own most likely occurred after he left St. Stephen's. Nevertheless Griesinger's description of Joseph's "tireless exertion" (p. 10) fits with his later self-descriptions. Late in life he complained about having to compose music for the line of text in *The Seasons,* "O Fleiss, o edler Fleiss, von dir kommt alles Heil!" ("O industry, O noble industry, from you comes all blessedness!"). With character-istic wit he said "that he had been an industrious man all his life, but that it had never occurred to him to set industry to music" (Griesinger, p. 40).

Dies's comment about knowing "how to profit" from Reutter's com-ments also rings true. The earliest of his compositions to have come down to us is a *Missa brevis* in F. In 1805 the seventy-three-year-old Haydn re-membered writing it in 1749, perhaps while he was still at St. Stephen's. There is nothing "monstrous" about it. It is scored for four-part choir plus two violins and continuo, a typical scoring at the time. But in addition he gave it two solo soprano parts, probably with the intention of having them sung by himself and his younger brother Michael, who by that time was also a choirboy at St. Stephen's. The part-writing is hardly free from errors, but the work still pleased Haydn when he was an old man. "What specially pleases me," he told Dies, "is the melody, and a certain youthful fire, and this stirs me to write down several measures a day in order to provide the voices with a wind instrument accompaniment" (p. 117). The old man's fondness for this youthful work notwithstanding, it is not the product of a prodigy. The greatness to come was still on the far side of lots of hard work and experience.

Near the end of his life Haydn heard the Esterházy choir sing in Vi-enna. After the performance the old, frail man, who had reached the pin-nacle of his profession serving the Esterházy princes for most of his adult life, told the boys: "I was once a choir-boy, Reutter took me from Hainburg to St Stephen's in Vienna. I was diligent. When my comrades went to play, I took my little *Clavier* under my arm and went up to the attic, where I could practice undisturbed. When I sang a solo, the baker next to St. Stephen's al-ways gave me a bun as a present. Go on being good and diligent, and never forget about God" (Landon 1, p. 60).

Joseph's time at St. Stephen's was not all hard work. Dies tells us that he had "many funny adventures," and proceeds to tell us one.

> Once, when the [Habsburg] court was building the summer palace at Schönbrunn, Haydn had to sing there in the choir during Whitsuntide. Except when he had to be in the church, he used to play with the other boys, climbing the scaffolds around the construction and raising a reg-ular row on the staging. What happened? The boys suddenly beheld a lady. It was the Empress Maria Theresa herself, who ordered somebody to get the noisy boys off the scaffolds and to threaten them with a thrash-ing if they dared to show up there again. The next day Haydn, driven

by curiosity, climbed the scaffold alone, was caught, and sure enough collected the promised reward. (p. 80)

Dismissal

Change of voice, a close call, and a prank all figured into Joseph's end as a choirboy at St. Stephen's. The voice-change, of course, was inevitable — or almost inevitable.

> At the time there were still many *castrati* employed at the court and in the churches in Vienna, and the director of the Choir School [Reutter] doubtless supposed he was making young Haydn's fortune when he came up with a plan to turn him into a soprano, and actually asked the father for his permission. The father, whom this proposal utterly displeased, set off at once on the road for Vienna; and thinking that the operation might perhaps already have been undertaken, he entered the room where his son was with the question, "Sepperl, does anything hurt you? Can you still walk?" Delighted to find his son unharmed, he protested against all further unreasonable demands of this sort, and a *castrato* who was present even strengthened him in his resolve. (Griesinger, p. 11)

The castration averted, nature took its course and dismissal was imminent. But a prank — undoubtedly not the only one Joseph ever played — hastened it.

> One of the choirboys, contrary to the usual costume of a choirboy at the time, wore his long hair in a pigtail. Haydn out of sheer mischief cut it off for him! Reutter called him to account and sentenced him to a caning on the palm of the hand. The moment of punishment arrived. Haydn sought every means to escape it and ended up declaring that he would rather not be a choirboy any more and would leave immediately if he would not be punished. "That won't work!" Reutter retorted. "First you'll be caned, and then get out!"
> Reutter kept his word, and thus the cashiered choirboy, helpless, without money, outfitted with three miserable shirts and a worn-out coat, stepped into the great and unknown world. (Dies, p. 89)

CHAPTER 3

From the Streets of Vienna to a Pilgrimage, and Then to a Wretched Attic

THE EARLY 1750S

When I was sitting at my old worm-eaten clavier, I envied no king his lot.

HAYDN

There was no lack of Asino, Coglione, Birbante [ass, cullion, rascal], and pokes in the ribs, but I put up with it all, for I profited greatly with Porpora in singing, in composition, and in the Italian language.

HAYDN

After St. Stephen's

Haydn was out on the streets — literally, according to the early accounts of his life. One story has him spending his first night out of St. Stephen's sleeping on the street in the cold November weather and then having the good fortune, the next morning, to meet a friend who offered him lodging! That in a nutshell characterizes Haydn's life during the 1750s. His situation was uncertain and precarious, but over and again the right people and the right opportunities came into his life at the right time.

The friend who rescued Haydn from the streets was Johann Michael Spangler, a tenor in the St. Michael's Church choir. He invited Haydn to live in his attic apartment with himself, his wife, and their nine-month-old baby. Whether this happened immediately after Haydn left St. Stephen's, as the story has it, or at a slightly later time, we do not know. But we do know that Haydn remembered the kindness the Spanglers showed him. Eighteen years later, when he was well established in the court of the Esterházy princes, he gave the Spanglers' second child a position as a singer in the court. She sang roles in at least two of his operas as well as his Italian oratorio, *Il ritorno di Tobia (The Return of Tobias)*.

"I Don't Want to Be a Priest"

Haydn was away from Vienna a good bit of the time during the first few weeks after his dismissal. Dies has him back home in Rohrau for a short time when his mother "showed her anxious cares with tears in her eyes" and took the opportunity to press upon him "the wishes and prayers of his parents to dedicate himself to the priesthood." But even the combination of his own piety and his mother's tears could not bring him to pursue that vocation. All he could say was, "I don't want to be a priest" (pp. 89-90), perhaps unable to articulate more specifically that his calling was to something else. Of course, that something else was music, but exactly what shape a career in music might take and how he might achieve it must have been hazy in his mind. And he might have had at least a suspicion that his practical parents might not approve of a career in music.

Pilgrimage to Mariazell

Soon after leaving St. Stephen's, probably in the spring of 1750, Haydn made a pilgrimage to Mariazell, a small town in the beautiful valley of Salza in the Styrian Alps about eighty-five miles southwest of Vienna. The object of this very popular pilgrimage was a shrine to the Madonna in the church at Mariazell. There is no reason to doubt that Haydn made the pilgrimage for spiritual purposes, but the thought of a few days of trekking through beautiful wooded hills and vales with fellow pilgrims must have been attractive in itself to a newly footloose young man. In addition, he seems to have held out some hope that there might be an opportunity to make his musical prowess more widely known, perhaps even leading to employment. In the event this might happen, he took a few of his compositions with him, went to the choirmaster of the church, told him that he was a student from St. Stephen's, asked to have his compositions performed, and offered his services as a singer. The choirmaster did not believe him, turned him down, and when Haydn persisted, dismissed him unceremoniously. "All kinds of riffraff," he said, "show up here from Vienna pretending to be discharged choirboys till it turns out they can't hit a single right note" (Dies, pp. 91-92). Undeterred, Haydn sneaked into the choir, struck up a friendship with one of the singers, and asked him for the music so he could sing in his place. The singer was fearful and turned him down. Haydn did not back down. According to Dies he

> pressed a piece of money into his hand, and kept standing near him until the music began and the young singer finally had to sing. Suddenly Haydn tore the part from his hands and sang so beautifully that the choirmaster was struck with wonder and apologized to Haydn when the music was over. The clergy sent to inquire who the good singer might be, and to invite him to dine. Haydn accepted the invitation with alacrity, stretched it out for a week, and — as he said — filled his stomach for some time to come. (p. 92)

Michaelerhaus

Physically nourished by a week of good eating, spiritually refreshed by the pilgrimage, and professionally encouraged by his reception as a singer, Haydn nevertheless had to face bleak prospects upon returning to Vienna. He could not expect financial support from his parents. They were probably not inclined to give what meager support they could afford to help him get started on a dubious career in music. But even if they had been so inclined, it is unlikely that they could have offered even meager support, especially since they had recently provided a dowry for their oldest daughter, Franziska, who was married in February 1750. However, Haydn did have lodging in the Michaelerhaus. Either this was where he had been living with the Spanglers before his Mariazell pilgrimage and they had since moved to a larger place to accommodate their growing family, or this was a new place for him. In any case he had a place to live, and thanks to a generous loan from a lace maker named Johann Wilhelm Buchholz, he could afford to pay rent and provide for his other basic needs. In his old age Haydn did not forget the kindness of the Buchholz family. He included their granddaughter in his will because, he said, "her grandfather lent me 150 gulden without interest in my youth and great need" (Griesinger, p. 59). He was quick to add that he had paid it back in full after a short time.

The Michaelerhaus had several floors. Its lodgers were accommodated on different floors according to their social status — the higher the rank the lower the floor. The first floor was occupied by the dowager Princess Esterházy. She was the mother of the first two princes for whom Haydn would work most of his career, but no connection seems to have been made at this time — and no wonder, since Haydn lived in the attic.

Dies describes Haydn's lodging as "a dark little attic five floors up under the eaves" (p. 91). Griesinger describes it as "a wretched little attic room without a stove in which he was scarcely sheltered from the rain" (pp. 11-12). But however dark and wretched the room, it proved to be a good place for Haydn to pursue his art. Living alone in his attic room he could practice his clavier to his heart's content — or as Dies put it, he could "play away his cares" (p. 91). Griesinger also mentions Haydn's clavier playing, but as an aspect of his budding compositional efforts rather than as solace during a difficult time. "Innocent of the comforts of life, he was industrious in the practice of composition, for [as he said] 'when I was sitting at my old worm-eaten clavier, I envied no king his lot'" (p. 12).

Studying C. P. E. Bach, Mattheson, and Fux

Griesinger goes on to say: "About this time Haydn came upon the first six sonatas of [Carl Philipp] Emanuel Bach. 'I did not come away from my clavier till I had played through them, and whoever knows me thoroughly must discover that I owe a great deal to Emanuel Bach, that I understood him and have studied him diligently'" (p. 12).

Dies also mentions Haydn's study of Bach but is vague about the time and differs from Griesinger by mentioning Bach's theoretical writing rather than his music. Wishing to "enable himself through serious study of theory to bring order (which he loved above all, as we already know) into the outpourings of his soul, he decided to buy a good book." So off he went to a bookstore where the bookseller "named the writings of Carl Philipp Emanuel Bach as the newest and best. Haydn wanted to look and see for himself. He began to read, understood, found what he was seeking, paid for the book, and took it away thoroughly pleased" (p. 95).

There is no doubt that Haydn later came to admire and learn from the music of Emanuel Bach, but he could not have known either Bach's music or his theoretical writing in the early 1750s. Although he would eventually get to know both, the theoretical writing probably had more influence than the music, especially with regard to some of his works of the fantasia/ capriccio type that culminated with his orchestral introduction to *The Creation,* "The Representation of Chaos."

Although Haydn's study of Emanuel Bach did not come until later, he had other sources for his musical study at this time. Dies tells about his self-study of music theory through Johann Mattheson's *Der vollkommener Kapellmeister* and Johann Joseph Fux's *Gradus ad Parnassum.* Griesinger, as we have seen, also mentions Haydn's study of the same two books but places it during Haydn's time at St. Stephen's — obviously too early. But chronology aside, what Griesinger wrote rings true: "With tireless exertion Haydn sought to comprehend Fux's theory. He worked his way through the whole method, did the exercises, put them by for several weeks, then looked them over again and polished them until he thought he had got them right" (p. 10). Fux wrote *Gradus ad Parnassum* in the form of a dialogue between teacher and student, making it ideal for self-study. In the foreword he described the type of reader for whom he was writing — and it fits Haydn to a T. His goal was "to help young persons who want to learn. I knew and still know many who have fine talents and are most anxious to study; however, lacking means and a teacher, they cannot realize their ambition, but remain, as it were, forever desperately athirst."[1]

So Haydn's "wretched attic" provided him with solitude to solidify and build on the musical foundation he had acquired at St. Stephen's. He could practice his clavier (and no doubt his violin too), continue his efforts at composition, and teach himself the music theory that had been neglected at St. Stephen's. Living in the attic gave him his own space in which to develop. But "no man is an island." Haydn needed work that would provide an income. He also needed teachers. As it turned out, his Michaelerhaus attic provided the link to both some income and a teacher. One of the residents of Michaelerhaus, living for a time a few floors below Haydn's attic room, in more commodious and comfortable rooms, was Pietro Metastasio, the imperial court poet and the most important opera librettist in the eighteenth century. The extent and nature of Haydn's contact with Metastasio is unclear, but whatever it was, it was through Metastasio that Haydn gained at least one very talented student and the opportunity to work for and learn from a famous Italian composer.

---

1. Johann Joseph Fux, *"Gradus ad Parnassum,"* in *The Study of Counterpoint,* trans. and ed. by Alfred Mann (New York: W. W. Norton and Co., 1965), p. 17.

Teaching

Haydn complained about teaching: "I had to eke out a wretched existence for eight whole years, by teaching young pupils (many geniuses are ruined by their having to earn their daily bread, because they have no time to study)" (Landon 2, p. 398). But teaching brought in some needed income, and at least one of his first students was highly gifted. That student was Marianna von Martinez, the seven-year-old daughter of a member of the papal embassy at the imperial court. Having left Michaelerhaus, Metastasio lived with the Martinez family and was in charge of Marianna's education. He engaged Haydn to teach her clavier playing and perhaps singing. Marianna would become a highly accomplished singer and clavier player, a favorite of the Empress Maria Theresa. She would also excel as a composer. Already at age seventeen she composed a mass that was performed at St. Michael's Church on Archangel Michael's feast day. The *Wienerisches Diarum* commented, "all the connoisseurs were amazed" by its excellence.[2] In 1773 she became the first woman to be elected to the Accademia Filarmonica of Bologna. She also became very active in Vienna's social life, hosting musical soirées that were attended by Haydn and Mozart. According to Michael Kelly, the tenor for whom Mozart wrote the roles of Don Basilio and Don Curzio in *The Marriage of Figaro*, "Mozart was an almost constant attendant at her parties, and I have heard him play duets on the piano-forte with her, of his own composition. She was a great favourite of his."[3] One would like to think that Haydn took some delight in teaching young Marianna, and that he later took pride in having been her teacher. But in his 1776 autobiographical letter he admits no exceptions to his begrudging attitude toward teaching young pupils who interfered with his study. However, in return for teaching Marianna, he received free board for three years.

Learning from Porpora

In the same letter in which he complained about teaching, Haydn wrote, "I would have never learnt what little I did, had I not, in my zeal for composition, composed well into the night; I wrote diligently, but not quite

2. Irving Godt, "Marianna in Vienna," *The Journal of Musicology* 16, no. 1 (Winter, 1998): 143.
3. Michael Kelly, *Reminiscenses,* vol. 1 (London: Henry Colburn, 1826), p. 252.

correctly" (Landon 2, p. 398). Again, acquaintance with Metastasio proved fruitful; it brought Haydn into contact with Nicola Porpora. Porpora's chief claims to fame were as a composer of Italian operas and as a teacher of singing. He composed nearly fifty operas — for a time he was Handel's main competitor in London — and his singing students included the great castrato Farinelli. Although he was semiretired and approaching seventy years of age when he moved to Vienna in the early 1750s, he was still much sought after as a teacher.

Going to Italy was still something of a *sine qua non* for a budding musician. As Daniel Heartz points out, other Viennese composers who had studied in Italy had the advantage over Haydn. But "by a stroke of fortune, Haydn, without leaving Vienna, studied with one of the last of the great Neapolitan masters."[4] Now Italy came to Haydn, as it were, in the person of Porpora. "At last," he wrote, "I had the good fortune to learn the true fundamentals of composition from the celebrated Herr Porpora" (Landon 2, p. 398).

Haydn was not a formal student of Porpora. Mainly he served as an accompanist for Porpora's students because, as Griesinger put it, "Porpora was too grand and too fond of his ease to accompany on the pianoforte himself" (p. 12). Haydn also served him as a valet. Nevertheless he learned much in the company of Porpora and readily acknowledged his indebtedness. He said that he "profited greatly with Porpora in singing, in composition, and in the Italian language," even though he had to endure "pokes in the ribs" and being called "*Asino, Coglione, Birbante* [ass, cullion, rascal]" (Griesinger, p. 12).

Other Musical Influences

Haydn's work for Porpora brought him into contact with some of the leading composers in Vienna. Among Porpora's singing students was the mistress of Pietro Correr, the Venetian ambassador.

Correr traveled in summer with the lady to the then much frequented baths at Mannersdorf, not far from Bruck. Porpora went there too in order to continue the lessons, and he took Haydn with him. For three

4. Daniel Heartz, *Haydn, Mozart, and the Viennese School: 1740-1780* (New York: W. W. Norton and Co., 1995), p. 237.

months here Haydn acted as Porpora's servant, eating at Correr's servant table and receiving six ducats a month. Here he sometimes had to accompany on the clavier for Porpora at Prince von Hildburghausen's, in the presence of Gluck, Wagenseil, and other celebrated masters, and the approval of such connoisseurs served as a special encouragement to him. (Griesinger, p. 12)

Heartz plausibly speculates that "the summer in question was probably 1754, the same during which the court visited Prince Hildburghausen's splendid residence of Schlosshof and witnessed the enchanting spectacle of Metastasio's *Le cinesi*, with Gluck's music. This was perhaps the first occasion that brought Gluck and Haydn together."[5]

At the same time Haydn may have met a teenaged musician in Prince Hildburghausen's retinue, Karl Ditters (later Ditters von Dittersdorf), who went on to become a virtuoso violinist and a highly regarded composer. Haydn and Ditters became good friends. At some later time

the two were roaming the streets at night and halted outside a common beer hall in which the musicians, half drunk and half asleep, happened to be fiddling miserably away at a Haydn minuet. The dancehall pieces that Haydn used to compose at that time found much favor on account of their originality.

"Come on, let's go in!" said Haydn.

"In we go!" Ditters agreed.

Into the taproom they go. Haydn places himself next to the lead violin and asks, very offhand, "Whose minuet?" The latter answers, still drier if not indeed snapping him off, "Haydn's!" Haydn moves in front of him and says, feigning anger, "That's a stinking minuet!" "Who says?" cried the fiddler, now angry himself, jumping out of his seat. The other players follow suit and are about to break their instruments over Haydn's head; and they would have if Ditters, a big fellow, had not shielded Haydn with his arm and shoved him to the door. (Dies, p. 93)

Ditters wrote in his autobiography:

I often came into contact with the amiable Joseph Haydn. What lover of music does not know the name and the beautiful works of this distin-

5. Heartz, p. 238.

guished writer? When we heard any new music by other composers, we criticized it between ourselves, praising, or the reverse, as we thought just.

I advise every young artist to found an alliance, at starting, with one of his colleagues, — stipulating that jealousies and envy are out of the reckoning. Haydn and I did this in a spirit of inquiry, and if all prejudices are laid aside, I maintain that nothing so materially assists a young musician's progress as mutual and friendly criticism of this kind.[6]

Haydn's varied musical activities during his "wretched existence" in Vienna — playing his instruments in his attic; working out counterpoint exercises and composing; teaching and accompanying; picking up what he could about singing, composing, and Italian from working with Porpora; and critical listening to the latest music with his musical friends — all served the budding composer well. Some of them even helped pay the bills, at least for a subsistent living.

---

6. Karl Ditters von Dittersdorf, *The Autobiography of Karl von Dittersdorf Dictated to His Son,* translated by A. D. Coleridge (London: Richard Bentley and Son, 1896), pp. 127-28.

CHAPTER 4

From Freelance Musician
to Music Director for Count Morzin

THE LATER 1750S

Haydn, you're the man for me! You must write me an opera!

BERNARDON

Fortune once again took a fancy to raise up the deserving.

DIES

Music Jobs to Eke Out a Living — and Further His Training

On occasion Haydn still sang in church choirs. His former teacher Reutter, who was now also in charge of the music in the Hofburgkapelle of the imperial court, engaged Haydn to sing with that choir for several services during Lent and Holy Week of the years 1754-56. At times he may also have sung at St. Michael's where his friend Michael Spangler sang. And sometimes he was employed in churches to play organ or violin. For a time he was simultaneously employed by three churches. At eight o'clock he played violin at the church of the Brothers of Mercy, at ten he played organ in the Chapel of Count Haugwitz, and at eleven he sang at St. Stephen's. The length of the services and the locations of the churches were such that it was possible for him to keep that tight schedule — but it took some scurrying!

Another kind of occasional employment that came Haydn's way was playing violin at balls that the imperial family arranged for their children and their friends during Carnival. His earliest surviving dance compositions, the "Seitenstetten" minuets, may have been written for those balls.

Accompanying singers, singing and playing in church, and playing at balls did not exhaust Haydn's music-making. He also participated in the street serenading that was popular at the time. The *Wiener Theater-Almanach* tells us that in the summer

> you may come upon serenades in the streets at all hours. They are not, as in Italy, a mere matter of a singer and a guitar. Here serenades are not meant for declarations of love, for which the Viennese have better opportunities. Such night music may be given to a trio or a quartet of wind instruments, and works of some extent may be played. The evening before the name day of some fair lady will produce a lot of this kind of entertainment; and however late a serenade is given, all windows are soon filled and in a few minutes the musicians are surrounded by an applauding crowd.[1]

In addition to being the source of a little income, playing serenades was a training ground for Haydn in a different kind of music — outdoor music featuring light, entertaining styles (primarily dance music), often involving wind instruments since they are more suited than strings for outdoor performance. Serenading was also a source of companionship — and an opportunity for a prankster. Dies tells of one of Haydn's pranks.

> Haydn once took a notion to invite a lot of musicians for a serenade at an appointed hour. The rendezvous was in the *Tiefer Graben*. There the musicians were to dispose themselves in front of some houses and in corners. There was even a drummer up on the high bridge. Most of the players did not know why they were there, and each had received orders to play whatever he wanted. Hardly had this frightful concert begun when the astonished residents of the *Tiefer Graben* opened their windows and began to scold, to hiss and whistle at the accursed hell-music. Meanwhile the watchmen had also come around. The players escaped just in time, except for the drummer and a violinist, who were both led away under arrest. Their freedom, however, was restored again after several days since they could not name the ringleader. (Dies, p. 92)

---

1. Quoted from Karl Geiringer, *Haydn: A Creative Life in Music,* 3rd rev. and enlarged ed. (Berkeley: University of California Press, 1982), p. 28.

Haydn's First Commission

Through serenading Haydn received his first composing commission. He and his fellow musicians were serenading the wife of the popular comic actor Kurz-Bernardon. Bernardon was so impressed by the music that he ran out into the street to find out who had composed it. Haydn admitted that he was the composer, whereupon Bernardon tried to convince him to compose music for his comic play *Der krumme Teufel (The Crooked Devil)*. Haydn protested, saying he was too young. (Griesinger has him nineteen, Dies twenty-one.) But Bernardon persisted. He brought him into his home, asking him to sit at the keyboard and accompany a pantomime of a person who fell into the water and was trying to save himself by swimming. As Dies tells it, Bernardon calls a servant, "throws himself flat on the stomach across a chair, makes the servant pull the chair to and fro around the room, and kicks his arms and legs like a swimmer, while Haydn expresses in six-eight time the play of the waves and swimming. Suddenly Bernardon springs up, embraces Haydn and practically smothers him with kisses. 'Haydn, you're the man for me! You must write me an opera!' " (Dies, pp. 97-98).

Haydn relented and wrote the opera. It was first performed in 1753 in the *Kärntnerthor,* the public German theater in Vienna (as opposed to the *Burgtheater,* the court theater for Italian operas). After a second performance, however, it was banned because some remarks in the text were deemed offensive. Neither the text nor the music survives. Haydn revised the opera around 1758 as *Der neue krumme Teufel.* That text survives, but again Haydn's music is lost.

Music Inspired by a Disappointment in Love

Two or three compositions seem to have originated as a result of Haydn's friendship with the Keller family. He first became acquainted with Georg Keller, a violinist. That in turn led to his friendship with Georg's brother Johann, a wig maker. Johann's family included two daughters, Maria Anna, the elder, and Therese. Haydn and Therese fell in love, but there would be no marriage because Therese became a nun. In 1755 she entered the Order of Poor Clares as a novice and took her vows the next year, apparently more because of her parents' wishes than her own. "In a document dated a few weeks after her entry, the parents professed that their daughter's vows were the result of their expressed wishes 'and for their spiritual comfort.' This document was accompanied by two very large sums of money, 500 gulden before and 500 gulden after Therese entered the Nunnery."[2]

Haydn wrote music — the *Salve regina* in E and the Organ Concerto in C (Hob. XVIII:1) — for the ceremony at which Therese took her vows, a ceremony that ended any hope he may still have had of marrying her. A half-century later he still had his autograph copies of those two pieces. He may have composed yet a third piece for the occasion. According to Landon, an 1803 letter from Griesinger stated that Haydn told him that he recently "found a concerto for the organ and one violin which he wrote fifty years ago for his sister-in-law when she took the veil." But as Landon explains: "Haydn seems to be talking of the Double Concerto for Organ, Violin and Orchestra in F, but the work he actually found in autograph was the Organ Concerto in C. Another work which turned up in his papers and was also post-dated 1756 was the *Salve regina* in E. The fact that Haydn took the trouble to keep these two very old autographs for very nearly half a century suggests that they had great sentimental value."[3]

Although it is possible that the Double Concerto in F was a third piece for the vow-taking ceremony in 1756, it is more likely that nearly fifty years after the event Haydn was simply confused about the occasion for it. Perhaps he had written it for Therese's entrance into the novitiate in 1755. In any case, there is little doubt that the other two works were written for the 1756 ceremony. The Concerto in C is fittingly festive for the occasion, and the *Salve regina* is an appropriately devotional prayer to the Virgin. James Dack calls it Haydn's "first masterwork."[4] It certainly is that, at least in the old sense meaning a work that demonstrates that an apprentice has achieved sufficient mastery of his craft to venture out on his own. The skill that went into *Salve regina* shows how much Haydn had benefited from the strict teaching of Porpora, and the work's expressiveness shows how much he picked up from Porpora's extensive experience in opera.

Haydn scored *Salve regina* for soprano soloist, choir, and strings. He divided the text into five movements.

2. H. C. Robbins Landon, *Haydn: Chronicle and Works,* vol. 1 (Bloomington, Ind.: Indiana University Press, 1980), p. 81.

3. Landon, *Chronicle and Works,* vol. 1, p. 81.

4. James Dack, "Sacred Music," in *The Cambridge Companion to Haydn* (Cambridge: The Cambridge University Press, 2005), p. 141.

1. Salve, Regina, Mater
      misericordiae,
   vita, dulcedo, et spes nostra,
      salve.

    Hail, Queen, Mother
      of Mercy,
   our life, sweetness, and hope,
      hail.

2. Ad te clamamus
      exsules filii Evae,
   ad te suspiramus, gementes et
      flentes
   in hac lacrimarum valle.

    To you we cry,
      exiled children of Eve;
   to you we sigh, mourning and
      weeping
   in this valley of tears.

3. Eia, ergo, advocata nostra,
      illos tuos
   misericordes oculos
      ad nos converte;

    Come then, our advocate,

   turn your eyes of mercy
      toward us;

4. et Iesum, benedictum
      fructum ventris tui,
   nobis post hoc exsilium ostende.

    and show us Jesus, the blessed
      fruit of your womb,
   after this exile.

5. O clemens, O pia, O dulcis
      Virgo Maria.

    O kind, O loving, O sweet
      Virgin Mary.

The first movement is a solo aria. Its beginning is especially expressive. Years later Haydn would return to the same opening musical gestures and the same rare key of E major for "Woman, behold your Son" in the *Seven Words of Christ from the Cross*. The second movement is a substantial soprano solo framed by the choir; and the third movement is again an aria. The short fourth section is a choral introduction to the last movement, which effectively alternates between elaborate music for the soloist and simpler, homophonic music for the choir. The choir ends with a quiet, peaceful cadence on the word "Maria."

Haydn's First String Quartets

Haydn's disappointment in love notwithstanding, his situation was definitely improving. He was gaining more students and receiving five florins instead of two per lesson. And his teaching led to some of his earliest compositions, in particular the easier keyboard sonatas and trios, which he wrote for his students. Griesinger tells us that Haydn had only a few of them still in his possession because "he gave them away and felt honored when they were accepted. Unaware that the music dealers were doing a good business in them, he lingered with pleasure before the shops where one or another of his works in print had been placed on display" (p. 15). Later, as his fame increased, his business savvy would also increase. Perhaps the memory of how dealers took advantage of his youthful naiveté prompted later sharp practices of his own.

One of his students was a Countess Thun, who may have been Haydn's connection to Baron Carl Joseph Fürnberg, an imperial official. Fürnberg employed Haydn to teach his children. His home in Vienna was near the Seilerstätte where Haydn was living at the time. While living there Haydn was the victim of theft.

> All his few possessions were stolen. He wrote to his parents to see if they might send him some linen for a few shirts; his father came to Vienna, brought his son a seventeen-kreuzter piece and the advice, "Fear God, and love thy neighbor!" By the generosity of good friends, Haydn soon saw his loss restored. One had a dark suit made for him, another presented him with underclothing, and so on, and Haydn recovered himself through a two-month stay with Baron Fürnberg that cost him nothing. (Griesinger, pp. 13-14)

In addition to his residence in Vienna, Fürnberg had a small castle, Weinzierl, about fifty miles west of Vienna. It was located in the scenic Danube valley and provided splendid views of the mountains. Griesinger tells us that Fürnberg "invited from time to time his parish priest, his estates' manager, Haydn and Albrechtsberger (a brother of the well-known contrapuntist, who played violoncello) in order to have a little music" (p. 13.) At Fürnberg's instigation, Haydn wrote his first string quartets for this group.

In 1757-58 Haydn performed his new quartets in his home town, Rohrau, in the castle of Count Franz Anton Harrach for whom Haydn's mother had worked as a cook. We know this from a story told by a Prussian army officer named Weirach. He had been taken captive by the Austrians during the Seven Years' War. Since officers were gentlemen and considered trustworthy, they were paroled to estates of Austrian nobility. Weirach happened to be kept at Rohrau Castle. He later told the composer Johann Friedrich Reichardt that he had heard Haydn himself playing his first quartets. Haydn, he said, "was modest to the point of timidity, despite the fact that everybody present was enchanted by these compositions, and he was not to be persuaded that his works were worthy of being presented to the musical world" (Landon 1, p. 230).

Haydn's earliest string quartets are in five movements — fast, minuet, slow, minuet, fast. The fast movements are lively and witty, with no shortage of surprises. As Daniel Heartz puts it, "The Haydn who could 'shock' like no one else, as Mozart reputedly said, is already before us."[5] The two minuets typically contrast with each other, one of them in a courtly, *galant* style, and the other more reminiscent of street music. The slow movements are like Italian love songs, the first violin being the "singer." These quartets were the first works to spread his reputation beyond the environs of Vienna. Four of them (Opus 1, nos. 1-4), along with two flute quartets not by Haydn, were published in Paris in 1764 in a collection titled "Six Simphonies ou Quatours dialogues par M^r. Hayd'en." These four plus two others became his Opus 1. According to Griesinger, Opus 1, no. 1 was Haydn's first string quartet. He quotes its opening theme and says that "it received such general approval that Haydn took courage to work further in this form" (p. 13). Indeed he did "work further in this form"! The quantity and quality of his eventual output of quartets would be unequaled.

Haydn's First Full-time Position

Haydn credited Fürnberg with getting him his first full-time position. In his 1776 autobiographical letter he wrote, "finally, by the recommendation of the late Herr von Fürnberg (from whom I received many marks of favour), I was engaged as *Directeur* at Herr Count von Morzin's" (Landon 2, p. 398). Various dates are given for this appointment. Griesinger puts it in 1759 but a year earlier is more likely.

Very little is known about Haydn's time at the Morzin court; in fact, so little has survived about the Morzin court around that time that we do not even know with certainty for which count Haydn worked, and we do not know precisely what his duties were. Haydn, of course, was pleased and thankful to have attained the position of Kapellmeister at the court of a count who was a passionate music lover. All Haydn recalled for Griesinger

5. Daniel Heartz, *Haydn, Mozart, and the Viennese School: 1740-1780* (New York: W. W. Norton and Co., 1995), p. 250.

are a couple of insignificant anecdotes. Once "he had fallen from a horse on the Morzin estates" (p. 20). That gave him a lifelong fear of riding horses. And another time he had experienced an embarrassing moment: "when he was sitting at the clavier and the beautiful Countess Morzin was bending over him to see the notes, her neckerchief came undone. 'It was the first time I had such a sight; it embarrassed me, my playing faltered, my fingers stopped on the keys' " (p. 15).

An Unhappy Marriage

On November 26, 1760, while still in the service of Count Morzin, Haydn married Maria Anna Aloysia Apollonia Keller, older sister of his beloved Therese. After Therese became a nun, the father offered Haydn Maria Anna instead. At first he turned down the offer, but finally, out of gratitude for Keller's help, he succumbed to persistent urging. That turned out to be a big mistake! Any love that developed between the two (Haydn told Dies that they "became fond of each other") did not last. Haydn said, "I soon discovered that my wife was very flighty" (p. 99). Griesinger described her as "domineering and unfriendly," and said she "loved to spend" and was indifferent (at best) to Haydn's music. "It is all the same to her," said Haydn, "if her husband is a shoemaker or an artist" (pp. 15-16). But the story we get of their marriage is far too skimpy for us to understand the real situation. No doubt the irritations and frustrations worked both ways. Regarding spending, Haydn complained that Maria Anna "was freer with charitable contributions than her situation warranted" (Griesinger, p. 16). But on her part, Maria Anna was as unhappy about Haydn's generosity to his relatives. Haydn also complained, "My wife was unable to bear children." When he added in his next breath, "I was therefore less indifferent to the charms of other ladies" (Griesinger, p. 15), it sounds as if he was making an excuse for infidelities. If so (and at least one affair is well-attested), we can only assume that Maria Anna was doubly troubled — by her childlessness (which must have troubled her as much as it did her husband) and by his unfaithfulness.

Haydn's Earliest Symphonies

We do not know Haydn's precise duties as music director for Count Morzin, but apparently writing operas and church music was not among them.

Equally apparent is that whatever the precise duties were, they required or allowed him to be productive as a composer of instrumental music. Problems with dating Haydn's early works make it impossible to know precisely what surviving works were written for the count, but fifteen (and perhaps as many as twenty) of his symphonies can be assigned with some certainty to his time at the Morzin court. Griesinger tells us that "as music director of Count Morzin, Haydn composed his first symphony" (p. 16), and he gives the opening theme of the symphony now known as no. 1. Since the numbering of Haydn's early symphonies is atrociously misleading chronologically, it is more or less accidental that Symphony no. 1 might actually be Haydn's first. (If no. 1 is not his first, then no. 37 is the next most likely candidate!) In any case, it was at the Morzin court that Haydn started writing symphonies, the genre that more than any other would secure his lasting fame.

Although posterity has bequeathed Haydn the well-deserved title "father of the symphony," he was not the earliest composer of symphonies. He had many precursors in Italy, Germany, and Austria, but it was he who elevated the symphony to the pre-eminent status it would hold in the late eighteenth and nineteenth centuries. As Brahms said, "After Haydn writing a symphony was no longer a joke but rather a matter of life and death."[6] He probably would not have said that about the fifteen or so symphonies Haydn wrote for Count Morzin. On the whole they are small-scale, lightweight, *galant* works. "Charming" is often the highest compliment critics pay them. But even if charm were the extent of their value, it must be said that the worth of their particular charm is by no means negligible. However, their worth extends beyond charm. Even though they are rarely, if ever, profound, on the whole Landon's more positive assessment is correct: "There is one outstanding quality that always characterizes these early symphonies: the innate, impeccable craftsmanship and the astoundingly sure sense of form. On the whole, these works do not plumb the emotional heights and depths of Haydn's later music, but there is a sense of object, of economical means (Haydn's music is *never* garrulous), that must have made his contemporaries sit up and take notice."[7]

At the time, symphonies most commonly had three movements in the

6. Quoted in David Lee Brodbeck, *Brahms: Symphony No. 1* (Cambridge: Cambridge University Press, 1997), p. 1.

7. H. C. Robbins Landon, *Haydn Symphonies* (Seattle: University of Washington Press, 1969), p. 13.

order fast-slow-fast, a pattern derived from the sinfonias (overtures) to Italian operas. Although that pattern is more prominent than any other in Haydn's Morzin symphonies, it accounts for only six of the fifteen, a fact that shows that Haydn was experimenting with different overall patterns of movements. He expanded seven of the symphonies to four movements by including a minuet, but in those seven symphonies he arranged the movements in four different ways. One of them, no. 11, recalls the old Baroque *sonata da chiesa* (church sonata) by beginning with a slow movement. Five others, nos. 3, 20, 32, 33, and 37, have what will become typical later in the century — fast outer movements framing a slow movement and a minuet. But the order of the inner movements varies; two of the five have the minuet second; three have it third. No. 15 is unique. Its last three movements are like two of the other four-movement symphonies — minuet-slow-fast. But its first movement is neither slow nor fast; it is both.

Symphony No. 15

Symphony no. 15 begins with a lovely serenade. The first violins "sing" a love song in D major accompanied by the lower stringed instruments, whose plucking suggests a guitar. Between phrases and at cadences we hear subdued horn calls. As the violins continue the song, they modulate to a new key whose arrival is heralded by "Scotch snap" rhythms and punctuated by a brief fanfare (still subdued) in the horns. The strings then linger leisurely in the new key while the horns quietly sustain the key note for them until the cellos and basses descend back to D major, the home key.

Back in the home key, the lower strings resume their guitar-like accompaniment with the same chord progression that began the piece — but with a surprise. They now accompany the horn calls instead of the love song, while the violins play the long-held note that the horns had just played. After a pregnant pause, the violins take over the melody again with the "Scotch snap" rhythms leading into a full cadence, again reinforced by a soft horn fanfare. But the full cadence is immediately followed by an extended half-cadence in D minor, leaving the listener wondering, "What next?"

Loud, fast, bustling music in D major, typical of fast first movements, bursts into the quiet serenade. (Pranksters, perhaps, interrupting the love song?) Its opening theme is given great energy by dissonances on all the strong beats as well as by the tremolos in the upper strings and a bouncing bass line in the lower strings. A series of different themes follows, all loud and full of energy. They reach a climax in running sixteenth notes in the new key of A major. But the new key is hardly established before there is a sudden change from loud to very soft — the first of many abrupt dynamic changes — and from major to minor, which makes the tremolos sound a bit scary. But it all changes back as abruptly as it was introduced.

More loud, bustling music (with brief, soft interjections) leads back to the home key — D major — and its opening theme. But it immediately takes an unexpected turn and leads to further development and more new keys before returning home again to D major (now for good) — but this time skipping the opening theme. Instead Haydn saved it for the end; the beginning becomes the ending — almost. It does lead to a full cadence, but no sooner has it done so than a sixteenth-note scale passage leads to a half-cadence on the same chord that ended the slow section. Again — what's next? This time it is the opening serenade, the love song; and this time it comes to a conclusive ending without further interruptions.

The second movement is a minuet featuring stately dotted rhythms, some surprising dynamic changes, and asymmetrical phrasing that in the end comes out balanced. The trio contrasts with the minuet in many ways. Except for a few accents it is entirely soft, and instead of stately dotted rhythms it features melodically smooth eighth notes slurred in pairs. The wind instruments are omitted while the strings play a dialogue between high and low instruments.

The third movement, like the trio of the minuet, dispenses with the wind instruments. It is also like the trio in its pervasive use of slurred pairs of notes. But the rhythmic movement is a little slower and the melodic style is very different. It is angular instead of smooth, frequently moving in leaps instead of in smooth steps like the trio. The paired notes are combined into motives and melodies of differing shapes and lengths and are presented in a variety of textures within a typical binary form: ‖: A :‖: B A′ :‖.

The finale is a ternary form — ‖ A ‖ B ‖ A ‖ — that reflects and balances the opening movement. But whereas the first movement is slow-fast-slow, the finale is fast throughout; and whereas the first movement was soft-loud-soft, the finale is loud-soft-loud. The soft middle section differs from the outer sections in key (D minor instead of major) and texture. The texture is particularly interesting. The wind instruments fall silent while the strings play quietly on three different rhythmic layers. The violas, cellos, and basses provide the foundation, moving in quarter and eighth notes. The first violins have the main melody on top, moving mostly in eighth notes. In the middle, the second violins have running sixteenth notes in perpetual motion.

The phrasing of the outer sections is subtly complex (see Diagram 4-1). By contrast, the middle section is very regular — eight, eight-measure phrases. But Haydn prevented the eight-measure phrases from getting tedious by combining them into three units of irregular length (xxyz / xyz / x), and by eliding phrase z with the return of phrase x. Phrase z's last two measures coincide with phrase x's first two measures (see Diagram 4-2). The first violin also mitigates the regularity of the phrasing with its unexpected rests and syncopations — not to mention its many large leaps.

Diagram 4-1

A^1 — 10 measures	A^2 — 10 measures	B — 12 measures	A^3 — 12 measures
(3+3+4)	(3+3+4)	(4+8)	(3+3+6)

Diagram 4-2

The letters represent phrases.
Each letter and dash represents one measure.

```
x-------x-------y-------z-------
                x-------y-------z-------
                                x-------
```

Landon calls Symphony no. 15 a technical "*tour-de-force* of the first magnitude."[8] But the technique is not an end in itself. With art that conceals art, Haydn unobtrusively takes the listener on a musical journey filled with beauty, excitement, and surprises. Like *Salve regina* in E, Symphony no. 15 reveals a composer whose work is more than charming and technically competent. It reveals, as well, a young composer already possessing a wide expressive range and a keen sense of form and drama.

8. Landon, *Chronicle and Works,* vol. 1, p. 290.

Moving On

Haydn's time at the Morzin court was short-lived. Sometime during 1760 or early 1761, financial difficulties forced Count Morzin to disband his orchestra, and Haydn's job went with it. But short as his employment with Morzin was, the time was fruitful. There is a great deal of uncertainty about which of his surviving works were for Morzin, but his compositions must have included some of the early keyboard sonatas as well as some miscellaneous chamber music and divertimentos. But we do know that he composed fifteen or more symphonies while working for the count. That in itself is sufficient productivity to call the time fruitful. While on the whole those symphonies do not clearly set him apart from his contemporaries, they do show signs of things to come. And one of them (which one, we do not know) was sufficiently impressive to lead to his next job.

CHAPTER 5

Vice-Kapellmeister at the Esterházy Court

1761-66

> *I was guided by an implicit faith in God's goodness: and there-*
> *fore led to the study of the most obvious and common things. . . .*
> *And in conclusion, I saw clearly, that there was a real valuable-*
> *ness in all the common things.*
>
> THOMAS TRAHERNE

> *The clutter of daily experience that we ordinarily apprehend*
> *as just that — clutter — may, on the contrary, be the epiphany*
> *of form — of the very order and harmony and serenity that we*
> *long for in our reveries.*
>
> THOMAS HOWARD

From Count Morzin to Prince Esterházy

After his work at the Morzin court ended, Haydn was not unemployed for long — if at all. Giuseppe Carpani, another of Haydn's early biographers, tells us that Prince Paul Anton Esterházy heard a Haydn symphony and asked Count Morzin to release Haydn to his service. The count was happy to do so since he was planning to disband his orchestra anyway. Whether it happened that quickly or not, on May 1, 1761, Haydn signed a contract to be the vice-Kapellmeister for the Esterházy family.

Even before the contract was signed, Haydn seems to have been some-what involved at the Esterházy court. Griesinger gives March 19, 1760, as the starting date of Haydn's employment. Obviously, that date is too early for the official beginning. Perhaps March 19, 1761 (not 1760), is the date Haydn started working for the Esterházy family before a contract made it official. There may have been some sort of trial period preceding Haydn's official appointment. Carpani mentions a delay in his account of Haydn's hiring. He tells us that a certain Maestro Friedberg (who is probably Carl Friberth, a tenor at the Esterházy court and a friend of Haydn)

> regretted this delay and had Haydn compose a solemn symphony to be performed on the Prince's birthday at Eisenstadt. When this was done, Paul Anton interrupted in the middle of the first allegro, and asked who wrote such a beautiful thing. "Haydn," answered Friedberg, and produced the trembling Giuseppe [Joseph] who stood, rooted to the spot, in a corner of the hall. The Prince, seeing him, said, "That blackamoor?" (Haydn did not in fact exactly have the colour of a lily.) "Well, blackamoor, from this moment you are in my service. What is your name?" "Giuseppe Haydn." "But you are already in my service, how is it that I've not seen you?" The timid Haydn remained silent, embarrassed. "Go and get dressed like a *maestro*," said the Prince. "I won't have you looking like that; you're too small and you look too insignificant; no, no, you must have new clothes, a wig with curls, the collar and red heels, but I want them high, as tall in stature as your knowledge." (Landon 1, p. 345)

The Esterházy Family

The Esterházys were the wealthiest and most powerful Hungarian noble family of the time. They were loyal supporters of the Habsburgs in the wars against the Turks, and like the Habsburgs, they were loyal supporters of the Catholic Church. Nicolaus I (1583-1645) established the tremendous wealth of the family from the spoils of war and through two financially advantageous marriages. Because of his military successes on their behalf, the Habsburgs gave him the title of count. Though born a Protestant, he was educated by Jesuits and converted to Catholicism.

Nicolaus's successor was his third son, Paul, who in 1687 became the first of the Esterházys to bear the title of Prince of the Holy Roman Empire. During his reign the Esterházy palace on the Wallnerstrasse in Vienna was built. Paul also converted the medieval castle in Eisenstadt into a Baroque palace, giving it the facade it still has today and building the spacious, high-ceilinged, and wonderfully resonant hall (now called the *Haydnsaal*) in which Haydn would present many of his works. In 1749 an Englishman described it as "a vast large House, built round a Court, & surrounded by a Mote, situated on an Eminence, at one End of the Village of Eysenstadt."[1]

Eisenstadt was a small town in the Austrian province of Burgenland located at the point of a nearly equilateral triangle about twenty-five miles south of Vienna and twenty-five miles southwest of Haydn's birthplace, Rohrau, which is about thirty miles southeast of Vienna. A town of ancient origin, it received the name Eisenstadt ("iron town") during the Middle Ages because of the iron mining in the area. In 1445 it came under the control of the Habsburgs, who, in 1622, leased its castle to Count Nicolaus Esterházy. In 1647 they sold it to the Esterházys.

Like his father, Prince Paul was a successful military leader, helping the Habsburgs in their Counter-Reformation campaign to bring Protestant areas of Central Europe back into the Catholic orbit. Staunchly Catholic, he erected Marian shrines throughout his lands and made the pilgrimage to Mariazell fifty-eight times. In Eisenstadt he built the St. Apollonia Chapel and an Augustinian nunnery, mainly for his three daughters. In the Oberberg district of Eisenstadt he built the *Kalvarienberg,* "a rugged shrine designed to evoke the Mount of Olives, typically baroque in its extravagant piety, and soon regarded as the 'eighth wonder of the world.' From the Marian chapel pilgrims chartered a course around a grotto, decorated with life-sized carved and colourfully painted figures representing the stations of the Cross, before emerging in the Chapel of the Cross."[2]

Paul loved the arts and lavishly supported them. He maintained a small ensemble of excellent musicians and was himself a poet, dancer, and harpsichordist. He was also a composer. His main work is a collection of fifty-five sacred cantatas titled *Harmonia Caelestis,* published in Vienna in 1711.

Michael, Paul's son, was next in line. Prince Michael continued the strong support of the arts, especially music, which his father had begun. He was succeeded by his half-brother Joseph, but an early death cut his reign short after only eleven weeks. His son, Paul Anton (1711-62), the first of the four Esterházy princes that Haydn would serve, succeeded him. Paul Anton studied law in Vienna and Leyden, writing a dissertation on an important work of Hugo Grotius, *De Jure Belli ac Pacis (On the Law of War*

---

1. Quoted from Rebecca Green, "A Letter from the Wilderness: Revisiting Haydn's Esterházy Environments," in *The Cambridge Companion to Haydn,* ed. by Caryl Clark (Cambridge: Cambridge University Press, 2005), pp. 19-20.

2. Gerda Mraz, "Eisenstadt," in *Oxford Composer Companions: Haydn,* ed. by David Wyn Jones (Oxford: Oxford University Press, 2009), p. 75.

and Peace). Like his predecessors, he had a distinguished military career in the service of the Habsburgs, especially when Maria Theresa, the last ruler from the House of Habsburg, was faced with a coalition of French, Bavarian, and Prussian forces during the War of the Austrian Succession (1740-48). He also fought in the Seven Years' War (1756-63) and served as imperial ambassador to Naples from 1750 to 1752.

Like his predecessors, Paul Anton had many cultural interests, especially music and literature. He amassed a large library of literature, opera librettos, and musical scores. He played violin, flute, and lute. During his minority, probably at his instigation, his mother appointed Gregor Werner to be the family's Kapellmeister. Werner served the Esterházys with distinction for nearly four decades, 1728 to 1766. He was a prolific composer of church music, both vocal and instrumental, but his output of popular instrumental music was negligible. By the time Haydn was brought in as vice-Kapellmeister, Werner was too old and infirm to turn his efforts in the direction of the new instrumental styles that were coming into fashion.

Haydn's Newly Created Position

Haydn's position, vice-Kapellmeister, was newly created by Prince Paul Anton so that he could hire Haydn without dismissing the aging Werner. Paul Anton made it clear in Haydn's contract that he appreciated Werner's decades of service, but that he also wanted his court to keep pace with the rest of Europe in the newly developing styles of music. The first item in the contract reads:

> Gregorius Werner, who having devoted many years of true and faithful service to the Princely house is now, on account of his great age and the resulting infirmities that this often entails, unfit to perform the duties incumbent on him, it is hereby declared that said Gregorius Werner, in consideration of his long service, shall continue to retain the post of *Ober-Capel-Meister,* while the said Joseph Heÿden, as *Vice-Capel-Meister* at Eisenstadt, shall in regard to the choir music depend upon and be subordinate to said Gregorio Werner, *quà Ober-Capel-Meister;* but in everything else said *Vice-Capel-Meister* shall be responsible. (Landon 1, p. 350)

Haydn's contract was for "at least three years," after which he could "seek his fortune elsewhere" upon giving six months' notice. But if he provided "complete satisfaction," he could "look forward to the position of Chief Kapellmeister." It was his duty "to compose such pieces of music as his Serene Princely Highness may command" but he was not to "communicate" them to anyone or "allow them to be copied, but to retain them wholly for the exclusive use of his Highness." Further, he was not allowed to compose music for anyone else without the prince's "knowledge and gracious permission." He was to inquire twice a day, morning and afternoon, "whether a high princely order for musical performance has been given," communicate those orders to the other musicians, "take careful charge of all the music and musical instruments," and "take care to practice all the instruments with which he is acquainted." In general, he was to "place the music on such a footing, and in such good order, that he shall bring honour upon himself and thereby deserve further princely favour." As "an honourable house officer in a princely court," he was to be "temperate" and "treat the musicians placed under him not overbearingly, but with mildness and leniency, modestly, quietly and honestly." In general he was "to conduct himself in an exemplary manner, so that the subordinates may follow the example of his good qualities" (Landon 1, pp. 350-51).

Haydn now had an excellent position, not only for the time being, but one with excellent long-term prospects. When he took up his first position with Count Morzin, he had lamented, "My good mother, who had always the tenderest concern for my welfare, was no longer living." But his father Mathias did live to see his son well-established in his chosen profession, not only in the lesser and short-lived position with Count Morzin, but also in the promising position with the rich and powerful Esterházy family. "Haydn's father," wrote Griesinger, "had the pleasure of seeing his son in the uniform of that family, blue, trimmed with gold, and of hearing from the Prince many eulogies of the talent of his son" (p. 16). However, he did not live to see more than the small beginnings of his son's success or of his fame that would spread throughout all of Europe and beyond. He died on September 12, 1763, after a wood pile fell on him and broke his ribs.

Haydn "had his hands full" in his new position. "He composed, he had to direct all music, help to rehearse everything, give lessons, even tune his own clavier in the orchestra. He oftentimes wondered how it had been possible for him to write so much when he was obliged to lose so many hours in mechanical tasks" (Griesinger, p. 16).

The Esterházy Orchestra

One of his first tasks was to upgrade the orchestra. The result was an expanded orchestra of about sixteen players, one of the best in Europe. In addition to the usual strings, it included flute, two oboes, two horns, and bassoon. Among the members were the violinist Luigi Tomasini and the cellist Joseph Weigl. Tomasini had been Prince Paul Anton's page since he was a young boy in the early or mid-1750s. He had received violin training in Italy, and in 1760 he studied in Salzburg with Leopold Mozart, Wolfgang's father. He first appeared on the list of Esterházy musicians in 1761 at the age of twenty. He soon — perhaps immediately — became the concertmaster and went on to become one of the leading violinists of his time. He remained with the Esterházys until the orchestra was disbanded in 1790. Thus Haydn's and Tomasini's musical careers with the Esterházys coincided exactly. The two not only had mutual respect for each other as colleagues, but they also became close friends. When the orchestra was disbanded, both Haydn and Tomasini received handsome pensions of 400 gulden annually.

Weigl, one year older than Tomasini, was also an outstanding performer. He became a member of the Esterházy orchestra in 1761 and remained at Esterházy until he became a member of the Kärntnerthor Theater orchestra in Vienna in 1769. In addition to these two outstanding string players to anchor the orchestra, Haydn was able to hire some excellent wind players. So from the beginning he had a first-rate orchestra with which to work. He later remarked, "I could, as head of an orchestra, make experiments, observe what enhanced an effect, and what weakened it, thus improving, adding to, cutting away, and running risks" (Griesinger, p. 17).

A Trilogy of Symphonies for Prince Paul Anton

The availability of such a fine orchestra bore immediate fruit in the first works Haydn wrote for Prince Paul Anton — a trilogy of symphonies (nos. 6, 7, and 8) titled *Le matin* ("morning"), *Le midi* ("noon"), and *Le soir* ("evening"). According to Dies, Paul Anton "gave Haydn the four times of day as a theme for a composition; he set these to music in the form of quartets, which are very little known" (p. 100). Dies was a bit confused. There are three works (not four), and they are symphonies (not quartets). But there can be little doubt that these three symphonies are the works he was referring to.

Program music was neither new nor uncommon at the time, and there is nothing unusual about the prince's choice of topic. The passage of time — the times of the day, the months of the year, the four seasons, and the ages of man — is a topic found in many works of art of the time. James Thomson's pastoral poem *The Seasons* (the inspiration for the libretto of Haydn's oratorio) is a fine literary example. Two musical examples were close at hand for Haydn. Vivaldi's famous tetralogy of concertos, *The Four Seasons,* was in the library of the Esterházy family, and Werner published a set of twelve instrumental suites in 1748, each suite depicting a month of the year.

Musical imagination and compositional virtuosity are what make Haydn's trilogy particularly impressive. His compositional virtuosity was not merely his ability to compose music that shows off the technical skill of its performers, although he did incorporate plenty of music in these symphonies to display the special skills of his newly hired virtuosi. Solo passages abound for violin, cello, and flute. Oboes, bassoons, and, occasionally, horns also get opportunities to come to the fore. Even the violone (string bass) gets solos. But Haydn's compositional virtuosity shows itself more in how well he incorporated the various solos into a symphonic, rather than a concerto, framework. He fused elements of the Baroque concerto grosso, a style of music much loved by Paul Anton, with the symphony, the new genre that Paul Anton was eager to have cultivated in his court. The solos are not merely "stuck in"; they are integral to the whole. Haydn did not sacrifice high standards of artistry in order to show off the talents of the orchestra members and satisfy his prince's tastes. He was already showing signs of his "uncanny ability to write music that pleased the patron (or audience) for whom it was composed and yet was uncompromising in technical, formal and instrumental level of standards."[3] In addition to showing Haydn's skillful fusing of concerto and symphony, the trilogy reveals him to be a composer with an unerring sense of musical form and an uncommon ability to recognize the developmental potential in simple musical materials.

Symphony No. 6

The first movement of Symphony no. 6 *(Le matin)* opens with a slow introduction that depicts a sunrise. It begins low and softly in the first violins alone. As the melodic line moves slowly up the D major scale more instru-

3. H. C. Robbins Landon, *Haydn: Chronicle and Works,* vol. 1 (Bloomington, Ind.: Indiana University Press, 1980), p. 555.

ments gradually join, the texture broadens, and the volume increases until a climax is reached on a bright A major chord pulsating through the full orchestra. It is all so simple, yet so very effective. (Toward the end of his career, Haydn will depict another sunrise. That sunrise, in his oratorio *The Creation,* while similar in construction to this one, surpasses it to represent the first dawn of God's perfect creation.)

In the eighteenth century, the times of day and the seasons as musical topics typically carried pastoral associations. The sunrise introduction reinforces that association; the main theme confirms it. It is played by a flute and an oboe, instruments with pastoral connotations — think shepherds playing panpipes (flute) and reed pipes (oboe). The main theme consists of a horn call (another stock pastoral figure) and a rapidly ascending scale in the flute, answered by the oboe. But the flute is the "wrong" instrument to give a horn call. Haydn rectifies his "mistake" when he later brings back the main theme. There, where we expect the flute to play that theme again, he gives it to the "proper" instrument, a subtle witticism in which the obvious — a horn playing a horn call — is a surprise! But since the valveless horns of Haydn's day could not convincingly play the rapid scale that follows the horn call, the horn has to drop out and let the flute take over — a bit of Haydnesque jesting with the horn player about the limitations of his instrument.

The movement, which Haydn developed out of a few simple musical ideas, is as bright and cheerful as a sunny morning in the country. The main theme has three components that are divided between its two phrases (see Example 5-1). The first phrase, played by the flute, is comprised of two components — a horn call (labeled "a" in Example 5-1) and a rapid ascending scale (labeled "b"). The oboe's answering phrase (labeled "c") begins with a motive similar in shape to the horn call. (Refer to Diagram 5-1 throughout the following analysis.)

EXAMPLE 5-1

Diagram 5-1

Main theme			Bridge			Second theme group							Codetta	
a	b	c	a	a	a (b)	(c¹)	c¹	c¹	x	a¹	(a¹)	birds (a²)	b¹	a³
			2 +	2 +	3	3	2 +	2 +						
4	–	4	–	–	7	–	–	7	–	3	–	4	6	–	–	–	5	–	–	–	4	–	–	–	=
7	–	–	–	–	7	–	–	7	–	4	7	–	–	6	–	–	–	5	–	–	–	4	–	–	=
8	–	–	–	–	–	–	–	–	–	–	–	–	–	8	–	–	–	–	=
21	–	–	–	–	–	–	–	–	–	–	21	–	–	–	–	–	–	–	–	–	–	=

a = horn call

b = scale

c = oboe answer to horn call

Each number marks the beginning of a phrase (or larger unit) and indicates the number of measures in the phrase.

Each number and each dash (–) represents one measure.

Underlined numbers show where phrases are elided, the last measure of one being the first measure of the next.

After the main theme, the full orchestra enters, playing a bridge passage that modulates from D major, the home key, to A major. The bridge is loud and bustling in contrast to the quiet, more relaxed main theme. In the midst of the loud bustle, the horn call (a) sounds three times, played by the flute and oboes.

After the third horn call, the flute and violins rush up the scale (b) to a climax, which is followed by a brief pause. A soft theme (c¹) in the strings, subtly reminiscent of the oboe's answer to the flute in the opening theme, confirms the new key of A major and leads, after a sudden loud and fast passage in the full orchestra (x), to another thematic idea that begins with the horn call (a¹) played twice as fast as it was in the beginning.

Next there is a passage featuring a short "warbling" motive, no doubt meant to suggest bird song. It is tossed back and forth by the woodwind instruments — including the bassoon, a seemingly unlikely "bird." The exposition ends with downward scales (b¹) that mirror the ascending scale of the flute in the opening theme. They lead to a statement of the opening horn call played in unison by the full orchestra and expanded to four measures (a³).

The phrase lengths are irregular — a typical Haydnesque trait. But the irregularity is not merely whimsical or arbitrary. It results in higher levels of order. Take, for example, the main theme and the bridge. The seven-measure bridge (2 + 2 + 3) exactly balances the eight-measure (4 + 4) main theme because the end of the main theme overlaps with the beginning of the bridge. Thus there are seven measures on each side of the point of juncture. The seven-measure bridge (2 + 2 + 3) is balanced by another seven-measure phrase at the beginning of the second theme group, and it too is organized as a 2+2+3 group of sub-phrases (see diagram 5-2).

Diagram 5-2

Main theme	Bridge	Second theme
7	/ 7	/ 7
1 – 2 – 3 – 4 / 1 – 2 – 3 – 4		
	1 – 2 / 1 – 2 / 1 – 2 – 3	
		1 – 2 / 1 – 2 / 1 – 2 – 3

Next comes a short three-measure unit (x) that is unique in two ways. First, it is the only section that makes no reference to any of the thematic ideas from the main theme, and second, it is the only section that has thirty-second notes, the fastest notes in the movement. It begins precisely in the middle of the exposition. Its energetic thirty-second notes rush to the climax, the highest and fastest statement of the horn call (a^1). That horn call marks the beginning of another seven-measure unit (again 4 + 4 = 7 because the phrases overlap) with which Haydn begins a systematic shortening of units from seven to six ("warbling birds") to five to four. The closing 5 + 4 (= 8 because of overlap) balances the opening 4 + 4 of the main theme. And note that the five-measure phrase prominently features *descending* scales *preceding* the horn calls of the codetta, thus mirroring the main theme where an *ascending* scale *follows* the horn call. Finally, note that this all results in twenty-one measures on either side of the juncture marked by the beginning of the unique section (x). All in all, this exposition is a fine example of what Charles Rosen calls "one of the basic satisfactions of eighteenth-century art" — namely, "symmetry withheld and then finally granted."[4]

The second movement, scored for strings only, begins like the first with a slow, ascending D major scale, here played by the first violins accompanied by the rest of the strings in a chordal, hymn-like texture. Some commentators have suggested that this represents a "singing lesson" *(do-re-mi-fa-sol-la)*. But the "students" have a problem — though the scale starts on D, it is harmonized in G major. This causes some confusion, and after six notes the scale ends in G minor on a B♭, a note not in the D major scale. As if to demonstrate the correct way, the solo violin (the "teacher") begins all over again, starting on the D and insistently repeating each note rapidly four times as he ascends six notes to a B-natural, which he then triumphantly harmonizes in triple stops with a G major chord. After five repetitions of that chord, the students, having caught on, confidently join in with four more repetitions of the chord.

The lesson having been learned, the "real" music can begin — and what lovely music it is! The solo violin plays the same six-note scale again, an octave higher and delicately ornamented with a few trills and turns, while the string orchestra accompanies with a harmonic progression featuring poignant dissonances. When the solo violin reaches the top, the first violins and lower strings take it back down in parallel thirds while the solo violin and the second violins decorate the descent, tossing ascending arpeggios back and forth. As Landon puts it, what began "as an amusing parody of a singing lesson" set the stage for Haydn to display "his mastery of polyphonic string writing" of a type "long known and cultivated by the

4. Charles Rosen, *The Classical Style: Haydn, Mozart, Beethoven* (New York: W. W. Norton and Co., 1972), p. 49.

Italians of the Corelli school," music that Paul Anton dearly loved.[5] In this way Haydn not only pleased his patron, but he also demonstrated splendor in the ordinary — a kind of musical alchemy, if you will. The musical "base metal" of *do-re-mi* gets transformed into the musical "gold" of the Corellian polyphony that Haydn composed so masterfully.

The "singing lesson" and Corellian polyphony are just the introduction to the central part of the movement, which features both violin and cello as solo instruments. It has the rhythmic feel, but not the form, of a slow minuet. After the "minuet," the Corellian polyphony returns, providing a conclusion that balances the introduction. It is based on the same "singing lesson" scale, but it is treated differently and shows yet more of the splendor latent in that ordinary scale. This time the scale is played in slow half-notes by the first violins, completely unadorned. When they reach the top of the scale, they turn around and descend, still in unadorned half-notes, past the D on which they started, all the way down to their lowest G. The harmonies are filled out by the second violins, and the rhythm of the passage is enlivened by a moving bass part. The long descent is given poignancy by a series of suspension dissonances in the second violins.

The third movement, in a livelier minuet tempo and in typical minuet form, features more solo instruments. A flute solo is prominent in the opening section, and a wind sextet (flute, two oboes, bassoon, and two horns) leads off the second section. The middle part of the movement features bassoon and string bass!

In the last movement the violin and cello return as the main solo instruments. The cello has substantial solos in the exposition and recapitulation. The violin has a very long and virtuosic solo that dominates the development section. It sounds a lot like a solo episode in a Vivaldi concerto and might be the most difficult part Haydn ever wrote for violin — no doubt to show off his friend Tomasini's talents.

Programmatic Readings of the 7th and 8th Symphonies

A detailed description of the 7th and 8th Symphonies would take us beyond the scope of this chapter, but a few of their features should be mentioned. The introduction to the first movement of Symphony no. 7 is in the French overture style — another example, like the Corellian and Vivaldian

---

5. Landon, *Chronicle and Works,* vol. 1, p. 555.

passages in Symphony no. 6, of Haydn's use of Baroque styles to enrich the simpler, currently fashionable, *galant* styles. French overture style, with its stately dotted rhythms and solemn pace, had associations with royal pomp and splendor. Here, at the beginning of *Le midi,* it represents the brilliance of the midday sun, which, in the words of Psalm 19, "comes out like a bridegroom from his wedding canopy . . . and nothing is hidden from its heat."

The most impressive movement of the whole trilogy is *Le midi's* second movement. Again Haydn appropriated something from the Baroque period, this time from vocal music. The movement consists of two distinct but connected parts — an "accompanied recitative" and an "aria." In other words, it is like a scene from a Baroque *opera seria,* but without words. In the recitative the solo violin "sings" the role of a deeply troubled tragic heroine. In the aria a cello (a heroic tenor) joins the violin in a duet that Daniel Heartz aptly characterizes as "blissful." The flutes featured in its accompaniment bring back pastoral associations, representing the consolations of nature. One thinks of later works like the "Scene by the Brook" in Beethoven's *Pastorale* Symphony and the part of Liszt's *Les Préludes* that he described as "the pleasant calm of rural life," which "a soul cruelly bruised seeks when the tempest rolls away."

At a deeper level, Landon, hearing the flutes as reminiscent of the famous "Dance of the Blessed Spirits" in Gluck's *Orfeo,* characterizes the aria as "Elysian."[6] Similarly, James Webster says the turn from the emotional turmoil of the recitative to the bliss of the aria "will have invoked in Haydn's listeners feelings about moving from a confrontation with death to salvation."[7] Within the context of the times of day, the movement resonates with Psalm 55 (Vulgate 54):17-18:

> Evening and morning and at noon
>   I utter my complaint and moan [the "recitative"],
>   and he will hear my voice.
> He will redeem me unharmed
>   from the battle that I wage,
>   for many are arrayed against me [the "aria"].

And since it occurs in *Le midi,* it is uncanny how closely it fits with words from St. Augustine's Exposition of Psalm 55 (54): "I will pray that at mid-

---

6. Landon, *Chronicle and Works,* vol. 1, p. 557

7. James Webster, *Haydn's "Farewell" Symphony and the Idea of Classical Style* (Cambridge: Cambridge University Press, 1991), p. 241.

day he who is seated at the Father's right hand may hear me. He who intercedes for us will hear my voice. What security this is, what comfort, what an encouragement in the face of faintheartedness and storm!"[8]

Just as Symphony no. 7 draws on Italian *opera seria,* Symphony no. 8 draws on French *opéra comique.* In this case the connection is literal: Haydn borrowed a tune from Gluck's opera *Diable à quarte (The Devil to Pay)* for the main theme of the first movement. Given this literal borrowing, it is tempting to read the first movement of *Le Soir* as depicting an evening at the theater. Indeed the character of the whole movement, not just the borrowed theme, suggests comic opera. Richard Will even went a step further and argued "that Haydn treated Gluck's song in such a way as to recall not just its general context but the specific confrontation implied by its text," namely, the confrontation between a husband and wife over her defiance of his ban on her use of tobacco.[9] But we do not need to hear the movement that specifically to hear that Haydn was developing a dramatic conception of the symphony, a conception that one must have in order to understand not only his symphonies, but also those of Mozart and Beethoven.

The last movement of Symphony no. 8 is the only movement in the trilogy that has a programmatic title. Haydn called it "La Tempesta." The evening that began at the theater for comic opera ends in a storm. The plausibility of such a reading, however, should not beguile us into trying to make everything in these three symphonies fit into a chronological narrative. To be sure, the beginning, middle, and end are marked by music that is clearly programmatic — the sunrise at the beginning of *Le matin,* the royal splendor of the midday sun at the beginning of *Le midi,* and the thunderstorm at the end of *Le soir.* In between we meet a variety of characters, events, and moods that we might encounter any day — but not necessarily on any given day, and not necessarily at specific times of the day. At the center of the trilogy is the turn from an emotionally turbulent "recitative" to the blissful "aria." That turn is obviously not there for chronological reasons, but for philosophical or, given Haydn's devout faith, theological reasons. In the midst of the multiplicity of daily life, from sunrise to storm (literally and figuratively), stand the hope and promise of bliss.

8. Saint Augustine, *Expositions of the Psalms,* vol. 3, trans. by Maria Boulding, O.S.B. (Hyde Park, N.Y.: New City Press, 2001), p. 71.

9. Richard Will, "When God Met the Sinner, and Other Dramatic Confrontations in Eighteenth-Century Instrumental Music," in *Music and Letters* 78, no. 2 (May 1997): 196-208.

CHAPTER 6

Symphonies and Baryton Music for Prince Nicolaus

1762-68

A king without diversion is a wretched man.

PASCAL

While Haydn, unbeknown to the Prince, was conducting an investigation into the nature of the baryton, he acquired a liking for it and practiced it, late at night because he had no other time, with a view toward becoming a good player, and in six months attained his goal.

The Prince knew nothing. Haydn could resist a touch of vanity no longer. He played openly in the presence of the Prince, in several keys, expecting to earn no end of applause. The Prince, however, was not at all surprised, and said merely, "You're supposed to know these things, Haydn!"

DIES

Prince Nicolaus Esterházy I

Haydn's three "times-of-the-day" symphonies must have pleased Prince Paul Anton, but he would not have the opportunity to enjoy much more of Haydn's music. He was ill during Haydn's first summer of employment and died the following spring, a month before his fifty-first birthday and less than a year after hiring Haydn. Because he died childless, his brother Nicolaus succeeded him as prince.

In many respects the two brothers were very much alike. Both had

[53]

studied law in Vienna and Leyden. Both had distinguished military careers fighting for Maria Theresa in the War of the Austrian Succession and the Seven Years' War. Nicolaus was decorated for his bravery in the Battle of Kolin, a key battle that saw Frederick the Great and his Prussian army go down to their first defeat in the Seven Years' War, a defeat that turned them back from advancing to Vienna. In 1764 Nicolaus became a captain in Maria Theresa's Hungarian Guard, a position he held until 1783. Like his brother, Nicolaus loved the arts, especially music. In fact, his interest in music was even greater than his brother's. He played cello and viola da gamba. He was especially fond of an unusual member of the gamba family called the baryton.

One way in which Nicolaus differed from his brother was his preference for the country over the city. Whereas Paul Anton preferred living in Vienna, Nicolaus preferred Eisenstadt. But his favorite residence was the Esterházy "hunting lodge" in Süttör (now Fertöd, Hungary), about fifty miles southeast of Vienna at the southern end of the Neusiedler Sea. A hunting lodge it may have been, but it had extensive gardens and forty-one rooms, including space and facilities for concerts, theater, and even some opera. Even before Paul Anton died, Nicolaus had plans for enlarging his favorite residence. Soon after Paul Anton's death, those plans became more ambitious, but it would take a few years for the hunting lodge to be replaced by a new summer palace called Eszterháza. In the meantime, while it was being built, Haydn and the musicians spent most of their time in Eisenstadt, but they also traveled with the prince to other Esterházy residences in Vienna, Pressburg, and Kittsee.

Haydn and Werner

When Nicolaus succeeded his brother, he raised Haydn's salary to 600 gulden per year. Paul Anton had hired Haydn as vice-Kapellmeister with a salary of 400 gulden per year, the same salary as Kapellmeister Werner was receiving. But Haydn was actually receiving more than Werner. "Documents show Haydn being paid a secret additional salary from the princely privy purse, the first for fifty gulden 'additional salary for the quarter 1 August–31 October'. In other words, Haydn received apart from his stated salary of 400 gulden another secret 200 gulden."[1] So when Nicolaus raised Haydn's

1. H. C. Robbins Landon, "Haydn and Eighteenth-Century Patronage in Austria and

stated salary to 600 gulden per year, he was simply making open what had been hidden: Vice-Kapellmeister Haydn was actually earning half again as much as Kapellmeister Werner!

Werner seems to have liked Haydn at first. According to an early-nineteenth-century report whose source was probably Haydn's student Ignaz Pleyel, "Werner conceived a liking for Haydn, and gave him lessons and advice" (Landon 1, p. 347). But as we shall see, the relationship deteriorated as Werner grew jealous of his younger, highly talented underling, a jealousy no doubt exacerbated, if not first ignited, by Haydn's higher salary. For his part Haydn maintained a lasting respect for Werner. In 1804 he made and published string quartet arrangements of instrumental introductions from six of Werner's oratorios. The title page reads: "published out of special regard for this celebrated master by his successor, J. Haydn."

Compositions for Nicolaus

Nicolaus's inauguration took place on May 17, 1762. Haydn probably wrote two works for the occasion, his first *Te Deum* (Hob. XXIIIc:1) and a lost cantata that he may have later reworked into his *Motetto di Sancta Thecla*. He would also write a few cantatas for occasions honoring Nicolaus, such as on his name day and upon his return from a journey. But on the whole, Haydn wrote very little vocal music during his first few years under Nicolaus. Since Werner was the Kapellmeister, entrusted with the church music at the court chapel, Haydn wrote only a handful of small church compositions. And prior to the completion of the opera house at Eszterháza in 1768, he was not heavily involved with opera either. His stage works from those years that have survived at least in part are *Acide* (1763, only fragments survive), an opera written for the festivities surrounding the wedding of Nicolaus's oldest son; *La marchese nespola* (1763), incidental music consisting of nine Italian arias for a spoken German play; and *La canterina* (1766), a two-act intermezzo. Even if we add two or three lost works to the list, the amount of vocal music is relatively small; instrumental music occupied the bulk of Haydn's time. Between 1762, when Nicolaus became prince, and 1768, when the opera house at Eszterháza was finished, Haydn

---

Hungary," p. 169. The Tanner Lectures on Human Values, Clare Hall, Cambridge University, February 25, 1983. Online at: http://www.tannerlectures.utah.edu/lectures/documents/Landon84.pdf.

wrote several divertimenti, a handful of keyboard sonatas and string trios, and concerti for various instruments including at least one each for violin, cello, keyboard, and horn. Several other concerti are known to be lost, including one for double bass, two for baryton, and one for two barytons. But two genres predominate: symphonies and baryton trios (works for baryton, viola, and cello).

Experimentation and Invention in Symphonies for Nicolaus I

Due to the uncertain chronology of Haydn's early symphonies, we cannot determine exactly how many symphonies he composed between the time Nicolaus succeeded Paul Anton as prince (1762) and the death of Werner (1766). Fourteen can be securely dated within that time, but approximately ten more can reasonably be added to their number. Even without counting the concerti, it is obvious that Haydn's orchestral output during these years was substantial.

During this time, even though Haydn was starting to settle into what would become the standard format for the symphony for the rest of the eighteenth century and beyond — four movements in the order fast-slow-minuet-fast — the number and pattern of movements he wrote still show variety. Of the fourteen symphonies whose dates certainly fall within this period, three have only three movements. No. 12 is in the old Italian sinfonia pattern of fast-slow-fast; the other two (nos. 9 and 30) are fast-slow-minuet. Of the thirteen four-movement symphonies, three (nos. 21, 22, and 34) have the old "church sonata" pattern beginning with a slow movement. ("Church sonata," it should be mentioned, does not necessarily indicate a work intended for liturgical use.) No. 34 is Haydn's first symphony to start with a movement in a minor key.

The standard instrumentation for Haydn's early symphonies is two oboes, two French horns, first and second violins, viola, cello, and string bass, but four symphonies from this time alter or expand that. No. 22 substitutes English horns for oboes, and nos. 13, 31, and 72 add a flute and increase the horn section from two to four. Writing for four horns was highly unusual at the time; it would not become standard until after Beethoven. After these three symphonies, Haydn would call for four horns again only once (in Symphony 39); Mozart called for them only twice in all his symphonies; and Beethoven called for three in his Third Symphony and for four in his Ninth.

Although by nineteenth- and twentieth-century standards Haydn's palette of instrumental colors was limited, he was masterful at exploiting what he had available. He used solo instruments to a greater extent than would be the norm for symphonies in the later eighteenth century and beyond. His fondness for solo passages for various instruments, which we saw in nos. 6 through 8, continued in some of the symphonies of this period. He was also very imaginative in coming up with unique textures and combinations of instruments. He even produced a unique color and texture by leaving out an expected instrument. In the trio of the minuet of Symphony no. 29, at the point where one would expect a violin or oboe solo, Haydn wrote drones for the horns and a bass-afterbeat ("oom-pah-pah") accompaniment for the strings, but no melody for a solo instrument. It is a case of an accompaniment seeking, and not finding, its melody! Given the soft dynamic level and the minor key with some archaic harmonic touches, the effect is quite haunting.

Other examples of Haydn's experimentation and inventiveness during this period are his use of a Gregorian chant as the basis for the first theme in Symphony no. 30, which is the reason for its nickname, *Alleluja*; the "chorale prelude" style of the first movement of no. 22, *The Philosopher*; the fugue finale of no. 40, a type of symphonic finale he had experimented with in no. 3 and would use only once more (in no. 70); the minuet with two trios in no. 30; and the theme and variation form in the finales of nos. 72 (for the first time in his symphonies) and 31. In both sets of variations Haydn emphasizes color and texture by having each variation feature a different solo instrument or group of instruments. The variations of no. 72 end with a delightful surprise, which Landon describes as follows: "Having taken the basic [variation] structure of the movement from the divertimento, Haydn now turns to the [dance] suite and introduces a Presto in a different metre and with entirely different music. In dance music of the period, this kind of procedure was known as the *Kehraus* ["break up" dance], the signal that it is time to go home."[2]

Symphony No. 21, 1st Movement

Sometimes Haydn's forms defy classification. The slow first movement of Symphony no. 21 is a good example. It is, A. Peter Brown says, "remarkable

2. H. C. Robbins Landon, *Haydn: Chronicle and Works,* vol. 1 (Bloomington, Ind.: Indiana University Press, 1980), p. 565.

for the way in which its materials create a new type of structure. If one were to attempt to explain it as belonging to one of the standard symphonic forms, one would fail miserably."[3] Even description and analysis that go beyond standard formal classification will fail to convey this music's (any music's) beauty, but they may help guide a listener's ears to be more perceptive.

The strings begin with a quiet, lyrical four-measure theme (see Example 6-1). The winds answer with a theme of their own (see Example 6-2). Then the strings repeat their theme and again the winds answer, this time taking the music into a new key. Next the strings begin to repeat their theme in the new key, but the winds interrupt after just two measures, only to be interrupted themselves after just one measure as the second violins reassert the string theme. They spin out the first measure of their theme in a descending sequence six measures long while the first violins play their own descending sequence ingeniously based on a variant of the part of their theme that the winds had cut off (see Example 6-3). The lower strings provide the whole passage with a repeated eighth-note accompaniment. When the sequence ends, the winds and strings join together in a concluding passage based on the winds' theme.

EXAMPLE 6-1

EXAMPLE 6-2

3. A. Peter Brown, *The Symphonic Repertoire*, vol. 2: *The First Golden Age of the Viennese Symphony* (Bloomington, Ind.: Indiana University Press, 2002), p. 86.

EXAMPLE 6-3

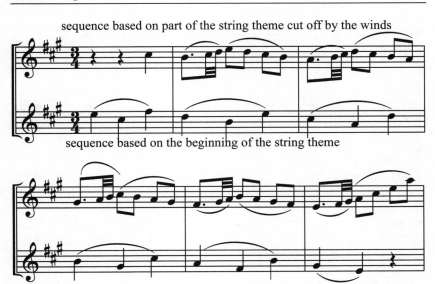

A brief transition leads back to the strings' theme, but this time upper strings have the accompaniment in repeated eighth-note chords while the cellos and basses play the melody. They begin as if they will spin out the melody in the same kind of descending sequence we heard just a few measures earlier. But soon the passage takes the first of several unexpected turns that stretch the journey out to thirteen measures before coming to a cadence.

After a conclusion similar to the previous one — which again is based on the winds' theme and played by the strings and winds together — Haydn has yet another way to develop the strings' theme. He presents it in close imitation starting with the first violins and working down to cellos and basses. The imitative statements begin on different beats of the measure creating rhythmic ambiguity (see Example 6-4). Up until this passage, the movement has been uniformly soft. Now it is softer yet — mysteriously soft, especially in the midst of rhythmic ambiguity. But the mysterious effect is suddenly interrupted by loud, repeated eighth notes, first in the lower strings, then joined by the upper strings, and finally by the full orchestra in an attempt to make a final cadence. The attempt fails and results in some more soft-loud exchanges before winds and strings together bring the winds' theme to a successful conclusion.

EXAMPLE 6-4

Two Symphonies with Four Horns

Brown says the first movement of Symphony no. 21 "represents Haydn at his very best, not only for the 1760s, but for his entire creative life."[4] I am

4. Brown, *Symphonic Repertoire,* vol. 2, p. 87.

not about to challenge his judgment. But if instead of a single movement I had to choose an entire symphony from this period that represents Haydn at his best, it would be a toss-up between nos. 31 and 13, two of the three symphonies with four horns.

Symphony no. 31, aptly nicknamed *Horn Signal,* is deservedly his best-known symphony of this period. Its four horns feature prominently in all four movements, always to their best advantage. At the beginning of the symphony they are heard in two successive, contrasting themes — first the loud, stirring fanfare previously mentioned, played by all four horns (see Example 6-5), and then a post-horn signal played by one horn, soft and haunting, as if from a distance (see Example 6-6).

EXAMPLE 6-5

EXAMPLE 6-6

The two horn themes reappear in prominent places throughout the movement: the post-horn theme, soft as always, at the end of exposition; the fanfare at the beginning of the development section; and the post-horn theme midway through it — in minor, even more haunting than usual. Just when the recapitulation is poised to return with the fanfare, Haydn has a surprise in store. Instead of the loud D major fanfare, the strings softly play a theme in D minor related to a countermelody that accompanied the post horn at the end of the exposition — but the post-horn theme itself is absent (see Diagram 6-1). Nevertheless, the D minor countermelody ends with the music again poised to return to D major with the expected horn fanfare — and again Haydn has a surprise in store. Instead of the fanfare, the soft post-horn theme returns. Except for the skipped fanfare, the reca-pitulation proceeds as expected, and it goes on to end (or so we think), like the exposition, with the soft post-horn theme. But that is not the end! The fanfare returns unexpectedly, but fittingly, as the conclusion, sounding all the more glorious for having been omitted from the beginning of the reca-pitulation, following rather than preceding the post-horn theme.

Diagram 6-1

Horn themes of Symphony no. 31, 1st movement, exposition and recapitulation

EXPOSITION	RECAPITULATION
	FALSE RECAP — <u>Fanfare in D major expected</u> but: — <u>Countermelody in D minor without post horn</u>
<u>1ST THEME GROUP</u>	<u>1ST THEME GROUP</u> — <u>Fanfare expected again</u> but:
— Fanfare (D major)	— [Fanfare omitted]
— Post horn	— Post horn
—	— . . . . . .
<u>2ND THEME GROUP</u>	2ND THEME GROUP
—	— . . . . . .
— Post horn with countermelody	— Post horn with countermelody
	— <u>Fanfare</u>

The second movement is a lovely pastorale in a graceful, lilting si-ciliano rhythm. Although it features solo violin and cello, the horns are also involved thematically, showing their lyrical side, in contrast to the fanfare and post-horn signal of the first movement. In the third movement, an aristocratic minuet, the horns have no independent material of their own; they simply enhance the sonority with their noble sound.

The last movement is in theme and variation form, and as mentioned above, the horns take their turn among the variations with other groups of instruments and soloists. Like the variations of Symphony no. 72, the last variation (here a string bass solo!) is followed by a *Kehraus,* a dance signaling that it is time to go home. But this time the *Kehraus* is not the end. Unexpectedly, the horns come to the fore again and close out the symphony with the rousing fanfare from the first movement!

The function of the four horns in Symphony no. 13 is entirely different from what it is in Symphony no. 31. In no. 31 they play a leading role; in no. 13, with one exception, their role is completely supportive; they fill out harmonies and enhance sonorities. Nowhere is their value in a supportive role more apparent than at the beginning. While all the strings play a trumpet-like motive in octaves, the winds (four horns, two oboes, and a flute) play sonorous, organ-like, sustained chords. This impressive beginning inaugurates a movement as festive as any Haydn ever wrote. Its energy is simply irrepressible.

The harmonies of the opening section come in three, three-measure blocks — three measures on the tonic chord, three measures on the dominant chord, and three measures back on the tonic chord. The strings play their trumpet-like motive through all nine measures. When the recapitulation comes around, it starts out just like the beginning. But there is a surprise at the third three-measure block. The lower strings drop out, the violins play the top notes of the chord in a vigorous syncopated rhythm, and the horns take over the trumpet-like motive. The passage is all the more impressive because Haydn saved the horns for thematic use until this moment.

In the second movement, a lovely serenity replaces the energetic festivity of the first movement. All the wind instruments are silent while the string orchestra accompanies a solo cello. In style it is similar to the slow movement of a sonata, except that the cello is accompanied by the orchestra rather than by a keyboard instrument.

The third movement is a witty minuet. It starts out noble and aristocratic — not to say a bit pompous. But the first phrase ends with impertinent little echoes that deflate the pomposity. The next phrase brings back the aristocratic aura, but it soon turns folksy with "Scotch snap" rhythms, and ends again with the impertinent echoes. Throughout the movement, pretentious pomposity never gets very far before it is deflated.

The last movement opens with a motive consisting of four half notes (see Example 6-7).

EXAMPLE 6-7

Mozart used the same motive to begin the last movement of his Symphony no. 41, *Jupiter*. Others have used it too. It is a series of pitches that was well-known from counterpoint exercises. It may have been derived from Gregorian chant (hence it is sometimes called the "Credo" theme). Whatever its origin, it was a motive with serious, "learned" connotations, which Haydn put in comic competition with a quite unserious theme, as Daniel Heartz describes:

> As serious as this whole-note [*sic*] theme in the strings seems to be, the winds erupt, as if in mockery, with their two measures of jubilation, which overlap the fourth measure of the theme. Thus the four-measure Credo theme is turned into a five-measure comedy. The dialogue becomes even funnier when the strings give in and repeat the wind figures, as if to say, "All right, have it your way." Haydn juggles both aspects, comic and serious, throughout the movement, keeping them in balance successfully until the inevitable final stretto, where the contrapuntal element comes to dominate.[5]

Although in contrapuntal sophistication the finale of Haydn's Symphony no. 13 cannot compare with the finale of Mozart's *Jupiter* Symphony (precious little can!), Haydn was proving to be preeminent as a symphonist, a composer who had already taken the genre well beyond its humble origins, and someone on his way to setting the standard for all future generations of symphonists. Already in the first half of the 1760s, composing a symphony was no joke, no matter how jocular Haydn's could be at times.

5. Daniel Heartz, *Haydn, Mozart, and the Viennese School: 1740-1780* (New York: W. W. Norton and Co., 1995), p. 279.

Prince Nicolaus and His Baryton

Prince Nicolaus should not have been any less pleased with the symphonies Haydn wrote for him than Paul Anton had been with the three "times-of-the-day" symphonies. But on November 3, 1765, he sent a communiqué to Haydn in which he "urgently enjoined" Haydn "to apply himself to composition more diligently than heretofore" (Landon 1, p. 420). Since Haydn's output during this time was nothing less than robust in quantity and stellar in quality, we might well wonder what precipitated this urgent injunction.

A month earlier Kapellmeister Werner had sent a letter to Nicolaus alleging that Haydn was neglecting his duties — a clear bit of evidence that the relationship between the Kapellmeister and vice-Kapellmeister had seriously deteriorated. The letter begins:

> I am forced to draw attention to the gross negligence in the local castle chapel, the unnecessarily large princely expenses, and the lazy idleness of the whole band, the principal responsibility for which must be laid at the door of the present director, who lets them all get away with everything, so as to receive the name of a good Heyden [a pun on the German word for "heathen"?]; for as God is my witness, things are much more disorderly than if the 7 children were about. (Landon 1, p. 418)

There follows a litany of complaints having to do with lack of discipline, sloppy care of the music and its cataloguing, negligence in keeping instruments in good repair, and the like. There are even accusations of theft and lying. Although Haydn's relaxed nature makes it easy to believe that his maintenance of discipline among the musicians was carried out amiably, it is obvious that the letter is full of the gross exaggerations of a bitter old man, jealous of his young, more gifted underling. Nicolaus understood the situation and responded by sending an order to Haydn. It was more a clarification of duties than a reprimand, but at the end Nicolaus added the seemingly unwarranted injunction for Haydn "to apply himself to composition more diligently than heretofore." Werner had not said anything about Haydn not composing enough. He would not have, of course, because a greater compositional output from Haydn would only have served to accentuate the talent gap between them. Yet Nicolaus obviously thought something was lacking, and he specified what it was: "such pieces as can be played on the gamba [baryton], of which pieces we have seen very few up to now" (Landon 1, p. 420).

The baryton is an unusual instrument. Even in its heyday (if it can be said to have had a heyday) it was unusual. It originated in the early seventeenth century, probably in England. It was known in the court of King James I (who ruled 1603-1625) and achieved a modicum of popularity in Austrian courts in the eighteenth century before it all but vanished by the early nineteenth century. Its unusual structure and difficult playing technique no doubt account for its lack of popularity and longevity. John Hsu, a leading authority and performer on the instrument, describes it as follows.

> The baryton is a modified viola da gamba with a broadened neck behind which metal strings are strung like a little harp along the length of the instrument. These harp strings are set either on a low bridge or on individual studs on the belly of the instrument. They are exposed within the open box-like back of the neck so that the left thumb can pluck them. Although the number of strings was not standardized, we know that the baryton of Haydn's patron Prince Nicolaus Esterházy had seven bowed strings and ten plucked strings tuned to the D-Major scale [which severely limits the number of keys the instrument can play in]. The technique of the baryton demands that the left hand function in two ways: fingering the bowed strings on the fingerboard and plucking the harp strings [with the thumb] behind the neck.[6]

Nicolaus had acquired his baryton in Innsbruck in August 1765, so Werner's letter in October gave him an opportune time to emphasize his desire for music that he could play on his new instrument. We do not know what sparked Nicolaus's interest in this unusual instrument, but Thomas Tolley gives a plausible explanation. He thinks it "stemmed from a belief that the baryton represented the closest modern equivalent to Apollo's lyre." He points out that the ceiling of the main hall at Eszterháza "was decorated with a huge fresco depicting Apollo, the sun god, driving his chariot across the sky bringing light to the world." Furthermore a treatise by G. B. Doni, published in 1763, shows an instrument of his own invention: "a double lyre, partly based on evidence drawn from antique sources associated with Apollo. The instrument bears a clear resemblance to the form of the baryton."[7]

---

6. John Hsu, CD notes for *Haydn Divertimenti, The Haydn Baryton Trio*, DOR-90233.

7. Thomas Tolley, *Painting the Cannon's Roar* (Burlington, Vt.: Ashgate Publishing Company, 2001), p. 83.

A Cornucopia of Music for Nicolaus and His Baryton

Whatever the reason, Nicolaus's enthusiasm for the baryton was great. His appetite for music to play on it was voracious, but its repertory was skimpy. So he issued a requirement for more music from an already-busy Haydn, a requirement that David Wyn Jones calls "one of the most indulgently self-interested in the history of musical patronage."[8] No matter how indulgently self-interested the request, Haydn complied with alacrity! In late 1765, he began composing chamber music that included a baryton. In the end, within a little more than a decade, he would compose at least 150 works for his prince to play, principally trios for baryton, viola, and cello. Haydn gathered 120 of the 126 known trios (122 extant and four lost) into five books of twenty-four trios each and had them lavishly bound in red leather for presentation to the prince. He compiled and presented the first three books in rapid succession between January 1767 and July 1768. Haydn may have written the first few trios soon after the prince obtained his instrument, and then he began to work in earnest when he received the order a few months later to compose more music for it. That means that he wrote most of the seventy-two trios in Books I through III in less than three years!

Nicolaus was already a competent cellist and gambist when he acquired his baryton, so he would have been able to adjust rather easily to playing the bowed strings on the fingerboard. But learning to play strings off the fingerboard — the "harp" strings that needed to be plucked with the left thumb — would have taken considerable practice. Therefore the trios in Book I do not require playing the plucked harp strings. In Book II, however, most of the pieces require playing the harp strings, and in general the musical and technical demands are greater. Increasing technical difficulty continued in Book III. The prince was obviously making progress on his new instrument.

After Book III, Haydn's pace slowed down. Book IV was not presented to the prince until December 1771, perhaps on his name day or birthday. The slowdown probably does not yet indicate that the prince's enthusiasm was waning. Two factors made it less incumbent on Haydn to supply new pieces. First, he had already supplied the prince with seventy-two trios, so he could no longer say "we have seen very few such pieces up to now." Sec-

---

8. David Wyn Jones, *The Life of Haydn* (Cambridge: Cambridge University Press, 2009), p. 56.

ond, other Esterházy musicians had started to compose works for baryton, including the violinist Tomasini and the cellist Weigl.

The slowdown between Books IV and V was much greater yet. Book V did not appear until November 1778. By then the prince's enthusiasm for the baryton had definitely waned, having been replaced by a waxing interest in opera. After the Book V trios, Haydn would write no more for the baryton. But by that time he had written so many works for the instrument that in the end they would outnumber the works in every genre in Haydn's oeuvre except his folksong arrangements.

The generic designation for each of the baryton trios is divertimento — music for diversion. The term suggests lightweight music for pleasant recreation, and indeed that is what the baryton trios are. They do not pretend to greatness; they are not "masterpieces" in the sense that they transcend time and place. But they are especially fine examples of what they were intended to be: music for the private playing pleasure of a musical prince. Because Haydn was a creative genius and his prince was musically knowledgeable, very few of the baryton trios, if any, are merely "throwaway" music. Were it not for the near extinction of the baryton, they could still give pleasure to competent amateur string players. And were it not for the same problem, some of them could even find a deserving place in modern chamber music concerts. Be that as it may, apart from any place they might occupy in our musical lives now, they remain a remarkable (if secondary) achievement. Amidst all his other activities, Haydn created an exceptionally large and musically distinguished repertory for a very particular recreational purpose.

Of course, Haydn wrote his symphonies, as well as the baryton divertimenti, for Prince Nicolaus's pleasure. But at least two differences gave the symphonies a better chance for an enduring life outside the Esterházy residences and beyond the eighteenth century. First, they were not limited by Nicolaus's technical capabilities as a baryton player; instead, Haydn wrote them to be performed by the highly skilled Esterházy orchestra. Second, they did not rely upon an unusual instrument for achieving long life and widespread popularity; instead, they were written for a type of ensemble that was becoming widespread throughout Europe and would have a long, distinguished history, thanks largely to Haydn, who was now well on his way toward deserving the title "Father of the symphony."

CHAPTER 7

Kapellmeister at Eszterháza Palace
and Composer of Church Music

1768-72

*It is perhaps a typical eighteenth-century concept to choose a
desolate, fever-ridden swamp as the place in which to construct
a fairy-tale castle with an opera house. It is, as it were, a gigantic Baroque conceit; the will of one man is forced upon, and
tames, rebellious nature.*

LANDON

*Art as elaborated at Versailles and in Paris had an all powerful
influence on court and society art, which is international, but
had no effect on religious and popular art.*

LOUIS RÉAU

Eszterháza Palace: "The Little Versailles of Hungary"

On January 3, 1766, Nicolaus informed his staff that "the castle at Süttör is
henceforward to be called Eszterház; accordingly the correct form of the address in future is determined as Eszterház by Süttör."[1] The huge project to turn
the "hunting lodge" Süttör into the palace Eszterháza had probably begun in
1762, soon after Nicolaus became prince, but it was not considered complete
until the large fountain in front of the palace was in operation in 1784. Two important intermediate stages in the building of Eszterháza were the completion

---

1. Quoted in David Wyn Jones, *The Life of Haydn* (Cambridge: Cambridge University
Press, 2009), p. 57.

of the opera house in 1768 and the opening of the marionette theater in 1773. But by the beginning of 1766, the project was close enough to completion that Nicolaus could anticipate moving into it for his summer residence.

"With the exception of Versailles, there is perhaps in the whole of France no place to compare with Eszterháza for magnificence," wrote Baron von Riesbeck in an account of his travels through Germany in the 1780s. The forty-one-room hunting lodge had become a 126-room palace. But sheer size was not its most impressive feature. Riesbeck reported that it was "bursting with luxurious things" and surrounded by gardens that contained "everything that human fantasy can conceive to improve or, if you will, undo the work of nature." "Pavilions of all kinds" stood "like the dwellings of voluptuous fairies." Everything, he wrote, "is so far removed from the usual human operations that one looks at it as if in the middle of a marvelous dream" (Landon 2, p. 99).

Eszterháza's fairyland appearance was heightened by the contrast with its marshy surroundings near the southern end of the Neusiedler See, a long, narrow, shallow lake on the plains of eastern Austria and western Hungary. At its normal size, the lake measures about twenty miles from north to south, has a maximum width of about seven miles, and reaches a maximum depth of only about six feet. Throughout history its volume and area have fluctuated considerably, even to the extent of drying up completely (as it did most recently in 1866). During Haydn's lifetime it dried up in 1740 but recovered to a record high in 1786. The lake was surrounded by marshland, especially the large Hanság marsh that extends south and east from the southern end and within which Eszterháza is located. "Anything more dull or depressing," wrote Riesbeck, "can hardly be imagined. The Neusiedler See, from which the castle is not far removed, makes miles of swamp and threatens in time to swallow up all the land right up to the Prince's dwelling." But another observer, writing at about the same time, saw the area in a more positive light. "The whole surrounding countryside is a flat field," he wrote, "and rich pasture-land alternates with fruitful arable country. Only at the edge of the lake, bountiful Ceres has yielded a piece of land to Bacchus, and quite a good wine grows there" (Landon 2, p. 102).

People may have viewed the surrounding area differently, but everyone marveled at the magnificence of the palace and its gardens. A member of the Hungarian Guard wrote:

Everything that a prince who was anxious to reflect the taste and spirit of the times needed was to be found in the palace and its environs, a large-scale Kapelle, library, picture gallery, armoury, state rooms decorated in white and gold or in the Japanese style, gold leaf, Chinese vases and pagodas, a porcelain room, a belvedere, a winter garden, an orangery, a cafe, an opera theatre, a marionette theatre, cascades, temples dedicated to the Sun, Venus, Diana and Fortune, a hermitage, *champs élysées,* a Dutch pavilion, a park for deer, pheasant, and wild boar, a *monbijou,* and a maze.[2]

Eszterháza became the summer residence for the Esterházy family, but Nicolaus was so fond of the place that "summer" expanded to as many as ten months. And of course that meant Haydn spent an increasing portion of the year there. Although he enjoyed the good hunting and fishing in the area around Eszterháza — Griesinger reports that "hunting and fishing were Haydn's favorite pastimes during his stay in Hungary" (p. 20) — one wonders how he felt about its opulence, courtly formalities, and isolation. There is no reason to doubt his sincerity in 1776 when he wrote that he wished "to live and die" in the service of the prince (Landon 2, p. 398). But there are indications in later letters that he sometimes chafed at the isolation.

Haydn Becomes Kapellmeister

Exactly two months after Nicolaus issued his proclamation about the impending move to Eszterháza, on March 3, 1766, Kapellmeister Werner died. It was almost a foregone conclusion that his position would become Haydn's — as indeed it did; and Haydn probably assumed that the new position would entail new responsibilities, especially in the area of church music. But the advance in rank hardly made a difference in his compositional activity. Whatever Haydn's expectations might have been after Werner died, Prince Nicolaus apparently had little inclination to make composing church music a substantial part of Haydn's work load. During the ensuing years, Haydn's instrumental composing would continue apace, and soon opera would loom large, but church music for the Esterházy court never would. Even so the seven years following Werner's death did see a significant increase in Haydn's engagement with church music, though we know of only one piece that he composed at Nicolaus's behest.

2. Quoted in Gerda Mraz, "Esterházy, Prince Nicolaus I," in *Oxford Composer Companions: Haydn,* edited by David Wyn Jones (Oxford: Oxford University Press, 2009), p. 88.

Church Music

After composing no church music during his five years as vice-Kapellmeister, Haydn, between 1766 and 1772, composed seven large-scale church works — four masses (each one very different from the others), the *Stabat mater,* the G minor *Salve regina,* and a large, congratulatory cantata for the abbot of the monastery at Zwettl on the fiftieth anniversary of his taking vows. Though the number of pieces is relatively small, the magnitude, diversity, and high quality of the works show a deep commitment to church music and suggest that Haydn would have liked it to be a bigger part of his work for the Esterházys. He may have taken on these major compositional challenges hoping to demonstrate to Nicolaus his competence as a church music composer, or he may have taken them on in order to prepare himself for a time when the prince might make it a higher priority. Or perhaps, as James Dack suggests, he took on the challenges more generally as "part of a larger desire to explore all branches of composition, which in sacred music posed challenges in the setting of text, large-scale musical structure, supra-movement coherence, mastery of a range of styles and techniques (including fugue and *stile antico*) and, not least, measuring up to tradition."[3]

Missa Cellensis in Honorem BMV

If these works were meant to demonstrate his competence to do hoped-for work in church music, or preparation for a time when it might be required, one would be hard-pressed to find two more stunningly successful pieces than the first two — the *Missa Cellensis in honorem BMV* and the *Stabat mater. Missa Cellensis in honorem BMV* is by far the biggest of all of Haydn's masses. At more than an hour in length, it is twenty to thirty minutes longer than each of the six great masses he wrote late in his life. But as Dack points out, the "most astounding" feature of the work

> is its mastery of the required range of styles and techniques: choral movements in Baroque ritornello structure (Kyrie I), modern symphonic style ("Gloria in excelsis"), and *stile antico* ("Gratias"); solo ritor-

3. James Dack, "Sacred Music," in *The Cambridge Companion to Haydn,* edited by Caryl Clark (Cambridge: Cambridge University Press, 2005), p. 142.

nello arias ("Christe," with choral interjections); affective movements for chorus and solo voices ("Qui tollis"); and choral fugues (Kyrie II; "In Gloria") carried out on the largest scale with the greatest assurance, all the more impressive in that these were among Haydn's earliest essays in fugue.[4]

Although we do not know of an occasion for which Haydn wrote *Missa Cellensis,* the title, "mass for the cell," might refer to Mariazell, the famous pilgrimage site to which he journeyed after being dismissed from the St. Stephen's boy choir and with which the Esterházy family had a long and close relationship. But since it could not have been performed at Mariazell due to insufficient resources, David Wyn Jones suggests that Haydn might have written it for "the annual service in the Augustinerkirche in Vienna on 8 September 1766 (a Marian feast day) organized by the Styrian confraternity and devoted, in particular, to celebrating the icon of the Blessed Virgin Mary at Mariazell."[5]

A story that surfaced in 1829 might refer to *Missa Cellensis.*

At the first mass which Haydn produced in Public, the Empress Maria Theresa was present — Hasse stood by her and she asked his opinion of the young composer.

Hasse told the Empress that Haydn possessed all the qualities that are required to form the highest style of writing, viz. beautiful and expressive melody, sound harmony, original invention, variety of effect, symmetrical design, knowledge of the powers of the different instruments, correct counterpoint, scientific modulation and refined taste. Hasse also predicted that Haydn would become one of the greatest Composers of the Age.[6]

At the time, Johann Adolph Hasse (1699-1783) was the leading German composer of opera and church music. Whatever mass of Haydn it was that elicited his high praise, he also would give high praise to Haydn's *Stabat mater.*

4. Dack, "Sacred Music," p. 142.
5. Jones, *The Life of Haydn,* p. 61.
6. Quoted in Jones, *The Life of Haydn,* p. 61.

Stabat Mater

The first performance of *Stabat mater* was in 1767. Most likely Haydn wrote it as a contribution to a long-standing tradition of performing *Grabmusik* (tomb music) on Good Friday in the chapel of the Ester-házy palace in Eisenstadt. Werner had contributed to the tradition, and Haydn may have been showing his readiness to continue the tradition. He took great pains with this work. He was particularly keen to express the words appropriately. So he sent the piece to Hasse for critique, especially with regard to the expression of the words, and reported Hasse's response to Nicolaus.

> You will recall that last year I set to music with all my power the highly esteemed hymn, called Stabat Mater, and that I sent it to the great and world-celebrated Hasse with no other intention than that in case, here and there, I had not expressed adequately words of such great importance, this lack could be rectified by a master so successful in all forms of music. But contrary to my merits, this unique artist honoured the work by inexpressible praise, and wished nothing more than to hear it performed with the good players it requires. (Landon 2, p. 144)

Later, in his autobiographical letter, Haydn again mentioned Hasse's complimentary response. "I shall treasure his testimonial all my life, as if it were gold" (Landon 2, p. 398).

Hasse's high esteem for the work must have been shared by the general public. *Stabat mater* became Haydn's most frequently performed and widely disseminated work during his lifetime. In 1784 an anonymous Englishman wrote that in *Stabat mater* Haydn "is like a heaven-born genius soaring to the *highest elevation* of his art, by adding his lays to those of poetry, and giving double force to language by the energy of his music. And here we behold him, not in a servile manner trying his genius on trifling airs, but imposing on himself a task worthy of his great mind. The subject he made choice of was the *Stabat Mater,* in which his talents found ample scope for that dignity and sublimity so essentially necessary in sacred music" (Landon 2, p. 497).

Stabat mater is one of the most beautiful and popular hymn texts from the Middle Ages. In twenty strophes, or sections of text, it moves from depicting the sorrowing Mary *(Mater dolorosa)* at the foot of the cross to a prayer for deliverance from the flames of hell and acceptance into the glories of heaven. Haydn's setting of the text calls for four soloists, choir, and a string orchestra plus two oboes (replaced by English horns in movements II and X). It is masterfully structured and poignantly expressive throughout. He organized the twenty strophes of text into thirteen movements. Five of the thirteen movements are choruses, placed strategically to articulate the beginning of each new section of text. (See Listener's Guide, pp. 76-79.)

Haydn was especially concerned that his music would adequately express the affect of the words. That is immediately apparent in the first movement. Its text, like the text of the entire piece, is full of words that call for affective settings — *dolorosa* ("grieving"); *lacrimosa* ("weeping"); *pendebat* ("hanging"); *gementem, contristatum et dolentem* ("lamenting, anguished and grieving"). His success in meeting this challenge certainly warranted Hasse's praise.

Changes of key from movement to movement also have affective significance and give structural coherence to the whole work. The changes are mostly down a third, alternating between minor and major keys (for example the first three movements progress from G minor to E♭ major to C minor). The downward movement of keys with their increasing number of flats is fitting for this sorrowful text. Movement IV interrupts the downward progression of keys. Had Haydn continued the initial pattern, movements IV and V would have been in A♭ major and F minor respectively (the major and minor keys with four flats). Instead, movement IV is in the doubly surprising key of F major (only one flat). Haydn skipped A♭ on the way to F, and then made it major instead of minor. F major, especially in this context, gives the music an appropriate feeling of gentle, pastoral compassion for the words "Who is not able to feel compassion contemplating the pious mother?"

Listener's Guide for Haydn, Stabat Mater

The scene: Mary grieving at the foot of the cross

		Key	Tempo / Notes
I. Chorus (strophes 1 & 2)	Stabat mater dolorosa iuxta crucem lacrimosa, dum pendebat Filius. Cuius animam gementem, contristatam et dolentem pertransivit gladius.	The Mother of Sorrows stood by the cross weeping, where her Son was hanging, whose lamenting soul, anguished and grieving, was pierced by a sword.	G minor (2 flats minor)	Largo. Note expressive/rhetorical emphasis on "dolorosa," "lacrimosa," "pendebat," and "gementem, contristatam et dolentem."
II. Alto aria (strophes 3 & 4)	O quam tristis et afflicta fuit illa benedicta, Mater unigeniti! Quae moerebat et dolebat et tremebat dum videbat nati poenas incliti.	O how sad and afflicted was that blessed one, Mother of the Only-begotten, who mourned and wept and trembled when she saw the pains of her glorious Son.	E♭ major (3 flats major)	Larghetto. English horns replace oboes.

Sympathy for Mary: two rhetorical questions; two descriptions of what she saw

		Key	Tempo / Notes
III. Chorus (strophe 5)	Quis est homo qui non fleret matrem Christi si videret in tanto supplicio?	Who is the one who would not weep if he saw the mother of Christ in so much torment?	C minor (3 flats minor)	Lento
IV. Soprano aria (strophe 6)	Quis non posset contristari piam Matrem contemplari dolentem cum Filio?	Who is not able to feel compassion contemplating the pious mother grieving with her Son?	F major (1 flat major)	Moderato. Pattern of keys descending by 3rds disrupted. F major after C minor gives the music a compassionate, pastoral feeling.

V. Bass aria (strophe 7)

Pro peccatis suae gentis vidit Iesum in tormentis, et flagellis subditum.	For the sins of his people she saw Jesus in torment and subjected to scourging.	B♭ major (2 flats major)

Allegro ma non troppo
Opening portrays the arrogant rebellion of the sinner. Note change to minor on "Jesus in torment."

VI. Tenor aria (strophe 8)

Vidit suum dulcem Natum moriendo desolatum, dum emisit spiritum.	She saw her sweet Son dying desolate as he gave up his spirit.	F minor (4 flats minor)

Lento, e mestoso
Deepest flat region in the whole piece – Jesus dying desolate.

Prayer to Mary, Part 1: Make me feel your grief and suffer with the Crucified

VII. Chorus (strophes 9 & 10)

Eia, mater, fons amoris, me sentire vim doloris fac, ut tecum lugeam. Fac ut ardeat cor meum in amando Christum Deum [fac] ut sibi complaceam.	Alas, mother, fount of love, make me feel the strength of your sorrow so that I may mourn with you. Make my heart burn in loving Christ my God [make me] so that I may please him.	D minor (1 flat minor)

Allegretto
The most distant key change between two adjacent movements articulates the change from observing and sympathizing with Mary to praying to her.
Note the rhetorical emphasis on "make me" towards the end. Haydn added an additional *fac* at the beginning of the last line and emphasized the final repetitions of it with two strong, isolated chords: *fac – – –, fac ut sibi complaceam.*

VIII. Soprano and tenor duet (strophes 11 & 12)

Sancta Mater, istud agas, crucifixi fige plagas cordi meo valide. Tui nati vulnerati, tam dignati pro me pati, poenas mecum divide.	Holy Mother, do this: drive the wounds of the Crucified deep into my heart. Of your wounded Son, who submitted to suffer for me, his pains with me share.	B♭ major (2 flats major)

Larghetto

IX. Alto aria (strophes 13 & 14)

Fac me vere tecum flere,
crucifixo condolere,
donec ego vixero.
iuxta crucem tecum stare,
et me tibi sociare
in planctu desidero.

| G minor |
| (2 flats minor) |

Make me truly weep with you,
and suffer with the Crucified,
as long as I shall live.
To stand beside the cross with you
and join with you
in weeping is my desire.

Lagrimoso
Return to key of opening movement.
The unusual tempo/expression marking points to
the affective similarity with the first
movement. Cp. "lagrimoso" with "lacrimosa,"
the key word of the first strophe.
Also note the long-held opening note in both
movements. In the first it is emphasized and
illustrated *stabat* ("stood"). Here it
emphasizes the key word of the prayer, *fac*
("make me"). Although it is not on the same
word, it (along with the other reminders of the
first movement) suggests *stabat* in this
movement in which the believer prays that
Mary will "Make me . . . to stand beside the cross
with you."

Prayer to Mary, Part 2: Let me bear Christ's death and be cherished in his grace

X. Quartet and chorus
(strophes 15, 16, & 17)

Virgo virginum praeclara,
mihi jam non sis amara,
fac me tecum plangere.
Fac, ut portem Christi mortem,
passionis fac consortem,
et plagas recolere.
Fac me plagis vulnerari,
cruce hac inebriari,
ob amorem filii.

| E♭ major |
| (3 flats major) |

Virgin of virgins resplendent,
to me now be not bitter,
let me lament with you.
Let me bear Christ's death,
share in his Passion,
and reflect upon his wounds.
Let me be wounded with his beatings,
inebriated by the cross
because of the love of your Son.

Andante
English horns replace oboes.
Note again (and more persistently) the rhetorical
emphasis on *fac* ("let me"). Cp. no. VII, the
opening chorus of the first prayer to Mary.

Movement	Latin	Translation	Key	Tempo / Notes
XI. Bass aria (strophe 18)	Flammis orci ne succendar, per te, Virgo, fac defendar in die iudicii.	So that I not burn in the flames of hell, by you, Virgin, let me be defended in the day of judgment.	C minor (3 flats minor)	**Presto** — The only truly fast tempo marking in the piece. The fast tempo, minor key, and string tremolos depict fear of judgment and hell fire.
XII. Tenor aria (strophe 19)	Fac me cruce custodiri, morte Christi praemuniri, consoveri gratia.	Let me be guarded by the cross, protected by Christ's death, cherished by grace.	C major (no flats major)	**Moderato** — Strong affective contrast with previous movement as the focus changes from fear of hell's flames to hope of heaven's grace.

The glory of Paradise

Movement	Latin	Translation	Key	Tempo / Notes
XIII. Chorus (strophe 20)	Quando corpus morietur, fac ut animae donetur paradisi gloria. Amen.	When my body dies, let my soul be given the glory of Paradise. Amen.	G minor/major (2 flats minor / 1 sharp major)	**Largo assai/Alla breve** — Threefold repetition of *fac* at the choral entrance. Change to G major for the long fugue on the last line of text. The only "sharp" key — the brightest key — in the piece. Fugue gives way to coloratura singing by soprano soloist.

Movement V in B♭ major (two flats) starts the flatward direction again. Its music has been criticized as being inappropriate for its text, *Pro peccatis suae gentis* ("For the sins of his people"). The major key and brash opening theme seem out of place. But the character of that opening is fitting as a description of proud sinners — "You will be like God," Satan promised Eve. The march-like repeated notes and boldly rising scale vividly portray arrogant rebellion, rebellion that led to Jesus' torment. So for the next line — "she saw Jesus in torment" — the music changes abruptly from major to minor.

Movement VI continues and accelerates the downward motion with a plunge to F minor (four flats). Haydn saved this key, the lowest key of any movement in the piece, for the text that speaks of Jesus "dying desolate." F minor would have been reached smoothly through A♭ major had the original sequence of keys continued — G minor, E♭ major, C minor, A♭ major, F minor. But since the F major and B♭ major of movements IV and V interrupted that sequence, the arrival of F minor is a surprise, an especially dark surprise following the two movements in major keys.

Having reached the nadir, the text shifts from describing and sympathizing with Mary to a prayer. The piece's biggest key change articulates this change in focus. The music jumps from F minor (four flats) to D minor (one flat). D minor then becomes the beginning of another downward sequence of keys (as if bowing down in prayer) analogous to the opening sequence, and, like it, ultimately reaching down to C minor — D minor, B♭ major, G minor, E♭ major, C minor.

A key word throughout the prayer is *fac* ("make me" or "let me"). In movement VII *fac* appears at the beginning of lines three and four. Haydn gave it special emphasis by adding it to the beginning of the last line and having it sung to two strong, isolated chords before completing the phrase: *fac — — —, fac — — —, fac ut sibi complaceam. Fac* next appears at the beginning of movement IX, where it is held for three long, slow beats. The long opening note not only emphasizes *fac,* but it also recalls the long note on *stabat* at the beginning of the whole piece. There the long note emphasized the word, and it also depicted Mary *standing* resolutely at the foot of the cross. It is not coincidental that the text of movement IX asks Mary, "Make me . . . *to stand* beside the cross with you." To further underscore the return of the standing-by-the-cross imagery, movement IX returns to the key of movement I (G minor) and has the unusual expression marking *lagrimoso,* a reminder of a key word, *lacrimosa,* in the first movement.

The emphasis on *fac* reaches its climax in movement X, the quartet with chorus that articulates the beginning of Part 2 of the prayer. Karl Geiringer says the movement is "especially stirring," even in a piece whose music throughout conveys an "atmosphere of restlessness and suffering superbly matching that of the text." "The soloists have the leadership, while the chorus, in somber responses, merely enunciates brief passages and frequently only single words. Most impressive are the moments when to the soloists' passionate utterance 'Passionis fac consortem — fac ut portem Christi mortem — fac me plagis vulnerari,' the chorus again and again adds the word 'fac,' like an urgent prayer."[7]

Movement XI is a climax of a different kind. It is the only fast movement in the whole piece. Its fast tempo, minor key, jagged leaps, and string tremolos depict the terror of the flames of hell on the Day of Judgment. But fearful C minor turns into joyful and reassuring C major as movement XII turns to thoughts of Christ's grace. Then in movement XIII, the music first drops back to G minor when thoughts turn to death *(morietur)*. But since those who die in Christ have his promise that they will be raised with him, another minor to major shift takes the music to G major (one sharp, the highest key of the piece) for the last line of text, *paradisi gloria,* set as a fugal chorus alternating with a coloratura soprano solo. Then at the *Amen,* coloratura takes over, first by the soprano soloist and then by the quartet of soloists punctuated by strong, confident chords sung by the choir.

Nicolaus would rarely, if ever, require his Kapellmeister to write sacred music, but had he done so, the *Missa Cellensis* and especially the *Stabat mater* make it clear that Haydn would have excelled in the genre. That Nicolaus never did so leaves posterity bereft of what would have been an especially rich addition to the repertory. But given what Haydn gave us instead, we certainly have no cause to lament.

7. Karl Geiringer, *Haydn: A Creative Life in Music,* 3rd revised and enlarged edition (Berkeley: University of California Press, 1982), p. 248.

CHAPTER 8

Sturm und Drang: *Symphonies*

1768-72

Let Music put on Protean changes now.

THOMAS CAMPION

*Haydn studied his art without ceasing. After he had composed
many works, he began again a complete course in composition
to affirm himself in his art and to know its secrets better.*

ANTON REICHA

A Generally Trouble-Free Life

Haydn told his biographer Dies that "the story of his life could interest nobody" (p. 75). By the time he said that late in his life, he had lived through
the French Revolution and Napoleonic Wars; he had rubbed elbows with
many of the rich, the powerful, and the famous of his day; and he was considered Europe's greatest living composer, his music loved and revered by
all. So his statement probably says more about his humility than about the
events and course of his life. Nevertheless, the implication that his life was
largely humdrum is not entirely false. During long stretches of time, he
routinely went about his business day after day, week after week, year after
year in isolated Eszterháza. Further, we know of no times of physical or
emotional crisis. No doubt he "had to struggle under manifold pressures
from without," as Griesinger wrote, but his personal life was "marked by
no great event" (p. 8). To be sure, big occasions arose at Eszterháza — such
as the visit from Empress Maria Theresa and her retinue in 1773. But even

though such occasions filled a few days with excitement, they also made Haydn busier. Besides, he was not one to be unduly impressed by the company of the great. "I have associated with emperors, kings, and many great gentlemen," he would say later, "and have heard many flattering things from them, but I do not wish to live on an intimate footing with such persons, and I prefer people of my own status" (Griesinger, p. 55). For Haydn, special occasions at Eszterháza, with all their glitz and glitter, were part of the humdrum.

Music historians, however, have long suspected some kind of personal crisis in the late '60s and early '70s, a time when he wrote an unusually large number of intensely expressive works in minor keys. But about all that can be found is an illness in 1770. At the time, the illness seemed severe enough for his brother Michael to ask for permission from his employer, the Archbishop of Salzburg, for leave to visit his sick brother. But the fact that Haydn recovered quickly enough so that Michael did not need to come suggests that the sickness may not have been as grave as at first it might have appeared. However, some twenty years later, Haydn's friend, Rev. Christian Ignatius Latrobe, wrote:

> Sometime about the year 1770 (but as to the particular year, I am not sure), Haydn was seized with a violent disorder, which threatened his life. "I was," said he, "not prepared to die, and prayed to God to have mercy upon me and grant me recovery. I also vowed that if I were restored to health I would compose a Stabat Mater in honour of the Blessed Virgin as a token of thankfulness. My prayer was heard and I recovered. With a grateful sense of my duty, I cheerfully set about the performance of my Vow, and endeavoured to do it in my best manner."[1]

But since *Stabat mater* had its first performance in 1767, Haydn must have been confusing it with another piece, perhaps the *Salve regina* in G minor. Many years later, Griesinger told how Haydn joked about the illness.

Haydn succumbed to a heavy fever, and the doctor strictly forbade him, during his gradual recovery, to occupy himself with music. Soon afterward, Haydn's wife went out to church, having first sternly impressed upon the maid that she must see her master did not go to the clavier.

---

1. Quoted in E. Holmes, "The Rev. Christian Ignatius Latrobe," *The Musical Times and Singing Class Circular* 4/88 (September 1, 1851): 256.

Haydn, in bed, pretended he had heard nothing of this order, and hardly was his wife gone when he sent the maid out of the house on an errand. Then he leaped in a hurry to his clavier. At the first touch the idea for a whole sonata came to him, and the first part was finished while his wife was at church. When he heard her coming back, he promptly pitched himself back into bed, and there he composed the rest of the sonata. (p. 19)

We need not be surprised that Haydn could both joke about it with one friend and tell another that he wrote a piece in honor of the Virgin as thanksgiving for his recovery. In any case, no matter how serious the illness may have been, it cannot have been the "crisis" that brought about an unusual spate of minor works, especially since some of those works preceded the illness.

An Unusual Concentration of Works in Minor Keys

Whether or not something in Haydn's life caused it, the spike in the number of compositions in minor keys between 1766 and 1772 is remarkable: five or six symphonies, four string quartets, and two keyboard sonatas. Those numbers hardly seem remarkable when compared with the total number of works Haydn wrote in those genres during the same period: sixteen or seventeen symphonies, eighteen string quartets, and perhaps as many as eight keyboard sonatas. Only about one in four is in a minor key. However, one in four is a large percentage when compared to the percentage of works in minor in his total output — only about one in eight out of all the works in those three major instrumental genres (including keyboard trios). If we add that only two of the 126 baryton trios are in minor (both, significantly, dating from about 1768-71) and that the number is similarly small among some one hundred-plus pieces in other instrumental genres, the percentage nearly dwindles to insignificance. But, of course, the smaller the percentage, the more the few stand out as extraordinary. So when music historians discovered that half of all Haydn's instrumental pieces in minor keys were concentrated in a short seven-year period within a career that spanned a half-century, they saw it as a phenomenon that had to be explained by something extraordinary. For a while, lack of evidence for something extraordinary did not stop speculation. One historian even speculated that Haydn, like Beethoven, was jilted by an unknown "immortal beloved." But when nothing extraordinary could be found in his life, the only recourse was to say it must have been caused by something "in the air," by the *Zeitgeist*. And since the pieces in question are not only in minor, but are especially intense and turbulent in character, the late '60s and early '70s came to be known as Haydn's *Sturm und Drang* (storm and stress) period, a brief stage in his life that seemed to presage the coming Romantic period.

Sturm und Drang

Sturm und Drang in the strict sense refers to a German literary movement that had a brief heyday in the mid and late 1770s. It is characterized by extreme emotionalism, subjectivity, and rebellion against social conventions. It took its name from Friedrich Maximilian von Klinger's 1776 play set in revolutionary America, *Sturm und Drang* (originally titled *Wirrwarr* — chaos, confusion). A statement Klinger made about himself reveals the main characteristic of *Sturm und Drang* — its emphasis on strong passion: "I am torn by passions; any other man would be destroyed by them. Any moment I would like to see mankind and everything devoured by chaos and then throw myself into it" (Landon 2, p. 271). Some of the more important works in the movement are Goethe's *Götz von Berlichingen* (1773) and *Die Leiden des junge Werther (The Sufferings of Young Werther)* (1774), and Schiller's *Die Rauber (The Robber)* (1781). But these all came *after* Haydn's so-called *Sturm und Drang* period. So the term is misleading insofar as it suggests that the literary movement had an influence on Haydn's music.

However, *Sturm und Drang* characteristics — or, more generally, proto-romantic characteristics — can be found in the arts and letters throughout Europe during the third quarter of the eighteenth century. Gothic novels came into vogue beginning with Horace Walpole's *Castle of Otranto* (1764). Several paintings reveal a delight in the frightening, the tempestuous, and the dark — for example Claude-Joseph Vernet's *The Seastorm* (1752), and *The Nightmare* by Henry Fuseli (1781). Jean-Jacques Rousseau ranked feelings above reason, and "natural" man (who is innately good) over "civilized" man (who has been corrupted). Johann Gottfried Herder (1744-1803) has been called the father of *Sturm und Drang*. Under the influence of the ballads collected by Thomas Percy in his *Reliques of Ancient English Poetry* (1765), Herder wrote poems that he called *Volkslieder* (folk songs) and claimed them to be "the true expression of the feeling of the whole soul." Robert Bareikis wrote that Herder's esthetics abandoned "traditional focus upon the effect of the work in favour of a concentration upon the person of the artist and the work of art *per se.*"[2] Similarly Edward Young's *Conjectures on Original Composition* (1759) contributed to the idea of the "primitive" artist as a genius uninhibited by the rules and morals of society.

James MacPherson's Ossianic forgeries (1762-63), an epic poem passed off as the product of Ossian, a natural, primitive genius, are filled with dark and gloomy scenes, heroic action, tragic deaths, and unmitigated grief.

Autumn is dark on the mountains; grey mist rests on the hills. The whirlwind is heard on the heath. Dark rolls the river through the narrow plain. A tree stands alone on the hill, and marks the grave of Connal. . . .

Here was the din of arms; and here the groans of the dying. Mournful are the wars of Fingal! O Connal! It was here thou didst fall. . . .

Dargo the mighty came on, like a cloud of thunder. . . . Bright rose their swords on each side; dire was the clang of their steel.

The daughter of Rinval was near; Crimora, bright in the armour of man. . . . She followed her youth to the war, Connal her much beloved. She drew the string on Dargo; but erring pierced her Connal. . . . He bleeds; her Connal dies. All night long she cries, and all the day, O Connal, my love, and my friend! With grief the sad mourner died.

Earth here incloseth the loveliest pair on the hill. The grass grows between the stones of their tomb; I sit in the mournful shade.[3]

The critic Hugh Blair, writing in 1763, said that Ossian's poetry "deserves to be styled, the poetry of the heart. It is a heart that is full, and pours itself forth. He did not write like modern poets, to please readers and critics. He sang from the love of poetry and song."[4]

Macpherson's pseudo-Ossian poetry was translated into German and published in Austria in 1768. A few years later, Goethe had the hero of his novel *Werther* exclaim (with obvious reference to the Ossian fragment quoted above):

2. H. C. Robbins Landon, *Haydn: Chronicle and Works,* vol. 2 (Bloomington: Indiana University Press, 1978), p. 269.

3. James MacPherson, *Fragments of Ancient Poetry.* Facsimile of the 1st edition of 1760 (Los Angeles: William Andrews Clark Memorial Library, University of California, 1966), Fragment 5, pp. 23-25.

4. Quoted in M. H. Abrams, *The Mirror and the Lamp* (Oxford: Oxford University Press, 1976), p. 83.

Ossian has superseded Homer in my heart. To what a world does the il-
lustrious bard carry me! To wander over the pathless wilds, surrounded
by impetuous whirlwinds, where, by the feeble light of the moon, we see
the spirits of our ancestors; to hear from the mountain-tops, mid the
roar torrents, their plaintive sounds issuing from deep caverns, and the
sorrowful lamentations of a maiden who sighs and expires on the mossy
tomb of the warrior by whom she was adored.[5]

Werther is ruled by passion. He is a social misfit, but "a hero who touched
an exposed sociological nerve of his time." He is "guided *entirely* by his emotions; he is completely alone; his inability to accept the social conventions of
his time leads inevitably to his destruction."[6] Along with such strains of irrationality and anti-sociality, Werther also deifies the creative process. As M. H.
Abrams puts it, "The divine Idea beamed from God into the soul's mirror,
thence to be projected on the written page, has become one of the erotic fanta-
sies and fevered emotions of the artist-hero of the *Sturm und Drang*."[7]

Sturm und Drang *Characteristics in Music*

Composers around this time — not just Haydn — wrote some intensely
passionate, even terrifying, works. Not surprisingly *Sturm und Drang* characteristics show up in opera, especially in accompanied recitatives, where
orchestral commentary heightens the passion of the words, and in ballet,
where bodily movement and gesture join music to raise the emotional intensity. A fine example of the latter is the remarkable finale of Gluck's *Don
Juan* (1761), which depicts Don Juan's descent into hell. Arias and ensembles in *Sturm und Drang* style also begin to appear more regularly (though
still infrequently). Like music in general, operas at the time were overwhelmingly major in tonality, but typically each one had a piece or two in
minor that stood out from the rest. Haydn's *La cantarina* (1766) and *Lo speziale* (1768) both have a *Sturm und Drang* aria. His next opera, *Le pescatrici*
(1769-70), uses *Sturm und Drang* style for Prince Lindoro's aria, "Varca il
mar" ("He crosses the sea"), the turbulence of the music reflecting not only

5. Johann Wolfgang von Goethe, *The Sorrows of Young Werther,* trans. by R. D. Boylan
(Boston: Francis A. Niccolls and Co., 1902), p. 87.

6. Barry S. Brook, "Sturm und Drang and the Romantic Period in Music," *Studies in
Romanticism* 9 (1970): 272.

7. Abrams, p. 44.

the stormy sea but also Lindoro's emotional state. Apart from opera, other large-scale vocal works also provided opportunities for *Sturm und Drang* style — recall, for example, the "flames of hell" movement in *Stabat Mater*.

But *Sturm und Drang* style was not limited to vocal music and ballet. Intensely expressive instrumental works in minor keys became more prevalent in the years surrounding 1770 than they were before or after. Examples include an A minor symphony by Haydn's friend Dittersdorf, a D minor symphony by Franz Beck (a Mannheimer working in Paris), and a symphony by the Italian Luigi Boccherini titled "La Casa del Diavolo," based on Gluck's ballet music for Don Juan's descent into hell. The best-known example, other than a few of Haydn's symphonies, is the seventeen-year-old Mozart's Symphony no. 25 in G minor (1773). Two centuries later, its *Sturm und Drang* character made it perfect background music for the opening scene of the film *Amadeus,* in which a suicidal Salieri has slit his throat.

Haydn's *Sturm und Drang* Works

Haydn's minor mode symphonies, quartets, and sonatas of this period fit with this broader picture of European proto-romanticism for which *Sturm und Drang* is an apt and commonly used (though chronologically misleading) designation. We do not know how much of this broader intellectual and artistic activity Haydn was aware of — probably little outside of music. But regardless of whether any of it had an influence on him (or he on it), it is clear that indeed there was something "in the air" that infected many artists and philosophers in various ways, all of which, however, were in some way a reaction against the Enlightenment's excessive faith in reason and its glibly optimistic view of the human condition. In Haydn's case the reaction may have simply been against the triviality and narrow emotional range of the *galant* music favored by the Enlightenment. His incorporation of Baroque ingredients into his generally *galant* earlier music is an indication that he was never entirely satisfied with *galant* simplicity. His increased use of Baroque contrapuntal techniques and his wide-ranging exploration of unusual tonalities and compositional techniques during the late '60s and early '70s suggest a growing dissatisfaction with what Charles Rosen calls the "simplification and destruction that attend any revolution."[8] But whatever Haydn may have had

8. Charles Rosen, *The Classical Style: Haydn, Mozart, Beethoven* (New York: W. W. Norton and Company, 1972), p. 45.

in common with *Sturm und Drang* or other proto-romanticisms of the time, it cannot be said that he abandoned "traditional focus upon the effect of the work in favour of a concentration upon the person of the artist," or that "he did not write like modern poets, to please readers and critics" or believed that his work was "the divine Idea beamed from God into the soul's mirror." In short, he was never infected by irrationality, anti-sociality, and the idea that the artist was the voice of God.

Each of Haydn's three main instrumental genres during this period shows examples of *Sturm und Drang* (in the limited stylistic sense), but the five or six minor-key symphonies are those most closely associated with *Sturm und Drang*. The earliest one is no. 39 in G minor. But since its two middle movements display no *Sturm und Drang* characteristics — instead they are decidedly *galant* in style — it is sometimes considered not truly representative. However, the next two — nos. 49 in F minor and 26 in D minor — are thoroughly *Sturm und Drang*.

Symphony no. 49 came to be titled *La passione*. Although the title was not Haydn's, it has stuck, no doubt because it begins with a slow movement (that is, it is in the old church sonata form), and its prevailing somber character makes it fitting for contemplating the suffering and death of Christ. But as noted before, church sonata form does not necessarily indicate that a work was intended for a church service. Furthermore, instrumental music was not used during Lent in Viennese churches. Nevertheless, Haydn may have written it for a non-liturgical, devotional occasion during Lent at Eszterháza or elsewhere.

There is no question about the liturgical connections in Symphony no. 26, though again this does not necessarily indicate a liturgical function for the work. It is called *Lamentatione* or, in at least one source, *Passio et Lamentatio*. The titles, though again not Haydn's, appear in many early copies and derive from Haydn's obvious incorporation of chant melodies in the first two movements. In the first movement he borrowed a melody used for the chanting of the story of Christ's Passion, and in the second, a melody used for chanting the Lamentations of Jeremiah.

Symphony no. 52 in C minor is probably the next of the minor symphonies. Though a fine work, it is not up to the standard of the two that preceded it or the two that followed it. Indeed the two that followed it, no. 44 in E minor and no. 45 in F♯ minor, are among Haydn's greatest works from any time in any genre. No. 45 in F♯ minor, nicknamed *Farewell*, is undoubtedly the best-known of all Haydn's earlier symphonies and the only one that never completely fell out of the orchestral repertory.

The Farewell *Symphony*

The story behind the *Farewell* Symphony is perhaps better known than the work itself. Here is Griesinger's version.

> In Prince Esterházy's orchestra were several young married men who in summer, when the Prince stayed at Eszterháza castle, had to leave their wives behind in Eisenstadt. Contrary to his custom, the Prince once wished to extend his stay in Eszterháza by several weeks. The fond husbands, especially dismayed at this news, turned to Haydn and pleaded with him to do something.
>
> Haydn had the notion of writing a symphony (known as the Farewell Symphony) in which one instrument after the other is silent. This was performed at the first opportunity in the presence of the Prince, and each of the musicians was directed, as soon as his part was finished, to put out his candle, pack up his music and, with his instrument under his arm, to go away. The Prince and the audience understood the meaning of this pantomime at once, and the next day came the order to depart from Eszterháza. (p. 19)

Those who have heard the story but do not know the symphony are likely to think: "Cute story. Typical Papa Haydn, up to his practical jokes." But if they listen despite their skepticism, one phrase of the music will quickly put an end to that notion. The full orchestra bursts in loudly in F♯ minor, the first violins playing a theme that angrily strides downward across nearly two octaves in just two measures. It is accompanied by driving eighth notes in the violas, cellos, and basses, shrill sustained chords in the oboes and horns, and agitated syncopation in the second violins. It is *Sturm und Drang* to the hilt! (See Example 8-1.) And the music continues with typical *Sturm und Drang* characteristics — strong dissonances, forceful accents, sudden changes of dynamics, wide leaps, unexpected key changes, and the like. But after several minutes of this, in the midst of the turmoil, without warning, "out of the blue," something very different appears. It happens about halfway through the development section after a long build-up has left the music poised to go on in the key of B minor. But after a moment of complete silence the upper strings enter alone with a quiet and completely new eight-bar theme in D major. (See Example 8-2.) For a moment all the turmoil has vanished, especially when the quiet theme is repeated an octave lower by all the strings in their rich, mellow range. An extension, now back in the higher range and with oboes added, leads to a tonally ambiguous and highly dissonant chord that fades into silence on its highest note.

EXAMPLE 8-1

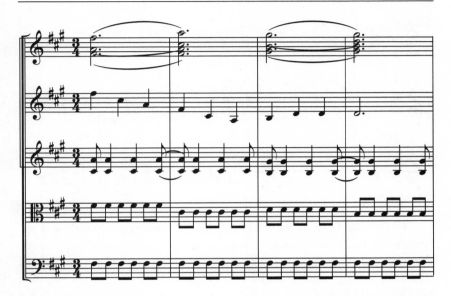

The loud F♯ minor theme from the beginning breaks the silence. But after just six measures Haydn expands that theme by turning it in new harmonic directions until the music, as in the middle of the development section, is again poised to go into B minor. This time, however, there is no silence and no tranquil theme in D major. Instead the music rushes ahead into a B minor statement of the opening theme, then modulates back to the home key of F♯ minor. The movement ends with no abatement of the *Sturm und Drang* turmoil.

All the fury of the first movement dissipates at the beginning of the second movement. Soft and slow A major replaces loud and fast F♯ minor. The dynamic marking at the beginning is *pianissimo,* and it never changes. The scoring is for strings only (violins muted) except for cameo appearances by the two oboes and two horns in only sixteen measures of the 190-measure movement. But behind the peace and serenity, uneasiness lurks in some passages of rhythmic ambiguity and slippage into minor keys.

EXAMPLE 8-2

The first and second violins begin the third movement lightly and op-timistically in F♯ major with what promises to be an untroubled minuet. But after only two measures they are rudely interrupted by a loud chord that has a "wrong" note in the bass — a D-natural that belongs in F♯ *minor,* not F♯ major. The violins, undaunted, try again. But again their little dance tune is interrupted after two measures by a loud chord. This time the chord is "right" but the rhythm is askew. The violins cannot find the downbeat; they keep putting the accent on the third beat of the measure. After four measures they find the downbeat, and, as in the beginning, they play alone. But they have abandoned the dance tune and simply play, in unison, a de-scending line that ends inconclusively near the bottom of their range on an A♯ instead of the tonic F♯, and on the weak third beat of the measure. As the minuet continues, there are more failed attempts to get things right. In the end the violins sink to the same inconclusive ending in the depths of their range.

However, the trio starts on a positive note with a stereotypical horn call. What could be more "right" than the notes of natural horns? In fact, the first two chords that they play are the correct chords that would have happened at the beginning of the minuet if the intrusive D-natural had not disturbed the harmony. As the trio progresses, all continues to seem right. But just when a safe arrival home in F♯ major seems assured, F♯ minor asserts itself insistently enough so that the trio seems about to end in minor. Then, as if hoping the F♯ minor threat will go away by simply ignoring it, the full orchestra ends the trio playing the opening F♯ major horn call — albeit softly. But, of course, the movement does not end with the trio. Trios invariably return to, and literally repeat, the minuet. So too here; again the minuet tune struggles to get things right, but with inevitable lack of success.

The last movement begins as another fast *Sturm und Drang* movement in F♯ minor. It proceeds as a normal sonata form until the end. But the coda, which should bring the movement to a firm conclusion, comes up short on a C♯ chord instead of a conclusive F♯ chord. Now what? Instead of a fast ending in F♯, the music resumes in A major in a slow tempo, a surprise analogous to the surprise in the middle of the development section of the first movement. The music then proceeds according to Haydn's programmatic "gimmick." Little by little players leave, blowing out the candles on their music stands as they go, until only two violinists are left — Tomasini and Haydn. But this is no gimmick. The systematic reduction of the orchestra and the not quite conclusive last chord (there is no bass note to anchor it) bring the music to a wistful close. James Webster says that this symphony is illogically called "farewell." Since "it engenders a psychological progression that corresponds to our feelings about a desperately longed-for journey home," he suggests a more apt nickname would be *Symphony of Longing*.[9]

The Trauer *Symphony*

As great as the *Farewell* Symphony is, Symphony no. 44 in E minor, nicknamed *Trauer* (mourning), is equally great. Its opening movement is constructed from an opening theme that contains two strongly contrasting motives, both introduced in stark unisons. The first two measures present loud, bold upward leaps (a), the next two present soft, sighing motives (b). The two motives are then combined in an accompanied melody in the next eight measures (c). (See Example 8-3.) A few measures later a countermelody joins the two motives in a loud G major passage. (See Example 8-4.) These two motives and the countermelody gave Haydn all he needed to construct a taut *Sturm und Drang* movement filled with strong

9. James Webster, *Haydn's "Farewell" Symphony and the Idea of Classical Style* (Cambridge: Cambridge University Press, 1991), p. 119.

EXAMPLE 8-3

EXAMPLE 8-4

accents and dynamic contrasts, canonic passages, a "piling up" version of the opening motive that sounds like the beginning of a stretto fugue, and driving rhythms, all to be performed "con brio" (with vigor) as Haydn instructed at the beginning.

A tense, canonic minuet in E minor and a serene and deeply moving slow movement in E major follow. Haydn is alleged to have requested that the slow movement be played at his funeral. The story is dubious, but as one wit said, "If he didn't request it, he should have!" (Princess Grace of Monaco did. It was performed at her funeral in 1982 in Monte Carlo.)

The last movement is back to E minor in a fast, driving *Sturm und Drang* style. (See Example 8-5.) As in the first movement, Haydn made significant use of counterpoint. Especially notable is the double canon that articulates the arrival of the G major section of the exposition and the return to E minor at the beginning of the recapitulation. (See Example 8-6.)

EXAMPLE 8-5

EXAMPLE 8-6

At the beginning of the development section, Haydn stretched out the opening motive into a long, ascending sequence. Remarkably, this motive is stated *nine* times, each time a step higher. Sequences of three or four repetitions are common; five or six repetitions feel like a real stretch. But nine? The build-up of tension is overwhelming, and it is made all the greater by a bass line pulling down while the upper parts are pulling up! Landon says this finale "is perhaps the most concentrated and overwhelming *Sturm und Drang* movement Haydn ever wrote."[10]

Other Haydn Symphonies of the Time

The striking character of the minor-key symphonies makes it understandable that they have overshadowed Haydn's other symphonies of the time — understandable but regrettable, because most of them, in their own ways, are fine works, products of the same fertile imagination and consummate skill. A few examples will have to suffice. Symphony no. 43 in E♭ major, nicknamed *Mercury,* is a chamber symphony, subtly expressive and technically sophisticated. In contrast, Symphony no. 48 is a C major symphony *par excellence,* displaying all the brilliance associated with symphonies in that key. Its second movement, a beautiful pastorale with tinges of sweet nostalgia, is all the more effective amidst its brilliant surroundings. Different again is Symphony no. 42 in D major. It is bright and cheerful throughout, from its effervescent first movement — it could be the overture to a comic opera — to its " 'hit tune' Finale" which contains "stylistic details dear to Haydn's famous rondos which conquered Europe in the next decade."[11] But the best of them all might be the two that he wrote in 1772, the same year as the *Farewell* Symphony, a truly remarkable year for symphonies. No. 46, in the unusual key of B major, might have been conceived as a companion for the *Farewell* Symphony. Among its many noteworthy features is the surprise return of the minuet theme toward the end of the fourth movement, a trick that Beethoven would use a generation later in his Fifth Symphony. The other 1772 symphony, no. 47 in G major, so attracted Mozart that he copied its opening theme, apparently with the intention of performing the work in one of his concerts. And well he might! He once wrote with great pride to his father about some of his own works:

10. H. C. Robbins Landon, *Haydn Symphonies* (Seattle: University of Washington Press, 1969), p. 27.

11. Landon, *Chronicle and Works,* vol. 2, p. 301.

These concertos are a happy medium between what is too easy and too difficult; they are very brilliant, pleasing to the ear, and natural, without being vapid. There are passages here and there from which connoisseurs alone can derive satisfaction; but these passages are written in such a way that the less learned cannot fail to be pleased, though not knowing why.[12]

No doubt Mozart was impressed by the same qualities in Haydn's Symphony no. 47. It satisfies "connoisseurs" and at the same time it pleases the "less learned." As a writer in a Pressburg paper wrote, Haydn's music "excites the admiration of experts and is nothing short of delightful for the listener" (Landon 2, p. 205).

12. *The Letters of Mozart and His Family,* trans. Emily Anderson (New York: Macmillan, 1962), p. 833.

CHAPTER 9

From Divertimenti to Sonatas and Quartets

THE LATE 1760S AND EARLY 1770S

The composer can do nothing better than to reach a mutual understanding with the consumers on their inarticulate desires and his ability of wisely and honestly gratifying them.

PAUL HINDEMITH

Music for Diversion

The dozen or more symphonies Haydn wrote during the late '60s and early '70s alone make it a fruitful period. But they are not the whole story. Far from it, for in the same period of time, he broke new ground in a series of more than a dozen large-scale keyboard works, and he "reinvented" the string quartet.

During the years surrounding 1770, Haydn's achievement in keyboard music was hardly less than it was in the symphony. As with the symphony, the style of his keyboard works changed decisively. Prior to 1766 they were generally short and unpretentious, modeled after the keyboard divertimenti of his older contemporary Georg Christoph Wagenseil. Then during the late '60s and early '70s "they became larger and correspondingly deeper in character." No longer merely "diversionary" divertimenti, they were now vehicles for "elevated thoughts."[1] Although Haydn continued to designate some of the works of this period as divertimenti, he also began using the term *sonata.*

---

1. A. Peter Brown, *Joseph Haydn's Keyboard Music* (Bloomington: Indiana University Press, 1986), p. 289.

The widespread use of the term *divertimento* during the mid-eighteenth century is significant. Multi-movement keyboard works were not the only ones Haydn and his contemporaries called divertimenti. They also used the term for multi-movement works written for a variety of instrumental ensembles. As we have already seen, Haydn used it for the more than one hundred twenty baryton trios he wrote for Nicolaus to play; he also used it for his early string quartets. In fact, he was still using the term for his Opus 20 string quartets, works that are much more than merely diversionary. (Likewise, as late as 1788, Mozart called one of his greatest works, the String Trio in E flat, a divertimento.) But even if the association of divertimenti with lightweight music that merely diverts is not always warranted, the term's widespread use during the last half of the eighteenth century indicates a general view of music during that time — a view typical of the Enlightenment. The Enlightenment favored music that was pleasing and moving, natural and simple, "an innocent luxury," as Charles Burney said, "unnecessary, indeed, to our existence, but a great improvement and gratification of the sense of hearing."[2] Immanuel Kant, in his *Critique of Judgment,* expressed a typical Enlightenment view of music when he said: "If we estimate the worth of the beautiful arts by the culture they supply to the mind and take as a standard the expansion of the faculties which must concur in the judgment for cognition, music will have the lowest place among them (as it has perhaps the highest among those arts which are valued for their pleasantness), because *it merely plays with sensations.*"[3]

Several post-Baroque musical styles reflecting Enlightenment ideals were in the foreground during Haydn's formative years. These various styles have in common the quality of *galanterie,* a word "derived from what the French called the *style galant,* which stemmed in turn from the old French verb *galer,* which meant 'to amuse' in a tasteful, courtly sort of way, with refined wit, elegant manners, and easy grace."[4] *Galant* music features simple melodies with clear phrasing supported by texturally and harmonically unobtrusive accompaniments. It is music that participates in the Enlightenment's trend toward simplification, a result of Enlightenment values such as innocent pleasure and immediate appeal. Contemporary writers praised *galant* music for its clarity, pleasantness, naturalness, and

2. Quoted in *Music in the Western World: A History in Documents,* selected and annotated by Piero Weiss and Richard Taruskin (New York: Schirmer Books, 1983), p. 303.

3. *Music in the Western World,* p. 297 (my emphasis).

4. Richard Taruskin, *The Oxford History of Music,* vol. 2, *Music of the Seventeenth and Eighteenth Centuries* (Oxford: Oxford University Press, 2010), p. 263.

other such qualities. They favored the minuet among dances because of its dignity, elegance, and decorum. In a general way, much of Haydn's music before the mid-1760s can be characterized as *galant,* though his folksiness and roguish sense of humor not infrequently offset dignity, elegance, and decorum.

Innocent pleasure, immediate appeal, and *galanterie* are not the highest goals for music, but they are not to be snobbishly scorned. Neither should they be valued too highly. Pleasure has a way of becoming the only goal, with the result that music gets "dumbed down," sinking to the lowest common denominator of taste. But Haydn never sank to that level, even when he quite obviously aimed to please his audience (including the performers). He would have said with Benjamin Britten: "I write music for human beings — directly and deliberately. I consider their voices, the range, the power, the subtlety, and the colour potentialities of them. I consider the instruments they play — their most expressive and suitable individual sonorities. I also take note of the *human* circumstances of music, of its environment and conventions."[5] And unlike composers whose primary aim is self-expression, or who believe art is for its own sake, he would have joined Britten in saying: "I find nothing wrong with offering to my fellow-men music which may inspire them or comfort them, which may touch them or entertain them, even educate them — directly and with intention. On the contrary, it is the composer's duty, as a member of society, to speak to or for his fellow human beings."[6]

But neither composer would go entirely down the path of succumbing to popular taste. Britten asked, "Where does one stop, then, in answering people's demands?" I expect Haydn would have substantially agreed with Britten's answer. "It seems that there is no clearly defined Halt sign on this road. The only brake which one can apply is that of one's own private and personal conscience; when that speaks clearly, one must halt; and it can speak for musical or non-musical reasons."[7]

5. Benjamin Britten, *On Receiving the First Aspen Award* (London: Faber Music in association with Faber and Faber, 1978), pp. 10-11.
6. Britten, p. 12.
7. Britten, p. 13.

Keyboard Playing and Keyboard Instruments

Haydn's early keyboard works are decidedly *galant* in their tunefulness and easy accessibility. They are ideal for their intended use as light entertainment or pedagogical material for his students. Most of the players were women, the wives and daughters of noble gentlemen. They generally had an abundance of free time, which they filled by cultivating "accomplishments" such as needlework, making artificial flowers, cutting out paper ornaments, and framing pictures. Keyboard playing was highly valued as a female "accomplishment."

The keyboard instruments they played were the harpsichord, the clavichord, and the fortepiano (or pianoforte). The sound of a harpsichord is made by quills plucking strings when keys are depressed. The sound of clavichords and fortepianos is made when strings are struck by hammers rather than plucked by quills. Since the strings are struck, the player has control of dynamics, a feature unavailable on a harpsichord. The force with which a key on a clavichord or fortepiano is depressed translates directly into the force that strikes a string — the greater the force, the louder the sound. Clavichords in general are smaller and quieter than fortepianos. Except for rare larger clavichords, their use was limited to very small, intimate gatherings and private practice.

The basic difference between a clavichord and a fortepiano is in the way the strings are struck. When a clavichord key is pressed down, a brass tangent at the other end of the lever rises up and strikes the string. As long as the key is held down, the tangent stays against the string. This causes the sound to decay very quickly. In a fortepiano, a wooden hammer, usually felt-covered, strikes the string and immediately bounces away. That allows the string to continue to vibrate so the sound decays much more slowly. But the clavichord has an expressive device that is unavailable on a fortepiano — vibrato. Since the brass tangent stays in contact with the string as long as the player holds the key down, it will wiggle when the player's finger wiggles. The wiggling causes slight changes in the tension on the string, which in turn causes vibrato.

Haydn's Keyboard Music of the Late '60s into the '70s

A few of Haydn's earliest keyboard sonatas surpass the majority in technical demands, expressive depth, and compositional sophistication. Significantly, Haydn called them partitas instead of divertimentos. They were apparently intended for quite advanced students. Three that stand out are nos. 2, 6, and 14. But during the late '60s and into the '70s, his keyboard music underwent a decisive change in style. These sonatas do not often get their due in comparison to the symphonies and string quartets of the same period, but seven surviving sonatas provide ample evidence that Haydn's keyboard music had reached an altitude comparable to that of his symphonies and string quartets. Had seven others that Haydn listed in his own catalogue of works survived, there can be little doubt that his achievements in keyboard music during the late '60s and early '70s would be considered as remarkable as those in the symphonies and string quartets during the same period.

The seven surviving sonatas are nos. 44-47 and 18-20. (Like Hoboken's symphony numbers, his sonata numbers are sometimes grossly misleading chronologically.) They are typically larger than their predecessors and are more idiomatically conceived for the fortepiano, which at the time was beginning to replace the harpsichord as the keyboard instrument of choice. The textures of these sonatas are more varied and their harmonic vocabulary is richer than earlier ones. They range more widely across the tonal spectrum as Haydn explores ever more possibilities within standard formal procedures. It is in the keyboard works of this period that the influence of C. P. E. Bach on Haydn is the most direct, particularly in his expressive ornamentation and in his integration of variation techniques into different forms.

Sonata No. 46 in A♭ Major

Brief descriptions of two sonatas will have to suffice to suggest something of the beauty, drama, expressiveness, and artisanship of these sonatas. The first movement of no. 46 in A♭ major begins with an eight-measure theme. That, of course, is normal. What is not normal is the way the eight measures are divided into phrases of 3 + 2½ + 2½ measures. Throughout the movement, phrases never fall into predictable patterns. They expand, contract, and overlap with a freedom that suggests improvisation. Also suggestive of improvisation are pauses that give the impression of thinking where to go next. Typically, the music goes somewhere unexpected. In the middle of the exposition, a pause occurs after a long build-up to a chord poised to resolve to the expected new key, E♭. Instead, the music goes to F minor only to turn back quickly, though not decisively, to E♭ major. Then, when E♭ major seems secure, it is seriously threatened by E♭ minor just before the cadence. But the threat does not materialize, the music cadences in E♭ major, and the closing theme anchors it there.

The development section begins in a normal way: we hear the opening three-measure phrase in E♭ major and then its repetition in F minor. The F minor statement expands by way of a canonic passage that leads to the longest part of the development — a virtuosic "improvisation" based on a bit of rapid keyboard figuration that until now had appeared only briefly as the extension of a cadence in the exposition. This seemingly inconsequential bit of figuration unexpectedly becomes prominent and takes us on a tonal journey into deep flat regions (all the way to A♭ minor — seven flats!) and back. The rest of the development section stays in F minor but with two pauses on an ambiguous chord that could, but does not, turn the music again into deeper flat regions. When the music finally returns home to A♭ major, we hear the opening theme, and all seems to be well again. But a shock awaits us. The opening theme repeats, but without warning it plunges back into A♭ minor. It stays there for only four measures, after which A♭ major returns and seems securely anchored. But can we be sure? If the music could plunge into minor without warning once, it could do it again. But it does not. Momentary threats of F minor and A♭ minor are quickly averted; the music stays in A♭ major.

The second movement is an adagio in D♭ major. At one time, scholars suspected the sonata was written as late as 1788 because this movement seemed to have been influenced by Mozart. We know now, however, that Haydn wrote it when Mozart was not more than fifteen years old, several years before the two composers met. If anything, this movement might have influenced Mozart. Haydn could be "Mozartian" before Mozart was. But whatever Mozartian flavor there might be in the movement, it also has an archaic, neo-Baroque flavor. It begins with a slowly moving bass supporting a lovely melody that climbs up the tonic triad in flowing eighth notes and then gradually descends, its eighth-note flow occasionally slowed by suspensions. The next four measures repeat the first four but with a third part added above, as if the piece were going to consist of variations over a repeated bass pattern in a trio sonata texture. The trio sonata texture — two melodic lines above a bass — and variations over a repeated bass are both typically Baroque. Although the bass variations do not continue, the Baroque trio texture does. Throughout the movement the flowing melodic lines are tinged with expressive chromatic notes and dissonances that reach a tortuous climax near the end. Charles Rosen numbers it among the pieces that are "on a level that no other composer of Haydn's time could equal or even approach."[8] I would add that not many at any time have equaled it. "Luminous beauty," "noble seriousness," "exquisite," "profound" — all of these and more expressions like them have been used to characterize this movement. All are accurate; all are inadequate.

This marvelous sonata ends with a high-spirited, invigorating contre-danse untroubled by complications beyond some playful extensions (one of them fourteen measures long!) that interrupt the regular four-measure phrases of the dance. It is Haydn at his effervescent best.

Sonata No. 20 in C Minor

The sonata from this period that has received the most acclaim, however, is no. 20 in C minor. By any standard it is a masterful work. Rosemary Hughes did not exaggerate when she called it "a masterpiece of tragic power."[9] It begins with a theme tinged with melancholy worthy of Brahms. After just eight measures the theme cadences firmly in C minor. Then a long passage begins with an unhesitating jump to E♭ major, but it never quite establishes the key convincingly. It never cadences securely in E♭ major, and threats of E♭ minor further destabilize the passage until it finally ends on a long-held dissonant chord whose most dissonant note is achingly suspended in the highest part. The tension is resolved as a vigorous new theme in E♭ major crashes in. It celebrates the firm establishment of a major key with lively "Scotch snap" rhythms and leads to an even livelier theme propelled by unrelenting, galloping triplets in the left hand. The music has made a deci-sive turn and seems to have dispelled the melancholy with which it began.

The development section seems to confirm this by beginning with a statement of the Brahmsian theme, now in major without its melancholic tinge. But after only two measures it is repeated in F minor. The alter-nation of light and shadow continues. Three measures later it brightens again, this time into A♭ major. But again the major key is barely established before it veers away and comes to a pause. After the pause, the once joyful theme from the end of the exposition charges ahead with its irrepressible

8. Charles Rosen, *The Classical Style: Haydn, Mozart, Beethoven* (New York: W. W. Nor-ton and Co., 1972), p. 146.

9. Rosemary Hughes, *Haydn* (London: J. M. Dent and Sons, 1978), p. 240.

galloping triplet rhythms in the accompaniment. But now it is in B♭ minor; the joy that had banished the melancholy is now itself banished. As the theme rushes on, it plunges into ever deeper flat regions — from B♭ minor to E♭ minor to A♭ minor. A♭ minor is the deepest tonal region the music reaches, and it takes some doing to wrest the music back to C minor for the return to the melancholy opening theme. Once back in C minor, any hints that the optimistic major themes from the exposition might return are immediately quelled. C minor prevails to the end.

The second movement consists of a long, wide-ranging melody that unfolds over a steady, walking bass. Although its tonality does not become clear until the second measure, it is a quiet, serene interlude in A♭ major between the C minor outer movements. Its serenity is sometimes disturbed, but never broken, by syncopated passages and mild chromaticism.

The finale is another tense C minor movement, the climax of the whole sonata. Tension is relaxed at the E♭ major end of the exposition as the music gets soft and flows along in smooth eighth notes in parallel thirds. The same thing happens at the end of the movement, but now in the key of C. However, there is some doubt whether the ending will be in minor or major. Major seems more likely until three measures from the end, when the music suddenly and loudly banishes any hint of major. As Hughes puts it, with "inexorable rage" the movement "asserts its somber tonality and defiant mood to the end."[10]

From Divertimento to String Quartet

We have already noted that Haydn "invented" the string quartet sometime during the 1750s in order to accommodate Baron von Fürnburg's gatherings of four stringed-instrument–playing friends, one of whom was Haydn himself. But those delightful, light-hearted works were not the sort whose invention posterity would hail as "one of the most telling and celebrated achievements in the history of Western music."[11] Haydn's return to string quartet composition after a hiatus of almost a decade marks the beginning of that achievement. We do not know what, besides his great affinity for the genre, prompted him to return to composing string quartets, but

10. Hughes, *Haydn,* p. 141.

11. Simon McVeigh, "Quartet" in *Oxford Composer Companions,* edited by David Wyn Jones (Oxford: Oxford University Press, 2009), p. 293.

during the late '60s and early '70s, he composed three sets of six quartets each. By 1774 they had all been published (without Haydn's authorization) and are now known by the opus numbers 9, 17, and 20.

The quartets of Opus 9, Opus 17, and Opus 20, unlike their predecessors, no longer betray their divertimento roots, though Haydn still called them divertimenti. Instead of having five movements of which two are minuets, they each have only four movements with one being a minuet. However, these four-movement pieces are longer than their five-movement predecessors. Obviously, then, individual movements must be substantially longer than their counterparts in Opus 1 and Opus 2. The greater length is not mainly due to additional material but to fuller development of the material. Since composing his early quartets, Haydn had attained greater skill and imagination in developing his musical ideas. This is particularly true of first movements, which are not only longer but more serious than the lightweight opening movements of the early quartets. Instead of a 3/8 or 2/4 meter in a fast tempo, a 4/4 meter in a moderate tempo typifies the quartets of this period. The broader meters and tempi gave Haydn greater rhythmic scope, which in turn opened up a wider range of expression.

Haydn most likely composed these quartets for Esterházy musicians, especially his friend, the virtuoso violinist Luigi Tomasini. That would explain features in the first violin parts like fast, florid passages, use of double stops, forays into the highest register, and opportunities to improvise concerto-like cadenzas. Though it is not fair to characterize these quartets as violin solos with string trio accompaniment, the virtuosic passages do give a degree of dominance by the first violin, and that probably accounts for their relative lack of popularity. They do not meet the expectation (an expectation that Haydn himself would establish) that in "true" chamber music all the parts must be equal in importance, or at least the first violin should be no more than "first among equals."

The charge that these quartets are "solo" quartets becomes less fair as we proceed through the three sets. The virtuoso passages for the first violin are less prevalent in Opus 17 than in Opus 9, and they essentially disappear in Opus 20. As that happens, of course, the lower three parts take on greater roles. Goethe famously compared listening to a good quartet to listening to a conversation between four intelligent people. Opus 9 or Opus 17 would not likely prompt that comparison, but it is definitely true for the Opus 20 quartets.

Opus 20

The tendency toward greater equality of parts actually became total equality in the fugues that serve as finales in three of the Opus 20 quartets — no. 2 in C major, no. 5 in F minor, and no. 6 in A major. Much has been made of these fugues, and rightly so. Donald Tovey called them Haydn's "reconquest of the ancient kingdom of polyphony,"[12] and Rosemary Hughes said they represent "a triumph for the equality and freedom of all four instruments."[13] True enough, but that triumph did not lead Haydn to write more fugues in string quartets or elsewhere. There will be only one fugal movement in the forty string quartets yet to come. However, even though independent fugues will not be a significant part of Haydn's future work, fugal writing will be a very important means for developing musical ideas.

What is most remarkable about the fugues in Opus 20, beyond Haydn's stellar artisanship, is their diversity. Haydn labeled them according to the number of subjects (themes) involved:

- *Fuga a due Soggetti* (that is, a subject and one countersubject) in no. 5 in F minor
- *Fuga a 3 Soggetti* (a subject and two countersubjects) in no. 6 in A major
- *Fuga a 4tro Soggetti* (a subject and three countersubjects) in no. 2 in C major

The diversity, however, comes not only from the systematic exploitation of increasing numbers of subjects, but even more from the widely differing character of the main subjects of each, and therefore from the widely differing character of the movements as a whole. The subject of no. 5 is serious and archaic. It bears a striking resemblance to the subject of Handel's fugue in *Messiah* on the words "And with his stripes we are healed." The subject of no. 6, on the other hand, with its dancing leaps and syncopations, is light-hearted, "a continual flow of gaiety, enthusiasm, and high spirits."[14] The subject for no. 2 is likewise light-hearted, but it starts with a mock-

12. Donald F. Tovey, "Haydn's Chamber Music," in *The Mainstream of Music and Other Essays* (Cleveland: The World Publishing Co., 1964), p. 45.

13. Rosemary Hughes, *Haydn String Quartets* (Seattle: University of Washington Press, 1969), p. 25.

14. C. S. Lewis's description of the tone of Charles Williams's conversation in *Essays Presented to Charles Williams* (Grand Rapids: William B. Eerdmans Publishing Co., 1966), p. xiii.

plaintive chromatic line before becoming a leaping gigue-like tune. The movement is a contrapuntal tour de force made to sound easy. As Daniel Heartz puts it, "Haydn's triumph is to turn the most learned genre of music into a finale so insouciant that it ranks with his greatest inspirations." It "dances from beginning to end like a scherzo and succeeds in totally beguiling us so that we forget all about its contrapuntal artifice; it is the will-o'-the-wisp of Op. 20."[15]

The diversity in the fugues of Opus 20 is a microcosm of the diversity of the entire opus. Texturally, the six quartets cover a wide gamut of possibilities for four stringed instruments, and harmonically they range as far afield as F♯ major (six sharps) and G♭ minor (nine flats). No. 5 in F minor foreshadows Beethovenian tragedy, while no. 6 in A major shows Haydn at his playful best. Minuets can be as tragic as the one in G minor or as exotic (and rhythmically bizarre) as the one in D major. Slow movements can express sweet delight as well as deep sorrow; their mode of expression can range from the theatrical to the intimate. The slow movement of no. 2 is an operatic *scena* beginning with an instrumental imitation of an impassioned "recitative" that leads to a consoling "aria." In contrast to the theatrical expression of this movement, there is the intimacy of the lovely F major slow movement of the F minor quartet (no. 5). Its graceful siciliano rhythm, gentle dissonant harmonies, and gossamer decorations combine to express a quiet serenity with a tinge of melancholy — all the more moving because of it dark and intense F minor surroundings.

If the inscriptions at the ends of the quartets in Opus 20 are any indication, Haydn was exhilarated by, and grateful for, what he was able to achieve. He often inscribed *laus Deo* at the end of his scores, but his inscriptions at the end of the Opus 20 quartets, though similar, are more effusive and different for each quartet.

- *Soli Deo et Cuique Suum* ("To God alone and to each his own")
- *Laus omnip. Deo* ("Praise the almighty God")
- *Laus Deo et B:V:M:cum S° S^{to}* ("Praise to God and the blessed Virgin Mary with the Holy Spirit")
- *Gloria in Excelsis Deo* ("Glory be to God in the highest")
- *Fine Laus Deo* ("Highest praise to God")

---

15. Daniel Heartz, *Haydn, Mozart, and the Viennese School: 1740-1780* (New York: W. W. Norton and Co., 1995), p. 343.

- *Laus Deo et Beatissimae Virgini Mariae* ("Praise to God and the most blessed Virgin Mary")

The magnitude of his achievement in Opus 20 certainly warranted his excitement and gratitude. After Opus 20, as Tovey wrote, "further progress is not progress in any historical sense, but simply the difference between one masterpiece and the next." And he added that if Haydn's career had ended with Opus 20, "no one could have guessed which of some half-dozen different lines he would have followed up."[16] What in fact followed during the next decade or so was a change in responsibilities that put opera at the center of his activities and new string quartets on hold.

16. Tovey, p. 49.

CHAPTER 10

Opera at Eszterháza

1768-83

Operas, I hardly need say, are sources of musical and dramatic enjoyment whether or not one perceives them as intellectual events. But there is much satisfaction to be had when one recognizes that they are also part of Western civilization. Opera can recount only part of our intellectual history, but it recounts that part with singular directness and power.

PAUL ROBINSON

Theater at Eszterháza under Prince Nicolaus I

If we divide Haydn's work into three categories — instrumental music, church music, and opera — we find that under Nicolaus his instrumental output fluctuated very little overall, that his church music was concentrated within the first few years after his promotion to Kapellmeister, and that his operatic work began slowly but became the dominant part of his workload after Nicolaus instituted a full-fledged opera season at Eszterháza.

Nicolaus's lack of interest in having his Kapellmeister heavily involved in church music is reflected in the architecture of Eszterháza. Its chapel could hold no more than twenty people, and there was space for the performance of only small church pieces. On the other hand, when completed, there were two opera theaters, the main one seating four hundred and a smaller one for marionette operas. Clearly, when it came to the arts, Nicolaus favored the theater over the church.

His interest in theater included both spoken drama and opera. Before the completion of the Eszterháza opera house, he often hired traveling theater companies whose repertories consisted mostly of improvisatory comic plays of the "Hans Wurst" (a coarse buffoon character) variety.

But, after 1769, Prince Nicholas succeeded in getting better companies, with a repertory of nonimprovised, "regular" dramas of high literary value by such playwrights as Molière, Voltaire, and Lessing. During 1770 and 1771, a similar repertory was performed at Eszterháza by the company of Franz Passer, whose performances are notable in German theatrical history as having contributed much to the transition from buffooneries to regular drama.

The golden age of spoken drama at Eszterháza came in the years 1772-77, when the company of Carl Wahr performed plays of high literary value, many of them being first performances in the German language. There were tragedies by Shakespeare, Goethe, Regnard, and others.[1]

Haydn's Operatic Activity before 1776

Given Nicolaus's great interest in theater, it comes as no surprise that under him Haydn's duties turned increasingly in the direction of opera. At first, between 1762 (when Nicolaus succeeded Paul Anton) and 1768 (when the opera house at Eszterháza was completed) Haydn's operatic output was modest. He composed three small-scale stage works: *Acide,* a thirteen-scene *festa teatrale* for a wedding in the princely family in 1762; a few arias for insertion into a spoken comedy in 1763; and a comic intermezzo, *La canterina,* in 1766. *La canterina* is the only work of these three to survive virtually intact. Four comic operas from this period are lost, but even adding those to the list, the output is not particularly noteworthy. Haydn was doing a typical Kapellmeister duty — composing occasional operas or smaller stage works for special courtly functions.

The impetus for change was the completion of the opera house at Eszterháza in 1768. For the celebrations accompanying the opening, Haydn composed *Lo speziale (The Apothecary),* an adaptation of a libretto by Carlo

---

1. Dénes Bartha, "Haydn's Italian Opera Repertory at Eszterháza Palace," in *New Looks at Italian Opera: Essays in Honor of Donald J. Grout* (Ithaca, N.Y.: Cornell University Press, 1968), pp. 173-74.

Goldoni, the librettist who more than any other established comic opera on an equal footing with serious opera during the mid-eighteenth century. More specifically, Goldoni established a type of opera called *dramma giocoso per musica,* which, though prevailingly comic, has serious characters and serious dramatic strands woven through the story. A typical *dramma giocoso* contains six or seven characters from a wide spectrum of social classes, the four main characters being a serious couple and a comic couple. However, Haydn used a revised libretto of *Lo speziale* in which the serious roles were cut, thereby making it a straight comic opera. But full-fledged *dramma giocoso* with its mixture of serious and comic elements would be the prevailing type performed at Eszterháza throughout the 1770s.

In 1769, a year after *Lo speziale,* Haydn completed another opera, *Le pescatrici (The Fisherwomen),* but his work in opera did not significantly intensify for a few more years. As we have seen, he was still adding considerably to Nicolaus's supply of baryton trios, his symphonic output was continuing apace, and he returned to string quartet composition with a flurry of new works. Further, he was in the midst of a series of major church compositions. But in 1773 his output of large-scale dramatic works picked up. He composed two operas, the comic opera *L'infedelta delusa,* and the marionette opera *Philemon und Baucis,* performed in Eszterháza's newly completed marionette theater. He composed no operas the following year, but did compose, for performance in Vienna, an unstaged dramatic work of greater magnitude than any of his operas thus far, the oratorio *Il ritorno di Tobia (The Return of Tobias).* Two more operas followed in 1775 — *L'incontro improvviso* and a marionette opera, *Dido.*

Most of Haydn's operas for Eszterháza continued to be written for special occasions, such as weddings and name days in the royal family and visits from members of ruling and aristocratic families. Such occasions stretched over three or four days and featured several types of entertainment — banquets, dances, plays, fireworks, hunts, and concerts in various locations indoors and out. The centerpiece of the festivities was an opera. Altogether, the events formed a sort of pageant glorifying the prince and displaying his wealth, power, and prestige. And if the visiting dignitary was of higher rank than the host, the pageantry would also pay homage and show loyalty to the visitor.

Empress Maria Theresa's Visit to Eszterháza

One such occasion was the visit in 1773 by Empress Maria Theresa accompanied by three of her children and a large retinue. They arrived on the morning of September 1, escorted by Nicolaus and greeted by state dignitaries and members of the Hungarian aristocracy. At some time during the festivities, Haydn was introduced to the Empress. He told Dies that he reminded her of the time when, as a choirboy, he had received a thrashing for disobeying her order not to climb the scaffolding on her summer palace at Schönbrunn. He said he "occasioned much laughter" when he "thanked her most humbly for the reward" (Dies, p. 88). That story rings true, but another one sounds like a hunter's "fish story." Haydn told Griesinger "that he once brought down with one shot three hazel-hens, which appeared on the table of the Empress Maria Theresa" (p. 20).

In the afternoon of the day of the empress's arrival, the imperial retinue toured the gardens and then saw a performance of Haydn's *L'infedeltà delusa*, a two-act comic opera that had also been performed a few weeks earlier for the name day of Nicolaus's widowed mother. Maria Theresa must have been impressed with the opera (unless she was merely engaging in polite hyperbole): "If I want to hear good opera," she said, "I go to Eszterháza."[2]

A masked ball in the Chinese Ballroom followed the opera. Haydn and his musicians performed in luxurious Chinese apparel. The party went on into the wee hours of the morning, but not for Maria Theresa. Though she was known for her love of dancing in her youth, the fifty-six-year-old Empress only watched for an hour and a half before retiring for bed, leaving the younger members of her retinue to dance till dawn.

The festivities resumed the next day with a formal banquet at which Haydn and his musicians provided more music. It was once thought that Symphony no. 48, nicknamed *Maria Theresa,* was composed for the occasion. But scholars now agree that it was composed no later than 1769. Nevertheless, it is possible that Haydn chose to perform it at this time for the Empress. Written in the regal key of C major and scored for high horns, it is music fit for royalty. But whatever was performed at the banquet was only the beginning of the music for the day. In the afternoon, the Empress

2. Quoted in Caryl Clark, "Haydn in the Theater: The Operas," in *The Cambridge Companion to Haydn,* ed. by Caryl Clark (Cambridge: Cambridge University Press, 2005), p. 182.

saw Haydn's first marionette opera, *Philemon und Baucis,* performed in the recently finished marionette theater. Again, the Empress seems to have been impressed. According to Dies it was a "favorite of Empress M. Theresa" (p. 107).

The opera consists of three parts. It begins with a prologue, *Der Götterrath (The Council of the Gods),* in which Venus extols lifelong marital faithfulness and virtue. But since evil behavior is the norm among mortals, Jupiter and Mercury disguise themselves as travelers and go to earth in search of a virtuous couple. The opera is based on a story in Ovid's *Metamorphoses* that tells of their search. Their search ends when they come to the hut of Philemon and Baucis, a poor peasant couple, in a village in Phrygia. Despite the couple's poverty and their deep sorrow over the recent deaths of their son and his fiancée, they provide food and hot baths for the travelers. Having found a virtuous couple, Jupiter brings their son and his fiancée back to life and turns the hut into a temple and the old couple into its priests. The neighbors, who had refused hospitality to the travelers, are frightened by the thunder that accompanies the metamorphoses. They fall down before Jupiter, who points to Philemon and Baucis and tells them: "Let this fate be a lesson to you." Then, accompanied by chorus, trumpets, and drums, the gods ascend back into heaven.

The story finished, the coat-of-arms of the Habsburg family appears on the stage surrounded by Glory, Clemency, Justice, and Valour. Then, according to an account in the *Pressburger Zeitung,*

> Fame came flying in, and crowned the coat-of-arms with a wreath. Divine Providence protected it with a shield, and Time embraced it. The Hungarian Nation approached, accompanied by Love of the Fatherland, by Obedience, Devotion, and Fidelity, and fell to its knees in veneration of the Imperial arms. Jupiter's temple disappeared, and the stage showed the central portion of the illuminated gardens at Eszterház. Here the neighbors changed into Hungarians too, joining in the final chorus, during which Happiness clasped the Imperial arms with one hand, and with the other showered Plenty upon the Nation from her cornucopia. (Landon 2, p. 197)

After a meal modestly called "supper" (though no doubt a lavish affair), the entertainment continued with a huge fireworks show, decorative lighting displays, and one thousand Hungarian and Croatian peasants, dressed in traditional costumes, singing, playing, and dancing their native music.

Haydn's Operatic Activity after 1776

Haydn's most intense period of operatic activity began in 1776 when Nicolaus launched a full-fledged opera season in the main opera house. Haydn's involvement in opera expanded enormously. He was in charge of two performances per week throughout a season that could stretch from March into December. In addition to composing and performing his own works, Haydn rehearsed and conducted works by Anfossi, Cimarosa, Paisiello, Sarti, Salieri, and Piccini, among others. And before rehearsing them and conducting them in performance, he edited them, made revisions, and composed new arias to suit the available singers. Even though the director of the marionette theater left in 1778, essentially putting an end to marionette opera at Eszterháza, and a fire destroyed the main opera house in 1779, neither event diminished Nicolaus's ardor for opera; if anything it only burned the hotter. Nicolaus wasted no time in having the opera house rebuilt. On February 25, 1781, it reopened with a performance of Haydn's *La fedeltà premiata*.

Although much of the archival documentation for the early years of full-fledged opera seasons was destroyed in the fire, fairly complete statistics have survived for the ensuing years. If the statistics in the years immediately preceding the fire were approaching the numbers we have for the following years (a reasonable assumption), a typical season consisted of four to eight new works (one of which was by Haydn) and four or five works repeated from previous years — all told a total of ninety to one hundred performances.

La vera costanza (True Constancy)

Haydn's last opera before the theater burned was *La vera costanza*. It is a typical *dramma giocoso* and a good example of his operas written at the peak of his operatic productivity. It is also a good example of how opera, as something more than mere diversion, participated in broader cultural currents of the time. In theme it is a "Pamela" opera — that is, it is a descendant of Samuel Richardson's popular novel *Pamela, or Virtue Rewarded* (1740), the story of a virtuous servant-girl who rebuffs all her master's attempts to ravish her. The novel was a huge success and it generated many spin-offs, including several operas. One of the Pamela operas was Mozart's *La finta giardiniera (The Pretended Gardener)*, first performed in 1775, four years before Haydn's *La vera costanza*. The description of *La finta* by opera historian Donald Grout contains the same kinds of criticisms that modern critics have typically leveled against Haydn's operas of the 1770s. "*La finta giardiniera* was an Italian opera buffa with a libretto which unhappily combined the new sentimental motif with a complicated and cumbersome array of secondary characters, disguises, mistaken identity, and farcical episodes inherited from the older Italian comedy. The music lacks dramatic continuity. Tragedy and comedy rub shoulders, but there is no sign of the synthesis of the two." But, he adds, the music "is extraordinarily attractive."[3]

Like *La finta giardiniera*, the music of Haydn's *La vera costanza* is extraordinarily attractive, and in typical *dramma giocoso* fashion, it mixes serious and comic characters and episodes. Its strong "sentimental motif" (definitely a serious element here) rubs shoulders with the farcical and, at least as traditional criticism would have it, "there is no sign of the synthesis of the two." But literary critic William Youngren provides a chronologically more appropriate perspective in which satire and ironic juxtaposition loom large. "In Haydn's operas," he writes,

> we are constantly encountering improbable characters placed in unlikely situations; yet the music explores the emotions of the characters at great length, and forces us to take both characters and emotions very seriously — even as we laugh at the improbabilities. Haydn's operas revel in the opportunities that their librettos provide for creating what literary critic Kenneth Burke once called "perspectives through incongruity." This should come as no surprise to us, for the eighteenth century was very fond of creating such perspectives.

In *La vera costanza,* Youngren continues, Haydn "took the totally improbable situation of the fishermaiden Rosina, who has somehow got herself secretly married to Count Errico, and brilliantly exploited the gap between the meaningless intrigue that seethes around her and her complex and varied emotions as she stands at the center of it all, affected yet unshaken."[4]

The opera begins with a three-part overture, the third part of which

3. Donald J. Grout, *A Short History of Opera* (New York: Columbia University Press, 1965), p. 276.

4. William H. Youngren, "The Operas of Haydn," *Atlantic*, vol. 252, issue 3 (September 1983): 114.

provides storm music (*Sturm und Drang* style) that leads directly into the opening scene. A small, storm-battered boat, shipwrecked near shore, carries four passengers: Baroness Irene, her maid Lisetta, Marquis Ernesto, and Villotto. They are helped to shore and given shelter by a fisherman named Masino and his sister Rosina, the "Pamela" character of the opera. Five years earlier Rosina had married Count Errico, Irene's cousin, and had borne him a son. The mentally unstable Errico had abandoned Rosina and their son. Irene is unaware of the marriage, but she had heard rumors that there was something between Errico and Rosina. In order to prevent an unsuitable marriage between her noble cousin and the lowly fishermaiden, she planned to foist Rosina off on Villotto, a wealthy fop. Though Rosina is the target of villainous scheming by Irene, Ernesto, and Villotto, confused by her unstable husband, and the victim of cruelty and misunderstandings all around, she never wavers in her love and loyalty to her husband and son. In the end, her virtue wins the day. Errico regains his sanity and reunites with his faithful wife, whose nobility is not a matter of birth but of character.

Haydn's music in *La vera costanza* wonderfully portrays the characters. Irene's opening aria is replete with all the trappings suggestive of nobility (of birth, that is, not necessarily of character); Villotto's music shows him to be vain and cowardly; Masino's is appropriately comic as he mocks Villotto's attempt to win Rosina; and Errico's shows his mental instability but also, in the end, the sincerity of his love for Rosina. Above all, Rosina's music depicts both her lower-class social station and noble character. Her music "retains the nobility of the high style" without its showy hallmark, brilliant coloratura. It "makes a direct and immediate appeal"[5] that conforms to late-eighteenth-century sensibility.

Eighteenth-Century Sensibility

The rise to primacy of sensibility during the eighteenth century was part of the romantic revolution against the primacy of reason in the seventeenth century. In the seventeenth century, as Nicolas Till points out, "the most powerful weapon against the obdurate authority of tradition and custom, or of religious dogma, had been reason." But the eighteenth-century bour-

---

5. Jessica Waldorf, "Sentiment and Sensibility in *La vera costanza*," in *Haydn Studies,* edited by W. Dean Sutcliffe (Cambridge: Cambridge University Press, 1998), p. 84.

geois Enlightenment "relocated its ethical authority where it could not be reached by others: within the inalienable feelings and instincts of the human body." It "demoted reason to the safer status of common sense and promoted the claims of the individual's experience of the here-and-now gained through the senses."[6]

Till calls Mozart's *La finta giardiniera* "one of the finest examples of operatic sensibility." The same could be said of Haydn's *La vera costanza*. Both operas place their composers "at the centre of a mid-eighteenth-century European bourgeois culture" that promoted an "aesthetics of Sensibility," which maintained that

> the purpose of art was, as Lessing argued, "to extend our capacity for feeling pity. The compassionate man is the best man, and he who makes us compassionate makes us better and more virtuous." "No appeal to the soul of man by impressions of pity and compassion can be too strong," the French sentimental playwright Mercier wrote, and the cult of Sensibility soon discovered that the most efficient method of triggering compassion was to represent, in ever more excessive forms, what Diderot readily identified as "the misfortunes of virtue."[7]

The misfortunes of Rosina as told in the libretto of *La vera costanza* might easily qualify as "excessive," but as for "triggering compassion," the chief agent is clearly the music that Haydn wrote for Rosina to sing. Any doubts about that can be erased by a simple experiment: first read the libretto without the music; then listen to the music.

One might wonder how an opera such as *La vera costanza* was received by Nicolaus, his family, and his friends of noble blood. Traditionally, the function of court operas had been to extol the virtues and show off the magnificence of royalty and nobility. But now the main genre had become *dramma giocoso,* in which traditional social distinctions get blurred. Those operas did not invariably reverse matters by placing virtue in lower-class persons and vice (or just plain silliness) in the aristocracy as clearly as in *La vera costanza*. But in the repertory as a whole we find virtue and vice, seriousness and buffoonery, cleverness and stupidity cutting across all social classes. As David Wyn Jones puts it, "Rather than glorifying a prince,

6. Nicolas Till, *Mozart and the Enlightenment* (New York: W. W. Norton and Co., 1993), p. 22.

7. Till, p. 23.

this was court opera that expressed wider Enlightenment values with verve and naturalness."[8] Nevertheless, Nicolaus must have enjoyed the operas mounted on his stage because if he did not, he could have had something else — whatever he pleased. Perhaps (though I think it unlikely) he thought operas were "just music" and ignored the "wider Enlightenment values" they embodied. Or perhaps he subscribed to those values, but failed to see (or chose to ignore) their implications for his own life. We will never know. But Caryl Clark presents a disquieting point to ponder. When *La vera costanza* was resurrected in 1785, its "overarching themes of constancy, marital fidelity and parental obligation would have reverberated at a court where both Prince Nicolaus and his Kapellmeister had mistresses."[9]

Haydn's Ventures into Other Operatic Genres

All of Haydn's operas up to and including *La vera costanza* were comic operas, mostly of the *dramma giocoso* type. But the next opera, *L'isola disabitata,* was different. Its libretto was by Pietro Metastasio, the great librettist from a generation before Haydn. (After being dismissed from St. Stephen's, you will remember, young Haydn lived in a "wretched attic" in the same building where Metastasio had an apartment on a lower floor.) Its genre, *azione teatrale,* is neither comic nor heroic.

> Metastasio artfully combined heroism and comedy in a pastoral setting. He used a desert island as a setting for the study of human nature, contributing to the 18th-century debate about the relative importance of birth and education in the formation of character. Viewing European civilization from afar, the opera is similar to the many essays and stories in which European intellectuals of the Enlightenment took on the personae of visitors from distant lands in order to comment on contemporary mores.[10]

Haydn returned to *dramma giocoso* for his next opera, *La fedelta premiata* (1780). But in his final two operas for Eszterháza, he again ventured

8. David Wyn Jones, *The Life of Haydn* (Cambridge: Cambridge University Press, 2009), p. 86.

9. Clark, "Haydn in the Theater: The Operas," p. 187.

10. John A. Rice, *"L'isola disabitata,"* in *Oxford Composer Companions: Haydn,* edited by David Wyn Jones (Oxford: Oxford University Press, 2009), p. 213.

into other genres. *Orlando paladino* (1782) is heroic-comic *(dramma eroico-comico)*, and *Armida* (1783) is an *opera seria* based on an episode in Tasso's great epic poem *Gerusalemme libertate (Jerusalem Liberated)*. It was his first and only *opera seria* for Eszterháza; it was also his last opera of any kind for Eszterháza. It also might be his best. He wrote to the publisher Artaria: "Yesterday my *Armida* was performed for the 2nd time with general applause. I am told that this is my best work so far" (Landon 2, p. 487). It was certainly his most frequently performed work at Eszterháza, being staged a total of fifty-four times between 1784 and 1788.

Although Haydn would write no more operas for Eszterháza after *Armida,* there was no slackening of his other operatic work. Editing, revising, writing new pieces for insertion, rehearsing, and conducting all continued to occupy a lion's share of Haydn's time. In fact, that work reached its peak in 1786, when seventeen operas were performed — eight premieres and nine operas repeated from previous years in a total of one hundred twenty-five performances!

At the peak, operas were offered twice a week all "summer" (which, as we have already noted, could extend from March to December). Performances were free of charge, but given Eszterháza's isolated location, it is questionable whether the surrounding area could provide steady audiences, even if small. Eszterháza attracted travelers from near and far, and they would have swelled the audience on occasion. Potential audience members nearest at hand on a regular basis were the estimated one thousand employees at court, but unless a fair number of them attended quite regularly, the audiences must have been small except for special occasions. According to one report, employees were permitted to attend even if they appeared "uncombed, drunk and disheveled." But one wonders how often they took advantage of Nicolaus's leniency. The same report notes that sometimes "apart from the servants" the prince "is the whole audience."[11]

The End of Opera at Eszterháza

Opera performances at Eszterháza came to an abrupt halt when Nicolaus died in 1790. His son Anton, who succeeded him as prince, did not share his father's musical interests. When he was installed as Lord Lieutenant

---

11. Thomas Tolley, *Painting the Cannon's Roar* (Burlington, Vt.: Ashgate Publishing Company, 2001), pp. 127 and 370, n. 6.

of Oedenberg in 1791, a celebration was held at Eszterháza. Haydn was in London at the time and could not honor his prince's request to compose an opera for the occasion. Instead, Haydn's godson, Joseph Weigl, composed the opera. (He was son of the cellist in the orchestra during Haydn's early years of working for the Esterházy princes.) It was the last opera performed in the Eszterháza opera house. In fact, the installation celebrations marked the last time the family used Eszterháza for large public functions. Anton and his successors resided in Eisenstadt and Vienna. Eszterháza fell into "increasing decay in the 19th century and by 1832, the centenary of Haydn's birth, the two opera houses were being used to store timber; the main theatre was demolished in 1870." Although since the mid-1950s "the main palace has been gradually restored and concerts are often held there, Eszterháza has remained isolated and off the main tourist beat."[12]

However, in 2005 the International Opera Foundation Eszterháza was created with these goals: "To rebuild the 1781 Opera House at Eszterháza with all of its original features, especially those concerning acoustics and stage machinery, with the aim to make this theatre a centre where eighteenth century opera can be performed true to the original [and] to resurrect the original Eszterháza repertoire of nearly one hundred operas, including the works of Haydn and other composers, which are rarely, if ever, performed today."[13]

A Haydn Opera Renaissance?

Since Haydn rarely traveled outside Eszterháza during the time he was writing operas, they got relatively little exposure elsewhere. His music "never featured prominently at the Habsburg court, which had its own group of favoured composers, and since the court continued to influence the running and, consequently, the repertoire of the main theatres in Vienna, the Burgtheater and the Kärntnerthortheater, Haydn's operas, the most important element of his duties at Eszterháza, were conspicuous by their absence."[14]

Haydn's operas have had the further misfortune of existing in the shadow of Mozart's incomparable late operas. So they have been, and still

12. David Wyn Jones, "Eszterháza," in *Oxford Composer Companions: Haydn*, p. 95.
13. http://www.eszterhaza-opera.com/index.php?p=2
14. David Wyn Jones, "Reception," in *Oxford Composer Companions: Haydn*, p. 324.

are, rarely performed. Until rather recently, even music historians gave them little attention. When they did, they typically dismissed them with faint praise. But what has never been questioned is the quality of their music. Nobody denied the music's beauty and wit, or its picturesque and expressive qualities, but criticism was, and still is, directed at the librettos and at what seem, to many, to be overly long arias that disrupt the dramatic pace.

Although performances of Haydn's operas are still rare and the criticisms persist, they are becoming better known, and more musicologists, performers, and critics are convinced that they have been misunderstood and unfairly judged. No one is about to take the operatic laurel wreath away from Mozart and give it to Haydn, and no one is about to rank any of Haydn's operas with *The Marriage of Figaro*. But if being ranked with *Figaro* were a prerequisite for being performed, precious few operas would be heard. As an old proverb says, "The forest would be a very quiet place if only the nightingale sang."

CHAPTER II

Symphonies and Sonatas during the Peak Opera Years

1773-81

> *The genius, fine ideas, and fancy of Haydn, Ditters, and Filtz, were praised, but their mixture of serious and comic was disliked, particularly as there is more of the latter than the former in their works.*
>
> A FRIEND OF CHARLES BURNEY

> *Chaucer is slapstick and profound. Chaucer is humane: the most humane of all our authors, with a deep wisdom about both the silliness and the significance of the human condition.*
>
> JOSEPH BOTTUM

An Odd Mixture of Styles?

In his autobiographical letter of 1776, Haydn named five of his compositions that had "received the most approbation" — three operas, the oratorio *Il Ritorno di Tobia,* and *Stabat Mater.* Then he went on to tell about the critical reception of his music in the "chamber-musical style," which we can assume included all his instrumental music — symphonies and sonatas as well as trios, quartets, and the like. He wrote:

> In the chamber-musical style I have been fortunate enough to please almost all nations except the Berliners; this is shown by the public newspapers and letters addressed to me. I only wonder that the Berlin gentlemen, who are otherwise so reasonable, preserve no medium in their

criticism of my music, for in one weekly paper they praise me to the skies, whilst in another they dash me sixty fathoms deep into the earth, and this without explaining why; I know very well why: because they are incapable of performing some of my works, and are too conceited to take the trouble to understand them properly, and for other reasons which, with God's help, I will answer in good time. *Herr Capellmeister von Dittersdorf*, in Silesia, wrote to me recently and asked me to defend myself against their hard words, but I answered that one swallow doesn't make the Summer; and that perhaps one of these days some unprejudiced person would stop their tongues, as happened to them once before when they accused me of monotony. Despite this, they try very hard to get all my works, as Herr Baron von Sviten [Swieten], the Imperial and Royal Ambassador at Berlin, told me only last winter, when he was in Vienna: but enough of this. (Landon 2, p. 398)

Criticism from North German writers ("the Berliners") was not new at the time Haydn wrote this. What particularly vexed them was the mixture of serious and comic elements in his chamber music. As early as 1768 Johann Adam Hiller had written that Haydn's music was a "curious mixture of the noble and the common, the serious and the comic, which so often occurs in one and the same movement."[1] In 1771, Johann Christoph Stockhausen said the problem was "getting out of hand," not only with Haydn, but with "Toeschin, Cannabich, Filz, Pugnani, Campioni." "You only have to be half a connoisseur," he wrote, "to notice the emptiness, the strange mixture of comic and serious, trifling and moving, that rules everywhere."[2] Stockhausen's inclusion of Italian composers in his criticism reveals the typical antipathy of North Germans toward Italian music — and toward South Germans and Austrians, whose music, they thought, was tainted by Italian frivolity.

Haydn's North German critics at the time thought the mixture of serious and comic resulted in confusion and was a symptom of degeneration from the serious art of the Baroque. As Daniel Chua puts it, "Haydn's mischievous mixture was precisely the sort of immiscibility that disrupted the rhetorical clarity of the Baroque aesthetic." It was "such a hotchpotch of

1. Quoted in Gretchen Wheelock, *Haydn's Ingenious Jesting with Art* (New York: Schirmer Books, 1992), p. 43.
2. Quoted in Mary Sue Morrow, *German Music Criticism in the Late Eighteenth Century* (Cambridge: Cambridge University Press, 1997), p. 54.

ingredients that it was more a recipe for disaster than for pleasure." Chua notes that Mozart was subject to the same criticism. "Mozart's music, said one critic, was 'too highly seasoned'; his 'almost unadulterated spicy diet,' said another critic, could easily spoil one's palate with its lack of unity. With its wayward mixture, the 'Classical style' signals the end of style, the ruin of taste. Indeed, its willful nature marks the end of the Baroque itself."[3]

But by 1776, when Haydn complained about his North German critics, their criticism had just about run its course. Haydn's growing popularity throughout Europe was making them want to claim him as one of their own. But the criticism never completely died out. In 1784, an English writer, the Rev. William Jones, found Haydn's music lacking both the unity of affect and the seriousness of purpose that characterized Baroque music. Not surprisingly Jones's standard of measurement, as in England generally, was Handel. He wrote: "As for Haydn and Boccherini who merit a first place among the moderns for *invention*, they are sometimes so desultory and unaccountable in their way of treating a Subject, that they may be reckoned among the wild warblers of the wood: and they seem to differ from some pieces of Handel, as the Talk and the Laughter of the Tea-table (where, perhaps, neither Wit nor Invention are wanting) differs from the Oratory of the Bar [law court] and the Pulpit."[4]

The Rev. Mr. Jones's critique continued to be the main theme whenever Haydn's music was undervalued, especially after European culture came to be dominated by a romanticism that equated the dark and the tragic with profundity and failed to recognize that wit and good humor are not necessarily signs of shallowness. Romantics might recognize that Haydn's music lacks "neither Wit nor Invention," but they cannot perceive the depth of its wisdom.

Haydn, as we have already seen, could write music that was pervasively dark and turbulent. One might even wonder if his *Strum und Drang* works were written in response to the criticism that he mixed "the comic and the serious, the trifling and the moving." Perhaps. But by the time he had written his autobiographical letter, he had already abandoned the *Sturm und Drang* style quite decisively. Throughout the rest of his career he would return to it only when it was a "topic" called for by a text in vocal music

3. Daniel K. L. Chua, *Absolute Music and the Construction of Meaning* (Cambridge: Cambridge University Press, 1999), pp. 71-72.

4. Quoted in Leonard Ratner, *Classic Music: Expression, Form, and Style* (New York: Schirmer Books, 1980), p. 27.

(for example, the stormy seas in *The Creation*), or as a momentary mood in the midst of music of very different character (for example, the surprising insertion of the first theme of the *Farewell* Symphony into the first movements of the 60th and 85th Symphonies). Even when his later instrumental works are in minor keys, they are quite different in character from his *Sturm und Drang* works.

Too Busy with Opera? The Symphonies of the Opera Years

Haydn's symphonies written between 1773 and 1781 have acquired the reputation of being inferior to those that immediately preceded them and all of those that followed. Their perceived inferiority is explained (and excused) on the grounds that they were written during the period of his most intense operatic activity. He simply could not put his best efforts into composing instrumental music. As busy as he was composing, editing, and directing operas, a drop in the quantity and quality of instrumental works was inevitable. At least so the story goes.

Haydn's busyness with opera did affect the quantity of his symphony production. From 1761, when he began working for the Esterházys, until about 1775, he composed symphonies steadily at the rate of about three per year. During the six or seven years after 1775, he composed only thirteen symphonies, and at least six of them have movements that are recycled opera overtures. Further, he took the music of one entire symphony from incidental music for a play. That symphony is no. 60, nicknamed *Il distratto* (*The absent-minded one*) after a play by Jean-François Regnard.

Symphony No. 60, Il distratto

Karl Wahr's troupe performed a German translation of Regnard's play at Eszterháza in 1774. Haydn wrote an overture, four entr'actes, and a finale for the play. They became the six movements of Symphony no. 60. A writer in the *Pressburger Zeitung* praised the play and its music. He wrote that "connoisseurs consider it a masterpiece." The music shows "the same spirit that elevates all of Heyden's work. His masterful variety excites the admiration of experts and is nothing short of delightful for the listener; he falls from the most affected pomposity directly into vulgarity, and H[aydn] and Regnard contend with one another in capricious absent-mindedness.

The play takes on a new and manifold worth. From act to act the music realizes the play's intention more closely, namely that of heightening the actor's absent-mindedness" (Landon 2, pp. 205-206).

But as a symphony, does the music stand on its own merits apart from its association with the play, or does it provide evidence for the alleged decline in quality of Haydn's symphonies during this period? The popularity of Symphony no. 60 with Haydn's contemporaries suggests that it can stand on its own merits. During his lifetime it became one of his most widely performed symphonies. However, Haydn himself does not seem to have been impressed. In 1803 he referred to it as "Den alten Schmarn" ("that old nonsense"). But that statement might simply be an example of his typical self-deprecation or just a slightly disgruntled (or amused?) complaint that this work was more popular than some other more deserving ones. In any case, A. Peter Brown seems too harsh when he characterizes the music as inane. Its "inanities," he wrote, "certainly match those of the play."[5] The most famous of them occurs in the last movement. The music has barely gotten underway when the absent-minded violinists discover that they have failed to tune their G strings. They have to stop midcourse and tune their lowest strings up a whole step from F to G. Granted, that is a bit of over-the-top silliness that goes beyond anything Haydn ever did in a "real" symphony. But other "inanities" such as "quotations from known sources, unusual juxtapositions, peculiar phrase extensions, touches of polytonality, use of national and regional styles, and interpolations of other characteristic allusions"[6] are not unique to Symphony no. 60. Similar things appear in dozens of his instrumental works that have no known connection to something extra-musical. Yet those works can be understood without explicit extra-musical crutches. So can Symphony no. 60; knowledge of the play is not necessary for it to be understood.

Equally important to its integrity as a stand-alone symphony is its musical coherence. Though the features Brown mentions may be more numerous (and occasionally more exaggerated) in Symphony no. 60 than is usual in other works by Haydn, they do not prevent it from being a coherent work. Gretchen Wheelock's analysis reveals "unifying threads that bind seemingly disparate materials in larger schemes of rhythmic, motivic, and harmonic relationships" throughout the work. Further, "gestures at home in theatrical comedy — surprising stops and starts, disjunctions and reversals, prolonged

5. A. Peter Brown, *The Symphonic Repertoire*, vol. 2 (Bloomington: Indiana University Press, 2002), p. 153.

6. Brown, *The Symphonic Repertoire*, vol. 2, p. 153.

delays and teasing anticipations, forgetful repetitions, and 'twisted' quotations — could be appropriated as signals of jesting intent in instrumental music independent of such a context." As she puts it, "Echoes of Leander," the absent-minded hero of the comedy, "are heard throughout Haydn's works."[7]

Music for Hamlet?

Of course, Haydn's music was often humorous before he wrote *Il distratto*, and it will often be humorous after it. But humor is not the whole of Haydn's musical persona. He could employ for serious purposes many of the same devices that he used so effectively for humorous purposes. Quotations from known sources, unusual juxtapositions, peculiar phrase extensions, surprising stops and starts, disjunctions and reversals, prolonged delays and excessive repetitions can be as effective for serious purposes as for humorous ones. The writer of a review of *Il distratto* in the *Pressburger Zeitung* knew that. After praising Haydn's music for heightening the comedy of the play he added, "We look forward to hearing music to Shakespeare's *Hamlet* by this adept composer" (Landon 2, p. 206).

A notice in the *Historisch-kritische Theaterchronik von Wien* of 1774 noted that "Haydn has also composed music especially for *Hamlet* as given by the Wahr troupe."[8] Wahr and his troupe of actors appeared regularly in Eszterháza during the summers from 1772 to 1777. According to Elaine Sisman, evidence suggests "that Wahr and Haydn were good friends. Moreover, theater journals identified Haydn as the music director of Wahr's troupe. The Gotha *Theater-Kalendar* of 1775 even commented that Haydn supplied the troupe with 'appropriate music for the entr'actes of nearly every noteworthy play.' "[9]

Symphony No. 64, Tempora mutantur

Unfortunately Haydn's *Hamlet* music is lost, unless he recycled some of it into a symphony — or, perhaps, vice versa. Whatever the direction of the recycling, Sisman suggests a relationship between the slow movement of

7. Wheelock, pp. 170-71.
8. Elaine Sisman, "Haydn's Theater Symphonies," *Journal of the American Musicological Society* 43, no. 2 (Summer 1990): 322.
9. Sisman, "Haydn's Theater Symphonies," pp. 320-21.

Symphony no. 64 and *Hamlet.* Its subtitle, probably provided by Haydn, is *Tempora mutantur* (literally, "the times are changed"). It comes from an epigram by the Elizabethan poet John Owen, known in Germany in the eighteenth century both in Latin and in German translation: "Tempora mutantur, nos et mutamur in illis; Quomodo? Fit semper tempore peior homo" ("The times are changed, and we are changed in them. In what way? Always in time man becomes worse"). Sisman relates this to *Hamlet's* famous line in Act 1, "The time is out of joint." She connects the symphony with Wahr's interpretation of Hamlet's character. "Wahr's interpretation of the title role was praised in Salzburg: 'Many actors entirely misunderstand Hamlet; they take him to be a passionate, courageous youth, whereas he is essentially the opposite. Hamlet must be presented as a cautious, serious, reflective youth, and that is how Herr Wahr played him.'" She also connects the symphony and Hamlet's character via a comment made by the protagonist in Goethe's novel *Wilhelm Meisters Theatricalische Sendung* (early 1780s). In a discussion of *Hamlet,* Wilhelm Meister "claimed that the key to Hamlet's entire behavior is the couplet that ends Shakespeare's first and Heufeld's [a German translator of Shakespeare] second act: 'The time is out of joint. O cursed spite,/ that ever I was born to set it right.'"[10]

Symphony no. 64, Sisman goes on to say, "reveals that the time is out of joint" and "actually calls attention to itself" with its title, *Tempora mutantur.* She aptly describes the slow movement as "an extended essay on time out of joint."[11] Her case for the connection between the music and the play is compelling. But the connection is not necessary in order to understand the music. Attentive listeners will hear displaced accents, distorted phrases, and cadences that do not end in the right place or at the right time. And they will hear repeated attempts fail to make things right. Overall, they will hear that something is seriously awry and that it is resolved only in the quiet, mysterious, and painfully prolonged — and achingly beautiful — final cadence.

A Multi-faceted Symphonic Output

Symphony no. 60 and Symphony no. 64 reveal two different facets of Haydn's musical persona, but they hardly exhaust them. His symphonies

10. Sisman, "Haydn's Theater Symphonies," pp. 325-26.
11. Sisman, "Haydn's Theater Symphonies," p. 327.

of this period range a gamut from deep seriousness to slap-stick humor. They show that opera had not sapped all his creative energies; if anything, it kept them flowing. They abound in characteristic Haydnesque features such as irregular phrasing, abrupt modulations, and various other kinds of surprises, and they show no diminishment in his imaginative use of instruments and inventiveness with form.

In the second movement of Symphony no. 51, Haydn used unprecedented extremes of the horn's range, both high and low. In Symphony no. 67 he called for *col legno* ("with the wood") bowing at the end of the second movement, and in the trio of the third movement the second violins need to tune their G strings down to F — just as in the last movement of no. 60, *Il distratto*. But in no. 67 the "wrong" tuning is not an absent-minded "mistake." Instead it allows the second violins to play two parts, a low drone on the F string along with the inner harmony below the high, muted melody of the first violins — an effect that Robbins Landon likens to that of the music of wandering gypsies in Kodaly's *Háry János.*[12]

In several symphonies Haydn expanded the role of the bassoon. Although he had given the bassoon some independence in early symphonies like nos. 6, 7, and 8, for the most part he had used it conventionally to play bass parts along with the cellos and string basses. Now he began to use it more regularly in solo passages and independently in combination with other instruments. He also made effective use of the bassoon to double melody-playing instruments. A particularly striking example is in the first movement of Symphony no. 54 where the bassoon doubles the first horn an octave lower while the second horn fills in the harmony between them. This passage is striking not only for its tone color, but also because it is the first theme of the movement, emerging out of an impressive slow introduction. The theme has two components — a trio and a fanfare — but each is performed by the "wrong" instruments. The melodious trio (typically for strings) is played by the horns and bassoon as described above, while the fanfare-like motive (typically for horns) is played by the strings.

Much in Haydn's symphonies of this period points to characteristics of his later ones (which is not to say that they are merely "forerunners"). For example, slow introductions to first movements become more common. Those for Symphony no. 50 and Symphony no. 57 in particular anticipate the slow introductions that will become standard in his later symphonies. Also antic-

---

12. H. C. Robbins Landon, *Haydn: Chronicle and Works,* vol. 2 (Bloomington: Indiana University Press, 1978), p. 314.

ipating some of his later achievements (and those of several later composers, including, most famously, Beethoven in his Fifth Symphony) are the slow movements with variations on two alternating themes — typically in alternating major and minor keys — such as the second movement of Symphony no. 63, *Roxelane*, a piece that became extremely popular in an arrangement for keyboard. But even more impressive, both technically and expressively, is the slow movement of Symphony no. 70, whose minor theme is at once a moving, cortege-like march and an exhibition of contrapuntal skill. Its two-part counterpoint is invertible — that is, the higher part can become the lower and vice versa — a feature that Haydn put to great expressive use.

The slow movement in variation form with a hymn-like theme is another type in these symphonies that anticipates some of his later works. The second movement of Symphony no. 75 is a lovely example. After a performance in London in March of 1792, Haydn wrote that an English clergyman, on hearing it, "fell into the most profound melancholy because he had dreamt the previous night that this piece was a premonition of his death. — He left the company at once and took to his bed." About a month later Haydn heard "that this protestant clergyman had died" (Landon 3, p. 152). Whatever role — if any — one thinks this movement might have played in the clergyman's death, there can be no denying the expressive quality of the music. Brown compares its "pastoral sadness" to an aria from Haydn's opera *La fedeltà premiata*.

Peaceful rivulets,
friendly flowered meadow,
sunny slopes,
dark and sad valleys,
tell me if you ever saw
a heart more unhappy
and tormented than mine.[13]

The fourth movements of Haydn's symphonies at this time provide numerous examples of his inventiveness. In the Symphony no. 51 and Symphony no. 55, Haydn explored the use of variation techniques within rondo form; in nos. 65 and 73 he explored the hunt topic — one that naturally lends itself to lively finales; and in no. 57 the thematic material comes from bird-song. He derived it from a seventeenth-century piece titled *Canzon*

13. Brown, *The Symphonic Repertoire,* vol. 2, p. 180.

und Capriccio über dass Henner und Hannergeschrey ("Canzona and Capriccio on the Cries of Hen and Rooster").

The fourth movement of Symphony no. 67 is a unique combination of forms. As in the first movement of the *Farewell* Symphony, Haydn here seems to have inserted something new and of differing character in the midst of a fast movement. It begins with what seems to be the exposition section of a typical sonata form. But following the exposition, Haydn introduced an adagio that seems at the moment to be an insertion in the development section. But it turns out to be very long — too long to be construed as part of a development section. There are, in fact, two adagios (call them X and Y). X is in F major; Y is in B♭ major. This sets up the expectation of a large ternary form in which X returns after Y: X (1st adagio in F) — Y (2nd adagio in B♭) — X (1st adagio in F). But at the place where we presume X will return, Haydn gives us the expected key (F major) but not the expected thematic material. Instead of a return to X, the music returns to the thematic material of the opening allegro (Z), which serves as the conclusion of both the sonata and ternary forms. (See Diagram 11-1.) At one and the same time Z functions as the recapitulation of the interrupted sonata form and a tonally satisfying, though thematically surprising, third section of the ternary form.

Another finale that is unique in form is the fourth movement of Symphony no. 70. Though the symphony is in D major, its finale begins in minor (an extreme rarity for a symphony in major), and it remains in minor until its brief conclusion. Furthermore, the bulk of the movement is a fugue — another rarity. Obviously, this is not a typical light, effervescent finale. But neither is it as thoroughly serious as its minor key and fugal form suggest.

The overall form can be construed as a double prelude and fugue with conclusion. (See Diagram 11-2.) Both preludes and the conclusion, says Brown, "present Haydn as a man of ironic wit."[14] They start with five high quarter notes played quietly by the first violins alone — a "whiff of the theatre" says Robbins Landon, who asks, "Harlequin softly opening the curtain?"[15] Indeed, there is something both comical and mysterious about the opening, and the half cadence at the end of Prelude 1 leaves us wondering — what next?

14. Brown, *The Symphonic Repertoire*, vol. 2, p. 177. Diagram 11-2 is from Brown, but I have substituted "prelude" where he has "exordium." His diagram has D major beginning at Prelude 2. This is undoubtedly a "typo" that proof-reading missed. Prelude 2 is unmistakably in D minor.

15. Landon, *Chronicle and Works*, vol. 2, p. 564.

Diagram 11-1

```
        ‖Allegro                ‖Adagio                                                    ‖Allegro
        ‖:F      to C          :‖:F  :‖:to C    to F  :‖:B♭        toF:‖ F    to B♭    | B♭ - g - E♭ - C    ‖F
SONATA  ‖:Exposition           :‖:- - - Development section replaced by two adagios and transition - - - -    ‖Recapitulation
                                  Adagio 1 in F    =    transition    =    Adagio 2 in B♭    =    transition
                                  ‖:       X       :‖                       Y          :‖                     Z
TERNARY
```

Diagram 11-2

[A]	[B]	[A]	[B]	[A]
Prelude 1	Fugue	Prelude 2	Fugue	Conclusion
26 measures	117 measures	18 measures	11 measures	22 measures
D minor...D major.........................				

"What next" are the repeated quarter notes again, but now they are played by the second violins two octaves lower and expanded into a theme that turns out to be the subject of a fugue. It is accompanied immediately by a countersubject in the first violins. Then, when the subject shifts to the first violins, the seconds take up the countersubject as the violas join with a second countersubject. So "what next" is a fugue on three subjects that Haydn labeled, in the terminology he used for the fugal finales in his Opus 20 string quartets, "a 3 soggetti in contrapunto doppio." And indeed this fugue can stand comparison with the masterful Opus 20 fugues. For that matter, the entire work can stand comparison with anything in Haydn's output. Among his works that have been unjustly overlooked by posterity, the neglect of Symphony no. 70 must rank among the most regrettable. It is a masterpiece. It is also one of the few symphonies from this period that we can date securely. Haydn wrote this celebrative symphony with its "whiff of the theatre" for the occasion of the laying of the cornerstone for the new opera house at Eszterháza on December 18, 1779, the old one having been destroyed by fire just a month earlier.

The symphonies Haydn wrote during the peak opera years show anything but a decline from his *Sturm und Drang* symphonies. In 1782, Hummel (a publisher in Amsterdam and Berlin) published six symphonies, nos. 75, 63, 70, 71, 62, and 74. A reviewer wrote that they "are full of the most original fancies, of the liveliest and most pleasing humour. Probably no composer has combined such originality and versatility with such charm and popularity as has Haydn: and few pleasing and agreeable composers have the good technique that Haydn has most of the time" (Landon 2, pp. 466-67). Another reviewer, writing a year later about Symphony no. 73, *La Chasse,* compared it to the symphonies Hummel had published, saying that it "is quite as worthy of its author and in no way needs our praise. In listening to it, the very beginning and the wonderful workmanship of the following parts reveal the hand of the great master, who seems to be inexhaustible in new ideas." He concluded with the hope "that Haydn will crown this great epoch of the symphony with more such wonderful pieces, and thereby reduce all bad writers of symphonies to silence, or to improving their superficial products, through which none but themselves can derive any pleasure" (Landon 2, p. 479).

Haydn would indeed compose "more such wonderful pieces" — twenty-nine more symphonies, many of which are (is it possible?) even more wonderful.

A Burst of Keyboard Composition

Even though the quantity of Haydn's symphony production tapered off during the years when his operatic work was reaching its peak, the tapering is more than balanced by a spike in the production of keyboard sonatas. During this period of less than a decade, he composed about twenty new keyboard sonatas. In other words, he composed about two-fifths of his output in the genre in less than one-fifth of his career. The sonatas of this period consist of two separate works (nos. 33 and 34) and three collections: nos. 21-26, nos. 27-32, and nos. 20 and 35-39.

Nos. 21-26, dedicated to Prince Nicolaus, were written in 1773 and published in 1774, the first works in any genre published with Haydn's authorization. Like the symphonies of this period, these sonatas have often been seen as a step back from the works that immediately preceded them around the turn of the century. To be sure, their rhetoric is less powerful and their forms less dramatic. Their style is quite pervasively *galant* and none are in minor keys — probably to better meet the demand for music for amateurs. They are, however, more advanced than Haydn's earliest (pre-1766) sonatas. Their style is more idiomatic for the keyboard and their forms are more sophisticated. Their balanced appeal for both the *Kenner* (connoisseurs) and the *Liebhaber* (amateurs) is exemplified by one of the most attractive of the set, no. 23 in F major. Its first movement features a jolly opening theme, passages requiring "nimble finger work," and "glimpses of the 'pathetic' mode." In contrast, the second movement is in F minor. Its minor key and graceful *siciliano* rhythms give it a sense of "delicate pathos." The third movement rounds out the cycle in a "*buffo* romp."[16]

The next set of sonatas, nos. 27-32, was not published at first. Instead

16. Michelle Fillion, "Intimate Expression for a Widening Public: The Keyboard Sonatas and Trios," in *The Cambridge Companion to Haydn,* edited by Caryl Clark (Cambridge: Cambridge University Press, 2005), pp. 128-29.

Haydn had them distributed in manuscript copies made by professional Viennese copyists. He listed them in his catalogue as "Six sonatas from the year 1776." Though an easy-going *galant* style is prominent, the set ranges from the thoroughly *galant* Sonata in G major (no. 27) to the intensely expressive Sonata in B minor (no. 32). Among the highlights is the beautiful, if archaic, middle movement of the Sonata in E major (no. 31) — an allegretto in E minor in a Baroque style in which a "walking bass" serves as the foundation for two lovely melodies that flow along in engaging counterpoint.

The set also shows Haydn exploring various aspects of form. The second movement of no. 31 moves without break into the third movement, and in no. 32 all three movements are joined without break. These are not isolated examples. Four other sonatas from this period — not of this set — contain run-on movements (nos. 33, 34, 37, and 38). But the form he seems most interested in exploring is strophic variation.

Strophic variation is a sectional variation form: a theme is followed by a series of variations with a break between each one. Throughout the variations, however varied they may be, the basic features of the theme's harmony, structure, and (usually) melody remain recognizable. It is a simple form that had its heyday in the mid- and late-eighteenth century. Charles Burney wrote disparagingly about the form, describing it as a series of "dull and unmeaning variations to old and new tunes"[17] — and in too many cases he was right. But Haydn took on the challenge of this unpromising form in five of the six finales of the 1776 sonatas. (During this same period he took on the challenge of writing strophic variations for slow movements in four symphonies.) Needless to say, Haydn rose to the challenge; his strophic variations are anything but "dull and unmeaning." They are never merely formulaic; each one shows an interesting permutation of the simple form. Indeed, Burney changed his tune when he heard Haydn's variations. He wrote that as the result of his "richness of imagination, by double counterpoint, and inexhaustible resources of melody and harmony," his variations are among "the most ingenious, pleasing, and heart felt of his admirable productions."[18] Granted, not all of Haydn's strophic variations of this period measure up to that high praise, but they were well on the way.

17. Quoted in Elaine Sisman, "Variation," in *Oxford Composer Companions: Haydn* (Oxford: Oxford University Press, 2009), p. 422.
18. Quoted in Sisman, "Variation," p. 422.

A New Contract and More Keyboard Sonatas

Before the 1780s, Haydn's music spread largely by way of manuscript copies and unauthorized publications. Even so, his reputation spread throughout Europe, but it would have spread more widely and penetrated the culture more deeply had his contract of employment not forbidden him to publish his music or accept commissions without Prince Nicolaus's consent. But that changed on New Year's Day of 1779 when Haydn signed a new contract that dropped the prohibition — this, fortuitously, just a few months after Artaria, a Viennese publishing house, expanded into music publishing.

Haydn and Artaria did not delay in taking advantage of the new situation. Already on January 31, 1780, he wrote to Artaria that he had sent a "6th pianoforte Sonata" and "will certainly deliver the 5th in the next few days." He sent the fifth on February 8 and asked Artaria to send him "all 6 once more for correction." He added that he hoped "to gain some honour by this work, at least with the judicious public; criticism of the works will be leveled only by those who are jealous (and there are many)" (Landon 2, p. 430). On February 25 he returned the corrected proofs, and on April 12 Artaria announced the publication in the *Wiener-Zeitung*. The publication contained six sonatas, nos. 35-39 and 20. The title page, in Italian, proudly proclaimed that the sonatas were composed by "the celebrated Mr. Giuseppe Haydn."

Haydn dedicated the collection to Katharine and Marianna von Auenbrugger, two of the six daughters of a highly respected physician from Graz. Katharine and Marianna were fine keyboardists. Leopold Mozart wrote that "both of them, and in particular the elder [Katharine], play extraordinarily well and are thoroughly musical."[19] And Haydn wrote: "The approval of the *Demoiselles* von Auenbrugger is most important to me, for their way of playing and genuine insight into music equal those of the greatest masters. Both deserve to be known throughout Europe through public newspapers" (Landon 2, p. 430).

Although the title page says these sonatas are for "Clavicembalo [harpsichord] or Forte Piano," Haydn seems to have had the fortepiano more in mind, not least because of the increased number of dynamic markings. Harpsichord was included on the title pages so as not to limit sales. It will

19. *The Letters of Mozart and His Family,* trans. by Emily Anderson (New York: Macmillan, 1962), p. 236.

continue to be found on most title pages of keyboard music until about 1800 even though by then the fortepiano had been the keyboard of choice by most composers for a couple of decades or more.

As many have noted, Haydn shrewdly compiled the collection for the marketplace of *Kenner* and *Liebhaber*. It includes both a C major sonata (no. 35) that is easily within the reach of a modestly accomplished amateur and a C minor sonata (no. 20, written earlier, see above, pp. 105-6) that Haydn called his "longest and most difficult." Michelle Fillion nicely sums up the set: "It includes the sternly conservative Sonatas nos. 36 in C# minor and 38 in E♭, three brilliant works in modern style in C, D, and G (nos. 35, 37, and 39), concluding with the large Sonata no. 20 in c minor of 1771. The collection exemplifies the striving for balance — between delight and edification, tradition and innovation, commercial expediency and artistic value, the capacities of the amateur and the discrimination of the connoisseur."[20] Indeed, provided "artistic value" is not limited to edification and innovation. Haydn did not put his artistry aside when he strove to delight, and he strove to delight not merely for the sake of commercial expediency.

20. Fillion, p. 129.

CHAPTER 12

"New and Special" String Quartets and a Special Friendship

THE 1780S, PART I

We now behold Haydn outstrip all his competitors.

European Magazine and
London Review, October 1784

Emperor: *"But what do you think of his chamber music?"*
Ditters: *"Why, it is making a world-wide sensation, and*
              most justly too."
Emperor: *"Is he not often too playful?"*
Ditters: *"He has the gift of sportiveness, but he never loses*
              the dignity of art."
Emperor: *"You are right there."*

DITTERS VON DITTERSDORF

Spreading Reputation

Haydn's reputation had been spreading throughout Europe since the 1760s. During the 1780s it became truly international. In 1784 an English writer observed a "vast demand for his works all over Europe" and "continual commissions from France, England, Russia, Holland, etc. for his compositions" (Landon 2, p. 497). Much of this was due to Haydn's newly won freedom to publish and accept commissions without Prince Nicolaus's permission.

A correspondent writing to Cramer's *Magazin der Musik* said he did not need to introduce Haydn with lavish praise. He could proceed "without further ado" because Haydn's fame was so widespread that his name "need merely be mentioned." His name alone expresses everything. The writer went on to say what many must have felt about Haydn's recently published Auenbrugger piano sonatas: they are "wonderful," an antidote "against sorrow and misfortune for many a piano player." So on behalf of "languishing violinists" he asked Haydn to compose "a little opus of violin sonatas for their empty larders." "If this sheet should come to his notice," he wrote, "may he fulfill the wishes of the German violin players who respect him" (Landon 2, p. 475).

Haydn composed no violin sonatas, so in that sense he did not fulfill the wishes of the writer and his fellow German violinists. But violinists from every country and every generation can be grateful for the impressive amount of wonderful chamber music he wrote during the next two decades, in particular his string quartets and his sonatas for clavier accompanied by violin and cello. (For the latter, see chapter 13).

Opus 33: "A New and Special Way"

Following release of the six keyboard sonatas dedicated to the Auenbrugger sisters, Haydn quickly linked up with Artaria for more publications. Within a year after the sonatas, Artaria published a collection of Haydn's songs and the six string quartets in Opus 33. Without diminishing the importance of either the Auenbrugger sonatas or the song collection, it is fair to say that Opus 33 is an achievement of greater magnitude. Haydn had long since proven himself to be the master of the genre, but almost a decade had passed since the (unauthorized) publication of his Opus 20 quartets. So the publication of six new quartets was of considerable historical moment.

In December of 1781, as the new quartets were nearing publication, Haydn sent out letters to potential patrons, offering pre-publication copies. One of the three surviving letters went to Johann Caspar Lavater in Zurich, a Zwinglian pastor, poet, and famous physiognomist.

> Most learned Sir and
> Dearest Friend!
> I love and happily read your works. As one reads, hears and relates,
> I am not without adroitness myself, since my name (as it were) is known
> and highly appreciated in every country. Therefore I take the liberty of

asking you to do a small favour for me. Since I know that there are in Zürich and Winterthur many gentlemen amateurs and great connoisseurs and patrons of music, I shall not conceal from you the fact that I am issuing, by subscription, for the price of 6 ducats, a work, consisting of 6 Quartets for 2 violins, viola and violincello *concertante,* correctly copied, and WRITTEN IN A NEW AND SPECIAL WAY (FOR I HAVEN'T COMPOSED ANY FOR 10 YEARS). (Landon 2, p. 454)

Haydn's reference to "gentlemen amateurs" points to a cultural phenomenon: clavier playing was a special domain for ladies; string quartet playing was a special domain for gentlemen. For reasons that now seem laughable, ladies did not play stringed or wind instruments. As Arthur Loesser explains:

When a woman plays the flute, she must purse her lips; and she must do so likewise when she blows a horn, besides also giving evidences of visceral support for her tone. What encouragement might that not give the lewd-minded among her beholders? When she plays a cello, she must spread her legs: perish the thought! When she plays the violin, she must twist her upper torso and strain her neck in an unnatural way; and if she practices much, she may develop an unsightly scar under her jaw. Moreover, eighteenth-century clothes fashions could seem especially inappropriate to certain instruments in contemporary eyes. [According to a writer in 1784] "It strikes us as ridiculous when we look at a female in a hoop skirt at a double bass; ridiculous when we see her playing the violin with great sleeves flying to and fro."[1]

Haydn's statement that he composed these quartets in a "new and special way" is sometimes dismissed as nothing more than a sales pitch. No doubt it was that, at least in part; Haydn knew the human craving for the novel. Others, however, see the "new and special way" as being so fundamentally different from what went before that it marks the beginning of the Viennese Classical style of Haydn, Mozart, and Beethoven — a style, says Charles Rosen, that "did not exist before the work of Mozart and Haydn in the late 1770s." That change in style was so great that to appreciate music of the '60s and '70s "we need all our historical sympathy." But

---

1. Arthur Loesser, *Men, Women, and Pianos* (New York: Simon and Schuster, 1954), p. 65.

ever since Haydn's Opus 33 quartets, "we have only to sit back and watch two friends [Haydn and Mozart] and their disciple [Beethoven] sweep almost every kind of music, from the bagatelle to the mass, into their orbit, mastering the forms of the sonata, concerto, opera, symphony, quartet, serenade, folk-song arrangement with a style so powerful that it can apply almost equally to any genre."[2]

There is truth in Rosen's assertion, and his prize-winning book, *The Classical Style,* provides perceptive analyses of features that define the essence of that style. But even if Haydn had erased all vestiges of the old in Opus 33, and granting that the new "is still in the blood of most musicians today," none of that could have been in his mind. He had sales and his current reputation in mind, not a grand idea about his place in music history. But it would be wrong to take his statement only as advertising. His parenthetical remark, "for I haven't composed any for ten years," seems to imply: "Surely you wouldn't expect my imagination to have dried up during ten very active years of composing. I've much more to say in this genre to which I've now returned." Later in life, with his energy waning and his health failing, he lamented about "how much is still to be done in this splendid art" (Griesinger, p. 65). But at this time in his life (and for many years to come) he had plenty of energy to do many amazing things "in this splendid art."

Donald Tovey wrote that after the Opus 20 quartets, no one could guess "which of some half-dozen different lines he would have followed up." Instead "something different happened";[3] Haydn indeed had something "new and special" to offer in Opus 33. At first glance, it might seem that Haydn was referring to the scherzos that he wrote instead of minuets in all six quartets. But the scherzos are not distinguishable from minuets in form and are barely distinguishable in other regards. But perhaps "scherzo" hints at something more general, not limited to the movements so labeled. "Scherzo" means "joke" or "jest," and critics have noticed from the beginning that these quartets show Haydn at his witty and humorous best more consistently than his earlier works. A 1783 review says they cannot be praised enough for "the most ingenious humor and the most lively, most agreeable wit that prevails in them."

Other critics, however, have seen "ingenious humor" and "lively wit"

---

2. Charles Rosen, *The Classical Style: Haydn, Mozart, Beethoven* (New York: W. W. Norton and Co., 1972), p. 47.

3. Donald Francis Tovey, "Haydn's Chamber Music," in *The Mainstream of Music and Other Essays* (Cleveland: Meridian Books, 1964), p. 49.

as a lapse from the seriousness of the Opus 20 quartets. Robert Sondheimer went so far as to say that "in his quest for applause," Haydn "shows an intellectual naivety which is indispensable to the acquisition of popularity."[4] But good humor is not necessarily a sign of shallowness, and popularity is not always a sign of dumbing down. From early on, Haydn had an uncanny ability to please his audiences without over-simplifying. At first the prince was his primary audience, but his audience grew to encompass the entire music-loving public throughout the Western world. From Opus 33 on, Haydn produced masterpiece after masterpiece whose special genius is that they appeal to both knowledgeable musicians and general music lovers — not in alternation but at one and the same time!

Haydn and Mozart's Friendship

Mozart, no mean critic, recognized that the Opus 33 quartets, for all their surface simplicity and good humor, were anything but intellectually naïve. Instead he saw them as works worthy of emulation. They challenged him to respond by composing six quartets of his own between 1782 and 1785 (K. 387, 421, 428, 458, 464, and 465) now known collectively as the *Haydn* quartets. Judging from the amount of time he spent on them, and the number of revisions in his manuscripts, the challenge proved to be more demanding than usual. What Brahms knew about Haydn's symphonies, Mozart knew about his string quartets — after Opus 33, writing string quartets was no joke.

Mozart dedicated the six quartets to Haydn. On the title page, Haydn's name appears above Mozart's, and both names are in the same sized lettering. Mozart's letter of dedication reads:

> To my dear friend Haydn,
>   A father, having resolved to send his sons into the great world, finds it advisable to entrust them to the protection and guidance of a highly celebrated man, the more so since this man, by a stroke of luck, is his best friend. — Here, then, celebrated man and dearest friend, are my six sons. — Truly, they are the fruit of a long and laborious effort, but the hope, strengthened by several of my friends, that this effort would,

---

4. Quoted in H. C. Robbins Landon, *Haydn: Chronicle and Works,* vol. 2 (Bloomington: Indiana University Press, 1976-80), p. 582.

at least in some small measure, be rewarded, encourages and comforts me that one day, these children may be a source of consolation to me. — You yourself, dearest friend, during your last sojourn in this capital, expressed to me your satisfaction with these works. — This, your approval, encourages me more than anything else, and thus I entrust them to your care, and hope that they are not wholly unworthy of your favour. — Do but receive them kindly, and be their father, guide, and friend! From this moment I cede to you all my rights over them: I pray you to be indulgent to their mistakes, which a father's partial eye may have overlooked, and despite this, to cloak them in the mantle of your generosity which they value so highly. From the bottom of my heart I am, dearest friend,

Your most sincere friend,

W. A. Mozart (Landon 2, p. 673)

This dedication was Mozart's most effusive, but by no means his only, expression of esteem for Haydn's music. Some of his earlier quartets were modeled after Haydn's Opus 20, and at some time in the early '80s he copied themes of three of Haydn's symphonies, nos. 47, 62, and 75, no doubt with the intent of performing them. His respect for Haydn could not be better expressed than it is in an anecdote told by Franz Xaver Niemetschek, Mozart's first biographer.

At a private party a new work of Joseph Haydn was being performed. Besides Mozart there were a number of other musicians present, among them a certain man who was never known to praise anyone but himself. He was standing next to Mozart and found fault with one thing after another. For a while Mozart listened patiently: when he could bear it no longer and the fault-finder once more conceitedly declared: "I would not have done that," Mozart retorted: "Neither would I, but do you know why? Because neither of us could have thought of anything so appropriate."[5]

We do not know when Haydn and Mozart first met. Their paths could have crossed in Vienna at various times during the '70s, but it is

5. Franz Xaver Niemetschek, *Leben des K. K. Kapellmeisters Wolfgang Gottlieb Mozart,* trans. as *Mozart: the First Biography* by Helen Mautner (New York: Berghahn Books, 2007), p. 59.

more likely that the meeting happened during the early '80s after Mozart took up permanent residence there, possibly at one of the concerts on December 22 and 23, 1783, in which music of both composers was featured; or perhaps at the performances on March 28 and 30, 1784, of Haydn's oratorio *Il ritorno di Tobia*. Whatever the occasion of their first meeting may have been, it led to a deep friendship that lasted until Mozart's early death in 1791.

Freemasonry

Friendship with Mozart may have prompted Haydn's interest in Freemasonry, though other Viennese acquaintances also could have prompted it. Whoever or whatever attracted him to Freemasonry, Haydn expressed great enthusiasm for joining. In a letter to the secretary of the lodge "Zur wahren Eintracht" ("True Harmony") he wrote: "The highly advantageous impression which Freemasonry has made on me has long awakened in my breast the sincerest wish to become a member of the Order, with its humanitarian and wise principles" (Landon 2, p 504).

The lodge's minutes of January 10, 1785, include Haydn among the aspirants and January 28 as his initiation date. But he missed the ceremony because word of the date did not reach Eszterháza until February 1. His rescheduled initiation took place on February 11. Unfortunately, Mozart was unable to attend because he was scheduled to play a concert that day. The speech given at the ceremony focused on the Masonic ideal of harmony, "the central point, the essential strength, through which Beauty is defined in the whole of Nature; without it Nature itself must fall, and the starry firmament must again sink with the earth into chaos." The speaker lauded Haydn as one who knew "especially well the designs of this heavenly gift, harmony; you know its all-embracing power in one of the most beautiful fields of human endeavour; to you this enchanting goddess has granted part of her bewitching power, through which she brightens melancholic and cloudy thoughts, and turns the heart of humans to joyful speculation; she not infrequently rises to the heights of passion herself — but to praise all her charms to you would be superfluous" (Landon 2, p. 507).

A Papal Bull in 1738 prohibiting Catholics from becoming Freemasons had little effect. By 1780 there were six lodges in Vienna. Among the members were many Catholics, not a few of them priests. It was Emperor Joseph II, fearing that the lodges might be breeding-grounds for antigovernment ideas, who brought about the closing of all Viennese lodges by 1794. That made little difference to Haydn. After his initiation, he never attended lodge meetings. No doubt busyness at Eszterháza made it difficult for him to attend meetings in Vienna, but had he been more committed to the Order (as Mozart was), he surely would have been able to make time for meetings, especially after Vienna became his year-round residence after 1790, or during his three years in London, where Freemasonry still flourished. It seems that his initial interest stemmed from a desire to belong to a club of respected, high-minded men rather than to an Order with quasi-religious rituals and esoteric beliefs. Unlike Mozart, he did not compose any music for Masonic rituals, and (again unlike Mozart, most notably in his *The Magic Flute*), none of his music contains Masonic symbolism. As David Wyn Jones puts it, "attempts to find specifically Masonic characteristics in Haydn's music smack of special pleading."[6]

Quartet Parties

Despite their deep friendship, scarcity of documentation suggests that Haydn and Mozart had little time together. String quartet parties sometimes brought them together. One is documented in the *Reminiscences* of Michael Kelly, an Irish tenor for whom Mozart composed the roles of Don Basilio and Don Curzio in the *Marriage of Figaro*. The host was Stephen Storace, an English composer and brother of Nancy Storace, the soprano for whom Mozart composed the role of Susanna in *Figaro*. Kelly wrote, tongue-in-cheek, that the players at this party were "tolerable," but, he added, in a classic understatement, "there was a little science among them." Indeed! The quartet included none other than Haydn and Mozart plus two other respected composers, Dittersdorf and Vanhal. "I was there," wrote Kelly, "and a greater treat or a more remarkable one cannot be imagined" (Landon 2, p. 491).

Quartet parties provided the opportunity for Haydn to hear Mozart's *Haydn* quartets prior to their publication. After one such party Leopold, Mozart's father, wrote to his daughter "that last Saturday Wolfgang had his 6 Quartets played to his dear friend Haydn and other good friends" (Landon 2, p. 509). A month later, after Haydn heard three of them again,

6. David Wyn Jones, "Freemasonry," in *Oxford Composer Companions: Haydn* (Oxford: Oxford University Press, 2009), p. 107.

Leopold reported: "Herr Haydn said to me: 'I tell you before God, and as an honest man, that your son is the greatest composer I know, either personally or by reputation. He has taste and, apart from that, the greatest knowledge of composition'" (Landon 2, pp. 508-509).

Haydn's Additional Quartets in the '80s

Opus 42

Artaria published Mozart's *Haydn* quartets in 1785. Haydn himself did not publish another set of six until 1787, five years after Opus 33. In a letter to Artaria dated April 5, 1784, he mentioned working on a set of short, three-movement quartets "intended for Spain" (Landon 2, p. 490). They are lost without a trace, unless the Quartet in D minor, Opus 42, is one of them. This is a short work not belonging to a set, but it has four movements, not three as the letter states. Two things set it apart from his other quartets around this time — its brevity and its slow first movement marked "Andante ed Innocentemente." But it is a fine work. Neither "innocence" nor brevity is a sign of weakness in a composer with a gift for terseness and whose surface innocence usually veils hidden depths.

Opus 50

Haydn's letter of April 5, 1784, might contain the first reference to the six Opus 50 quartets, but they were not completed until 1787. From February through July of 1787, he wrote several times to assure Artaria that quartets were, or soon would be, in the mail despite "lack of time." "Opera rehearsals," he wrote, "detain me" (Landon 2, pp. 696 and 689).

His letters also referred to the dedication of the quartets to Friedrich Wilhelm II, nephew of Frederick the Great, whom he succeeded as King of Prussia in 1786. Haydn had recently sent him his six *Paris* Symphonies (see chapter 14). The Royal Prussian Minister informed Haydn that the king was "especially pleased." He wrote: "There is no doubt that His Majesty has always appreciated *Herr Kapellmeister* Haydn's works, and will appreciate them at all times. To provide concrete assurance of the same, he sends him the enclosed ring as a mark of His Majesty's satisfaction and of the favour in which he holds him" (Landon 2, p. 692).

Haydn was pleased by the king's reception of his music. On May 19, 1787, he wrote to Artaria: "Now here is something important I have to tell you: you know that I received a beautiful ring from His Majesty, the King of Prussia. I feel deeply in His Majesty's debt because of this present, and for my part I can think of no better and more fitting way to show my thankfulness to His Majesty (and also in the eyes of the whole world) than by dedicating these 6 Quartets to him" (Landon 2, p. 693). On December 19, 1787, Artaria advertised the publication of Opus 50 in the *Wiener Zeitung*. The dedication read: "A Sa Majesté/FREDERIC GUILLAUME II/ROI DU PRUSSE."

Some Shady Business Practices

All had not gone well in the meantime. In the early years of music publishing, there was much dishonest dealing. In this case, Haydn was guilty of double-dealing. In August he offered the six quartets to the London publisher Forster with the claim that he had not yet given them to anyone. Forster accepted the offer and published them ahead of Artaria. To make matters worse for Artaria, a Viennese copyist was selling manuscript copies as early as October. Artaria blamed Haydn's copyist, and Haydn blamed one of theirs. When they called out Haydn for selling to Forster, Haydn blamed them for delaying publication and not granting rights to their own London associates, Longman & Broderip.

Though Haydn was clearly in the wrong, the circumstances make his duplicity understandable, though not justifiable. Publishers were all too ready to take advantage of composers. During the previous two decades they had made significant profits from unauthorized publications of Haydn's music, from which he had received nothing. They would continue to do so whenever they could. Further, they frequently attributed the works of others to him in order to reap greater profits through the use of his famous name. No doubt, as W. Dean Sutcliffe says, such practices fuelled "Haydn's drive to capitalize on his musical products" and "to 'catch up' on his lost earnings." In a letter to Artaria, Haydn asserted the principle that he had "a greater right to get this profit than the other dealers." As Sutcliffe rightly notes: "It was Haydn's aggressive insistence on his rights and growing appreciation of his 'clout' that was initiating a major change in the status of composers. The major credit in this process is commonly given to Beethoven, just as many of Haydn's musical innovations are still associated with their imitation in his pupil's works; the new ground he broke seemingly unnoticed was to be reclaimed by Beethoven."[7]

Although "Haydn's drive to capitalize on his musical products" would become a necessity when freelance composing replaced patronage as the main means of earning a living, not all composers were ready to become salespeople. A German composer named Joseph Martin Kraus, whom Haydn regarded very highly, visited Eszterháza in 1783. In his travel diary he wrote: "In Haydn I got to know a right good soul, except for one point — that's money. He simply couldn't understand why I didn't provide myself with a drawer full of compositions for my trip, so as to plant them whenever necessary. I answered quite drily that I wasn't cut out to be a Jewish salesman" (Landon 2, p. 478).

Wit and Creativity

King Friedrich Wilhelm II of Prussia, the dedicatee of Opus 50, was a fine cellist. In 1789 he commissioned Mozart to write a set of quartets, which Mozart fulfilled with his final three string quartets (K. 575, 589, and 590). These, like Haydn's Opus 50, were known as the *Prussian* quartets. Mozart flattered the king by including long cello solos in his quartets, but Haydn, in his, does not seem to have had the royal player very much in mind. To be sure, the cello is an independent voice among the four instruments. Sometimes it carries the melody or plays elaborate figuration, but it is never showy. As Rosen puts it, "The solo cello passages placed as a tactful homage to the royal amateur call forth complementary solo displays from the other instruments."[8] If Haydn intended the cello parts as homage to the king, the first instance of it is a not-so-subtle joke at the king's expense. The first two measures of the first quartet display the cello alone playing eight quarter notes on the same pitch — not the stuff to show off the king's virtuosity! When the upper strings enter in measure three, they play a lightly decorated cadential figure, another joke — cadences are endings, not beginnings.

Haydn may have begun the movement with a couple of jokes, but the piece is not funny; it is serious in character, not jocular. It exhibits Haydn's wit not so much as humor but as agility of mind and fertility of imagina-

---

7. W. Dean Sutcliffe, *Haydn: String Quartets, Op. 50* (Cambridge: Cambridge University Press, 1992), p. 35.

8. Rosen, p. 138.

tion that can take stable, conventional elements, use them in unexpected places or in surprising conjunction, and bring incongruity into unsuspected congruity.[9] In this sense wit is closely allied to notions of genius and imagination, as in Pope's famous line: "Wit and Judgment often are at strife." It is hard, as C. S. Lewis points out, to find a word that expresses what wit clearly means here. "But what is hard to express is easy to understand. What is being talked about is the productive, seminal (modern cant would say 'creative') thing as distinct from the critical faculty of *judicium;* the thing supplied by nature, not acquired by skill *(ars)*. It is what distinguishes the great writer and especially the great poet. It is therefore very close to 'imagination.' "[10]

Despite Lewis's dislike for the word "creative," it seems to me that this term comes as close as any to describing Haydn's "wit" or "genius" or "imagination" in the first movement of the first quartet of Opus 50. Only God can truly create — if that means to bring something into existence out of nothing. But in this movement and hundreds more, Haydn creates something out of next to nothing. After the first statement of the cadential figure, Haydn repeated it two steps higher instead of one step lower as expected, thus evading an all-too-early cadence. Then, out of two minimal and commonplace ingredients — the throbbing repeated note and the short cadential figure (and its variant in triplets) — Haydn built the whole movement. The paucity and commonplace nature of the musical materials do not lead to boring uniformity. On the contrary, Haydn's lively imagination and keen awareness of the potential of his material enabled him to build a movement full of variety and subtle tensions that are resolved in the end.

The terse economy of the opening movement of the first Opus 50 quartet has often been taken as typical of the whole set. Indeed, that is a general tendency, but if it suggests sameness throughout the set, nothing could be further from the truth. Haydn may tend strongly toward the terse rather than the expansive, but that does not limit his range of expression, nor does it force his forms into a few prefabricated molds. The music can be as jolly as the first movement of no. 5 in F major or "lose itself in pathos"[11] like the last movement of no. 4 in F♯ minor, the "quietest and deep-

9. See Gretchen A. Wheelock, *Haydn's Ingenious Jesting with Art* (New York: Schirmer Books, 1992), pp. 22-25.
10. C. S. Lewis, *Studies in Words* (Cambridge: Cambridge University Press, 1967), p. 92.
11. Rosen, p. 138.

est of all the few instrumental fugues since Bach."[12] In form the music can be as thoroughly monothematic as the first movement of no. 1 in B♭ major or grow out of sharply contrasting themes as in the first movement of no. 2 in C major. "From op. 50 onwards," says Tovey, "there is no dealing with Haydn's first movements [or, I would add, any others] except by individual analysis."[13] His music never came out of predetermined forms; it grew out of the musical materials he invented, whose potential for development his perceptive ears so readily detected.

Twelve More Quartets

After completing Opus 50, Haydn took no significant hiatus in string quartet production. Soon after finishing, he began work on six more, finishing them sometime in 1788. He sent them to Paris via Johann Tost, a violinist in the Esterházy orchestra. They were published there by Jean-Georges Sieber in June of 1789 in two sets of three as Opus 54 and Opus 55. Then by late 1790 he had finished another set of six, now known as Opus 64. These were dedicated to Tost and published in Vienna by Leopold Kozeluch, a once-successful composer turned publisher. Kozeluch advertised them in April of 1791; Sieber in Paris followed with an edition in June. With twelve quartets following so closely on the heels of the six in Opus 50, one might wonder if the new ones might be somewhat formulaic. But as James Webster says, "It bears repeating: Haydn never repeated himself."[14]

Opus 54, No. 2

Opus 54, No. 2, in C major is the quartet in this group that is most obviously different. It begins with a strong, almost symphonic, antecedent phrase followed by a grand pause. The expected consequent phrase follows with another grand pause. What next? The opening phrase again, but now in the unexpected, distant key of A♭ major! (One could be excused for thinking this is Schubert.) This time the theme is not interrupted by a

12. Tovey, "Haydn's Chamber Music," p. 61.
13. Tovey, "Haydn's Chamber Music," p. 55.
14. James Webster, *Haydn's "Farewell" Symphony and the Idea of Classical Style* (Cambridge: Cambridge University Press, 1991), p. 334.

grand pause. It goes on, finally extracts itself from A♭, and makes a strong cadence in C major — only to pause again and repeat the cadence softly an octave higher. Twenty-nine measures into the music and it is still in C major. After yet another pause we hear the opening theme again — this time in A minor! Perhaps now the music will finally make the normal modulation to G major, the dominant key. But after ten measures it seems to be back in C. However, the next eight measures convince us that the return to C major was only a passing illusion on the way to G major. That, in fact, turns out to be the case, but only after being delayed by a passage in G minor.

This description has brought us only to measure fifty-six of the exposition. There are thirty-two measures to go before the development section, but enough has been said to more than hint at the adventure that lies ahead.

Adventurous as it is, the first movement is the least surprising of the four — at least in its broad outlines. The second movement — again in its broad outlines — is also unsurprising. It is a slow movement in rounded binary form — ‖: A :‖: B A′ :‖. It begins innocently, but tragically, with a slow eight-measure melody in C minor. It is harmonized hymn-style and ends with a half-cadence. The same melody is repeated but transferred from the first to the second violin, freeing the first violin to play what is the most striking feature of the whole movement: a very florid, rhapsodic lament in Hungarian Gypsy style. Underneath the rhapsody, and completely obscured by it, the three lower instruments continue with the remaining parts (B A′) of a rounded binary form. A′ (unlike A, which is antecedent) should be consequent. But when it gets to its presumed end, it cadences deceptively on A♭. Then instead of an extension that "should" bring the music to a cadence on C, it proceeds instead to a half-cadence on G, which leads without break to the third movement.

The third movement is a surprisingly light-hearted and bouncy minuet in C major. In stark contrast, its trio begins with a brusque, unison phrase in C minor that turns very soon to a sighing motive. The sighing motive is developed into an anguished plaint with dissonant harmony that makes one wonder whether Wagner knew this work.

The fourth movement defies description. Instead of the usual fast finale, we hear what sounds like the beginning of a slow movement. Might it be a slow introduction to a fast movement? It does not take long before it becomes obvious that this will not be an introduction, and as the music progresses it sets up more expectations, all of which need to be changed as the music progresses further. James Webster quotes Edward T. Cone, who says that Haydn created "a series of mistaken interpretations cleverly ordered in such a way that the subsequent corrections of each merely exposes the listener to the next error." Webster then adds: "Over the course of the movement, these continual reversals create a chain of defeated expectations, reinterpretations, and contradictions, which reaches stability only at the very end."[15] Fifty-six slow measures into the movement, long after expectation that this is an introduction has gone away, the music comes to a half-cadence where, as Webster puts it, "we indeed actively expect 'something new,' although by now we no longer have any concrete idea which it might be." And what is it? "A rollicking Presto! — precisely the sort of music which, before the finale began, we supposed we would hear, but which in the meantime we have entirely forgotten."[16] But the rollicking presto turns out to be far too short and inconsequential to be construed as the main part of the movement. So another reinterpretation is needed — and it will not be the last!

In all of music, the finale of Opus 54, No. 2 is exceptional in the extent to which Haydn manipulated the conventions of musical form. But his music generally is full of surprises. To say it differently, his music is dramatic, and his dramas vary greatly in the type of "characters" (the musical materials) they involve, in how they interact, and in how it all turns out. "The drama is in the structure," as Charles Rosen so succinctly puts it.[17] But in order for structure to be dramatic, there have to be conventional structures that carry with them certain expectations. No composer understood that better than Haydn, and no composer could play with musical structures more imaginatively to produce new and compelling dramas, even when major works were coming from his pen as quickly as the eighteen quartets during the last part of the '80s. No less than the Opus 33 quartets, these works are all "new and special."

---

15. Webster, *Haydn's "Farewell" Symphony,* p. 301.
16. Webster, *Haydn's "Farewell" Symphony,* p. 306.
17. Rosen, p. 76.

CHAPTER 13

New, Revived, and Unique Genres

THE 1780S, PART 2

Happy is he whose words can move,
Yet sweet notes help persuasion.
Mix your words with music then,
That they the more may enter.

THOMAS CAMPION

Now, from a remote corner of the Continent, he had received
a commission which no artist might dare to carry out solely by
means of technical dexterity.

ROBERT SONDHEIMER

Haydn Enters a New Field, Song

So far, we have heard nothing about Haydn as a song composer. The reason is simple: he did not write songs before 1781. In this respect he was not alone among Austrian composers. Although the composition of lieder (German songs with clavier accompaniment) had flourished since mid-century among composers of the so-called first Berlin School, C. P. E. Bach being chief among them, it was not until the end of the '70s that Austrian composers entered the field. In 1778, Emperor Joseph II established the German National Theater, a significant event in the movement in Austria to promote German language and literature over the Italian and French that prevailed in opera and plays. The movement was a stimulus for lied composition by Austrian composers. A further stimulus was the eagerness of publishers to cash in on a genre perfectly suited for a sizeable market — the clavier-playing ladies who sang as they accompanied themselves, or who accompanied a singer during a social gathering. Between 1778 and 1782 the publisher Joseph Kurzböck issued several collections with a dozen songs in each.

As we have previously noted, Haydn was now under a new contract with Prince Nicolaus that no longer required him to receive the prince's permission to publish his music or accept commissions. We have also noted that the Viennese publisher Artaria had recently expanded into music publishing. Eager for a piece of a burgeoning market, Artaria requested lieder from Haydn. Thus it was that a new genre entered Haydn's compositional portfolio. On July 20, 1781, Haydn wrote to Artaria, "I send you herewith the first 12 *Lieder,* and will endeavour to send you the second dozen, good Sir, as soon as possible" (Landon 2, p. 448).

Haydn and Hofmann

Haydn was pleased with the first-fruits of his new endeavor. He wrote that his lieder, "by their variety, naturalness, beauty, and ease of singing, will perhaps surpass all others" (Landon 2, p. 446). In particular he was pleased with three of his songs whose texts had been previously set by Leopold Hofmann, Kapellmeister at St. Stephen's. Haydn was quick to point out that his choice of those texts was intentional. He wanted to show that his own settings were much better than Hofmann's and thereby assure Artaria that they were entering a competitive market with a superior product. He wrote that the three texts "have been set to music by *Capellmeister* Hofmann, but between ourselves, miserably; and just as this braggart thinks that he alone has ascended the heights of Mount Parnassus, and tries to disgrace me every time with a certain high society, I have composed these very three *Lieder* just to show this would-be high-society the difference." His own songs, he claimed, "are not the street songs of Hofmann, wherein neither ideas, expression nor, much less, melody appear" (Landon 2, p. 449).

Haydn's antipathy toward Hofmann is uncharacteristic. As Allan Badley puts it, "Hofmann has the dubious distinction of being one of only a handful of musicians whom Haydn is known to have disliked." He speculates that Haydn might have been envious of advantages Hofmann had because his "father was a highly educated court official whose contacts were wide and varied."[1] But however much Haydn disliked Hofmann, he was not merely bragging or putting down a rival; his songs are clearly superior. A. Peter Brown says it bluntly: Haydn's songs "do not compete" with Hofmann's; "they belong to another realm."[2] "Hofmann's melodies are eminently forgettable, Haydn's memorable; Hofmann's harmonies are bland, Haydn's colourful; Hofmann slavishly follows the accentuation of the text, Haydn modifies it; and Hofmann has no grasp of poetic structure, Haydn understands its potential."[3]

Romantic Criticism

Although Haydn's lieder were successful at the time, posterity has not shown them much appreciation. What happened to Haydn's lieder is the same thing that happened to so much of his voluminous output: they were overshadowed by later music (including his own). Haydn's lieder became the victim of changing tastes and the all-too-common prejudice that presumes that later is better. With the advent of Romanticism, his lieder simply went out of style and were judged inferior for not being something they were never meant to be.

Beginning with North Germans of his own time, critics have taken issue with Haydn's choice of poems. But the history of song is replete with examples that prove that a poor poem does not necessarily make a poor song. The quality of a song cannot be judged by reading its text. However, the problem goes deeper. Even when the critics sound as if they are objectively criticizing a poem strictly as poetry, they are all too often objecting to a *kind* of poetry they simply do not like. In the poems of Haydn's lieder they do not like what Marshall Brown calls their "remoteness from experiential immediacy." Haydn's contemporaries, unlike the romantics, preferred "implication to immediacy" and a "rhetoric of suggestion" over a "rhetoric of declaration."[4] Eighteenth-century rhetorical and aesthetic preferences

---

1. Allan Badley, "Hofmann, Leopold," in *Oxford Composer Companions: Haydn* (Oxford: Oxford University Press, 2009), p. 156.

2. A. Peter Brown, "Notes on Haydn's Lieder and Canzonettas," in *For the Love of Music: Festschrift in Honor of Theodore Front on His 90th Birthday,* edited by Darwin F. Scott (Lucca, Italy: Lim Antiqua, 2002), p. 80.

3. A. Peter Brown, "Song," in *Oxford Composer Companions: Haydn* (Oxford: Oxford University Press, 2009), p. 367.

4. Marshall Brown, "The Poetry of Haydn's Songs: Sexuality, Repetition, Whimsy,"

fit the social occasions in which Haydn's songs were typically performed. As Brown explains, "Concealment rather than passionate utterance is a core value of Enlightened manners and of the lyric poems that correspond to them. Good breeding hides emotions." A widely read etiquette book of Haydn's day puts it this way: "Conversation requires a certain equanimity, and the self-denial capable of suppressing every outbreak of passion."[5]

Style and Content for Amateurs

In the intimate social settings for which Haydn's lieder were written, the same person often sang and played the clavier. Haydn himself sang and played his lieder in salons in fashionable homes. "I shall sing them myself," he wrote to Artaria, "in the critical homes" (Landon 2, p. 449). Their published format is conducive to that type of performance. The title page calls them *Lieder für Pianoforte* ("Songs for Pianoforte"). They look like keyboard pieces, and indeed the keyboard "accompaniment" is complete in itself. Performed without a singer they are "songs without words" two generations before Mendelssohn. The words are printed between the staves of the keyboard "part." The singer simply sings them to the melody in the upper stave. The keyboard thus provides an ideal support for the amateur singers for whom the music was intended, and the arrangement of the score was especially friendly when singers accompanied themselves.

The lieder collections include a wide variety of feelings attractive to buyers. In a letter of October 18, 1781, Haydn asked Artaria to send him "three new, gentle *Lieder* texts, because almost all the others are of a lusty character. The content of these can be melancholy, too: so that I have shadow and light" (Landon 2, p. 453). Although love songs dominate both the 1781 and 1784 collections — in fact all the songs of the 1781 set are love songs — there is plenty of variety, ranging from melancholy to jocular, from serious to trivial. Whatever the proper emotion and whatever the proper tone, Haydn's music deftly captures (or provides) them.

Even songs with the same topic show great variety. Take, for example, three songs of unrequited love in the 1781 collection. In "Das strickende Mädchen" ("The Knitting Maid"), a male suitor's expressions of love are

---

in *Haydn and the Performance of Rhetoric,* edited by Tom Beghin and Sancer M. Glodberg (Chicago: University of Chicago Press, 2007), pp. 233 and 238.

5. Quoted in M. Brown, "The Poetry of Haydn's Songs," pp. 238-39.

simply ignored. Each stanza ends with the refrain, "Phyllis, without speech or word, sat and quietly continued her knitting." In the refrain after the last stanza her silent treatment is made final; the verb "sat" is changed to "left" — end of story! And we are left to imagine (with hints from the music) the rebuffed suitor's feelings and reaction.

In "Die Verlassene" ("The Abandoned Woman") it is the woman who has been jilted. The song expresses her anguished reaction with great intensity. Her faithless lover, she sings, mocks her poor, beating heart. Nevertheless she "cannot hate him" because she, like all women, has a "weak heart." So she asks Nature, "Why did you create us so meek and men so hard?" and then begs her to teach men "the desires of true love!"

"Der Gleichsinn" ("Indifference") presents yet a third picture of rejection, now sung by a young man who has apparently experienced it many times. Each stanza ends with the insouciant refrain, "What do I care how pretty (gentle, pious, rich) she is?" In the last stanza the refrain is modified: "If your heart is not mine,/ What do I care whose it is?"

In the 1784 set, five of the twelve lieder are on themes other than love. "Auf mein Vaters Grab" ("On my father's grave") is sentimental, pastoral, and religious. "Lob der Faulheit" ("In praise of laziness") is satirical. In laborious tones the singer sings that he must now praise laziness. He tries to do his best, but in the second (last) stanza he becomes increasingly worn out by the task and asks laziness to forgive him. After all it is laziness that prevents him from being enthusiastic in his praise of laziness!

Two songs present contrasting views of life. "Zufriedenheit" ("Contentment") asks "Why wish to be the king?" Since all the evil throughout the kingdom rests on his shoulders and all his advisors lack brains, the king is a slave who gets no rest from his work. So the song concludes: "I would not want to be the king for anything in the world." The other song, "Mein Leben ist ein Traum" ("My life is a dream"), presents life as meaningless. We slip into the world and float around in a confused foam; love and jokes are empty and disappear; we think, we doubt, and we grow wise; but in the grave the answer is the same: "Life is a dream."

The fifth non-love song, "Geistliche Lied" ("Sacred song"), is devotional. The singer would draw near to God, to "the throne of highest majesty," and add his prayer of thanks to the jubilant tone of the seraphs. But he is mere dust of the earth; sin and death are in him. Even so, he can join the seraphs because of Jesus' death. Words are not thanks enough, but noble deeds mixed with cross and tears are the offering God loves. This will be the thanks he offers every hour until he reaches the gate of Eternity.

Haydn Reenters an Old Field, Keyboard Trios

Another genre about which we have so far heard nothing in the late 1780s is the keyboard trio (that is, works for keyboard, violin, and cello). Unlike song, however, which was new in Haydn's output at this time, keyboard trios were not. Ten of his forty-plus surviving keyboard trios date from very early in his career, before being employed by the Esterházy family. Some may have been composed for the chamber music evenings at Count Fürnberg's castle, for which he wrote his first string quartets, and others may have been written for Countess Morzin. Like the early solo keyboard pieces, the early keyboard trios were given the generic designation divertimenti (or partitas).

Just as the newly flourishing music publishing business and Haydn's newly granted freedom to receive commissions and publish his works without the prince's consent brought about his turning to song writing, so too they brought about his return to composing keyboard trios. Now, like the solo keyboard works, they are called sonatas — more precisely, "sonatas for harpsichord or pianoforte accompanied by a violin and cello," clearly indicating their generic relationship to the solo keyboard works and the primacy of the keyboard instrument in the trios. Haydn did not answer the call from publishers for this newly popular form of chamber music as quickly as he did their call for songs. He was still too busy with opera to respond immediately with larger works. In July 1782 he wrote to Artaria: "As to the pianoforte Sonatas with violin, you will have to be patient a long time; for I have to compose a new Italian opera [*Orlando Paladino*], and the [Russian] Grand Duke and Duchess and perhaps His Majesty the Emperor will be coming here for it" (Landon 2, p. 464) — a visit which, by the way, did not materialize. In June 1783 he wrote again: "As to the pianoforte Sonatas with violin and bass [cello], you must still be patient, for I am just now composing a new *opera seria* [*Armida*]" (Landon 2, p. 476).

More Shady Business

In 1784 Haydn finally sold a set of three keyboard trios, nos. 3-5, to the English publisher William Forster. However, two of the three, nos. 3 and 4, were not written by Haydn but by his student Ignaz Joseph Pleyel. From ages fifteen to twenty (1772-77), Pleyel had studied with Haydn in Eisenstadt. Pleyel's patron, Count Ladislaus Erdödy, gave Haydn a carriage and

two horses. Haydn informed Nicolaus the gift was due to Erdödy's "satisfaction with the pupil he entrusted to me." But since the horses were ex-
pensive to maintain, Haydn asked the prince "in his serene graciousness to
grant him hay and oats" (Landon 2, p. 397).

Haydn and Pleyel would be good friends for life, but their friendship
had to survive Haydn's dishonesty and the ensuing legal battle. Pleyel had
sent the two keyboard trios to Haydn as an act of homage. Some time after
receiving the trios, the publisher Forster asked Haydn for three new trios
and offered a good price if he could get them soon. Haydn was busy composing *Armida,* but he did not want to turn down Forster's offer. So he sent
the two Pleyel had given to him along with one of his own that he had just
composed. At about the same time Longman, another London publisher,
bought some works of Pleyel and asked particularly that the two trios written for Haydn be included. Pleyel at first refused but later consented, not
knowing that they had already been published under Haydn's name.

The two publishers sued each other. Forster sued Longman for publishing the supposed Haydn works under the name of Pleyel, and Longman sued Forster for publishing Pleyel's pieces under Haydn's name.
Haydn and Pleyel, neither one wanting to embarrass the other, told the
judges the truth. The end result was an out-of-court settlement and the
two composers remained friends.

More Keyboard Trios

The one genuine Haydn trio from the 1784 set marked the beginning of a
flurry of keyboard trio composition. Twelve more were published between
1786 and 1790. In 1786 Artaria published a set of three (nos. 6-8); so did
Forster (nos. 2, 9-10), but no. 2 was an earlier work. They received high
critical acclaim. A reviewer of the Forster collection wrote: "Among the
many excellent compositions by this great man, these three sonatas claim
one of the foremost places. The initial Adagio from the first one in A major
[no. 9] has an inexpressible charm and makes a very pleasing contrast with
the following Vivace. However, the most beautiful sonata among these
beauties is still the third one in E-flat major [no. 10], in which Haydn's genius soars to its greatest heights. It is also harder to play than the previous
ones" (Landon 2, p. 703).

In August 1788, Haydn wrote to Artaria: "Since I am now in a situation where I need some money, I am offering to write for you by the end

of December either 3 new quartets or 3 new *Clavier* sonatas with violin accompaniment" (Landon 2, p. 708). Artaria chose the trios, and Haydn, as he wrote in reply, bought a new fortepiano "in order to compose your 3 *Clavier* sonatas well" (Landon 2, p. 710). This clearly indicates that Haydn was moving away from a generic keyboard style that could be performed on either harpsichord or fortepiano to a style that required the touch sensitivity of the newer instrument. It also shows how serious Haydn was about writing idiomatically for the instrument. He wanted to learn about the capabilities of this relatively new type of instrument from first-hand experience.

Haydn delivered on his promise and Artaria published three new keyboard trios (nos. 11-13) in 1789. Again they met with high critical acclaim: "The original style of this composer, his beautiful modulations, and his wealth of ideas are too well known to require anything further on our part for the recommendation of these works here announced. Neither the principal [keyboard] part, nor the accompanying [violin and cello] parts are encumbered with difficulties such as would require especially trained players for these sonatas" (Landon 2, p. 723).

Another reviewer wrote that "no sonatas have appeared which could rival the superior qualities of these three." He praised "the well-known originality of their composer," the "excellent working-out" they display, and the way they show "how attractive a common theme can be made by masterly development." He also mentioned their "frequent modulations to remote keys," which require a skilled player. But even "if one cannot immediately play them at sight, one will be very richly rewarded for their effort. For if played nicely in all the parts and performed with the proper expression, they provide the greatest enjoyment which this kind of music can produce" (Landon 2, p. 723).

In 1790, four more were published. Bland (in London) published two in June (nos. 15-16); Artaria's publication in October was a set of three, adding no. 14 to the two already published by Bland; and shortly thereafter Bland published another set of three, adding no. 17 to the two he had already published. Nos. 15-17 have the distinction of being scored for flute instead of violin (although violin is an option). As befits the flute, they are lighter, more *galant* in style than the earlier ones from this time. They also make more concessions to the technical level of amateur players, yet they are never simplistic. Just as the more complex and technically difficult ones do not cross the border into the esoteric, neither do the simpler pieces cross the opposite border into the trivial.

Haydn's keyboard trios, as the reviewer said, "provide the greatest enjoyment which this kind of music can produce." At every turn there are formal innovations, striking textures and colors, unsuspected modulations and satisfying resolutions, lyrical melodies and rollicking dance tunes — beauties and delights of every sort. It is no wonder publishers made more requests than he could meet. But today his keyboard trios have long since fallen into neglect. As Charles Rosen wrote, "Haydn's piano trios are a third great series of works to set beside the symphonies and the quartets, but they are the least known of the three groups for reasons that have nothing to do with their musical worth."[6] The reason for their neglect is that they are misconstrued as failed chamber music. That is, they are not like Beethoven's or Brahms's piano trios, in which the three performers all get roughly the same billing. But that is not the type of piece Haydn was writing. As the title pages make clear, he was writing sonatas for keyboard with violin and cello accompaniment, and that is how they should be listened to. Such an adjustment in our conception will certainly help us to hear the pieces for what they are worth.

Haydn clearly intends a hierarchy among the three instruments; they are not all equal, but they are all important. Rosen describes them as "solo piano works with added solo violin passages."[7] At least in terms of virtuosity, the keyboard is more prominent. Virtuosity belonged to the keyboard, while the violin was best displayed in lyrical passages. That contrast in roles is demonstrated most vividly in the slow movement of the A♭ major trio (no. 14). Its first section is a lyrical violin solo with keyboard accompaniment — a beautiful "song without words." The second section is a brilliant, rhapsodic keyboard solo accompanied by pizzicato strings.

And what about the cello? To be sure it mostly serves to double the keyboard's bass part, but it does have moments of independence, though they are rare and usually very brief. However, the case for the cello's importance cannot be made on the basis of its momentary independence. Its importance lies rather in its sustaining power, which, in most cases, makes it more accurate to say the keyboard's bass line merely doubles the cello rather than vice versa. As Michelle Fillion puts it, "The cello parts are far from optional, leading rather than following the keyboard left hand by virtue of its singing voice and sustaining power. And all three players must

6. Charles Rosen, *The Classical Style: Haydn, Mozart, Beethoven* (New York: W. W. Norton and Co., 1972), p. 351.
7. Rosen, p. 351.

bring considerable understanding to bear on the signal musical demands."[8] In addition to all the other musical values that these works have in such abundance, the values of imaginative texture and sensitive orchestration must be added. Haydn was a master of orchestration, whether he was working with full symphony orchestra, a wind ensemble, or a string quartet. His mastery is no less evident when working with keyboard, violin, and cello.

Two Commissions for Sacred Works

We have already noted that Prince Nicolaus made few, if any, demands on Haydn for sacred music. Although early in his career under Nicolaus Haydn had undertaken the composition of several substantial liturgical works, once his operatic duties became full-blown, his composition of sacred music nearly dried up. But in the first half of the '80s, during which his composition of operas (though not his other operatic duties) came to a stop and his new contract allowed him to accept new commissions, Haydn composed two major liturgical works. Both were composed for outside commissions. The first commission, in 1782, was for a mass. The result was the *Missa cellensis,* also known as the *Mariazeller Mass.* A retired army officer, recently promoted to nobility status, commissioned it. Nothing is known about when or where it was first performed. Despite its nickname, it is not likely that it could have been performed by the small cappella at the church at Mariazell. Plausible speculation has it performed at a church in Vienna that had a connection with the Mariazell pilgrimage, perhaps to celebrate the officer's ennoblement or for some occasion relating to the pilgrimage.

The second commission was unusual. It came from Cadiz, Spain. It provided Haydn with what he called "one of the most difficult tasks" of his career and resulted in a work that is truly unique. Griesinger tells the story as he got it from Haydn.

A canon in Cadiz requested Haydn, about the year 1785, to make an instrumental composition on the Seven Words of Jesus on the Cross which was to be suited to a solemn ceremony that took place annually during

8. Michelle Fillion, "Intimate Expression for a Widening Public: The Keyboard Sonatas and Trios," in *The Cambridge Companion to Haydn,* ed. Caryl Clark (Cambridge: Cambridge University Press, 2005), p. 131.

Lent in the cathedral at Cadiz. On the appointed day the walls, windows, and piers of the church were draped with black, and only a single lamp of good size, hanging in the middle, illuminated the darkness. At the appointed hour all doors were locked, and the music began. After a suitable prelude the bishop mounted to the pulpit, pronounced one of the Seven Words, and delivered a meditation upon it. As soon as it was ended, he descended from the pulpit and knelt down before the altar. The music filled in this pause. The bishop entered the pulpit a second, a third time, and so on, and each time the orchestra came in again at the end of the talk. (Griesinger, p. 21)

The difficulty of the task was "to make out of thin air, with no texts, seven adagios following one another that would not weary the listener but stir in him all the feelings inherent in each of the Words uttered by the dying Saviour" (Griesinger, p. 21). As one reviewer wrote, "The idea of expressing these thoughts by purely instrumental music is curious and daring and only a genius like Haydn would take such a risk" (Landon 2, p. 618).

Haydn framed the seven slow movements that followed each of the seven spoken meditations with a solemn, majestic introduction and a tumultuous presto conclusion that represents the earthquake that followed Jesus' death. Haydn himself, as Griesinger reports, "oftentimes declared this work to be one of his most successful" (p. 21). His success amounted to more than merely overcoming the challenge of writing seven adagios without, as Haydn put it, "fatiguing the listeners" (Landon 2, p. 616). The whole — Jesus' words, the spoken meditations, and Haydn's music — succeeds simply and directly in stirring "the feelings inherent in each of the Words" and in promoting further contemplation of the spoken meditations that they follow. David Wyn Jones describes it as "a masterly aural equivalent to the paintings and sculpture of rococo churches throughout Catholic Europe, inducing penitence and peace of mind in equal measure."[9] The music, in its simplicity and humility, expresses a grateful and hopeful faith. "Far from diminishing its spiritual impact, this simplicity and this humility actually serve to underline the artist's serene and unshakable faith. More than the horror of Christ's agony, it is his touching and profound gratitude towards this sublime testimony to divine love that Haydn wished to express. Thus hope and internal peace always have the

---

9. David Wyn Jones, *"Seven Last Words of Our Saviour on the Cross,"* in *Oxford Composer Companions: Haydn* (Oxford: Oxford University Press, 2009), p. 360.

last word, which explains why only one of the seven adagios ends in the minor key."[10]

The Seven Last Words is an expression of faith over against the liberalism of the time. Jones notes that Haydn composed it "in the middle of an increasingly liberal decade in Austria."

> Both as a musician and as a traditionally minded Austrian Catholic, Haydn may well have viewed with some concern the new restrictions on church music and the accelerated decline in the number and the wealth of the monasteries, for though he dabbled with fashionable Freemasonry, becoming a member in 1785, the composer remained a committed and orthodox member of the Church. If he had misgivings about recent trends, *The Seven Words* seems to re-assert the potency of his faith and the part music can play in affirming that faith.[11]

The Seven Words spread rapidly throughout Europe. The original orchestral version was published in Vienna, London, and Paris. Arrangements that would broaden its spread soon followed in 1787 — one for string quartet (made by Haydn), and another for keyboard (made with Haydn's approval), no doubt intended for fortepiano. In 1795, as he was returning from London, Haydn heard an arrangement for choir, soloists, and orchestra. He liked the idea of such an arrangement but thought the one he heard could be improved. He enlisted Baron van Swieten to work on the text while he himself improved the musical arrangement. Their version had its first performance in 1796. After its publication in 1801, it became the most frequently performed of all the versions.

---

10. Henry Halbreich, CD Notes for *Joseph Haydn, Les sept dernières paroles de notre Rédempteur sur la Croix, Le Concert des Nations,* Jordi Savall, cond., Astrée ES 9935, p. 17.

11. H. C. Robbins Landon and David Wyn Jones, *Haydn: His Life and Music* (Bloomington: Indiana University Press, 1988), p. 191.

CHAPTER 14

Music for London, Vienna, Paris, and the King of Naples

THE 1780S, PART 3

*The symphonies of the immortal Haydn stand out so won-
drously that the pen can only feebly describe them. Elevated in
expression, inexhaustible in invention, new in every musical
thought, unexpected and astounding at every turn, their mild
harmoniousness melted the senses of connoisseurs and laymen
alike.*

Pressburger Zeitung

A Visit to England Delayed

In July 1783 Haydn wrote to the publisher Boyer in Paris telling him that
"last year I composed 3 beautiful, elegant and by no means over-lengthy
Symphonies" (Landon 2, p. 477). He wrote them anticipating a trip to England. His music had been known in England at least since 1765 when his
Opus 1 quartets were advertised in London. During the '70s the amount of
his music available in London increased steadily, and by the early '80s his
popularity in England was so great that English writers were calling him
the Shakespeare of music. But the anticipated trip did not materialize.

The earliest known attempt to bring Haydn to England was made in
1782. Since 1764 Johann Christian Bach (Johann Sebastian's youngest son)
and Carl Friedrich Abel, two of the leading composers in England, had
been giving a series of concerts in London. But on New Year's Day, 1782,
Bach died. Abel tried to carry on with the concert series but financial difficulties forced him to withdraw the next year. A group of gentlemen, led by
Willoughby Bertie, the Fourth Earl of Abingdon, took over the series with

ambitious plans, including bringing Haydn to London. In July 1782 they advertised a series of concerts in the Hanover Square Rooms and claimed that Haydn had been engaged. From that time until February 1783, newspapers carried various reports and rumors, some that Haydn was coming, others that he was not. On February 17 the *Morning Chronicle* reported that "we have yet got neither him nor his music," and it speculated that although "the music is certainly to come, the musician, most probably, will remain in Vienna."[1] The speculation was correct. Haydn did not come but his music did, and it was performed on ten of the twelve concerts in the series.

Rumors of Haydn's coming were kept alive well into the '80s. Reasons given for his not coming were sometimes utterly fantastic and tainted with more than a little chauvinism and religious bigotry, such as the following from the *Gazetteer & New Daily Advertiser*:

> This wonderful man, who is the Shakespeare of music, and the triumph of the age in which we live, is doomed to reside in the court of a miserable German Prince, who is at once incapable of rewarding him, and unworthy of the honour. *Haydn,* the simplest as well as the greatest of men, is resigned to his condition, and in devoting his life to the rites and ceremonies of the Roman Catholic Church, which he carries even to superstition, is content to live immured in a place little better than a dungeon, subject to the domineering spirit of a petty Lord, and the clamorous temper of a scolding wife.[2]

The writer even went so far as to wonder whether kidnapping might be in order. "Would it not be an achievement equal to a pilgrimage, for some aspiring youths to rescue him from his fortune and transplant him to Great Britain, the country for which his music seems to be made?"

The 76th through 81st Symphonies

Haydn's first visit to England was still almost a decade away when he offered the 76th, 77th, and 78th Symphonies to Boyer, but there can be little question that he had London audiences in mind when he wrote them. In

---

1. Quoted in Christopher Roscoe, "Haydn and London in the 1780s," *Music and Letters* 49, no. 3 (July, 1968): 204.

2. Quoted in Roscoe, "Haydn and London," p. 205.

his letter to Boyer he explicitly mentioned that they were "for the English gentlemen" (Landon 2, p. 477). But apart from what he might have known of the music of Bach and Abel, he probably knew little about English taste at the time. More likely he wrote the symphonies for a general, international audience. And not knowing the special capabilities of the orchestras that might perform them, he composed them for a capable but not virtuosic orchestra. So he wrote, "they are all very easy, and without too much *concertante*," and assured Boyer that "these 3 Symphonies will have a huge sale" (Landon 2, p. 477).

These were the first of Haydn's symphonies to be published with his authorization. Their sale again reveals Haydn's sharp business practices. After he sold them to Boyer in Paris, he also sold them to William Forster of London in 1784, and shortly thereafter they were also published by Torricella in Vienna. Whether or not Boyer profited from the "huge sale" Haydn promised in his letter, Haydn certainly profited by selling them to three different publishers. The three symphonies are worthy predecessors of the famous twelve he later wrote for London (nos. 93-104). Nevertheless, they have been neglected by posterity because, like so many of his other works, they stand in the shadow of his later works.

The next three, nos. 79-81, have not fared much better. Haydn composed them in 1784 for a Lenten program given in Vienna on March 13 and 15, 1785. The proposed program included all three symphonies, plus an aria and two choruses (probably from his own oratorio *Il ritorno di Tobia*), a concerto, and a Psalm by Mozart. But Mozart did not finish the Psalm in time, so his cantata *Davidde penitente* was performed instead. Because of the cantata's great length it replaced not only his unfinished Psalm but also one of Haydn's symphonies.

Farewell to *Sturm und Drang*

Of the six symphonies Haydn wrote during the years 1782-84, two are in minor — no. 78 in C minor and no. 80 in D minor. And in 1785 or 1786 he composed a third — no. 83 in G minor. This is striking against the background of the symphonies of the previous decade. After Haydn's last *Sturm und Drang* symphony in 1772, none composed in the ensuing decade were in minor. But the three minor symphonies from the first half of the '80s do not signal a return to *Sturm und Drang*, or, if it is a return, it is only to say farewell.

No. 78 in C minor begins with a strong, angular, unison theme — an unmistakable *Sturm und Drang* opening. (See Example 14-1a.) It is a theme with a long lineage. It is most widely known as the fugue subject of the chorus "And with his stripes" from Handel's *Messiah*. (See Example 14-1b, which is transposed into the same key as Haydn's theme for easier comparison.) Haydn used a similar version of the theme as the fugue subject of the last movement of his F minor Quartet, Opus 20, no. 5. (See Example 14-1c, also transposed.) For Symphony no. 78, Haydn put Handel's theme in three-quarter time and turned it upside down. (Compare examples 14-1a and 14-1b.) A few years later, in his C minor Piano Concerto, Mozart further transformed the theme of Symphony no. 78. He expanded it by two notes, which moved the distinctive leap at the end a fifth higher. (Compare examples 14-1a and 14-1d.) Mozart knew Haydn's theme. In May of 1784 he wrote excitedly to his father, "I *really* possess the last three symphonies he wrote."[3]

EXAMPLE 14-1a, Haydn, Symphony no. 78

EXAMPLE 14-1b, Handel

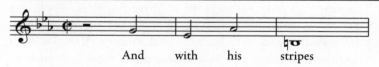

And   with's   his   stripes

EXAMPLE 14-1c, Haydn, Quartet, Opus 20, no. 5

EXAMPLE 14-1d, Mozart, Piano Concerto in C minor

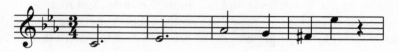

3. Quoted in Robert Marshall, *Mozart Speaks: Views on Music, Musicians, and the World* (New York: Schirmer Books, 1991), p. 65.

By inverting the theme Haydn gave it a strong upward thrust, especially with the ascending diminished seventh at the end, and changed its
character from plaintive to agitated — even angry. Further contributing
to the change in character are the increased amount of melodic dissonance
and the abruptness caused by the change to three-quarter time. The strong
accents and use of driving repeated eighth notes in the continuation of the
opening gesture are additional *Sturm und Drang* features. In short, this
movement is *Sturm und Drang* to the hilt.

The second and third movements generally turn away from *Sturm und
Drang*. The second movement is in the relative major key, E♭. Although it
begins with a loud sigh, the movement is quiet and gentle, generally untroubled by minor keys, strong dissonances, chromaticism, or loud out-
bursts. There are a few intrusions such as a loud chord hammered home in
rapid repeated notes and a short harmonic progression in minor played in
a loud tremolo. But such intrusions are few, just enough to make us wonder
whether the storm has really passed or only subsided temporarily.

The third movement is a joyous C major minuet that seems confident
that the storm has indeed passed. The second section starts in C minor, but
before there is time to worry that it might be a portent of darker things,
it slips easily into E♭ major. However, E♭ major can just as easily slip back
into C minor; indeed, it soon threatens to do just that. But it is a bluff. The
opening C major theme returns as joyous and confident as ever, and in the
trio there is not the slightest whiff of C minor.

Commentators tend to hear the fourth movement as a return to *Sturm
und Drang*. The first theme is in C minor but nothing else about it is *Sturm
und Drang;* rather, it has the character of a slightly rowdy folk dance. It is
paired with a second theme in major. Both themes are lively and full of
good-natured fun. The minor one is a bit rougher than the major one, and
the second time around it turns into a wild romp. But the movement ends
with a major dance in all its gaiety. It teases for a moment near the end, and
then concludes with *opera buffa* festivity.

Symphony no. 80 dismisses *Sturm und Drang* very early on. At the end
of the exposition of the first movement a simple closing theme gleefully
mocks the stern and agitated *Sturm und Drang* opening. Although there are
attempts to reassert *Sturm und Drang,* they are all quickly deflated by the
same little mocking tune.

The first movement of Symphony no. 83, like that of Symphony no.
80, has a powerful *Sturm und Drang* theme and a humorous contrasting
theme, but its dramatic course is entirely different. Its first theme, in ad-

dition to the *Sturm und Drang* gesture with which it begins, has another element — dotted rhythms — which by way of its association with the French overture suggests high and noble character, albeit here in a fierce, perhaps even brutal, tone. By the end of the opening theme, the dotted rhythms have taken over completely. They also figure prominently in the bridge passage, as does the opening *Sturm und Drang* gesture. Together the two components of the main theme lead to a fanfare-like second theme in B♭ major, which in turn leads to a humorous closing theme.

The clucking sound of the closing theme is what gave the symphony its nickname, *La poule* ("the hen"). After being played once, the "hen theme" is played again, this time with an oboe adding a continuous string of dotted rhythms above it. Ironically, the usually noble-sounding dotted rhythms here add to the humorous effect of hens clucking and pecking for food. The dotted rhythms continue into the codetta and close out the exposition, now definitely sounding noble again.

The hen theme gets heard twice early in the development section (the second time in minor), but the opening gesture of the *Sturm und Drang* theme, against a countermelody derived from the fanfare theme, dominates throughout. Near the end of the development section several versions of the *Sturm und Drang* gesture, without the countermelody, are stated softly for the first time before leading to the recapitulation in G minor.

But G minor and *Sturm und Drang* do not last long before the fanfare theme returns in G major. The recapitulation then continues its normal course: "hen theme," "hen theme" repeated with the string of dotted rhythms added, and codetta. But before the codetta can run its course, it is interrupted by a forceful statement of the *Sturm und Drang* gesture — but now in G major, its *Sturm und Drang* character almost transformed into true nobility. But there is still a note of harshness. So when it is about to come to a cadence, there is another interruption. Instead of the expected G major chord, there is a long-held ambiguous chord — a question mark rather than a period. It is answered by the opening *Sturm und Drang* gesture played softly in sweet parallel thirds by the violins alone, completely shorn of all its harshness. Then it is repeated by the full string section, still softly, with the first violins playing the string of dotted rhythms — now heard as both noble and lowly. A third statement has the violins continuing the string of dotted rhythms while the opening gesture in parallel thirds moves up to the oboes, who modify it to lead back to the place where the codetta had been interrupted. The transformation is now complete. The codetta picks up where it left off, and the movement concludes with triplets rushing joyfully to the final G major chord, which is repeated in dotted rhythms that now sound a note of true nobility.

The second movement is sheer loveliness, a picture of true feminine nobility (one might think of the Countess in *The Marriage of Figaro*). The minuet contains Ländler-style dances, bucolic in character. And after this celebration with folk dancing, we hear, in the finale, the music of the hunt, nobility's favorite pastime. Its unrelenting gigue rhythm suggests the chase ("la chasse") and also picks up on the celebratory triplets from the end of the first movement. It is "altogether a very outdoors piece, the kind of music which, arranged for wind band, one might have expected to hear at someone's hunting picnic."[4]

A. Peter Brown summarizes Haydn's accomplishment in the *Hen* Symphony as a convergence of "surface and intellectual brilliance, wit, and endless facile skill" that reaches "a height not achieved in any previous Haydn symphony." With this and the other five symphonies known as the *Paris* Symphonies (nos. 82-87), he says "we begin to build the canon of Western instrumental art music."[5]

Haydn's Music in Paris

The *Paris* Symphonies were composed to fulfill a commission from Paris. As in London, Haydn's music began to spread to Paris as early as the 1760s. The Opus 1 quartets were available in Paris in 1764, and some symphonies were available from Parisian publishers and were performed by the *Concert des Amateurs* not much later. Founded about 1770, the *Concert des Amateurs* had a short life, disbanding in 1781. But during that time it did much to promote instrumental music in Paris, in particular orchestral music. In 1771 the *Journal de musique* said that the organization was "composed almost entirely of amateurs whose great talents are in no way inferior to those of the cleverest professors [professionals]." And in 1775 the *Almanach musical* proclaimed that its forty-eight musicians made up "the best orchestra for symphonies that there is in Paris and perhaps in Europe."[6] (Note

4. H. C. Robbins Landon, *Haydn: Chronicle and Works,* vol. 2 (Bloomington: Indiana University Press, 1978) p. 610.

5. A. Peter Brown, *The Symphonic Repertoire,* vol. 2 (Bloomington: Indiana University Press, 2002), p. 216.

6. Jean Mongrédien, "Paris: the End of the Ancien Régime," in *Man and Music: The Classical Era* (Englewood Cliffs, New Jersey: Prentice Hall Inc., 1989), pp. 68-69.

that at forty-eight, it was more than double the size of Haydn's orchestra at Eszterháza at its largest.) By the time it disbanded in 1781, Haydn's symphonies were a significant part of its repertory.

The *Concert Spirituel,* an older society that provided concerts, also figured significantly in the growth of Haydn's popularity in Paris. Founded in 1725, it organized the first subscription concerts in France and became the most dominant institution in the musical life of Paris. At first it offered concerts of sacred music during Lent and other days in the church year when the theaters were closed. Very soon, however, its repertory extended beyond sacred works to include instrumental music. Even after secular vocal music entered the repertory, instrumental music, since it did not have explicit secular content, remained prominent. Haydn symphonies entered the *Concert Spirituel* repertory in the late '70s, and during the '80s they became dominant, easily the most popular items on the programs. In 1789 there were forty Haydn performances. All told, forty-four symphonies by five different composers were performed; thirty-seven of them were by Haydn![7]

Surprisingly, the work that stimulated the big upswing in Haydn's popularity in Paris was not a symphony but a sacred work, his *Stabat Mater* of 1767. When the *Concert Spirituel* introduced it to Parisians in 1781, it was intruding on sacrosanct territory owned by Pergolesi's *Stabat Mater* since the '50s. Nevertheless, it was a great success, something that Haydn was quick to report to Artaria. On May 27, 1781, he wrote: "Monsieur Le Gros, *Directeur* of the Concert Spirituel, wrote me the most flattering things about my *Stabat Mater,* which was performed there four times with the greatest applause; the gentlemen asked permission to have it engraved. They made me an offer to engrave all my future works on the most favourable terms for myself, and were most surprised that I was so singularly successful in my vocal compositions" (Landon 2, p. 447).

The *Concert des Amateurs* and the *Concert Spirituel* played a crucial role in fostering Haydn's popularity in Paris, but it was the *Concert de la Loge Olympique* that commissioned the *Paris* Symphonies. When the *Concert des Amateurs* disbanded in 1781, Parisian Freemasons formed the Loge [lodge] Olympique, whose principal stated goal was "the establishment in Paris of a concert organization which may in some respects replace the loss of the

---

7. Bernard Harrison, *Haydn: The 'Paris' Symphonies* (Cambridge: Cambridge University Press, 1998), pp. 14-15.

Concert des Amateurs."[8] They certainly succeeded! Within three years of their founding their concert series

> had proved so popular that it had moved its venue from the Hotel de Bouillon in the rue de Coq Héron to the guard room at the Palais des Tuileries; at the last concert in the old venue, on 13 April 1784, Haydn's "Farewell" symphony was given. With a total complement of 67 players the orchestra of the Loge Olympique was over three times the size of the orchestra at Eszterháza and its members included amateurs as well as professionals. In order to boost the quality of music-making leading performers were made nominal Freemasons, and a lodge of Adoption, that is a lodge of lady Freemasons, was established in order to provide female singers.[9]

The prime mover was the Count Claude-François-Marie Rigoley d'Ogny. He was a cellist in the orchestra and an avid collector of musical scores. His music library, which may represent the repertory of the *Concert des Amateurs,* contained around two thousand works, including thirty-four symphonies attributed (some falsely) to Haydn.

Also involved was another musician, Joseph Bologne Chevalier de Saint-Georges, one of the more colorful characters of the time. He was born in Guadeloupe, son of a plantation owner and an African slave. When the father was accused of murder, the three of them fled to Paris. Educated in Paris, Joseph became renowned for his athletic and musical prowess. John Adams, second President of the United States, wrote in his diary that he was "the most accomplished man in Europe, in riding, running, shooting, fencing, dancing, music. He will hit the button — any button on the coat or waistcoat of the greatest masters. He will hit a crown-piece in the air with a pistol-ball."[10] Musically he became a renowned violin virtuoso and a composer of some stature. He debuted as violinist with the *Concert des Amateurs,* playing two of his violin concertos. With the demise of the *Concert des Amateurs,* he became the founder of the *Concert de la Loge Olympique* and the intermediary who negotiated the commission of the six *Paris*

8. *Annuaire de la Société Olympique pour 1786.* Quoted in Mongrédien, "Paris: the End of the Ancien Régime," p. 69.

9. Marc Vignal, "Paris," in *Oxford Composer Companions: Haydn* (Oxford: Oxford University Press, 2009), p. 267.

10. *Diary and Autobiography of John Adams,* edited by L. H. Butterfield (Cambridge, Mass.: Harvard University Press, 1961), vol. II, p. 374.

Symphonies with Haydn, offering the extravagant fee of twenty-five louis d'or for each symphony plus another five louis d'or for publication rights. He may have been the conductor of the premier performances that probably occurred during the 1787 concert season.

The Paris *Symphonies*

The *Paris* Symphonies were soon performed at the *Concert Spiritual* as well as the *Concert de la Loge Olympique,* and they were published in close succession in Vienna, Paris, and London. The Artaria publication (December 1787) was first on the market, followed by Imbault in Paris (January 1788) and Forster in London (later 1788). As we have seen before, Haydn was dishonest with the publishers in promising each of them exclusive rights. Needless to say, he profited handsomely; but so did publishers! The sale of unauthorized parts, from which Haydn profited nothing, sprang up almost immediately and was widespread. By the end of 1788, orchestral parts from several publishers had appeared, and new editions continued to appear for several decades. In addition, symphonies reached the public in another way; publishers sold chamber music arrangements of them. This kind of dissemination of Haydn's symphonies "happened with remarkable speed. In 1788 alone arrangements for keyboard trios and quartets (Boyé & Le Menu), for string quartet (Artaria), and for keyboard and violin (Longman & Broderip) had appeared, and these heralded a host of similar arrangements which appeared regularly into the 1790s and beyond."[11]

The *Paris* Symphonies make up the first set of symphonies written specifically for publication, and like sets of keyboard sonatas and string quartets written for publication, they display lots of variety to enhance market appeal. In contrast to no. 83 already discussed (pp. 171-73), no. 82 is a festive symphony in the tradition of Austrian C major symphonies, no. 84 begins with a movement that sparkles with the gaiety of comic opera, and no. 85 begins with a slow introduction in the majestic style of the French overture.

Slow movements are equally diverse. No. 85's is a set of variations on a popular French song in the style of a gavotte, "La gentile et jeune Lisette," and no. 87's is based on a hymn-like tune — a movement whose "poignant, lyrical passages" convey "a strong sense of autumnal beauty."[12] No. 86's

11. Harrison, *The 'Paris' Symphonies,* p. 3.
12. Landon, *Chronicle and Works,* vol. 2, p. 607.

slow movement might be the most remarkable movement in the whole set. Unique in form and mysterious in character, Haydn labeled it "Capriccio."

Minuets tend toward the rustic and folksy — for example no. 85 with its "Scotch snap" rhythms and Ländler-like trio — but they can also be courtly and learned. The third movement of no. 86 is a courtly minuet expanded into a small sonata form with a wonderful contrapuntal passage in its development section.

The *Paris* Symphonies exhibit Haydn's mastery of the art of orchestration at every turn. Two examples will have to suffice. In the second movement of no. 85, the third variation on "La gentile et jeune Lisette" features a flute descant over the simply harmonized tune in the strings. At first it consists of wide-ranging arpeggiated eighth notes played staccato. But in the middle it turns to a short, ornamental figure suggesting a bird call — a delicate, pictorial touch in a movement that is pervaded by a bucolic, Arcadian atmosphere. Another delicious example occurs near the end of the second movement of no. 84. The music comes to a pause like those that typically set up a cadenza in a concerto. But cadenzas do not belong in symphonies or in theme and variation forms. Since it is not a concerto, there is no solo instrument to improvise a cadenza. So what next? A lovely composed cadenza for woodwind quintet (flute, two oboes, and two bassoons) accompanied by pizzicato strings.

Of course, Haydn did not simply string all these surface delights and beauties together in medleys or pour tunes into pre-cast formal molds. His sense of balance and proportion, of contrast and continuity, of drama and symmetry — in a word, form — is as keen as ever, and his ear is as alert as ever — if not more so — to the developmental possibilities of his themes. His sonata forms tend toward monothematicism without losing any of the contrast or conflict that is essential to the form. His rondos often take on characteristics of sonata form, and variation procedures permeate all forms. His mastery of the art of composition is nothing less than astounding, yet he wears his technical sophistication lightly so it never obscures the simple delights. And on the other side of the coin, the simple delights do obscure his displays of technique, which is what the ancient Roman rhetorician Quintilian called the perfection of art: "art concealing art."

A 1788 review in the *Mercure de France* states:

> Symphonies by M. Haydn were performed at practically all the concerts. Each day one is more aware of, and consequently one admires more, the work of this great genius, who, in each of his pieces, knows so

well how to draw such rich and varied developments from a single subject; so unlike those sterile composers who continuously move from one idea to another for lack of knowing how to present one [idea] in varied forms, and mechanically pile up effect on effect, without connection and without taste.[13]

Earlier in this chapter I quoted Brown saying that the *Paris* Symphonies mark the beginning of "the canon of Western instrumental art music." They are also, not coincidentally, the works in which Haydn fulfilled, more completely than ever before, the Enlightenment ideal of satisfying the whole spectrum of music lovers — *Kenner und Liebhaber,* learned and unlearned, professionals and amateurs, princes and common folk throughout the Western world.

Symphonies between the Paris and London Sets

In 1788 two more Haydn symphonies (nos. 88 and 89) made their way to Paris, this time via the Eszterháza violinist Johann Tost. And by 1789 Haydn had composed three more (nos. 90 through 92). They were apparently commissioned by Count d'Ogny. Although these five all have a connection to Paris, it does not appear that Haydn had Paris specifically in mind in composing them. For posterity they were in danger of getting lost between two mountain ranges — the six *Paris* Symphonies that preceded them and the twelve *London* Symphonies that followed them. Nevertheless, two of them, nos. 88 and 92, have risen above their companions to achieve lasting popularity — most deservedly so in both cases. Of no. 88 Tovey said, "The quality of Haydn's inventiveness is nowhere higher and its economy nowhere more remarkable."[14] Its second movement prompted Brahms to say, "I want my ninth symphony to be like this!"[15] And of no. 92 Landon wrote, it "artlessly presents the greatest contrapuntal mind since J. S. Bach, embedded within the popular classical style, which with this work achieved a peak of matchless perfection."[16] It is no surprise that Haydn would later take this work with him to London and perform it at

13. Quoted in Harrison, *The 'Paris' Symphonies,* p. 22.

14. Donald Francis Tovey, *Essays in Musical Analysis,* vol. 1 (London: Oxford University Press, 1965), p. 140.

15. Quoted in Tovey, *Essays in Musical Analysis,* vol. 1, p. 142.

16. Landon, *Chronicle and Works,* vol. 2, p. 635.

a concert in connection with his being awarded an honorary doctorate by Oxford University (hence its nickname, *Oxford* Symphony).

Music for an Unusual Instrument and an Eccentric King

Eleven symphonies, nineteen string quartets, and seven keyboard trios, all composed in the last half of the '80s, and all showing rare mastery of the art of composition, constitute an artistic achievement whose equal is hard to find. Yet during that time Haydn still found the time and energy to fulfill two unusual commissions. Both came from a singularly peculiar king — Ferdinand IV, King of Naples. He was rough, uncouth, vulgar, and virtually uneducated. Having become king at age eight, his education was entrusted to his chief governor and a tutor. The governor "felt that physical culture was sufficient education for any gentleman," and his tutor "was more interested in retaining the favor of the court than in imparting a sound education to his charge."[17]

At age seventeen he was married to Maria Carolina, a daughter of Empress Maria Theresa. A year later, in 1769, Emperor Joseph II visited his sister and wrote an account of his time in Naples, including a good bit about the antics of his brother-in-law at a court ball. Joseph wrote that Ferdinand greeted him with "a great salute on my behind at the moment I least expected it, in the presence of more than four people." And in imitation of riding on Joseph's back when he was small, Ferdinand "came and put his arms over my shoulders, slackening his whole body so that it dragged after me." And he did this "more than twenty times." The procession to the ball began with a solemn march, but apparently Ferdinand became bored and "began to shout like the postillions and kick the bottoms lustily right and left, which seemed the signal to start galloping." When the emperor asked what the ladies did on such occasions, he was told "that when the King gallops they gallop too, so that all these good old dames follow the procession out of breath."[18]

Not surprisingly Ferdinand's musical taste ran toward *opera buffa*. But due to the influence of Queen Maria Carolina, German and Austrian instrumental music, including Haydn symphonies, had a substantial place

17. Harry R. Edwall, "Ferdinand IV and Haydn's Concertos for the 'Lira Organizzata,'" *The Musical Quarterly* 48, no. 2 (April, 1962): 192.

18. Edwall, p. 193.

in the music of the court. It was the Queen who interested him in learning to play an unusual instrument called the *lira organizzata,* a type of hurdy-gurdy that had strong pastoral and rustic associations.

In the 17th century French taste for the pastoral and rustic had brought about a revival of the hurdy-gurdy. But even though its pastoral associations made it attractive, its technical limitations caused dissatisfaction that resulted in the invention of hybrids such as the *lira organizzata.* As with a hurdy-gurdy, a player operated a *lira organizzata* by turning a crank with the right hand. The crank turned a wheel that rubbed against the strings like a bow. A keyboard enabled the player to play a melody on one of the strings; the rest of the strings simply played drones. In addition, the *lira organizzata* was equipped with a set of organ pipes. They were attached to the keyboard and also to bellows that provided air. The bellows were activated either by turning the crank or by foot pedals. Adding organ pipes to a hurdy-gurdy sounds strange to us, but the practice was not new, and by the late eighteenth century "the custom was so widespread that a person buying a piano could choose one with or without pipes." Although we do not know who first thought of adding organ pipes to a hurdy-gurdy, such a hybrid seems to have been in existence by the middle of the eighteenth century. "The peak of its popularity was reached around 1780." But it soon declined rapidly so that "even before the death of Louis XVI [in 1793] the instrument had fallen into disrepute and soon thereafter it returned to the provinces from whence it had come."[19]

King Ferdinand learned to play this clumsy instrument, and in 1786 he commissioned Haydn to compose concertos for it. We do not know how Haydn greeted this commission to compose music for an unusual instrument with severe limitations in the midst of all his busyness at the time. But whether he viewed it as an annoying duty or an interesting challenge, the result is music as bright and joyous as he might have imagined a sunny day in Italy to be. He probably composed six concertos, though only five have survived. All are scored for two *lire organizzate,* two horns, violins I and II, violas I and II, and cello (probably doubled by string bass). They are all in simple keys (C, F, and G major) and stay within the modest technical limits of King Ferdinand's strange instrument. Since the commission was for concertos, the technical limitations of the putative solo instrument posed an all-the-greater challenge. Haydn solved it by writing the pieces more like orchestral concertos than like solo concertos. They work more

19. Edwall, pp. 191–92.

by pitting section against section than solo instrument against orchestra. So there is a lot of interplay between the pairs of *lire,* violins, and violas, although Haydn found subtle ways to make the *lire* "more equal." He also tilted the style in the direction of the lighter divertimento by using dance forms, a feature practically non-existent in concertos.

The King must have been pleased. Two years later he commissioned Haydn to write some notturni (divertimenti) for a small ensemble that included two *lire.* Again Haydn complied, writing nine notturni (one is lost). Haydn must have been pleased too. He thought highly enough of the concertos to reuse movements from them in the 89th and 100th Symphonies. And when he finally went to London, he brought some notturni with him, five of which he performed in the concerts in the Hanover Square Rooms. For performance in London he substituted two flutes (recorders work as well) or oboe and flute for the *lire* parts.

CHAPTER 15

From Vienna to London

1790-91

My language is understood all over the world.

HAYDN

Music [at Oxford] has still made further strides towards per-
fection. Vulgar annual songs were once considered as almost
a part of the institution. Handel's portrait is now to be seen
among the sages of the Bodleian repository, and his music is
enjoyed, well understood, and even performed by thousands
in the University! Can anything exhibit the improved taste in
that divine science so justly, as the degree just given to the mod-
est Haydn by the University?

A correspondent to the *European Magazine*

Loneliness, Unremitting Work,
and Another Special Friend

Robbins Landon calls the Adagio of the 1790 Notturno in G major (Hob.
II:27) "possibly the greatest single movement of all the Notturni." He hears
"summery melancholy" in its C minor section. "We seem to be with Haydn
in the garden of Eszterháza on a hot summer's afternoon, watching the
slow passing of huge white clouds above the yellow and green of the castle.
The Prince is in Vienna and the garden empty. A profound sadness over-
comes Haydn, which wells out of this marvelous Adagio in its measured

quavers, the interweaving parts slowly moving in a modulation that seems to foretell Brahms."[1]

Many have noticed a sense of loneliness and melancholy in Haydn as the '80s were coming to an end. In 1776 he had written that he wished "to live and die" in the service of his Prince (Landon 2, p. 398). Just five years later he complained, "My misfortune is that I live in the country" (Landon 2, p. 447). But that complaint should not be construed too broadly. It was prompted by the Director of the *Concert Spirituel* in Paris, who expressed surprise at Haydn's success in vocal composition, in particular in his *Stabat Mater*. That surprise, wrote Haydn, was due to the fact that his operas were unknown in Paris, which in turn was due to his isolation "in the country" at Eszterháza.

During the '80s, Haydn's circle of Viennese friends and acquaintances grew considerably. He had dealings with publishers, played string quartets with fellow musicians, and became acquainted with many leading citizens at the salons where he sometimes performed his songs. In that sense he was actually becoming less isolated. But since he was still stuck in Eszterháza most of the year, his feeling of isolation was growing stronger. He expressed that feeling with uncommon openness in letters to Maria Anna von Genzinger, wife of Prince Nicolaus's doctor. She was well-educated, a fine pianist and singer, and mother of five children. The Genzingers frequently hosted musical gatherings, which Haydn attended when he could. But since he had to be at Eszterháza so much of the year, opportunities to visit the Genzinger home were limited. Instead, a flourishing correspondence developed.

Starting in 1789, Haydn and Frau von Genzinger corresponded frequently. In June 1789, she wrote to Haydn about a keyboard arrangement she had made of one of his orchestral works. For a while the correspondence mainly dealt with musical matters, but soon Haydn started to open up to her about his feeling of isolation and complain about his unremitting work schedule. In a letter of January 23, 1790, he wrote with obvious delight about "the arrangements for the little quartet party we agreed to have this coming Friday" (Landon 2, p. 736). But more often than not, Haydn could not attend such parties. On February 3 he declined an invitation to one of them. "I regret this very much," he wrote, "and from the bottom of my heart I wish you, not only tonight but for ever and ever, the most

1. H. C. Robbins Landon, *Haydn: Chronicle and Works,* vol. 2 (Bloomington: Indiana University Press, 1978), p. 655.

agreeable and happy of gatherings. Mine are over — tomorrow I return to dreary solitude" (Landon 2, p. 737).

A few days later he sent her another letter containing a lengthy and more explicit complaint: "Well, here I sit in my wilderness — forsaken — like a poor waif — almost without any human society — melancholy — full of the memories of past glorious days — yes! past alas! — and who knows when these days shall return again? Those wonderful parties? Where the whole circle is one heart, one soul — all these beautiful musical evenings — which can only be remembered, and not described." He went on to complain about the mess in his room, sleeping poorly, and cold weather. "I could only sleep very little, even my dreams persecuted me; and then, just when I was happily dreaming that I was listening to [Mozart's opera] *The Marriage of Figaro,* that horrible North wind woke me and almost blew my nightcap off my head." And he complained about the food: "instead of that delicious slice of beef, a chunk of a cow 50 years old; instead of a ragout with little dumplings, an old sheep with carrots; instead of a Bohemian pheasant, a leathery joint." Of course this is hyperbole; even Haydn seems to have realized he was getting carried away. "Forgive me, kindest and most gracious lady, for filling this letter with such stupid nonsense, and for killing time with such wretched scrawl, but you must forgive a man whom the Viennese terribly spoiled. I am gradually getting used to country life, however, and yesterday I studied [composed] for the first time, and quite Haydnish" (Landon 2, pp. 737-38).

Composing was consoling. In the midst of "many annoyances from the Court," he wrote, "being eagerly disposed to work" was "the only consolation left" (Landon 2, p. 741). Nevertheless, the heavy workload of nearly three decades was taking its toll, especially after the death of Princess Maria Elizabeth, Nicolaus's wife. On March 14 Haydn wrote to Frau von Genzinger that his delay in responding to two letters was due to "the many things I have to do for my most gracious Prince in his present melancholy condition. The death of his wife so crushed the Prince that we had to use every means in our power to pull His Highness out of this depression, and thus the first 3 days I arranged enlarged chamber music every evening with no singing; but the poor Prince, during the concert of the first evening, became so depressed when he heard my Favourite Adagio in D that we had quite a time to brighten his mood with other pieces" (Landon 2, p. 739).

The extra music-making continued for some days before settling back into the normal (but ever-busy) routine. On May 13 he wrote that "business doesn't permit me to go to Vienna" (Landon 2, p. 741). A couple of weeks later he complained that it is "scarcely credible" that he "cannot go to Vienna even for 24 hours." But, he added hopefully, "the day will come when I shall have the inexpressible pleasure of sitting beside Your Grace at the pianoforte, hearing Mozart's masterpieces, and kissing your hands for so many wonderful things" (Landon 2, pp. 741-42).

Freedom

Haydn's lament continued into the summer, but a big change was not far off. On September 28 Prince Nicolaus died. His son Anton succeeded him, and one of his first actions was to disband the Esterházy musical establishment. Finances, cultural changes in Austrian courts, and his personal indifference toward music all figured in Anton's decision. He also preferred living in Vienna and Eisenstadt instead of Eszterháza. In August 1791 he was installed as Governor of the County of Oedenburg. That was the last time the family used Eszterháza for a public occasion.

Haydn was now free. He had a good pension from Nicolaus and earnings from commissions and publications. He also had a salary from Anton, who kept him on the payroll but required very little from him. He could live wherever he wanted and was free to accept other employment. He moved to Vienna immediately, taking rooms in the house of a friend. He would never return to Eszterháza, save for one short visit. But as welcome as this new freedom was, he did not forget how supportive the Esterházy family — especially Nicolaus — had been. Late in his life he told Griesinger, "My Prince was content with all my works, I received approval." He even recognized with gratitude the role Eszterháza (his "wilderness") had played in his development: "I was set apart from the world, there was nobody in my vicinity to confuse and annoy me in my course, and so I had to be original" (p. 17).

Johann Peter Salomon

But now what to do with his newly acquired freedom? Had the French Revolution not recently broken out, he might have gone to Paris. But a trip to that musical capital where his music was so much loved would never happen. He would have been heartily welcomed at the court of the King of Naples, but as it turned out, a trip to Naples or anywhere else in Italy would never happen either. The Prince of Oettingen-Wallerstein also would have welcomed him, and he had an offer to be Kapellmeister at the court of Prince Grassalkovics (Nicolaus's son-in-law) in Pressburg. In December he was still weighing his options when, as Dies tells it, "a strange man one day walked unexpectedly into his room and said bluntly, 'I am Salomon from London and have come to fetch you. Tomorrow we shall conclude an agreement' " (p. 119).

Johann Peter Salomon was a German, born in Bonn, Beethoven's home town. But now he was a violinist and impresario living in London. He was on his way back to London from a recruiting trip in Italy when he heard of Nicolaus's death. Back in 1787 he had tried to lure Haydn on behalf of the manager of the King's Theater in London. Now, upon hearing the news about the prince, he seized the opportunity and went immediately to Vienna. It did not take Haydn long to accept. Already on December 8 he had agreed to Salomon's generous terms. Dies tells us that Haydn's friends tried to dissuade him. "They reminded him of his age [fifty-eight years], of the discomforts of a long journey, and of many other things to shake his resolve. But in vain! Mozart especially took pains to say, 'Papa!' as he usually called him, 'you have no training for the great world, and you speak too few languages.'

" 'Oh!' replied Haydn, 'my language is understood all over the world!' " (Dies, pp. 119-20).

Journey to a New Life in London

Haydn and Salomon set out for London on December 15. Dies tells of Haydn and Mozart saying farewell. "Mozart on this day never left his friend Haydn. He dined with him, and said at the moment of parting, 'We are probably saying our last farewell in this life.' Tears welled from the eyes of both. Haydn was deeply moved, for he applied Mozart's words to himself, and the possibility never occurred to him that the thread of Mozart's life could be cut off by the inexorable Parcae [fates] within the following year" (p. 121).

On their trip to Calais, France, where they would embark for England, Haydn and Salomon arrived at Bonn on Christmas Day. The following morning, the Feast of St. Stephen, they went to mass, where Haydn was surprised and flattered to hear his own music. After mass he was invited to the oratory, where Elector Maximilian greeted him and introduced him to the musicians. One of the musicians was an up-and-coming composer — the twenty-year-old Ludwig van Beethoven.

Haydn and Salomon arrived at Calais on December 31. They attended early mass on New Year's Day, 1791, and then sailed for England. The trip, of course, was Haydn's first experience of sea travel. It turned out to be quite an adventure, which he described in some detail for Frau von Genzinger. They embarked at 7:30 a.m. At first they had almost no wind. The ship went so slowly that in four hours they had traveled only one of the twenty-four miles between Calais and Dover. It looked as if they would have to spend the night at sea. But around 11:30 a favorable wind arose that brought them to Dover by 4:00 p.m.

Haydn enjoyed the trip. "I remained on deck during the whole passage," he wrote, "so as to gaze my fill at that mighty monster, the ocean. So long as it was calm, I wasn't afraid at all." But nearing Dover, as "the wind grew stronger and stronger, and I saw the monstrous high waves rushing at us, I became a little frightened, and a little indisposed, too." And since it was ebb tide, the large ship he was on could not reach the pier. So while still fairly far out at sea, the passengers and their luggage had to be transferred into two smaller ships that had come out to meet them. "I overcame it all," he wrote, "and arrived safely, without vomiting, on shore" (Landon 3, p. 36). But he added that he needed two days to recover.

London

London at the time was three to four times as large as Vienna. Haydn called it "this endlessly huge city." He was "quite astonished" by its "various beauties and marvels" (Landon 3, p. 36). While in London he kept notebooks[2] that he filled with miscellaneous observations, including:

- National debt of England is estimated to be over two hundred millions. A convoy of waggons to pay this sum in silver would reach from London to Yorck, that is, 200 miles, presuming that each waggon could not carry more than £6000.
- 8 days before Pentecost I heard 4,000 charity children in St. Paul's Church sing. No music ever moved me so deeply as this devotional and innocent [singing].

2. *The Collected Correspondence and London Notebooks of Joseph Haydn,* ed., trans., and annotated by H. C. Robbins Landon (Fair Lawn, N. J.: Essential Books, 1959). The excerpts below are on pp. 253, 261, 275, 278, 257, and 275 respectively.

- In England, a large man-of-war is reckoned according to the number of its cannon. Each cannon is estimated at 1,000 lbs.
- Madam Mara was hissed at Oxford because she did not rise from her seat during the Hallelujah Chorus.
- Oranges from Portugal arrive in the middle of November, but they are quite pale and not so good as they are later.
- If anybody steals £2 he is hanged; but if I trust anybody with £2000, and he carries it off to the devil, he is acquitted.
- The city of London keeps 4,000 carts for cleaning the streets, and 2,000 of these work every day.

A Social Whirlwind and New Friends

Haydn also copied this proverb into his notebook: "In solitude, too, there are divinely beautiful duties, and to perform them in quiet is more than wealth."[3] But in London he found very little solitude. A whirlwind of activity followed his arrival — "necessary calls" to ambassadors, making the "round of all the newspapers," concerts, and seemingly limitless dining out because "everyone wants to know me" (Landon 3, p. 36). The friends and acquaintances Haydn made in London ranged "from the Duchess of York to 'Mister March a dentist, coach-maker and dealer in wines, a man 84 years old with a very young mistress'; from Dr. Burney to the Earl of Abington; from the violent revolutionary poet and playwright Thomas Holcroft to the gentle Mistress Schroeter; from the banker Nathaniel Brassey to the naval captain who had the delighted Haydn to lunch on his East India merchantman 'with six cannon.'"[4]

On January 18, the Queen's birthday, Haydn attended a court ball. The *Daily Advertiser* reported a "remarkable Circumstance." "Mr. Haydn came into the Room with Sir John Gallini, Mr. Wills and Mr. Salomon. The Prince of Wales first observed him, and upon bowing to him, the Eyes of all the Company were upon Mr. Haydn, every one paying him Respect" (Landon 3, p. 43). The Prince of Wales was an enthusiastic supporter of music. He played cello — "quite tolerably," in Haydn's words — and organized private concerts held regularly in the morning. More occasionally,

3. *The Collected Correspondence*, p. 267.
4. H. C. Robbins Landon, *Haydn: Chronicle and Works,* vol. 3 (Bloomington: Indiana University Press, 1976), p. 22.

he also organized evening concerts, some of which had featured the first London performances of Haydn's *Paris* symphonies.

At a concert on February 7, Haydn met Charles Burney, a minor musician and a major writer about music who had long admired Haydn's music. Based on his extensive travels, Burney published interesting accounts of *The Present State of Music in . . .* the various countries of Europe. His magnum opus is his four-volume *General History of Music,* published shortly before Haydn came to London. Burney sent a copy to Haydn upon his arrival. After the February 7 concert Burney wrote: "Having met the good great man, by accident, at the Professional Concert soon after he had rec^d my present, he took the opportunity of making *fine speeches* innumerable" (Landon 3, p. 45). Two days later they met again at another concert: "I afterwards met him at the Concert of Anc^t Music in Tottenham street, whence I carried him home when it was over; & then he repeated & added more *fine things* on my present" (Landon 3, p. 45) Haydn and Burney became close friends, sometimes making music together. Burney wrote to Rev. Thomas Twining: "I spent the day yesterday with the dear great & good Haydn, whom I love more & more every time I see as well as hear him. In a small party chiefly of my own family, we prevailed on him to play the Ist Violin to his Instrumental Passione. Its effect was admirable as executed by him, in a most chaste & feeling manner" (Landon 3, p. 67). The "Instrumental Passione" Burney referred to is the string quartet version of *The Seven Last Words.*

Burney introduced Haydn to another longtime admirer, the Rev. Christian Ignatius Latrobe, an ordained Moravian minister and a fine musician. He was described by a contemporary as a musical Samuel Johnson, "as social and conversational, and as full of geniality" who exhibited "great sweetness and dignity, cheerfulness and benevolence." He performed "well-directed services in aid of the diffusion of musical taste," in particular as one "who, in a catholic spirit, first introduced fine sacred music, whether of the Reformed or Romish Church, to the immediate notice of musical families, giving them delightful objects of study, elevating the taste, and purifying the enjoyments of home."[5]

Latrobe described his first introduction to Haydn (Landon 3, pp. 57-58). "I was introduced to him by Dr. Burney, who well knew the value I should set upon the personal acquaintances of a man whose works had been a feast to

---

5. E. Holmes, "The Rev. Christian Ignatius Latrobe," *The Musical Times, and Singing Class Circular,* September 1, 1851, p. 249.

my soul. I had at that time made scores of about twenty-five of his quartettos, from the printed parts, and continued to play them on the pianoforte."

Already at their first meeting, Latrobe's "admiration of him as the first of composers, soon rose to sincere affection for him as a most amiable man." Not long after, Haydn paid Latrobe a visit.

When he entered the room, he found my wife alone, and as she could not speak German, and he had scarcely picked up a few English words, both were at a loss what to say. He bowed with foreign formality, and the following short explanation took place. *H.* Dis Mr. Latrobe's house? The answer was in the affirmative. *H.* Be you his woman? (meaning his wife) "I am Mrs. Latrobe," was the reply.

After some pause, he looked around the room, and saw his picture, to which he immediately pointed, and exclaimed, "Dat is me. I am Haydn!" My wife instantly sent for me. Of course I hastened home, and passed half an hour with him in agreeable conversation.

Haydn gave Latrobe his address and invited him to call on him whenever he pleased. They met often. "Sometimes," Latrobe wrote, "I met him at friends' houses, but never enjoyed his company more than at his own lodging." On one occasion Haydn heard some sonatas that Latrobe had composed. Haydn urged him to publish them. Latrobe agreed to do so if Haydn would agree to be the dedicatee.

Latrobe wrote about Haydn's religious character and about the impact Haydn's *Stabat Mater* had on his own musical development.

He appeared to me to be a religious character, and not only attentive to the forms and usages of his own church, but under the influence of a devotional spirit. This is felt by those, who understand the language of music, in many parts of his Masses and other compositions for the church. I once observed to him that having in the year 1779, when a youth, obtained the parts of his *Stabat Mater* from a friend, who had found means to procure them at Dresden, I made a score, and became enchanted with its beauty. The study of it, more than of any other work, helped to form my taste, and make me more zealous in the pursuit of this noble science. He seemed delighted to hear my remarks on a composition, which he declared to be one of his own favourites, and added, that it was no wonder, that it partook of a religious savour, for it had been composed in the performance of a religious vow.

Haydn found a congenial kindred spirit in Latrobe. He found a different kind of kindred spirit in Mrs. Rebecca Schroeter. She came from a wealthy family and played the clavier well. When Haydn came to London, she was a forty-year-old widow. Against her family's wishes, she had married John Samuel Schroeter, a talented musician who died in 1788 at age thirty-eight.

What we know about the friendship between Mrs. Schroeter and Haydn comes from twenty-two letters she sent to Haydn.[6] Curiously, they only survive in copies that Haydn made of them. If he wrote to her, his letters are lost. The first of Mrs. Schroeter's letters is dated June 29, 1791. It is a request for music lessons. Future letters, however, say nothing more about lessons. Her next letter was not written until February 8, 1792. In it she expressed regret that she did not see Haydn in the morning and hoped he could come the next day. She inquired about his health and hoped he did not fatigue himself "with too much application to business." She addressed him as "My Dear" and signed off as "your Faithful." From March into the summer the letters continued with increasing frequency into June. The themes are the same: regrets at not seeing him, invitations to dine, expressions of concern about his health, sleeplessness, and business, plus expressions of great appreciation for his music, and ardent avowals of love and affection — "my heart WAS and is full of TENDERNESS for you, but no language can express HALF the LOVE and AFFECTION I feel for you, you are DEARER to me EVERY DAY of my life." Since we have no letters from Haydn to her, it is impossible to say how he responded. Fifteen years later Haydn showed the letters to Dies and remarked that "although she was already sixty years old [sic], she was still a beautiful and amiable woman whom I might very easily have married if I had been free then" (Dies, p. 157). But that hardly sheds more light on the nature of their relationship.

Composing an Opera and Symphonies for Salomon's Concert Series

London dazzled Haydn, and he enjoyed the company and adulation of its citizens. But he had work to do amidst all the social demands. Already on January 8 (if the date is correct), he wrote to Frau von Genzinger that, although the socializing "was very flattering," he wished he "could fly for a time to Vienna, to have more quiet in which to work, for the noise that the

---

6. All the letters are in *The Collected Correspondence*, pp. 279-86.

common people make as they sell their wares in the street is intolerable. At present I am working on symphonies, because the libretto of the opera is not yet decided on" (Landon 3, p. 37).

John Gallini, manager of the King's Theatre, had commissioned Haydn to compose an Italian opera. Haydn had also contracted to compose six symphonies for Salomon's series of concerts given in the Hanover Square Rooms. Salomon's concerts took place on twelve Friday evenings — every Friday from March 11 through June 3, except Good Friday. But the opera was the first order of business. It was to be a full-scale *opera seria* based on the story of Orpheus and Eurydice titled *L'anima del filosofo (The Spirit of Philosophy)*. Given this story's prominence in the history of opera and the current status of Gluck's *Orfeo ed Euridice,* this was a daunting — and prestigious — assignment. As a result Haydn composed only two symphonies, nos. 96 and 95 (in that order), for the 1791 season. But he had taken with him other recent works that were new to the London audience: the 90th and 92nd Symphonies, the Opus 64 string quartets, a concert aria, and some of the *notturni* for the King of Naples, arranged for a woodwind ensemble in which clarinets played the violin parts and flute and oboe the lira parts. So there was "new" music by Haydn at all the concerts. As it turned out, however, the opera did not get performed, because Gallini had not obtained a license for performing opera in the King's Theatre. Haydn completed the opera, but he would never see it performed. He did, however, receive the promised payment.

Concerts were long and mixed. The program of the first Salomon concert is a typical example.

Part I

Overture — Rosetti

Song — Signor Tajana

Concerto Oboe — Mr. Harrington

Song — Signora Storace

Concerto Violin — Madame Gautherot

Recitativo and Aria — Signor David

Part II

New Grand Overture — Haydn

Recitative and Aria — Signora Storace

Concertante, Pedal Harp and Pianoforte — Madam Krumpholz
and Mr. Dusseck,

Composed by Mr. Dusseck.
Rondo — Signor David
Full Piece — Kozeluck
Mr. HAYDN will be at the Harpsichord
Leader of the Band, Mr. SALOMON.

Haydn and Salomon shared the "conducting" responsibilities, Haydn at the keyboard (probably a fortepiano, not a harpsichord), a vestige of Baroque continuo practice, and Salomon from his concertmaster's chair. The chief attraction was the "New Grand Overture" (symphony) by Haydn. Since the programs give only generic titles, we are usually left to guess the specific identity of the pieces. In the case of this concert, the best we can do is say that the New Grand Overture was either the newly composed Symphony no. 96 or one of the symphonies Haydn took with him from Vienna, nos. 90 and 92. If we assume the reviewer for the *Morning Chronicle* knew a rondo when he heard one, the "New Grand Overture" was Symphony no. 96 because in his review he called the fourth movement a rondo, and Symphony no. 96 is the only one of the candidates that meets that description. In any case, the piece was a great success. A reviewer wrote:

The First Concert under the auspices of HAYDN was last night, and never, perhaps, was there a richer musical treat.

It is not wonderful that to souls capable of being touched by music, HAYDN should be an object of homage, and even of idolatry; for like our own SHAKSPEARE, he moves and governs the passions at his will.

His *new Grand Overture* was pronounced by every scientific ear to be a most wonderful composition; but the first movement in particular rises in grandeur of subject, and in the rich variety of *air* and passion, beyond even of his own productions. (Landon 3, p. 49)

For an English writer at that time to put a foreign artist in the same class with Shakespeare was high praise indeed. Another one wrote that as a "musical Shakespeare," Haydn "can equal the strains of a Cherub, and enchant in all the gradations between those and a ballad — a genius whose versatility comprehends all the powers of harmony, and all the energy, pathos, and passion of melody! Who can stun with thunder, or warble with a bird!" (Landon 3, p. 93). "Thus," writes Elaine Sisman, "Haydn had become the epitome of original genius." His music spans "a continuum from the most elevated (Cherub's singing) to the commonest (ballad), from the most scientific and learned (harmony) to the most inspired rule-free invention (melody), from the sublime (thunder) to the beautiful (bird song)."[7]

Other Concerts

Salomon's concert series was hardly the only show in town. Musical performances of all sorts, public and private, professional and amateur, proliferated to an unprecedented level. Haydn, of course, was frequently in attendance. At the end of the 1791 season, he attended a concert that had a special impact on him. From May 23 to June 1 a gigantic Handel Festival took place at Westminster Abbey. Haydn had some knowledge of Handel's music by way of performances put on by Baron van Swieten in Vienna, but they seem to have had little impact on him. On June 1 Handel's *Messiah* was performed by more than one thousand musicians. Haydn, in attendance, was greatly moved. During his remaining time in London he would hear more of Handel's music. "He is the father of us all," he exclaimed to Giuseppe Carpani. He also told Carpani "that when he heard Handel's music in London, he was so struck by it that he began his studies all over again as if he had known nothing until that time. He mused over every note and extracted from these learned scores the essence of real musical magnificence."[8] Carpani was prone to hyperbole, and there is little in Haydn's music that shows the stylistic or technical influence from Handel. But there can be no doubt that Haydn learned a great deal about "the essence of real musical significance" — or, more specifically, of the musical sublime.

Dr. Haydn

In July, Oxford University honored Haydn by bestowing on him an honorary Doctor of Music degree. In addition to the formal ceremony, there was a "Grand Musical Festival" consisting of three concerts. At the second concert Haydn conducted Symphony no. 92, hence its nickname, *Oxford*. "A more wonderful composition never was heard," wrote the reviewer from

---

7. Elaine Sisman, "Haydn, Shakespeare, and the Rules of Originality," in *Haydn and His World,* edited by Elaine Sisman (Princeton: Princeton University Press, 1997), p. 24.

8. Quoted in Vernon Gotwals, *Haydn: Two Contemporary Portraits* (Madison, Wisc.: The University of Wisconsin Press, 1968), p. 235, n. 88.

the *Morning Herald*. "The applause given to HAYDN, who conducted this admirable effort of his genius, was enthusiastic; but the merit of the work, in the opinion of all the Musicians present, exceeded all praise" (Landon 3, p. 90). It was indeed an appropriate work for the occasion, a splendid example of Haydn's matchless combination of learned artistry and popular appeal.

CHAPTER 16

Life in London and a Return to Vienna

1791-93

*The commonplace had not exactly gone from her form and
face, the robe had taken it up, as a great composer takes up a
folk tune and makes of it a marvel, yet leaves it still itself.*

C. S. LEWIS

*This Haydn is like a child. You never know what he is going to
do next.*

JOHN KEATS

Ambivalence

In a letter to Frau von Genzinger on September 17, 1791, Haydn expressed
some ambivalence about his new freedom. Even though he had "often
sighed for release," he acknowledges that he had had "a kind prince." But
now, even though he has a measure of release, he is "burdened with far
more work." Yet the continuing busyness is somewhat compensated for by
knowing that he is no longer a "bond-servant" to the prince. On the other
hand, "dear though this liberty is to me, I should like to enter Prince Esterházy's service again when I return." But he doubts that it will be possible
because "my Prince strongly objects to my staying away for so long, and
absolutely demands my speedy return; but I can't comply with this, owing
to a new contract which I have just made here" (Landon 3, pp. 97-98).

In July Haydn had written to Prince Anton asking permission to extend his leave. The Prince refused and ordered him to return; apparently

he had some duties for his Kapellmeister in connection with the ceremonies for his installation as Governor of the County. But Haydn had already signed a new contract with Salomon; so he defied his prince and stayed in England — and consequently worried that a return would not be possible.

Summer Vacation in the Country

During August and early September Haydn had an extended stay in the English countryside. After the social and musical busyness of the preceding months, culminating in his being awarded an honorary Oxford doctorate, he found the change of pace most welcome. In his notebook he wrote: "On August 4th, I went to visit Herr Brassy, the banker who lives in the country, 12 miles from London. Stayed there 5 weeks. I was very well entertained. N.B.: Herr Brassy once cursed, because he had had too easy a time in this world" (Landon 3, p. 96).

Apparently Herr Brassy's "curse" was a suicide attempt. Dies tells us that Haydn "frequently entertained the company with descriptions and anecdotes of his previous life, which was not infrequently at considerable variance with the brilliantly fortunate life the banker had lived." This drove Brassy to threaten suicide. After his family intervened, he explained that "he wanted to shoot himself because he never knew trouble, misery and poverty; and as he now realized he was not really happy, for all he knew how to do was to stuff himself and drink; he had been surrounded with plenty, and it now disgusted him" (Landon 3, p. 96).

Despite this troubling incident, Haydn's stay in the country provided much needed peace and quiet after the hustle and bustle of London. He wrote: "I am alright, thank the good Lord! except for my usual rheumatism; I work hard, and when in the early mornings I walk in the woods, alone, with my English grammar, I think of my Creator, my family, and all the friends I have left behind" (Landon 3, p. 97).

The refreshment must have been conducive to composing. He had time to get at least a good start on the 93rd and 94th Symphonies for the 1792 season that would begin in February. But he also took on another compositional project — a large but not very taxing one. In May he had met a publisher, William Napier. Napier's business was not doing well, even though he had followed a recent fad by publishing a collection of Scottish folksongs. Although sales were good, they were not good enough for Napier to support his wife and twelve children. So he had to declare bankruptcy. Haydn promised to compose accompaniments for one hundred songs without charge. The accompaniments consisted of a violin part plus a figured bass part for pianoforte. The volume was announced in November with the claim that "the whole of the Harmony to the Original Melodies will be supplied by Mr Haydn, who has already composed the greatest part of it" (Landon 3, p. 129). After some delay, the collection appeared in June. It did well enough so that Napier's business turned around. In 1795, Napier would publish a third volume to which Haydn contributed fifty more arrangements.

Back to the Busyness of London

After his stay with the Brassy family, Haydn returned to London. Although his social schedule was not as crowded as it had been earlier in the year, there were still many invitations. Some, but not all, were to Haydn's liking.

On November 5 Haydn was a guest at a dinner given in honor of the new Lord Mayor of London. The food, Haydn wrote in his notebook, was "very nice and well-cooked." Just about everything else was annoying. After dinner, at about 9:00 p.m., the dancing began.

> Nothing but minuets are danced in this room; I couldn't stand it longer than a quarter of an hour; first, because the heat caused by so many people in such a small room was so great; and secondly, because of the wretched dance band, the entire orchestra consisting only of two violins and a violoncello. The minuets were more Polish than in our or the Italian manner. From there I went to another room, which was more like a subterranean cavern, and where the dance was English; the music was a little better, because there was a drum in the band which drowned the misery of the violins. (Landon 3, p. 106)

Back at the great hall "the band was larger and more bearable. The dance was English, but only on the raised platform." The tables were all occupied "by men who, as usual, drank enormously the whole night." But the "most curious thing" was "that a part of the company went on dancing without hearing a single note of music, for first at one table, then at another, some were yelling songs and some swilling it down and drinking toasts amid terrific roars of 'Hurrey' and waving glasses. The hall and all the other rooms are illuminated with lamps which give out an unpleasant odour" (Landon 3, p. 106).

Much more to Haydn's liking were the two days he spent at Oatland, country seat of the Duke of York, brother of the Prince of Wales. Haydn described it as a "little castle, 18 miles from London," situated on a slope that "commands the most glorious view" (Landon 3, p. 109). He wrote enthusiastically to Frau von Genzinger about his visit with the prince, the duke, and the duke's new seventeen-year-old wife.

> I must take this opportunity of informing Your Grace that 3 weeks ago I was invited by the Prince of Wales to visit his brother, the Duke of York, at the latter's country seat. The Prince presented me to the Duchess, the daughter of the King of Prussia, who received me very graciously and said many flattering things. She is the most delightful lady in the world, is very intelligent, plays the pianoforte and sings very nicely. I had to stay there 2 days, because a slight indisposition prevented her attending the concert on the first day. On the 2nd day, however, she remained continually at my side from 10 o'clock in the evening, when the music began, to 2 o'clock in the morning. Nothing but Haydn was played. I conducted the symphonies from the pianoforte, and the sweet little thing sat beside me on my left and hummed all the pieces from memory, for she had heard them so often in Berlin. The Prince of Wales sat on my right side and played with us on his violoncello, quite tolerably. (Landon 3, pp. 117-18)

Haydn and Pleyel: Friendly Rivals

Back in London in December, Haydn learned that he had competition that could prove uncomfortable. Salomon's chief rival, the Professional Concert, had engaged Haydn's former pupil, Ignaz Pleyel, for their own concert series. Pleyel arrived on December 23 and dined with Haydn the next day. "So now," Haydn wrote, "a bloody harmonious war will commence between master and pupil. The newspapers are full of it" (Landon 3, p. 125). But despite the tension, the two principals in the competition remained friends. They were often together. They attended the opera together and Haydn often attended Pleyel's concerts with the Professional Concert. Nevertheless, Haydn felt the pressure. He complained about the heavy workload — "my labours have been augmented" — and the ensuing strain on his eyes and sleepless nights. He even sounds a bit paranoid at times: "I realized at once that a lot of people were dead set against me. I must be the victim and work the whole time." But "with God's help," he added, "I shall overcome it all." He and Pleyel could both share their "laurels equally and each go home satisfied" (Landon 3, p. 141).

Salomon's 1792 Concert Season

For the 1791 season Haydn had written only two new symphonies, nos. 95 and 96, no doubt because composing an opera had taken up so much of his time. For Salomon's 1792 season, thanks to having a summer and fall to prepare and no opera to write, he produced four symphonies, nos. 93, 94, 97, and 98, and the *Sinfonia Concertante.* Although the programs still listed nothing but generic titles, there is enough information from other sources so that, unlike for the 1791 season, we can deduce what dates the symphonies were performed. Symphony no. 93 was performed at the first concert, February 17. The critic for *The Times* was most enthusiastic about the new symphony "from the pen of the incomparable *Haydn.*" "Such a combination of excellence," he wrote, "was contained in every movement, as inspired all the performers as well as the audience with enthusiastic ardour. Novelty of idea, agreeable caprice, and whim combined with all *Haydn's* sublime and wonten grandeur, gave additional consequence to the *soul* and feelings of every individual present" (Landon 3, p. 134).

Haydn, however, was not totally pleased. He wrote to Frau von Genzinger that the last movement needed to be altered, "since it is too weak compared with the first. I was convinced of this myself, and so was the public, when it was played the first time last Friday; notwithstanding that it made the most profound impression on the audience" (Landon 3, p. 140). He never did revise the movement, and modern critics are divided about its need for improvement. I side with Simon McVeigh: "It is hard to imagine a negative response to the existing one, for it is one of Haydn's wittiest and most ingenious rondo variants, making great play with audience expectations."[1] In any case, if there are minor weaknesses in the movement, they are, as A. Peter Brown says, "more than made up for by the first three movements, which represent the composer at his very best"[2] — especially the second movement. It is justly famous for its "Great Bassoon Joke," a joke that ranks with Haydn's

1. Simon McVeigh, "Symphony," in *Oxford Composer Companions: Haydn* (Oxford: Oxford University Press, 2009), pp. 408-9.

2. A. Peter Brown, *The Symphonic Repertoire,* vol. 2 (Bloomington: Indiana University Press, 2002), p. 256.

best. But it is unfortunate if the joke detracts from the movement's manifold beauties that range from the charming to the sublime.

Symphony no. 98, performed on March 2, was the next of the new symphonies to be performed. Mozart had died three months earlier on December 5. Haydn was likely working on Symphony no. 98 when he heard the news. On December 20 he wrote to Frau von Genzinger that he was looking forward to going home and embracing all his good friends. But he deeply regretted "that the great Mozart will not be among them, if it is really true, which I trust it is not, that he has died" (Landon 3, p. 118). Other than chronological coincidence, there is no evidence that he thought of Symphony no. 98 as homage to his dear friend. However, the poignant outcries and overall solemnity of the slow movement beg to be heard as Haydn's memorial to Mozart, all the more so because, intentionally or coincidently, its hymn-like theme has clear resonances with the theme of the slow movement of Mozart's *Jupiter* Symphony.

After its first performance, Symphony no. 98 was repeated the next week — "by desire," as Salomon's announcement in the papers proclaimed. The new work by Haydn on that program was his *Sinfonia Concertante*. Then at the next concert, March 16, the *Sinfonia Concertante* was repeated (again "by desire"), as were five other pieces by Haydn. The unusually high concentration of works by Haydn pleased the reviewers (and no doubt the audience). One wrote: "There has hardly ever been a more beautiful musical treat than the fifth performance of SALOMON'S Concert, at the Hanover-Square Room, last night. No less than six Pieces of HAYDN were performed, exhibiting a richness and variety of genius that far exceed all modern Composers" (Landon 3, p. 147).

Symphony No. 94, *Surprise*

Haydn's best-known work, the work that defines him for most people, received its first performance on March 23. That work, of course, is Symphony no. 94, nicknamed *Surprise*. The surprise is a single loud chord that comes unexpectedly in the midst of a very soft, very gentle theme in the second movement. Both the unexpected loud chord and the simple theme it disrupts do, in fact, represent (but do not exhaust) two important aspects of Haydn's art: its wit and its surface innocence. But the wit involves more than the momentary surprise of the loud chord, and the innocent surface belies the masterful artistry that went into its making.

Example 16-1 shows a hypothetical first draft of Haydn's famous melody. It is rounded binary in form — ‖: X :‖: Y X′ :‖ — normal in every respect, conventional and boring. The first two measures of X merely outline the notes of the tonic chord — C, E, G, E. The next two measures outline the descending notes of its closest relative, a dominant 7th chord — F, D, B, G. Then the next two measures repeat the first two, and the last two, in the most obvious way, make a cadence on G — a conventional antecedent ending. After the repeat of X, the first four measures of Y make two attempts to get back to C — first by descending in quarter notes from F, then by descending in eighth notes from A. Both come up short of the goal, getting only as far as D. The goal, C, is reached at the beginning of the next measure, whereupon the music does a modified repeat of X (X′) with the cadence altered to make a consequent ending on C.

EXAMPLE 16-1

Now compare that with what Haydn wrote. (See Example 16-2.) In the X part he makes only two small changes to the hypothetical original; but they make a big difference. The first change is the high C instead of A in measure 7. It is at once surprising and logical. It is logical because it is the goal of the ascending C-E-G that begins the melody. Haydn could have put it quite convincingly on the last beat of measure 6, and from there it could progress satisfactorily to the cadence. But he did not put it there. He simply turned the music back down to E (as in measure 2) and then jumped up to C a beat later (on the first beat of measure 7). So we get the expected climax but in an unexpected place. By putting it one beat later than expected, Haydn not only gave us a minor surprise, but he also made the climactic C more emphatic because it is rhythmically stronger (it is on the first beat of the measure) and reached by a large leap.

EXAMPLE 16-2

The second change is hardly noticeable. In measure 8, instead of holding the G, Haydn dropped it down an octave on beat two. Then he immediately put that seemingly insignificant change to good use. He used the drop to the low G to enliven the rhythmically boring beginning of section Y. But a problem remains. At the end of measure 12, the melody is poised to return to X with the cadence altered to end on C. And that is what it does in our hypothetical example — and a boring ending it is! But just as the D is about to resolve to the C, it turns upward through D♯ to E. Now the music can go on and repeat the ascending chord from the beginning, but with two differences. It now starts a notch higher — on E instead of C — and then continues its ascent through the whole octave to a high E, making a higher climax than the C in the first part. And notice how Haydn reinforced the ascent to the climax in measures 13-14. He did not abandon the melody of the opening measure. He kept it, but put it in the second violin part. So the violins ascend together in parallel motion from two different starting points, the seconds from the original C and the firsts from the E. In addition, Haydn has the violas and cellos start from the same two notes (C and E) and do the same thing as the violins — but going down instead of up. And from this expanding, full-textured climax, the music is set up to make a final cadence on the high C.

With a few seemingly insignificant strokes, Haydn was able to turn a nondescript melody into a small but perfectly chiseled jewel, a jewel whose various facets he will show in the ensuing variations through a variety of textures, colors, rhythms, dynamics, and countermelodies. And through it all, the tune never loses its simple, innocent, pastoral character.

But what about the famous surprise? First of all, Haydn knew exactly where to place it for the greatest possible effect. In the beginning we hear the first eight measures of the theme played softly in a very sparse texture. When they are repeated, they are played even more softly. Then just as the phrase is about to end, on the weakest beat of the whole phrase, at the place where the violins had dropped to their almost inaudible low G, the full orchestra, *fortissimo,* plays the surprising chord. One observer said "the whole auditorium was profoundly shocked, especially the ladies" (Landon 3, p. 151). Haydn may or may not have said he did it so "the ladies will jump," but given the pastoral character of the theme, indeed of the symphony as a whole, it is not surprising that one reviewer heard it in a pastoral context. "The surprise," he wrote, "might not be unaptly likened to the situation of a beautiful Shepherdess, who lulled to slumber by the murmur of a distant waterfall, starts alarmed by the unexpected firing of a fowling piece" (Landon 3, p. 150).

Although the most obvious effect of the loud chord is a momentary surprise or shock, it has a subtle effect on the rest of the movement. If Haydn did it once, he might do it again. But when? Since four variations on the theme follow, there are several opportunities to do it again in an analogous place — but he does not. Of course, he might also do it at some other unexpected moment. Again he does not; but we cannot be sure that he will not until the final, quiet chords of the wistful, minor-tinged coda have faded away.

Wrapping Up the Concert Season

Haydn's last new symphony for the 1792 season, no. 97, was not performed until his May 3 benefit concert, or the next evening at the tenth of Salomon's concerts — or perhaps both. Although his composing obligations to Salomon were now finished, he still needed to stay to conduct the remaining concerts, the last of which was to have been on May 18. But "to gratify the wishes of his Subscribers," Salomon added a thirteenth concert that was given on June 6.

Haydn was eager to return to Vienna, but his English friends no doubt urged him to stay longer. Besides, Prince Anton had ordered him to be in Frankfurt to attend the coronation of Franz II as Holy Roman Emperor on July 14, and by remaining in London a little longer he could stop in Frankfurt on the way back to Vienna. Being out from under his musical obligations, an additional month in London offered leisure for more sightseeing and visits. On June 14 he saw Windsor Castle and its chapel. Its altars and stained-glass (and their cost!) impressed him greatly. The next day he went to the horse races at Ascot and described them in great detail in his notebook. From there he went to Slough where he visited William Herschel, at one time a musician of some note, now a famous astronomer, discoverer of the planet Uranus and two of its moons. Herschel had built a forty-foot telescope that impressed Haydn greatly, especially its "machinery," which, he wrote, is "very big, but so ingenious that a single man can put it in motion with the greatest ease" (Landon 3, p. 176). No doubt he looked through the telescope, but he wrote nothing about what he saw. He certainly was not impervious to natural beauty. On his voyage to England he was awed by "that mighty monster, the ocean," and in his notebooks he often remarked about beautiful scenery — for example, the "divine" view from the terrace of Windsor Castle. Perhaps he was so awestruck by the view of the heavens that he was at a loss for words. His reaction to the splendor of the stars had to wait for expression until his music would give it eloquent voice in *The Creation*.

Back to Vienna

Back on the continent in early July, Haydn first stopped in Bonn where he met Beethoven again. He made plans for Beethoven to come to Vienna in November to be his student. He also made plans for Beethoven to go with him when he returned to London in 1793. As it turned out, Haydn did not return in 1793 as planned. And by 1794, when he did return, the plan for Beethoven to accompany him had been abandoned or forgotten.

From Bonn, in order to concur with Prince Anton's wish, Haydn went to Frankfurt for the coronation of Franz II. His appearance in Frankfurt was little noticed, and little of consequence happened; also, when he returned to Vienna later in July, his arrival went unnoticed in the Viennese newspapers. He moved back into the lodgings he rented after leaving Eszterháza, where his wife was still living, and it seems that his first order of business was to return to Eszterháza to retrieve the belongings he had left there when he hastily left after Anton disbanded the musical establishment.

After the disbandment, the singer Luigia Polzelli had gone to Italy. She had been Haydn's mistress for a time during the '80s. While Haydn was in London, letters between the two discussed having Luigia's oldest son, Pietro, study with him. Now back in Vienna, he took Pietro in as a boarder and student. On October 22, Pietro wrote to his mother, "*il Sigre Maes.* Haydn has found a place for me in his own home," and in a postscript Haydn added, "Your son has been very well received by my wife" (Landon 3, p. 199). But a more important student would soon arrive. As planned in Bonn, Beethoven came to Vienna in November to study with Haydn.

Haydn and Beethoven

Beethoven had been in Vienna in 1787 to study with Mozart. But he was soon called back to Bonn to attend to his sick mother. By the time he was able to return to Vienna, Mozart had died. So now Beethoven hoped, as his patron Count Waldstein put it, he would "receive the spirit of Mozart from

Haydn's hands" (Landon 3, p. 192). But Beethoven was dissatisfied with Haydn's teaching — at least so the story is commonly told. He is even supposed to have said that he never learned anything from Haydn. The story expands beyond dissatisfaction with Haydn's teaching to tell of a relationship that was fraught with jealousy and disrespect. But many of the sources of this story are late and anecdotal, and since some of the anecdotes are demonstrably false, it is hard to separate fact from fiction in the whole lot of them. They are rendered even more suspicious by the fact that chronologically they coincide with, and conveniently fit into, the later mythology of "Papa Haydn" (in the patronizing sense of that nickname) and "Heroic Beethoven."

The sources, when critically scrutinized, do point to some tension in the relationship, especially during the few years around the turn of the century when both were at critical, but opposite, junctures in their careers. Beethoven's star was rising, but he was aware of the onset of progressive deafness that "threatened (he believed) to subject him to the scorn and contempt of his rivals and enemies." At the same time Haydn's *Creation* (1798) was an "unexpected hurdle" for Beethoven to surmount on his way to ascendancy. And Haydn, for his part, after *The Creation* and *The Seasons,* became frustrated that he was "no longer able to summon up the strength and concentration to complete musical compositions, but was still attempting to do so."[3]

Any serious friction between the two great composers, then, likely occurred during a short but particularly sensitive time within the two decades when their relations were otherwise cordial and respectful. Whatever uncertainty we may have about the depth of their friendship, or about the quality of Haydn's formal teaching (or Beethoven's receptivity) in their early pedagogical relationship, there can be no question about the ultimate effect of Haydn on Beethoven. As Barry Cooper puts it, "When Beethoven remarked that he had never learnt anything from Haydn, he was clearly not referring to the inspiring example of Haydn's music."[4]

3. James Webster, "The Falling Out of Haydn and Beethoven: The Evidence of the Sources," in *Beethoven Essays: Studies in Honor of Elliot Forbes* (Cambridge: Harvard University Department of Music, 1984), pp. 23 and 26

4. Barry Cooper, "Beethoven, Ludwig van," in *Oxford Composer Companions: Haydn* (Oxford: Oxford University Press, 2009), p. 20.

Return to London Delayed

Beethoven stayed on as Haydn's student until Haydn returned to London at the beginning of 1794. The original plan was for Haydn to return for the 1793 season. On New Year's Day, 1793, the London *Morning Post* announced that Salomon would again feature Haydn in his series. But on January 11, the *Morning Chronicle* was less definite about Haydn's return. He would "fulfill his engagement as soon as there is a possibility of his undertaking the journey" (Landon 3, p. 212). As it turned out, he stayed in Vienna the whole year. The French Revolution was in full swing — King Louis XVI was guillotined on January 21, 1793 — so Haydn may have had concerns for his safety on a trip back to England. Furthermore, he had returned to Vienna a tired sixty-year-old man, not ready to plunge back into a hectic schedule of composing, concerts, and social obligations. But the reason given in the London papers was that he needed surgery. According to the *Morning Herald*, "Poor Haydn continues in Germany very ill: but composing for England and promising to come over when he can. He is afflicted with the tedious and painful disorder, a *polypus* in the nose, for which he is immediately about to suffer an operation" (Landon 3, p. 214).

Haydn had long suffered from the polyp. Griesinger wrote that earlier in his life, "when it became embedded and threatened his breathing, a surgeon from the Order of the Brothers of Mercy in Eisenstadt had tied it up, three times in thirty years, and had thus always rendered it harmless for a long time" (p. 43). And Dies tells us that as the result of an operation by "the celebrated Brambilla," surgeon to Emperor Joseph II, Haydn "had been so unfortunate as to forfeit a piece of the nasal bone without being wholly freed of the polyp" (p. 151). Shortly before returning to Vienna, Haydn's London friend Dr. John Hunter, Surgeon General and Inspector General of Hospitals, offered to remove the polyp. But the surgery did not take place. Haydn told Dies: "After the first greetings several big strong fellows entered the room, seized me, and tried to seat me in a chair. I shouted, beat them black and blue, kicked till I freed myself, and made it clear to Mr. H, who was standing all ready with his instruments for the operation, that I would not be operated on. He wondered at my obstinacy, and it seemed to me that he pitied me for not wanting the fortunate experience of his skill. I excused myself for lack of time, due to my impending departure" (p. 152).

Less dramatically, Griesinger simply reports that Haydn was afraid the surgery might have "evil consequences," so he was stoically resolved to live with the polyp. "I'll have to leave it to rot under the earth now,"

Haydn said. "My mother suffered the same ailment, without ever dying of it" (p. 42). But now in Vienna he seems to have decided to go ahead with surgery. At least it provided a credible excuse for delaying his trip.

The extra year gave Haydn a good opportunity to get a head start on composing music for the London concerts. In Vienna, he did not receive the adulation he received in London, so his social life was nothing like the whirlwind it had been in London. Of course, many of his friends were still in Vienna, but Mozart was not. And after January 20, 1792, neither was his dearest friend, Frau von Genzinger. She died at age forty-two, the mother of five. In addition to a slower social life, he was not involved as composer or performer in any concert series — though he did mount a concert that included three of the four symphonies he had written for the 1792 season in London. So in much-welcomed peace — albeit tinged with sorrow — Haydn composed for the second visit: the six string quartets of opus 71 and opus 74; Symphony no. 99; and substantial parts of the 100th and 101st Symphonies. He also composed a little music for use in Vienna. He composed twelve minuets and twelve German dances for a masked ball given by the Society of Visual Artists for the benefit of widows and orphans. And he composed the Andante and Variations in F minor, one of his greatest keyboard pieces. He dedicated it to Barbara von Ployer, a former student of Mozart and now one of the outstanding keyboardists in Vienna. It is the only solo keyboard piece he wrote between 1789 and 1794. Could it be that he wrote this isolated and deeply moving piece in memory of his two Viennese friends who had died?

CHAPTER 17

Back in London

1794-95

This was a dance, a dance ordered and graceful, and yet giving an impression of complete and utter freedom, of ineffable joy.

MADELEINE L'ENGLE

Creativity represents a miraculous coming together of the un-inhibited energy of the child with its apparent opposite and enemy, the sense of order imposed on the disciplined adult intelligence.

NORMAN PODHORETZ

Unrecognized in Germany

On January 19, 1794, Haydn again set out for London, this time in a coach lent to him by Baron van Swieten and accompanied by his copyist, Johann Essler. There are no letters from Haydn describing the trip. He told Dies that they went at "top speed" so that he "had no time to halt along the way and strike up acquaintance with any celebrities" (p. 167). But two anecdotes from the trip bear retelling, the first by Griesinger, the second by Dies.

> When he was going through Schärding on the Austrian border, the customs officials inquired about his character. Haydn answered that he was a *Tonkünstler* [musician]. "What is that?" asked the one. "A potter!" [*Ton*, clay; *Künstler*, artist] answered the other. "Exactly," Haydn agreed,

"and this man sitting next to me in the carriage (his servant) is my journeyman" (pp. 28-29).

In the inn [in Wiesbaden] where Haydn had stopped he heard next his room the beloved Andante with the Drum Stroke [from the *Surprise* Symphony] being played on a pianoforte. Counting the player a friend, he stepped politely into the room where he heard the music. He found several Prussian officers, all great admirers of his music, who, when he finally made himself known, would not take his word for it that he was Haydn. "Impossible! Impossible! You Haydn? — Already such an old man! — That doesn't rhyme with the fire in your music! — No! We shall never believe it!"

In this doubting vein the men persisted so long that Haydn produced a letter received from their King which he had fortunately brought along in his trunk. Then the officers overwhelmed him with their fondness, and he had to stay in their company till long past midnight (pp. 167-68).

Compositions for Salomon's 1794 Concert Series

Haydn arrived in London on February 4 and soon thereafter learned that Prince Anton had died on January 24. He moved into a house on Bury Street, about a ten-minute walk from both Hanover Square and Rebecca Schroeter's house. (The close proximity of their residences is the explanation usually given for the total lack of correspondence between them during Haydn's second stay in London.)

The pace of Haydn's life during this second visit was slower and less tense. He was more familiar with the whole scene, he had had more time to prepare, and there was no competition from the rival concert series because the Professional Concert had gone out of business. For the 1794 season he needed only six new instrumental compositions and no vocal works, and, as previously noted, he had already composed the six string quartets of Opus 71/74, all of Symphony no. 99, and substantial parts of Symphony no. 100 and Symphony no. 101 while still in Vienna.

Already on February 10, six days after his arrival, he performed Symphony no. 99. The reviews were no less effusive in their praise than they had been in 1791-92. One called it "one of the grandest efforts of art that we ever witnessed. It abounds with ideas, as new in music as they are grand

and impressive" (Landon 3, p. 234). Another declared it "a composition of the most exquisite kind, rich, fanciful, bold, and impressive." But the highest praise came from a critic who found words inadequate "when the *chef d'oeuvre* of the great HAYDN is the subject." So he called upon silence: "Come then, expressive SILENCE, muse his praise" (Landon 3, p. 234).

At the second concert a week later, Symphony no. 99 was repeated and one of the Opus 71/74 quartets received its premiere performance. Like the symphonies, the quartet received enthusiastic praise. It "gave pleasure by its variety, gaiety, and the fascination of its melody and harmony throughout all its movements." At the third concert there were no new Haydn works, but at the fourth, Symphony no. 101 made its debut. It was customary then for audiences to ask for immediate encores of movements that especially delighted them. A reviewer reported that "the first two movements were encored, and the character that pervaded the whole was heartfelt joy." He went on to marvel at Haydn's continuing fertility of imagination at a time when one might expect him to rest on his laurels. No one would have been surprised if, at his advanced age, and after such a long, productive career, his creativity might be exhausted. As the reviewer wrote, with every new symphony "till it is heard, we fear he can only repeat himself; and we are every time mistaken." So again on this night "as usual the most delicious part of the entertainment was a new grand Overture [symphony] by HAYDN; the inexhaustible, the wonderful, the sublime HAYDN" (Landon 3, p. 241).

Symphony No. 101, Clock

Symphony no. 101 soon received the nickname *Clock,* a name that refers to the "tick-tock" accompaniment that begins and pervades the entire second movement. The same reviewer made special mention of that accompaniment: "The management of the accompaniment of the andante, though perfectly simple, was masterly" (Landon 3, p. 241) — as, of course, was his management of every other aspect of the movement. It is in a simple rondo form, and the rondo theme is in a simple ternary form. (For a detailed diagram of the movement, as described in the following, see Diagram 17-1, pp. 213-14.) It begins with one measure of the "tick-tock" accompaniment alone, which sounds like a typical vamp-till-ready opening. The "tick-tock" will pervade the rondo theme in each of its three appearances as well as the second episode and the coda. Although it will be absent through most of the first episode, even in its absence its presence is felt.

Diagram 17-1

Haydn, Symphony No. 101, Clock, 2nd movement

Rondo theme

X		Y		X¹		
1 + 2-5 (1 + 4)		6-10 (5)	11-15 (5)	16-19 + 20-23 (4 + 4)	24-28 (5)	29-34 (6)

||: a – antecedent / a¹ – consequent :||: b – antecedent / c – antecedent // a – antecedent / a² – consequent :||

G major

Episode I

Note the increasing rhythmic and textural complexity, which builds to a peak of intensity in section 3 and then subsides step-by-step in sections 4-6.

34-39	40-49	50-55	56-59	60	61-62
|| section 1	/ section 2	/ section 3	/ section 4	/ section 5	/ section 6 ||
G minor to B♭ major	*B♭ major*	*modulatory*	*G minor (dominant pedal point)*		

Rondo theme (varied)

The flute takes the upper notes of the "tick-tock" accompaniment, but by the end of phrase a it has become a countermelody. Note that throughout this statement of the rondo theme the flute subtly shifts back and forth between accompaniment and countermelody.

X		Y		X¹			
63-67	68-72	73-77	78-81 + 82-85		86-90	91-96	97
|| a – antecedent	/ a¹ – consequent || b – antecedent	/ c – antecedent // a – antecedent	/ a² – consequent			|| pause ||
G major							

Episode II (98-110)

Starts with one measure of the "tick-tock" accompaniment in G minor but immediately changes key when the rondo theme enters in E♭ major. Only the beginning of phrase a is heard as it soon gives way to scale passages and rhythmic patterns reminiscent of Episode I.

Rondo theme (varied)

This variation of the rondo theme is loud except for the Y section. It has 16th-note triplets running continuously throughout, sometimes as accompaniment figures but usually as decoration of the melody.

X		Y		X¹	
111-115	116-120	121-125	126-129 + 130-133	134-138	139-144

‖ a – antecedent / a¹ – consequent ‖ b – antecedent / c – antecedent ‖ a – antecedent / a² – consequent ‖

G major

Coda (144-150)

16th-note triplets continue as descending scales against the "tick-tock" accompaniment in the bassoons. The scales begin in the violas and are then picked up in order by the 2nd violins, 1st violins, and then flutes and oboes. Finally the cellos and basses play the scales, now ascending, and lead to the last three chords, which are an augmentation and inversion of the first three.

Like the famous theme of the *Surprise Symphony,* the rondo theme is simple. But due to its greater rhythmic variety, it is a few levels of sophistication higher. (See Example 17-1.) It unfolds as a typical four-measure antecedent phrase which would normally be followed by a four-measure consequent phrase. And that, at least for two measures into the consequent phrase, is exactly what seems to be happening. But then, after the surprising leap to a high C in measure eight, the music needs an extra measure to reach the expected cadence on G. So the phrases are unbalanced — four measures (not counting the vamp) followed by five.

EXAMPLE 17-1

At this point there is the customary repeat. But instead of repeating back to measure two where the melody begins, Haydn has the repeat include the seemingly superfluous vamp-till-ready measure. It sounds like a mistake until we realize that the extra measure brings balance to the theme — five (counting the vamp) and five. The first measure, as it turns out, is not merely a vamp-till-ready opening; it is an integral part of the theme that Haydn will include every time the theme returns.

The Y section of the rondo theme develops the various rhythmic motives of the X section and leads to the return of X (X′). The antecedent phrase of X′ is repeated verbatim, except that the flute joins the violins in playing the melody. But again the consequent phrase has a surprise in store. It leaps up to the high C already in its first measure, and by the time it has made the long descent to the cadence on G it has taken six measures. This might seem to upset the balance again, but it brings to a conclusion the expansion of phrases that began in X with four measures expanding to five. Now five measures expand to six.

The first episode presents a strong contrast. A loud minor passage bursts into the scene even as the soft major theme is arriving on its final chord. The texture is full, employing the entire orchestra, and counterpoint has replaced accompanied melody. But it is not totally unrelated to the rondo theme. It takes the rondo theme's dotted rhythms and radically transforms their slightly coquettish character into stern seriousness. However it soon modulates to B♭ major, at which point the stern dotted rhythms give way to lively thirty-second notes (another rhythmic motive from the rondo theme). At this bright, lively moment, Haydn reintroduces the "tick-tock" accompaniment. But instead of oscillating gently back and forth over a narrow range, the "clock" becomes exuberant. Narrow oscillation gives way to wide leaps and every "tick" and "tock" is reinforced by off-beats in the woodwinds. (See Example 17-2.)

EXAMPLE 17-2

Each of the first three sections of Episode I is more intense than the previous one by virtue of increased rhythmic activity and greater complexity of texture. After reaching the peak of intensity in section three, it gradually subsides in the last three sections as the rhythm slows and the texture simplifies down to the first violins alone.

The first return of the rondo theme features the addition of a flute part above the theme in the strings. At first the flute takes the place of the first bassoon in the accompaniment — two octaves higher! But after three measures of "tick-tock," it becomes a lyrical countermelody. And from there it subtly shifts back and forth between accompaniment and countermelody.

At the end of the rondo theme, the music comes to a cadence that could mark the end of the movement — though not a very convincing one. Everything stops as if Haydn were trying to make up his mind whether to go on — and if so, how. After one measure of silence he does go on, and he seems to have decided on a tried-and-true formula: play the rondo theme in minor. So the episode begins with the "tick-tock" accompaniment in G minor, but we soon encounter one surprise after another. First, G minor lasts only through the one "tick-tock" measure before turning to E♭ major when the melody enters. Second, the melody remains intact for only two measures before it breaks up into scale patterns reminiscent of Episode I. And third, after a few measures of seemingly being stuck in E♭ major, a surprising chord, hammered out in the stern dotted rhythms of Episode II, forces the music back to G major.

After a long lead-in, the rondo theme returns in a variation for full orchestra featuring continuous running sixteenth-note triplets. Starting in the accompaniment, they move up to decorate the melody. All the while the "tick-tock" accompaniment is going on, though it is somewhat lost in the excitement. But as the excitement subsides in the coda, its presence (in the bassoons, as at the beginning) is clearly noticed again. The coda ends softly on three chords that are an exact augmentation (twice as long) and inversion (the top and bottom parts trade places) of the opening "tick-tock."

Rejoicing in the Passage of Time

Imaginative handling of the simplest of materials is one of the hallmarks of Haydn's music. Another is that surface simplicity often masks depth of meaning. Charles Rosen draws a parallel between Haydn's compositional style and the literary pastoral, a popular genre at the time. Just as "the rustics in pastoral speak words whose profundity is apparently beyond their grasp, and the shepherds are not aware that their joys and sorrows are those of all men," so do Haydn's melodies "seem detached from all that they portend, unaware of how much they signify."[1] So, perhaps there is

---

1. Charles Rosen, *The Classical Style: Haydn, Mozart, Beethoven* (New York: W. W. Norton and Co., 1972), p. 162.

more to be said about the "tick-tock" accompaniment than that it lent itself to Haydn's compositional virtuosity; perhaps it portends more than its surface simplicity suggests.

What can be more homely and ordinary than the ticking of a clock? And yet, what has more profound implications for our lives? The writer of Psalm 90 says what everybody knows but would rather not face: our days are swept away "as with a flood"; they are "like a dream"; our life is like grass; "in the evening it fades and withers." We return "to dust." So the psalmist prays: "Teach us to number our days that we may get a heart of wisdom." Such thoughts about the passing of time more often than not bring on sadness, melancholy, fear, maybe anger — emotions that are not even hinted at in this symphonic movement. But Haydn, like the psalmist, believed that those who trust in God's steadfast love "may rejoice and be glad all their days." Even as the clock ticks, they can rejoice in the passage of time, living in the sure hope that there will be eternal joy when the ticking stops.

Symphony No. 100, Military

The next new symphony to appear on Salomon's concert series was the *Military* Symphony (no. 100). For a time it would be even more popular than the "Surprise" Symphony. Its popularity owed something to the political situation in Europe at the time. The Reign of Terror was going strong. Mass executions that would reach into the tens of thousands had already included Marie Antoinette and Louis XVI among its victims. News of the Terror was reaching London, not only through the newspapers but also from the many French refugees, some of them musicians, arriving in England. The number of refugee musicians was large enough to prompt one reporter to write, "Nothing less than the demolition of one Monarchy, and the general derangement of all the rest, could have poured into England and settled such a mass of talents as we have now to boast. Music as well as misery has fled for shelter to England" (Landon 3, p. 214). Haydn no doubt heard of the atrocities from musicians he worked with, as well as from daily conversations all around him. Burney wrote that "There is no talking or thinking of anything else but the tremendous increase of discontent, danger, & unheard of profligacy & and horrors. Peace, tranquility, content, benevolence, humility, politeness, and all religious & social virtues, are not only neglected, but regarded as vices!" (Landon 3, p. 240).

In this environment, Haydn performed his *Military* Symphony, so called because of the second movement, which begins as a "suspiciously light, . . . dainty march" — an army in full colors on parade (a real army to an eighteenth-century listener, not the toy soldiers that the music might suggest to us!). It all sounds so very confident as the parade proceeds in orderly fashion for fifty-six measures to a full cadence. But then "a sudden switch to the minor key unleashes a barrage of percussion instruments, wholly unprecedented in Haydn's symphonies (or, indeed, anybody else's) and which proceed to cast a dark shadow over the rest of the movement; at a later point a solo fanfare on trumpet leads to another outburst. For Haydn's audience this symphony captured the mood of the day perfectly."[2]

I suspect that not many audiences today hear the horrors of war in this movement, accustomed as they are to far more terrifying noises in the music they hear. But the sudden plunge into minor, along with the banging on percussion instruments never before heard in a symphony, certainly was a shock to eighteenth-century Londoners. The march itself already had military connotations, and the loud percussion instruments (which had clear "Turkish" connotations) introduced not only unprecedented, but more importantly, discordant sounds. As one reviewer wrote: "The reason of the great effect they [the percussion instruments] produce in the military movement is that they mark and tell the story: they inform us that the army is marching to battle, and, calling up all the ideas of the terror of such a scene, give it reality. Discordant sounds are then sublime; for what can be more horribly discordant to the heart than thousands of men meeting to murder each other?" (Landon 3, p. 251). Perhaps with the help of a little historical imagination we can overcome our jaded sensibilities and again hear these sounds as terrifying. And maybe we do not even need historical imagination in order to feel terrified when we hear the solo trumpet fanfare and drum roll near the end.

The *Military* Symphony was repeated on April 7, a week after its premiere, then at the May 2 benefit concert for Haydn, and again on May 12 for Salomon's last concert of the 1794 season. Although Salomon's season was over, there was a flurry of other concerts during the rest of May and early June. There were no new pieces by Haydn, but some of his earlier works were performed, and he still "presided" at the keyboard.

2. David Wyn Jones, *The Life of Haydn* (Cambridge: Cambridge University Press, 2009), p. 165.

Haydn's English Songs

On June 2 an advertisement appeared for Haydn's "Six Canzonettas," English songs with keyboard accompaniment. The poems are by Anne Hunter, widow of the surgeon who attempted to remove the polyp on Haydn's nose at the end of his first stay in London. During that first stay, Haydn had lived within easy walking distance of the Hunters' home. He often dined with them and attended Anne Hunter's salon where literature, art, and music were the usual topics of discussion. She was an accomplished poet whose lyrics were well-suited for musical settings, some of which she gave to Haydn. Now at the end of the 1794 concert season he published six that he had set to music and dedicated them to her.

Like the German lieder that he had composed in the 1780s, his English songs were written for amateurs for home entertainment. Unlike his lieder, the voice parts of these songs were written on a separate staff above the two keyboard staves, an indication that the voice has some independence from the accompaniment. Further, the English songs make somewhat greater demands on both singer and accompanist, and in general they are more expansive and elaborate than their German counterparts. Although strophic forms are still common, they are not exclusive. It is plausible to see Haydn's English songs as forerunners (but not "mere" forerunners) of nineteenth-century German lieder.

A. Peter Brown observes that when "looking at Anne Hunter's volume *Poems,* it becomes clear that her muse was aroused by family, friends, and contemporary events."[3] This is apparent in many of the titles, such as, "To a Friend on New Year's Day," "To My Daughter on Being Separated from Her on Marriage," "To My Son at School," and "William and Nancy." The text of the second of Haydn's "Six Canzonettas," titled "Recollection," is an elegy Mrs. Hunter wrote on the death of her husband.

> The season comes when first we met,
> But you return no more.
> Why cannot I the days forget,
> Which time can ne'er restore?
> O days too fair, too bright to last,
> Are you indeed forever past?

---

3. A. Peter Brown, "Musical Settings of Anne Hunter's Poetry," *Journal of the American Musicological Society* 47 (1994): 64.

Brown plausibly suggests that the "Six Canzonettas" form an incipient song cycle which progresses "from the joy of the mermaid [in 'The Mermaid's Song'] to the mournful in 'Recollection,' 'A Pastoral Song,' and 'Despair,' to the gradual recovery found in 'Pleasing Pain' and 'Fidelity.' The order of the poems is then suggestive of a narrative that could be related to the poet's own biography, which seems especially appropriate for a writer whose verses record so faithfully her life's events."[4] Autobiographical or not, the six songs in this collection, each very fine in its own right, present a cogent and moving sequence that transcends the individual parts. It culminates in "Fidelity," which, amidst all the F minor *Sturm und Drang* of life, ends in F major pledging eternal faithfulness.

> But whatsoe'er may be our doom,
> The lot is cast for me,
> For in the world or in the tomb,
> My heart is fix'd on thee.

Caecilia Maria Barthelemon, daughter of one of Haydn's musician friends in England, tells of Haydn singing "Recollections." "Often have I sat with him when he play'd his Sweet Canzonetts & and used to shed tears *when he sang* 'The Season comes when *first we met* but you return no more' & I said to him, 'Papa Haydn, Why do you cry?' & he said, 'Oh! *My dear Child.* I do not like to leave my English Friends, they are so kind to me!' " (Landon 3, p. 169). But at the time the song was published Haydn still had another year with his English friends ahead of him and a relatively relaxed summer and fall awaited him before the 1795 concert season arrived.

Summer and Fall Break, 1794

With the first of June came a great victory for the British navy over the French. One Londoner wrote to a friend:

> I cannot resist the temptation of wishing you all Joy of our great and splendid Victory at Sea. Lord Howe had two actions with the French Fleet; in the last on ye Ist of June he brought them to close Action and

---

4. Brown, "Musical Settings of Anne Hunter's Poetry," pp. 64-65.

took seven Sail of Line of Battle Ships. Six are coming home; one sunk after she surrendered, and one is supposed to have gone down during the Engagement.

We received this News last night at the Opera where Morichelli was singing a favorite song. She was silenced in a Moment, and Rule Britannia called for, which was repeated at least a dozen times, the Audience standing and huzzaing. (Landon 3, pp. 258-59)

Haydn mentioned the victory in his notebook, but he sounds a little less than pleased with some of the celebrating that went on. "On 11th June the whole city was illuminated because of the capture of French warships; a great many windows were broken. On the 12th and 13th the whole city was illuminated again. The common people behaved very violently on this occasion. In every street they shot off not only small but also large guns, and this went on the whole night" (Landon 3, p. 259).

In July, Haydn took a trip to Portsmouth, where he saw some of the spoils of Lord Howe's victory. His notebook tells us that on the way he saw "the old Royal Castle at Hampton Court, which is very large and has a garden like that at Estoras [Eszterháza], with three principal allées" (Landon 3, p. 262). Judging from his notebook entries, the Portsmouth visit intrigued him a great deal. He saw the barracks where thirty-five hundred Frenchmen were quartered, he "inspected the fortifications" and found them "in good repair," and he "went aboard the French ship-of-the-line called *le just*," noting its "80 cannon." "The ship is terribly shot to pieces," he wrote. "The great mast, which is 10 feet 5 inches in circumference, was cut off at the very bottom and lay stretched on the ground. A single cannon-ball, which passed through the captain's room, killed 14 sailors" (Landon 3, pp. 262-63). He took notes on various distinguishing features of frigates, brigs, and cutters. He also described a fire-ship and even made a sketch of it.

From Portsmouth it was on to the Isle of Wight, where he was a guest of the governor. He noted that the governor's country house "commands the most magnificent view over the ocean." Later in the summer he visited Bath ("one of the most beautiful cities in Europe") and Bristol ("rather dirty" with many churches "all in the old Gothic style"). Ever cost-conscious, he noted that "the trip there and back cost me 75 Viennese Gulden" (Landon 3, pp. 266 and 269). He also saw the ruins of the six-hundred-year-old Waverley Abbey and confessed, "whenever I looked at this beautiful wilderness, my heart was oppressed at the thought that all this once belonged to my religion" (Landon 3, p. 269). And on the way to visit Lord Abington, he traveled with a bridal pair. "The man was named Lindley, organist, 25 years old; his wife 18, with very good features — but both of them stone-blind. The old proverb, 'Love is blind', does not apply here. He was poor, but she brought him a dowry of £20,000 Sterling" — to which Haydn added the wry comment, "Now he doesn't play organ any more" (Landon 3, p. 270).

Haydn's Final Concert Series in London

Sometime during the summer, word reached Haydn that Prince Nikolaus II had named him "as his Kapellmeister and wished to re-establish the entire chapel." According to Dies, "Haydn received this news with greatest pleasure" (p. 171). But, of course, his obligations in London extended through the 1795 concert season, so however pleased he was when he received the news — and we might doubt that his feelings were as unmixed as Dies portrays them — his time in London was still far from over. Even after his composing obligations were fulfilled, and even when his own music was not being performed, he was still obligated to "preside" at the keyboard.

His obligation to compose symphonies was nearly complete. During the summer and fall he had completed no. 102 and much of nos. 103 and 104, and a new development lessened any further compositional expectations. Instead of mounting his own series at the Hanover Square Rooms, Salomon joined with some of his former competitors in a series at the newly finished concert room of the King's Theatre. The hall was larger, seating eight hundred instead of the Hanover's five hundred. The orchestra was also larger, numbering about sixty instead of forty. And now Haydn was only one of four resident composers, though clearly *primus inter pares*. But even when his own music was not being performed, he conducted from the fortepiano. The schedule was not as regular as it had been during the previous seasons. There were weekly concerts on Mondays from February 2 to March 16. After a break they resumed on April 13 with regular subscription concerts following on April 27, May 11, and May 18. A benefit concert for Haydn took place on May 4. The 102nd and 103rd Symphonies were performed at subscription concerts. No. 104, his final symphony, was performed at the benefit concert along with the ever-popular *Military* Symphony and some of his vocal music.

"His Genius Is Inexhaustible"

It is hard to talk about Haydn's latest symphonies (or, for that matter, his latest works in any genre) without simply repeating superlatives. But with repetition superlatives grow weak — and eventually meaningless. So when one reads the reviews of the 1795 season and finds in them the same superlatives as in the reviews of the preceding three seasons, one feels their force rapidly waning. And one might be excused for thinking that maybe the symphonies have become as formulaic as the reviews. But nothing could be further from the truth. Each symphony is unique; each one takes the listener on a new adventure, spins out a new dramatic narrative, and opens vistas that reveal new beauties. With "the various powers of his inventive and impassioned mind," wrote one reviewer, "this wonderful man never fails" (Landon 3, p. 303). "His genius," wrote another, "is inexhaustible" (Landon 3, p. 236).

Haydn's inexhaustible genius can perhaps be best illustrated by what we can almost literally call "creativity." In a scathing review, Hugo Wolf said that Brahms, "like God Almighty, understands the trick of making something out of nothing." But as Leonard Bernstein retorted, that is not a sign of weakness but, on the contrary, the very thing that makes Brahms great. For making something out of nothing "is exactly what Brahms did — well, not out of *nothing*, to be accurate; that, in Wolf's words, is reserved for God Almighty. But out of *almost* nothing — out of ideas and themes that in themselves might seem uneventful but that turn out to be loaded with symphonic dynamite."[5] The same is true of Haydn, as one of his reviewers understood. He wrote that "no man knows like HAYDN how to produce incessant variety without once departing from [his theme]" (Landon 3, p. 241). There is no better example of that kind of creativity than the last movement of Symphony no. 103.

Symphony No. 103, Last Movement — Creation Out of (Almost) Nothing

The form of the last movement of Symphony no. 103 can best be labeled a monothematic sonata-rondo. Sonata form developed during the last half

5. Leonard Bernstein, "Brahms: Symphony 4 in E Minor," in *The Infinite Variety of Music* (New York: Simon and Schuster, 1966), p. 230.

of the eighteenth century when surface variety — contrasting themes, textures, keys, etc. — became the ideal. It developed, as Kenneth Levy cogently explains, "to contain within a single instrumental movement an esthetically satisfying mix of the contrasting whims and textures that Classical composers prized."[6] Contrasting themes are so common in sonata form that it came to be typical (though not entirely accurate) to describe the form largely in terms of contrasting themes. But Haydn became increasingly fond of monothematic sonata form; that is, he took a form noted for its contrasting themes and turned it into a form in which all or most of the themes are derived from one theme.

Contrast is important in rondo forms as well. Contrasting episodes occur between statements of a rondo theme. Haydn also became fond of combining features of sonata form with those of rondo form. Most typically sonata-rondo forms have a sonata-like exposition (with contrasting themes) in place of the opening rondo theme. In a monothematic sonata-rondo form like the last movement of Symphony no. 103, everything — the contrasting themes of sonata form and the contrasting episodes of rondo form — is derived from one theme! And yet there are as much variety and contrast in this movement as there are in any movement with several contrasting themes. And not only does all the variety in this movement come from one theme, but it also comes from a theme made up of the most minimal of materials — a few repeated notes followed by descending and ascending scale segments. The melody is accompanied by a simple horn call involving only the basic notes of the natural (valveless) horn. (See Example 17-3.) Nothing could be more commonplace and seemingly devoid of potential, and no one but a consummate artist could turn it into one of the glories of Western musical art. The movement comes as close as anything I know to being creation out of nothing. But contrary to the way many of his contemporaries were thinking of human creativity as something divine, Haydn simply viewed his talent as a gift from God. "Once the clavier-player ——— from P. visited him. 'You are Haydn, the great Haydn,' he began with theatrical bearing. 'One should fall on his knees before you! One should approach you as a being of the highest sort!' — 'Oh my dear sir,' countered Haydn, 'don't talk to me like that. Consider me a man whom God has granted talent and a good heart. I push my claims no further'" (Griesinger, p. 55).

---

6. Kenneth Levy, *Music: A Listener's Introduction* (New York: Harper and Row, 1983), p. 158.

EXAMPLE 17-3

Haydn's Last London Compositions

Haydn's last public appearance in London was at a benefit concert for a musical friend, Andrew Ashe, on June 8. Haydn noted: "Madam Mara [the star singer] gave a 2nd concert under the auspices of the flautist Ashe. The house was quite full; I sat at the pianoforte" (Landon 3, p. 313). Although this concluded his obligations, he stayed in England two more months before returning to Vienna. If we can judge from the paucity of notebook entries from these two months, he did not do as much socializing and traveling as he had previously. Instead, he had time to wrap up some composing projects that were not part of his contractual agreements. He published a second set of English songs ("canzonettas"). Anne Hunter again worked with him on the selection of poems to be set, but this time only one of them was written by her. That one, "The Wanderer," like some of her poems from the first set, prompted a high romantic style from Haydn.

Wonderful as his songs are, Haydn's greatest London compositions, apart from the symphonies, are his keyboard works. London was filled with highly accomplished keyboardists, both amateur and professional; and it was the home of one of the leading fortepiano builders, John Broadwood. This flourishing keyboard world inspired Haydn to return to keyboard composition after a brief hiatus during the late '80s and early '90s. He composed three fortepiano sonatas for Therese Jansen, a former student of Muzio Clementi, and now one of the leading professional pianists in London. The sonatas are the last three (nos. 50-52), and, like the London symphonies, they are the crowning glory of Haydn's output in the genre. Although all three are surpassingly great, only no. 52 in E♭ major has received anything approaching the attention it deserves. Among Haydn's keyboard works, as Michelle Fillion points out, "it has dominated the concert stage and the critical literature, eclipsing all Haydn's other London piano music." But the features that make it "so beloved — brilliance, sublime wit, wide emotional palette, daring harmony, and architectural sweep — are matched by other equally formidable works of this time."[7]

Just as great as the last three sonatas, and far more numerous during the second London visit, are the keyboard trios. In 1794 and 1795, London publishers issued three sets of three Haydn trios — nos. 18-20 published by Broderip in 1794, nos. 21-23 by Preston in 1795, and nos. 24-26, again by Broderip in 1795. The Preston set was dedicated to Rebecca Schroeter and the second Broderip set, like the sonatas, to Therese Jansen. In no other area of Haydn's vast output is the gap between merit and reception as wide as it is in the keyboard trios; they are indeed "one of the best-kept secrets of Haydn's instrumental music."[8]

---

7. Michelle Fillion, "Intimate Expression for a Widening Public: The Keyboard Sonatas and Trios," in *The Cambridge Companion to Haydn* (Cambridge: Cambridge University Press, 2005), p. 136.

8. Fillion, p. 137.

CHAPTER 18

Back to Vienna: A Fruitful Final Harvest

1795-1802

Thanks to Heaven, a harmonious song was the course of my life.

from "Der Greis"
("The Old Man") by J. W. L. Gleim

Leaving London

Before Haydn left England, Anne Hunter lamented his departure in a poem. Haydn set it to music, but it was not published until 1806. It has since become one of his best-known songs.

> O tuneful voice I deplore,
> Thy accents, which I hear no more,
> Still vibrate on my heart.
> In echo's cave I long to dwell
> And still to hear that sad farewell
> When we were forced to part.

Many, including King George III and Queen Charlotte, tried to persuade Haydn to stay. But their entreaties were to no avail. Haydn was resolved to return to Vienna. He was tired and looking forward to a quieter life; and he still felt loyalty toward the Esterházy family. Dies wrote of his "hearty affection for the Esterházy princes, who had assured his daily bread and given him the opportunity to develop his musical talents." Continued freedom and the promise of greater fame and fortune could not entice him to stay in England. "His love and his gratitude" for the Esterházys "met every objection and moved him to accept the proposal of Prince Nikolaus with joy and to return to his fatherland" (p. 171).

After he had fulfilled his contract with Salomon, he delayed his departure for a couple of months, closing some business deals and prolonging his goodbyes as he made preparations for the return trip. When he departed from London on August 15, he sailed across the North Sea to Hamburg instead of crossing the Straits of Dover to Calais. According Dies he took this route "expressly to make the personal acquaintance of C. P. E. Bach" (p. 174). But Bach had died seven years before, and it seems impossible that Haydn would not have heard the news. More likely he altered his return trip because the war made it dangerous to travel through territory now ruled by France. In any case, he was able to visit Bach's daughter and express his esteem for her father from whom he had learned much.

Haydn Buys His Last House and Visits His First House

Between his two stays in London, Haydn had purchased a house in Gumpendorf, a quiet suburb of Vienna. His wife had discovered the house during his first stay in London. In a letter she asked him for money to buy it. He did not send her the money, but when he got back to Vienna, he found that the "still and solitary situation" of the house pleased him. He bought it and contracted to have "a story added to it" during his second stay in London (Dies, p. 133). But when he returned to Vienna, he had to find temporary lodging because the remodeling was not quite finished. When the house was ready he moved in and lived there with his wife until she died in 1800. When she had asked him to send her money for the house, she called it a "favor" that would provide her with a "house to occupy in the future when she was a widow" (Dies, p. 133). As it turned out, Haydn would live there for nine years as a widower.

Haydn paid a visit to Rohrau, his hometown, and saw the monument that the Count had recently erected in his honor. He also saw the house in which he was born. Profoundly moved at seeing both his humble birthplace and a monument proclaiming him "the deathless master of music," he stooped to kiss the threshold of the house.

Final Orchestral and Keyboard Compositions

On December 18, 1795, he put on a concert for the Viennese public. It included three of his symphonies, and Beethoven played his own Second Piano Concerto. More performances of his symphonies took place during the next year, but we know of no performances of his symphonies in Vienna in 1797. The musical infrastructure of impresarios and concert organizations in Vienna was much weaker than London's. Haydn must have realized that he would not be composing a series of "Vienna" symphonies. So his twelve "London" Symphonies turned out to be his final harvest in that genre. A more fruitful harvest is beyond imagining. He had long since secured his reputation as the "Father of the Symphony" and set a standard for the genre that has yet to be surpassed.

His only purely orchestral work after London was his famous Trumpet Concerto. Concertos were not a major part of Haydn's output, although he wrote several in the '50s and '60s. They are generally undistinguished, the exception being his brilliant Concerto for Cello in C Major (Hob. VIIb:1), written for Joseph Weigl, the principal cellist in the Esterházy orchestra. After the '60s, apart from the concertos for the King of Naples' unusual instrument and perhaps a lost concerto or two for baryton, Haydn wrote only three concertos — another cello concerto (Hob. VIIb:2), a very fine keyboard concerto (in D major, Hob. XVIII:11), and, in 1796, the Trumpet Concerto. He wrote it for a newly invented keyed trumpet that provided the means for playing the notes in the gaps between the notes of the overtone series, the only notes available on a natural trumpet.

As with his orchestral music, Haydn wrote no more solo keyboard sonatas after London. But his composition of keyboard trios, the larger part of his output stimulated by the flourishing London keyboard culture, overflowed into his early years back in Vienna. As noted in chapter 17, in 1794 and 1795 he published three sets of three keyboard trios (nos. 18-26), the last set dedicated to Rebecca Schroeter. He had also begun composition on his final set of three trios (nos. 27-29) while still in London, but since they were not published until 1797, it seems likely that he put finishing touches on them after returning to Vienna. He dedicated them to Therese Jansen, one of the finest professional keyboardists in London, who was also the dedicatee of the C major and E♭ major sonatas (nos. 50 and 52).

He composed his final keyboard trio (no. 30) in Vienna. It and the Jensen trios are the crowning glory of the genre — and its last chapter. Of course composition of trios for keyboard, violin, and cello did not die out, but composition of the eighteenth-century type of keyboard trio — more aptly described as accompanied keyboard sonatas — came to an end with Haydn.

Final String Quartets

Not so with the string quartet. After Haydn, string quartets would continue to be composed along the lines he established, and they would be measured by the standards he set. No doubt that would have been true even if he had not composed eight more quartets after he returned from London. But thanks to two music-loving noblemen, he composed the six quartets of Opus 76 and the two of Opus 77. Since Haydn rarely composed unless he had a specific reason, one wonders whether he would have composed these quartets without the commissions. But perhaps more germane to the question is his waning strength as he approached seventy years of age. His creativity was not waning, but his energy was. In fact, his energy gave out before completing the second commission. He finished only two instead of the usual set of six. He did begin what he might have intended to be a third quartet in the set, but he finished just two movements (now listed as Opus 103). When they were published in 1806, the publisher printed the first phrase from the poem "Der Greis" ("The old man") on the title page: "Hin ist alle meine Kraft, alt und schwach bin ich" ("Gone is all my strength, old and weak am I"). Haydn had set "Der Greis" to music as a vocal quartet in 1796, and in his later years he had the text and melody of the first phrase printed on his calling cards.

Even though Haydn already had had a long and busy career and was just coming off an exhausting time in London, Count Joseph Erdödy had enough confidence in his remaining creative powers and energy to commission six string quartets. A few years later Prince Lobkowitz showed the same confidence. Neither misplaced his confidence. Even though Prince Lobkowitz had to settle for a smaller quantity, the quality of each of the two in Opus 77 is equal to any of the six in Opus 76. In both collections Haydn was as good as ever. A Swedish diplomat wrote of the Opus 76 quartets that they are "more than masterly and full of new thoughts" (Landon 4, p. 255). And Charles Burney wrote that they seem like the products of "a sublime genius who had expended none of his fire before" (Landon 4, p. 483).

In these last eight (or eight and one-half) quartets, as in most of his

earlier ones as far back as Opus 20, there are "intellectual depths and freedom of form that are among the inexhaustible experiences of art."[1] Until
his physical power ran out, Haydn remained as inventive as ever regarding
colors and textures, and as sensitive as ever regarding all aspects of harmony, being especially adventuresome in making abrupt key changes and
in taking harmonic journeys to far-flung regions. His mastery of counterpoint was as complete as ever, his phrasing as subtle as ever, his sense
of form and balance and proportion as keen as ever, and his mind and
ears as alert as ever to the developmental possibilities of simple themes.
Tovey even went so far as to say that Opus 77, No. 2 "is perhaps Haydn's
greatest instrumental composition." And concerning the andante of the
unfinished Opus 103 he wrote: "With this Haydn bids us farewell, not in
terms of the quotation from his part-song, *Der Greis,* which he issued as
a visiting-card, complaining of age and weakness, but rather in terms of
the end of that song, which says, 'Thanks to Heaven, a harmonious song
was the course of my life.' Power and eternal youth remained in these last
and gentlest strains that the venerable creator of the sonata style allowed
his pen to record."[2]

The best-known of the eight late quartets is Opus 76, No. 3, the *Emperor* Quartet. The reason for its popularity is its second movement, a set
of variations on one of Haydn's greatest tunes, "Gott erhalte Franz der Kaiser" ("God save Franz the Kaiser"). The song originated at a time when
Austria and Britain were the only remaining allies against the French. An
Austrian government official commissioned Lorenz Leopold Haschka to
write the words and Haydn to write the music for an Austrian national
anthem. Haydn, fresh from England where he had been impressed by the
role that "God Save the King" played in engendering national pride and
loyalty, was eager to compose the music for an anthem that would play a
similar role in Austria. The tune he wrote served his country well. It was
Austria's national anthem until 1918, when the monarchy was abolished.
Unfortunately, in 1841 Haydn's music also became associated with the text
"Deutschland, Deutschland über alles" ("Germany, Germany over all"),
which the Nazis later conscripted. But it also served the church well as a
hymn tune, most notably for John Newton's "Glorious Things of Thee Are
Spoken" (1779):

1. Donald Francis Tovey, "Haydn's Chamber Music," in *The Mainstream of Music and
Other Essays* (Cleveland: Meridian Books, 1964), p. 64.
2. Tovey, "Haydn's Chamber Music," p. 64.

Glorious things of thee are spoken,
Zion, city of our God!
He, whose word cannot be broken,
Form'd thee for His own abode.
On the Rock of Ages founded,
What can shake thy sure repose?
With salvation's walls surrounded,
Thou may'st smile at all thy foes.

Haydn, I am sure, would have been pleased to find this text with his tune.

A Return to the Composition of Masses

None of Haydn's music discussed so far in this chapter was written for Prince Nicolaus II. Even though he had reestablished the Esterházy musical enterprise and brought Haydn back to active duty as Kapellmeister, his primary artistic interest was painting, not music, and the only compositions he required from Haydn were masses. In 1799 Haydn wrote, "My present young Prince issued the moderate command four years ago that in my old age I must compose a new mass once a year." Although Haydn mentioned no specific occasion for the masses, scholars assume that the prince ordered them for the name day of his wife, Princess Marie Hermenegild. He had married Marie, the former Princess of Liechtenstein, in 1783 when he was eighteen and she was fifteen. The marriage was a sham. Although Marie bore two sons and a daughter, Nicolaus carried on most of his procreating with others. David Wyn Jones describes him as "serially unfaithful and rampantly promiscuous, with one commentator suggesting that he had two hundred mistresses and one hundred children."[3] If the relationship between Nicolaus and Marie makes it seem unlikely that the masses were meant for Marie's name day, Jones suggests that Nicolaus made her name day "the focal point of extended celebration" in order to compensate for her "marital solitude."[4] We do know that the name day celebrations for Princess Marie were very elaborate, and we know that some, but not all, of Haydn's last six masses were first performed on her name day.

3. David Wyn Jones, *The Life of Haydn* (Cambridge: Cambridge University Press, 2009), pp. 177-78.
4. Jones, *The Life of Haydn*, p. 178.

Although the *Missa Sancti Bernardi* was first performed on Princess Marie's name day, Haydn composed it for the Feast of Saint Bernard of Offida, a seventeenth-century Capuchin monk beatified in 1795. The Capuchins celebrated his feast on September 11, which in 1796 happened to coincide with the Feast of the Most Holy Name of Mary, which was also Marie's name day.

The *Missa in tempore belli (Mass in the Time of War)* was first performed on December 26, 1796, at the ordination of a priest. It was performed again on September 29, 1797, but a new mass by another composer was performed on September 10, Marie's name day (a date that moved from year to year with the Feast of the Most Holy Name of Mary).

Haydn began composing the *Missa in angustiis (Mass in Troubled Times,* nicknamed the *Nelson Mass)* on July 10, 1798. Since he normally took three months to compose a mass, this was a late start for a work intended for performance in early September. The delay was probably due to Haydn's exhaustion after presenting the first performances of *The Creation* in April and May. Nevertheless, he finished by August 31, perhaps hurrying to have it ready for Marie's name day, September 9 that year. But if he was aiming to meet a deadline for the name day, he failed. Nine days was not enough time for copying parts and preparing a performance, so the first performance took place two weeks after the name day.

Haydn gave no names to his final three masses. He simply called them *Missa.* They have all acquired nicknames, but they give no hints about the occasion for which they were written. The *Theresienmesse* was probably performed on Princess Marie's name day in 1799, but there is no concrete evidence for this, and the reason for the nickname is unknown. Both the *Schöpfungsmesse (Creation* Mass) and the *Harmoniemesse (Wind-band* Mass) were first performed on Princess Marie's name day in 1801 and 1802 respectively. The *Creation* Mass got its nickname because Haydn quoted from *The Creation* in the "Gloria," and the *Wind-band* Mass got its nickname because of the prominence of the wind instruments.

Since Princess Marie's name day usually coincided with the Feast of the Most Holy Name of Mary, a feast instituted in 1683 to commemorate the victory at the Battle of Vienna, it would not be surprising if the masses performed on that day bore some relationship to war. But as we have seen, the two masses whose names or nicknames suggest a relationship to war were not first performed on that day.

The Missa in Tempore Belli

The *Missa in tempore belli* was composed in 1796 at a time when Austrian troops were under attack. Napoleon had defeated the Austrians at the Battle of Lodi and then drove them out of Lombardy. In addition, fighting was going on against the French for control of southern Germany. Jones describes the situation and its effect on church music.

> For the first time since the Turkish threat in 1683, Austria sensed an imminent invasion of its heartland. The resonance of 1683, when the infidel was repulsed, was a strong one in Austrian folk memory, commemorated every September in Vienna by a public procession and associated church service. Church music, especially masses and settings of the Te Deum that have unusually prominent parts for trumpets and timpani, sometimes invoked the threat and the triumph of war. Haydn's *Missa in tempore belli,* his *Missa in angustiis,* and Beethoven's *Missa Solemnis* are three well-known examples of the mingling of the bellicose and the religiously triumphant sentiments reignited during the Napoleonic period.[5]

In the *Missa in tempore belli,* musical references to war appear already in the introduction to the "Kyrie," when quiet supplication is interrupted by pounding timpani and trumpet fanfares. The surprisingly bellicose entrance in minor at "Pleni sunt coeli" in the "Sanctus" may also refer to the war, but the most obvious references to the war come in the last two movements, "Agnus Dei" and "Dona nobis pacem." The ominous, soft drumbeats and harsh trumpet blasts in "Agnus Dei" are frightening; they clearly signal war. Haydn told Griesinger that the timpani sound "as though one heard the enemy coming already in the distance" (p. 62). Then in the "Dona nobis pacem" the trumpets and timpani turn from bellicose to triumphant, anticipating victory and an answer to the prayer for peace.

The Missa in Angustiis

The *Missa in angustiis* does not have the kind of specific musical references to war that the *Missa in tempore belli* has, and neither does its title neces-

---

5. David Wyn Jones, *"Missa in tempore belli,"* in *Oxford Composer Companions: Haydn* (Oxford: Oxford University Press, 2009), pp. 240-41.

sarily refer to war. But of course its nickname, the *Nelson* Mass, suggests a connection with Lord Horatio Nelson, the famous British admiral. The popular notion that Haydn composed the *Nelson* Mass to celebrate Nelson's victory over Napoleon's fleet in the Battle of Aboukir Bay (also called the Battle of the Nile), August 1-3, 1798, cannot be true. By the time news of Nelson's victory reached Austria, Haydn had already completed the work. The nickname may have originated in connection with Nelson's visit to Eisenstadt in early September of 1800. According to Griesinger, Nelson "asked for a worn-out pen that Haydn had used in his composing, and made him a present of his watch in return" (p. 47), but there is no evidence for the oft-told story that Haydn performed the mass in Nelson's honor at the time of his visit. (But his second *Te Deum*, Hob. XXIIIc:2, may have been written for that occasion.) Nevertheless, from its stirring D minor opening to its joyful D major conclusion, the *Missa in angustiis* is a splendid piece of music that is fitting for "troubled times" whether the trouble is war or something else.

As musically splendid as Haydn's six late masses are, their reception has been mixed, largely because the character of the music is sometimes at odds with the text — a problem not unique to Haydn. "The eighteenth century," as Charles Rosen points out, "is filled with complaints of unnaturally brilliant and inaptly jolly settings of the *Kyrie* and the *Agnus Dei*."[6] The problem is made especially acute by the eighteenth-century preference for first and last movements that are fast and brilliant or fast and light, characteristics clearly at odds with the first and last words of the mass — "Lord have mercy" and "grant us peace." If, as Rosen suggests, the function of music vis à vis the text is simply celebrative, there is no problem. But if an expressive fittingness is required, "Kyrie" and "Agnus Dei" need to be "quiet and pleading in character."[7] Haydn was aware of the problem. He made some attempts to meet both the demands of celebration and expression, for example by beginning "Kyrie" with a slow, solemn section before launching into a lively allegro (just as he did in the first movements of most of his late symphonies). But they remain "uncomfortable compromises." For example, the "Kyrie" of the *Missa in tempore belli* "opens with an expressive Largo introduction, but the Allegro moderato that follows has passages that can only have sounded as trivial to Haydn's contemporaries as

6. Charles Rosen, *The Classical Style: Haydn, Mozart, Beethoven* (New York: W. W. Norton and Co., 1972), p. 367.

7. Rosen, p. 367.

they do to us today."[8] And just as Haydn's juggling of two opposing musical functions fails to convince, so does his explanation that the disconnect is the result of his being a joyful Christian. "I prayed to God not like a miserable sinner in despair but calmly, slowly. In this I felt that an infinite God would surely have mercy on his finite creature, pardoning dust for being dust. These thoughts cheered me up. I experienced a sure joy so confident that as I wished to express the words of the prayer, I could not suppress my joy, but gave vent to my happy spirits and wrote Allegro above the *miserere, etc.*" (Dies, p. 139).

His sincerity cannot be doubted, but the expressive disconnect between music and text remains.

The Creation

Fortunately, shortly before his composing days were over, Haydn was given a religious text that lent itself perfectly to his greatest gifts as a composer. While in England, inspired by Handel's oratorios, he began to think of composing an oratorio. He asked his friend and colleague François Hippolyte Barthelemon for advice concerning a subject for an oratorio. Barthelemon picked up a Bible and said, "There, take that, and begin at the beginning" (Landon 4, p. 117). As it turned out, that is what Haydn did — quite coincidentally. Just before he left England, he received a libretto on the subject of the Creation written by an unknown English author who had probably intended it for Handel. We do not know why Handel did nothing with it — or even if he received it. It probably came to Haydn via Salomon. Haydn took the libretto with him back to Vienna. Baron van Swieten, who had first introduced Haydn to Handel's oratorios back in the '80s, was as enthusiastic as Haydn about the project. Swieten translated the original English libretto into German, and then, after Haydn had composed the music to the German text, he adapted the original English text to fit the music. The score was published in 1800 with both the German and English texts set to the music.

The Creation is divided into three parts. (See the Appendix for an outline of the entire oratorio.) Part I tells of the first four days of Creation, Part II of days five and six, and Part III of Adam and Eve in the Garden of Eden. The core text of Parts I and II comes from the Creation story in Genesis 1 and

8. Rosen, p. 369.

2:7. Each day begins with a secco recitative in which one of the three soloists (each representing an angel) tells, directly from Genesis, what God did that day. Their proclamation of God's creative act is followed by two types of response: first, amazed and delighted description (accompanied recitative or aria); then, grateful praise (chorus). Books VII and VIII of Milton's *Paradise Lost* were the source of inspiration for some of the response texts, and nos. 12, 13, and 27 are from the Psalms. Although each day includes all three components — proclamation, description, and praise — the musical structure of each day varies considerably. Only the second and fourth days follow the "typical" structure of secco recitative (proclamation), accompanied recitative or aria (description), and chorus (praise).

Part I

Part I begins with one of Haydn's greatest challenges — an instrumental depiction of chaos — which resulted in one of his greatest achievements. Just as the disordered elements in the dark void struggled for form before God spoke, so do the empty C octave at the beginning and the disordered musical elements that follow struggle for sonata form and the "light" of C major tonality. Both the cosmic and the musical struggle are futile until God speaks a creative word: "Let there be light." The blazing C major chord on "light" is the greatest surprise in all of Haydn's music, just as light devouring darkness at God's word was the greatest surprise in the creation story.

The telling of God's act on Day One is followed by an aria with chorus in which description and praise are combined. The tune the choir sings on the words "A new created world" is one of Haydn's simplest, and yet most profound. Like Donald Tovey "I am proud to ally myself with the company of persons who are as completely bowled over by it as by anything in Bach's B minor Mass."[9]

Day Two illustrates the "typical" structure, and Day Three follows with what might be called a double version of the typical structure: act — description/act — description — praise. The double structure is due to the two parts of God's act on that day — the creation of bodies of water and dry land. In addition Day Three has a recitative that introduces the cho-

---

9. Donald Francis Tovey, *Essays in Musical Analysis,* vol. 5, *Vocal Music* (London: Oxford University Press, 1968), p. 127.

rus of praise. Day Four follows, again with the typical structure. Although Haydn gave it no special structure, he did underscore its special position as the end of Part I by framing it with two of the highlights of the oratorio — the orchestral depiction of the sunrise at the beginning, and at the end, the splendid and ever-popular chorus celebrating cosmic order, "The heavens are telling the glory of God." The chorus not only concludes Day Four; it is also the climax of praise that marks the end of the creation of inanimate things.

Part II

Both of the days in Part II have variants of the double structure. Day Five has the creation of fish and birds, but there is a different reason for its double structure. God's words on this day include the command, "Be fruitful." So Haydn omitted description of the fish. Instead he composed an arioso for God's words (uniquely scored for violas I and II, cellos I and II, and string basses). That is followed by an introduction to a trio in which the angel soloists contemplate God's work prior to the angelic chorus of praise.

The sixth day — the creation of animals and humans — has the most elaborate structure of all for two reasons: it includes the creation of humans, and it meditates on the whole of God's "glorious work." So after the description of animals (no. 21) there is another aria (no. 22) that briefly summarizes the whole and introduces the creation of Adam.

> Now heav'n in fullest glory shone;
> earth smiles in all her rich attire.
> The room of air with fowl is fill'd,
> the water swell'd by shoals of fish;
> by heavy beasts the ground is trod.

But for all its glory, "the work was not complete."

> There wanted yet that wond'rous being,
> that grateful should God's pow'r admire,
> with heart and voice his goodness praise.

After this introduction, the creation of Adam is presented in the normal pattern of proclamation (no. 23) and description (no. 24), but the third component, praise, is enlarged considerably. First, it is preceded by an introductory recitative (no. 25), which turns our attention back to the whole with the words from Genesis 1:31 — "And God saw ev'ry thing that he had made; and behold, it was very good," and an allusion to Job 38:7 — "and the heav'nly choir, in song divine, clos'd the sixth day." This is followed by the expected chorus of praise. But there is more. After the chorus, the three angels meditate on God's power and mercy in the words of Psalm 104:27-30. Then the angel chorus returns with the previous chorus's words and music ("Achieved is the glorious work"). But soon the chorus goes on to a glorious climax with new words ("Glory to his name forever") and new music (a mighty fugue).

Part III

The story from Genesis 1 finished, the librettist turned to Books IV and V of *Paradise Lost* for the picture of Adam and Eve in Eden in Part III. With just six numbers, it is by far the shortest of the three parts. It has a double structure like the fifth and sixth days, but God's glorious work has already been completed, so the first component of the pattern, God's act, is missing. Instead it begins with an accompanied recitative whose function is both descriptive and introductory. As usual in Haydn's descriptive recitatives, the orchestra depicts the words instrumentally before they are sung. Here a ravishingly beautiful flute trio accompanied by pizzicato strings depicts the "rosy mantle" of "morning young and fair" and the "pure harmony" that descends "from the celestial vaults" upon the newly created earth. Then the recitative (sung by Uriel) turns our attention to the "blissful pair" who will utter "a louder praise of God," and invites all the angels to join them: "Then let our voices ring, united with their song!" Indeed they do! Adam and Eve, the angel choir, and all creation join in singing what Tovey called the greatest movement that Haydn ever wrote!

After this one cannot help but think the rest can only be anti-climactic and superfluous. It may be anti-climactic, but it is not superfluous. The human creature is unique in all creation. Genesis points out that uniqueness by telling us not only that Adam was created out of the dust of the earth on the same day as the animals, but also that God breathed into him the breath of life and made him in God's own image. For want of better terminology, we can say that human nature has a "high" and a "low" aspect, provided we do not denigrate the "low." Like everything else, God pronounced it good. So the next two numbers complete the picture of the human creature by showing its "low" aspect. Adam and Eve now sing by themselves to each other, not, as in their previous duet, to God with the angels. Their music is correspondingly "lower" — more earthy and folksy — without any suggestion that "lower" somehow falls outside of that which God pronounced good.

Theologian Helmut Thielicke wrote that Genesis "recognizes our earthy, beastly side." If *The Creation* ended with the great duet and chorus (no. 30), it would have presented a one-sided view of humans as (in Thielicke's words) "a spiritual being who somehow hovers above all that is creaturely." But by going on to nos. 31 and 32, it affirms the biblical view that "the whales, the sparrows, and Homo sapiens are all created together on the same sixth day of creation and thus included in a whole." Therefore the "struggle of nature also determines our human life, that we too are controlled by instincts and urges, needs and desires, just as are the birds and the beasts of the field." Haydn said and believed that "an infinite God would surely have mercy on his finite creature, pardoning dust for being dust." And he added, "These thoughts cheer me," just as Thielicke said he was cheered "beyond all measure" that "the Lord's Prayer does not pretend that we are only religious people, but that we have the urge to eat — again like the animals — that we must have our daily ration of bread."[10]

The picture of humanity completed, a final chorus of praise is in order. But first a small recitative precedes it — not to introduce it, but to give listeners a warning, a much-needed warning at a time when there was much "enlightened" optimism about human nature.

> O happy pair, and always happy yet,
> if not misled by false conceit,
> ye strive at more, as granted is,
> and more to know, as know ye should.

The Seasons

The Creation crowned Haydn's incredible career. After its enthusiastic reception, he was not looking for another big project. But Swieten was.

---

10. Helmut Thielicke, *How the World Began: Man in the First Chapters of the Bible* (Philadelphia: Fortress Press, 1961), pp. 64-65.

Buoyed by the great success of *The Creation*, he hoped for a sequel, and James Thomson's epic nature poem, *The Seasons*, gave him the idea for a new libretto. He completed it and persuaded a reluctant Haydn to set it to music. According to Griesinger, "Haydn often complained bitterly over the unpoetic text. When he came to the place *O Fleiss, o edler Fleiss, von dir kommt alles Heil!* [O industry, o noble industry, from thee springs every good!], he remarked that he had been an industrious man all his life, but that it had never occurred to him to set industry to music." Haydn even said that "the strain that composition of *The Seasons* cost him" was the reason for "the weakness that grew ever greater from this time" (p. 40). But despite Haydn's complaints about weariness and the weakness of his old age, *The Seasons* shows no sign of waning creativity. Carl Friedrich Zelter, a distinguished conductor, teacher, and composer, said it best when he wrote to Haydn, "Your *Seasons* is a work youthful in power and old in mastery" (Landon 5, p. 285). Haydn's mastery of the art of composition enabled him, at the end of his career, to create one of the great works of pastoral art of all time, a hymn of gratitude for the beautiful, hospitable world God made and placed us in.

The Seasons combines the pastoral with the topic of time. Much of the oratorio is given over to "painting" pastoral scenes — a farmer tilling and sowing, a summer storm, a hunt, a harvest celebration, women spinning by the fire, and the like. But the seasons are also an allegory of the passage of time and the stages of life. Throughout most of the oratorio allegory operates beneath the surface, but it becomes explicit at the end of winter in the aria "Behold, o weak and foolish man, the picture of thy life!" Bleak winter shows "at last the yawning tomb." But just as winter awakes to spring (as it did at the beginning of the oratorio), death, in the words of the last chorus, "awakes us to second life, from pain and death forever free." In Swieten's text this awakening — this salvation — comes through human effort. "Virtue," in Simon's final aria, is "our guide to happiness on high," and the final chorus includes a close paraphrase of Psalm 15.

> The heav'nly gates are lifting up;
>   the hallow'd mount appears,
>   and on its brow the holy tent where peace eternal dwells.
> Those gates to pass, who may proceed?
>   The man, whose life was incorrupt.
> The sacred mount, who may ascend?
>   The man, whose tongue spoke no deceit.

Within the tent, who shall abide?
He that to want and grief lent aid.

The chorus, like the Psalm, is in harmony with Christian theology only if it is heard in a Christological context. As a devout Christian, Haydn knew this. Although this context is missing in *The Seasons,* in the choral version of his *Seven Last Words of Our Savior on the Cross,* which he and Swieten made a few years earlier, it is explicit right from the opening movement: "For us and for our salvation Thy Son has shed his blood." Heard within that context, as Haydn no doubt did, the promise of a "second life, from pain and death forever free" can be affirmed with "Amens" and celebrated with the fanfares in what Tovey called "one of the most overwhelmingly energetic closes I have ever heard."[11]

---

11. Tovey, *Essays in Musical Analysis,* vol. 5, p. 161.

CHAPTER 19

Infirmity and Death

1803-09

*How often one might have liked to speak to Haydn in the last
years of his life the words of Agamemnon to Nestor:*

*The general burden of age weighs hard on thee. O gods!
Would that another bore it, and thou a youth shouldst go
forth!*

GRIESINGER

*I am no more use to the world. I have to be nursed and looked
after like a child. It's high time that God called me to Him!*

HAYDN

Finished and Unfinished Works and a Final Performance

When Haydn complained to Griesinger that composing *The Seasons* caused
"the weakness that grew ever greater" from that time on, it was not the first
time he referred to the problems of old age. In 1799 he had written to the
publisher Breitkopf:

> The older I get the more business I have to transact daily. I only regret
> that on account of growing age and (unfortunately) the decrease of my
> mental powers, I am unable to dispatch but the smallest part of it. Every
> day the world pays me compliments on the fire of my recent works, but
> no one will believe the strain and effort it costs me to produce them:
> there are some days in which my enfeebled memory and the unstrung

state of my nerves crush me to the earth to such an extent that I fall prey
to the worst sort of depression, and thus am quite incapable of finding
even a single idea for many days thereafter; until at last Providence re-
vives me, and I can again sit down at the pianoforte and begin to scratch
away again. (Landon 4, p. 468).

After that letter he did write an impressive *Te Deum* in 1800, and in
1802 he completed the *Harmoniemesse*. But other composition plans went
uncompleted. He finished two movements of the Opus 103 quartet by 1803
— he told Griesinger it was his "last child" (p. 47) — and then struggled
for three more years to compose the remaining movements before giving
up and having the two completed movements published.

Back in the mid '90s, he had ventured into what was a new genre for
him — partsong. He planned to write a set of twenty-four, and by 1796
he had completed nine of them. But then he composed only four more
before finally giving up on finishing the project. The thirteen completed
songs were published in 1803. Their contents are mixed and by various poets. They include, appropriately enough given the circumstances, J. W. L.
Gleim's "Der Greis" ("The Old Man"), whose first lines, as we have seen,
provided the postscript to the unfinished Opus 103 quartet. The published songs also include four texts by Haydn's favorite poet, Christian
Fürchtegot Gellert (1715-1769), whose *Geistliche Oden und Lieder* (1757) was
the source for texts of fifty-five songs by C. P. E. Bach and of the six songs
in Beethoven's Opus 48. The titles of the four Haydn chose to set reveal
their serious and religious content: "Betrachtung des Todes" ("Contemplation of Death"), "Wider den Übermut" ("Preserve Me from Insolence"),
"Aus dem Danklied zu Gott" ("From the Song of Thanks to God"), and
"Abendlied zu Gott" ("Evening Song to God"). The latter two, prayers to
God at the end of this earthly life, must have been especially meaningful
to Haydn as he approached the age of seventy. With his music carrying the
words of the devout Protestant poet, the devout Catholic Haydn prayed
(in "Abendlied"):

Herr, der du mir das Leben	Lord, you who have given me life
Bis diesen Tag gegeben,	up to this very day,
Dich bet ich kindlich an.	to you I pray like a child.
Ich bin viel zu geringe	I am much too unworthy
Der Treue, die ich singe,	of the faithfulness of which I sing,
Und die du heut an mir getan.	and which you show to me today.

Concerning the "Danklied" Carl Fridrich Zelter, a composer and conductor in Berlin, wrote to Haydn: "I do wish I could give you the pleasure of hearing your choruses sung here, and find edification in the peace, piety, purity and reverence with which they sing your beautiful chorus, 'Du bist's dem &c.' The best and finest youths of Berlin assemble here with their fathers and mothers, like a heaven filled with angels, praising in joy and honour the glory of Almighty God, and practicing the works of the greatest master the world has yet seen" (Landon 5, p. 285).

One other project occupied Haydn during the first half-decade of the nineteenth century — supplying accompaniments for folksongs. As previously noted, he first did some of this while in London. Back in Vienna, he did a lot more. In 1799, the Scottish publisher George Thomson contracted him to compose accompaniments to Irish, Welsh, and (mostly) Scottish folksongs — including songs by Scotch literary luminaries Robert Burns and Walter Scott. (Later Thomson would also contract Beethoven.) Haydn enjoyed this less taxing work and supplied some two hundred arrangements for Thomson and another sixty-five for William Whyte, a publisher in Edinburgh. Most, if not all, of them were done by 1804. Though they were all published under Haydn's name, he had assigned the composition of some of them to a couple of his students, Friedrich Kalkbrenner and Sigismund Neukomm.

Like his composing, Haydn's conducting ceased before the middle of the decade. On December 26, 1803, Haydn conducted the *Seven Last Words* in a charity concert for St. Marx hospital. It was his last public performance.

Visitors and Honors

Haydn received many visitors during his last years. Princess Marie Esterházy, who was especially fond of Haydn, visited him and even persuaded the prince to increase his stipend to offset medical expenses. On November 26, 1806, the prince wrote to Haydn: "My wife, the Princess Marie, has brought me your wish to receive six hundred gulden yearly from me besides the present emoluments, adding that its fulfillment would greatly quiet and content you. I hasten with pleasure to meet this opportunity to convey to you my esteem and friendship, impart to you herewith the assurance by which you will receive from my court treasury, which is being so notified at once, three hundred gulden half-yearly" (Dies, p. 165).

Of course many of his visitors were musicians. Among them were his students, his Esterházy musician friends, and some of the leading composers of the time such as Reicha, Clementi, Tomaschek, Cherubini, Hummel (now Konzertmeister for the Esterházys), and Weber. Weber wrote that he visited the "unforgettable Haydn" several times. "Except for the weaknesses of old age, he is still cheerful and in a good humour, speaks very gladly about his affairs and is especially pleased to talk to pleasant young artists: the real stamp of a great man" (Landon 5, p. 279).

Honors came to him from all over Europe, including Sweden, St. Petersburg, and Paris. When a French ambassador saw a gold medal presented to Haydn by the *Concert des Amateurs,* he said to Haydn, "You should receive not this medal alone but all the medals awarded in the whole of France" (Landon 5, p. 360). But Haydn seems to have been especially pleased by an award from close to home. The "twelve-fold golden citizens' medal" was given by the Vienna City Magistracy "as a small token of the gratitude felt by the poor male and female citizens of St. Marx" (Landon 5, p. 260). In response Haydn wrote: "When I endeavoured to help in support of old and impoverished citizens, by placing at their disposal my knowledge of the art of music, I esteemed myself very fortunate in having thus fulfilled one of my most agreeable duties, and could not flatter myself that the worthy Magistracy of the Imperial and Royal capital city would deign to bestow on me so distinguished a mark of their consideration, in return for my modest exertions" (Landon 5, p. 261).

Losses, War, and a Final Public Appearance

In 1805, word that Haydn had died went around England and France. Believing it to be true, Cherubini composed "Chant sur la mort de Joseph Haydn." The rumor turned out to be false. Haydn would linger on a few more years, but his brother Michael died the next year leaving Joseph as the last living sibling. Their older sister, Franziska, had already died in 1781, but the other three siblings died within in the half-decade before Michael's death.

During that half-decade the situation in Austria was becoming more precarious. In the fall of 1805, Napoleon's troops advanced along the Danube toward Vienna. They entered Vienna on November 12 after a peaceful surrender. Napoleon established his headquarters in the Schönbrunn Palace, only about two miles from Haydn's house in Gumpendorf. (Recall that as a choirboy Haydn had received a thrashing for climbing the scaffolding around that palace.) Napoleon would soon move on to defeat a coalition of Austrian and Russian troops at Austerlitz. This resulted in the Treaty of Pressburg, which required Austria to cede several of her territories to France. It also resulted in Emperor Francis II abdicating his title as Holy Roman Emperor; he was reduced to being Francis I of Austria.

Haydn's health and strength continued to decline, but for his seventy-sixth birthday a gala performance was planned. The Amateur Concerts would perform *The Creation* in the University Hall in Vienna. Antonio Salieri would conduct. Griesinger expressed surprise that Haydn, "considering his failing health," planned to attend. "Consideration for my health could not stop me," Haydn told him; and it did not (Landon 5, p. 358). On March 27, 1808, Haydn made his last public appearance. Prince Esterházy ordered a carriage to bring Haydn from Gumpendorf into Vienna. Princess Esterházy and other royalty and nobility were there to greet him. So, according to one source, was Beethoven. Dies tells us:

> The crowd was very large, so that a military guard had to see that order was kept. Now Haydn, sitting on an armchair, was borne along aloft, and at his entrance into the hall, to the sound of trumpets and timpani, was received by the numerous assemblage and greeted with the joyful cry, "Long live Haydn!" He had to take his place next the Princess Esterházy. Next to him on the other side sat Fräulein von Kurzbeck. The greatest nobility of that place and from afar had chosen their places in Haydn's vicinity. It was much feared lest the weak old man catch cold, so he was obliged to keep his hat on (p. 177).

And when Haydn felt a draft, Princess Esterházy put her shawl around him, and several other ladies followed suit.

Both Carpani and Griesinger report what happened when the music burst forth at the creation of light. Griesinger wrote: "At that point which is imperceptibly prepared, and which suddenly surprises one, progressing with the brightest and most splendid harmonies: 'And there was light!' the audience as usual broke into the loudest applause. Haydn made a gesture of the hands heavenward and said, 'It comes from there!' " (p. 49). Carpani, who was sitting close behind Haydn, describes the moment with more dramatic flair. Tears were "streaming down Haydn's pallid cheeks and as if overcome by the most violent emotions, raised his trembling arms to Heaven, as if in prayer to the Father of Harmony" (Landon 5, pp. 361-62).

The excitement and emotion proved to be more than Haydn could handle. He had to leave after "The Heavens Are Telling the Glory of God," the glorious chorus that concludes Part I. Two men carried him out in his armchair. When they reached the door he signaled for them to stop. "The porters obeyed," wrote Carpani, "and turned him round to the public; he thanked them with the usual gestures of acceptance, then, looking at the orchestra with the most intense expression, he raised his eyes and his hands to heaven, and with tears in his eyes he blessed his children" (Landon 5, p. 362).

Final Days

Napoleon's first conquest of Vienna had been peaceful, but his troops returned in 1809 when Francis I of Austria declared war on France in an attempt to regain some of the territory Austria had lost. In April 1809, Vienna had to defend itself against an invading French army. On the morning of May 10, the French moved into Vienna. Johann Elssler, Haydn's longtime copyist and servant, wrote about it in a letter to Griesinger. He and the cook were getting Haydn out of bed when four cannon shots "exploded one after the other, and really, we kept a ball that fell in the courtyard as a souvenir, because of these explosions the door to the bedroom blew wide open and all the windows rattled, our good Papa was shocked and cried in a loud voice, 'Children, don't be afraid, for where Haydn is, nothing can happen'" (Landon 5, pp. 385-86). On May 13, Vienna surrendered.

In the ensuing days, Elssler tells us, Haydn played his *Kayser Lied* three times a day. On May 24, a French officer visited him and sang the aria from *The Creation* that follows the creation of Adam.

> In native worth and honour clad,
> With beauty, courage, strength adorn'd,
> To heav'n erect and tall he stands
> A man, the Lord and King of nature all.

It was the last time Haydn heard someone perform his music.

On May 26, Haydn played the *Kayser Lied* for the last time. As usual, Elssler tells us, he played it "three times over, with such expression and taste, well! That our good Papa was astonished about it himself and said he hadn't played the Song like that for a long time." On the morning of the 27th, he was unable to get out of bed, "and so our good Papa didn't leave his bed any more." At 12:40 on the morning of May 31, 1809, "our good Papa went quietly and peacefully to sleep" (Landon 5, p. 386). He was buried the next day, and the following day Michael Haydn's Requiem Mass was sung for him. The turmoil of war, including disruption in the conveyance of news, resulted in sparse attendance at both of these events. But two weeks later, Mozart's Requiem was performed in Haydn's memory in the Schottenkirche. Such was the world's respect for Haydn that the large number who attended this performance even included many French officers.

> *Requiem æternam dona eis, Domine;*
> *et lux perpetua luceat eis;*
> *cum Sanctis tuis in æternum,*
> *quia pius es.*

CHAPTER 20

Music for Troubled Times

*I was guided by an implicit faith in God's goodness: and there-
fore led to the study of the most obvious and common things.
And in conclusion, I saw clearly, that there was a real valuable-
ness in all the common things.*

THOMAS TRAHERNE

"Can you sing?" [asked Denethor].

*"Yes," said Pippin. "Well, yes, well enough for my own peo-
ple. But we have no songs fit for great halls and evil times, lord.
We seldom sing of anything more terrible than wind or rain.
And most of my songs are about things that make us laugh; or
about food and drink, of course."*

*"And why should such songs be unfit for my halls, or for
such hours as these? We who have lived long under the Shadow
may surely listen to echoes from a land untroubled by it. Then
we may feel that our vigil was not fruitless, though it may have
been thankless."*

J. R. R. TOLKIEN

Held in High Regard

When Haydn died, his music was known and loved around the world. His biographer Carpani was not exaggerating when he said that Haydn's music "is performed at this day, from Mexico to Calcutta, from Naples to London, from the suburb of Pera to the saloons of Paris." An obituary published in the *Diario de México* heaped typical praise upon him. "All of the natural gifts that can possibly distinguish an artist are united in Haydn: fluency of invention, immense facility, boldness to expand the limits of his art, variety of resources which lend freshness to his compositions, and above all the most delicate taste that prevents him from passing those limits beyond which genius degenerates into extravagance."[1] During his lifetime Haydn achieved something no composer has achieved since. As Charles Rosen puts it: "There have been composers who were as much admired [by the musical cognoscenti] and others whose tunes were as much whistled and sung during their lifetimes, but none who so completely won at the same time the unquestioned and generous respect of the musical community and the ungrudging acclaim of the public."[2]

Diminishing Stock

For a short while after his death, Haydn's reputation and his music did more than linger. His nickname, "Papa," continued to express the same love and whole-hearted respect it had during his lifetime when it was used by Esterházy musicians and fellow composers — not the least of whom was Mozart. "Papa" was the "father" mentioned by the Vienna Tonkünstler-Societät when they awarded him lifelong membership for "his extraordinary merit as father and reformer of the noble art of composition." But during the generation after his death, his stock fell and "Papa" started to take on patronizing overtones. An influential early step in that direction was taken by E. T. A. Hoffmann in his 1813 essay, "Beethoven's Instrumental Music."[3] Haydn's symphonies, he wrote, "lead us into vast green woodlands, into a merry, gaily colored throng of happy mortals" — a world "be-

---

1. Quoted in Thomas Tolley, *Painting the Cannon's Roar* (Burlington, Vt.: Ashgate Publishing Company, 2001), pp. 20 and 21.

2. Charles Rosen, *The Classical Style: Haydn, Mozart, Beethoven* (New York: W. W. Norton and Co., 1972), p. 329.

3. The quotations from Hoffmann's essay in this paragraph are taken from *Strunk's*

fore the Fall." Mozart's music takes us deeper; it "leads us into the heart of the spirit realm." But Mozart, like Haydn, was merely a stepping stone for Beethoven. "Mozart and Haydn," wrote Hoffmann, were "the creators of our present instrumental music, were the first to show us the art in its full glory; the man who then looked on it with all his love and penetrated its innermost being is — Beethoven!" Haydn grasps "what is human in human life"; Mozart calls for the "superhuman." But it is Beethoven's music that "sets in motion the lever of fear, of awe, of horror, of suffering, and wakens just that infinite longing which is the essence of romanticism."

Certainly Hoffmann had high regard for Haydn, but his characterization of Haydn's music is one-sided. Daniel Chua's pithy retort could well be aimed at Hoffmann: "If you hear only happiness in Haydn, the joke is simply on you."[4] But there is a deeper problem than one-sidedness. Hoffmann's view of the history of music is evolutionary — "Ever further and further onward," he wrote.[5] He saw evolution in technical progress: "obviously, the new musicians far exceed the old ones in technical skill" (which is manifestly false in the case of Haydn and Beethoven). But beneath the surface of technical progress Hoffmann saw a deeper, spiritual evolution. As Carl Dahlhaus points out, Hoffmann "refused to consider technical progress without spiritual development." For Hoffmann, instrumental music was the "onward driving world spirit itself that has cast this splendor into the mysterious art of the newest age, an age working its way toward inner spiritualization." "Put bluntly," writes Dahlhaus, "Beethoven's symphonies are 'religious' music." They are the most advanced stage of the transformation of "a sharply defined Christianness" into "intimations of the 'wonders of the distant realm.'" Hoffmann made the Haydn-Mozart-Beethoven succession into an ideal example of the evolution toward "inner spiritualization," moving from "human" Haydn to "superhuman" Mozart and then to Beethoven — the one who "penetrated the inmost being" of the art that was the "onward driving world spirit" of the "age working its way toward inner spiritualization."

Hoffmann's art-religion was not new. The *Sturm und Drang* movement

---

Source *Readings in Music History,* rev. ed., vol. 6, *The Nineteenth Century,* ed. by Ruth A. Solie (New York: W. W. Norton and Co., 1998), pp. 152-53.

4. Daniel Chua, *Absolute Music and the Construction of Meaning* (Cambridge: Cambridge University Press, 1999), p. 216.

5. All the quotations from Hoffmann in this paragraph are taken from his 1814 essay "Old and New Church Music" as quoted in Carl Dahlhaus, *The Idea of Absolute Music,* trans. by Roger Lustig (Chicago: The University of Chicago Press, 1989), pp. 91-95.

contained a strand of it, and by the early nineteenth century it was in full bloom. Ludwig Tieck wrote: "For music is certainly the ultimate mystery of faith, the mystique, the completely revealed religion."[6] In 1830, Emile Barrault wrote: "Henceforth the fine arts are the religion and the artist is the priest."[7] Five years later Franz Liszt was prophesying that "art shall say: 'Let there be light.' "[8]

In a climate like that, it is no wonder that Haydn's stock diminished. When evolution is a ruling idea, forerunners quickly become "mere" forerunners. Even a forerunner like Haydn, who continued to be numbered among the masters, soon becomes an "old master," behind the times and irrelevant. As Robert Schumann complained, "Haydn's music has always been played here regularly; we can learn nothing from him. He is like a regular house-guest who is always welcome and respectfully received; but he no longer holds any deeper interest for our age."[9] (One wonders what his good friend Brahms might have said to that!) Interestingly, Schumann's statement reveals that Haydn's music was still "lingering on." The fact that the music of an old master was still being performed more than what Schumann thought was warranted is what prompted his peevish outburst. And however much the likes of Schumann were disturbed because too many people were spending too much time with the music of a less "advanced" composer like Haydn, it was more disturbing that they were not advancing "further onward" in humanity's spiritual evolution.

Time for a Resurgence of Appreciation

This is not the place to rehearse more than two centuries of Haydn reception. It goes without saying that Haydn's stock has had its ups and downs along the way and that the reasons are complex. Suffice it to say that in recent decades there has been a resurgence of interest and appreciation, especially among composers (*contra* Schumann's "we can learn nothing from him"), performers, and scholars. During his lifetime Haydn was admired

6. Quoted in Dahlhaus, *The Idea of Absolute Music,* p. 89.

7. Quoted in Conrad L. Donakoski, *A Muse for the Masses* (Chicago: The University of Chicago Press, 1977), p. 177.

8. Quoted in Piero Weiss and Richard Taruskin, *Music in the Western World* (New York: Schirmer Books, 1984), p. 367.

9. Quoted in James Garratt, "Haydn and Posterity" in *The Cambridge Companion to Haydn,* ed. by Caryl Clark (Cambridge: Cambridge University Press, 2005), p. 232.

and respected by all. Now he has regained a good measure of that respect from the professional musical community, but public acclaim still merely lingers relative to many of his successors.

The number of recordings available can serve as a rough-and-ready indicator of Haydn's current popularity relative to the other two members of Hoffmann's trio of composers. In three of four main genres — symphonies, chamber music, and solo piano — Beethoven is clearly in the lead, followed by Mozart, with Haydn, at a considerable distance, bringing up the rear in numbers of recordings. The only genre in which Beethoven does not come in first is opera, where Mozart is the clear leader. But Mozart's lead there is easily explained. Beethoven wrote only one opera, whereas Mozart wrote more than a dozen, including at least three that are among the best ever written. Hoffmann's evolutionary ranking of the three great classical composers still holds sway. Even apart from sheer numbers, Haydn's current status at the bottom of that hierarchy is indicated by the fact that his music, when it is programmed, is rarely placed last, the position usually reserved for the most "profound" or "important" work on the program.

But what does it matter? It matters because Haydn has something to offer that is sorely lacking in our world. To put it in language as seemingly naïve as what Haydn himself used, our world needs more art that makes it a happier place. As theater and music critic Terry Teachout observes, in the current art world "a considerable number of contemporary artists seem to think that art must be grim and/or preachy (preferably both). They have a point — up to a point. Tragic works of art tell disquieting truths that illuminate the darkest corners of the human condition. The trouble is that the world is already full of over earnest creatures who believe that great art can do nothing else. No one seems to have told them that art has another, equally important function." That function, he says, is "one that Goethe summed up pretty well when he said that it should be 'life-enhancing' and that Johnny Mercer hit dead center in 'Ac-Cent-Tchu-Ate the Positive': 'You've got to spread joy up to the maximum.' "[10]

Teachout quotes from a play by Arnold Bennett in which two of the characters are discussing one of their friends. "What's he done?" asks one. "Has he ever done a day's work in his life? What great cause is he identified with?" The other replies, "He's identified with the great cause of cheering us all up." That was Haydn's cause too. A few years before his death he wrote in a letter:

10. Terry Teachout, "The Smiling Genius," *Wall Street Journal,* July 24, 2010.

Often, when struggling against obstacles of every sort which opposed my labours: often, when the powers of mind and body weakened, and it was difficult for me to continue in the course I had entered on; — a secret voice whispered to me: "There are so few happy and contented people here below; grief and sorrow are always their lot; perhaps your labours will once be a source from which the care-worn, or the man burdened with affairs, can derive a few moments' rest and refreshment." This was a powerful motive to press onward, and this is why I now look back with cheerful satisfaction on the labours expended on this art. (Landon 5, p. 233)

But does not this play right into the hand of those who contend that Haydn's music is basically trivial, a mere diversion from the serious affairs of this world — pleasant, charming, humorous, and ultimately inconsequential? And maybe even worse than inconsequential. Is it not dishonest, painting as it does a false view of reality? Or a drug, deadening our senses to the way things really are?

Thomas Howard addresses these questions from within the framework of what he calls the "old myth" ("everything means everything") and the "new myth" ("nothing *means* anything").[11] He addresses them as they relate to poetry, but his discussion is equally applicable to music. In the new myth, poetry, if it is not of the "grim and/or preachy type" that Teachout talks about, "is a fanciful diversion, a charming way to escape briefly from the real business of life." For believers in the new myth, poetry is lying when it leads people "to believe that there are joy and naiveté and rhythm in life." For those so beguiled, the "whole experience of life will be a relentless dashing of all these notions." But believers in the old myth believe "what the human imagination suspects — that the formal disposing of common things may not be misleading." In the old myth, poetry (and I would add music) "knows that our attention is cudgeled by functional concerns morning, noon, and night, and it suspects that this is not the desideratum. But it does not call us away from the 'real' world of function into a garden of fancy that never existed anywhere." On the contrary, its "high office is to ransom us from thrall to the deadly myth that life is cluttered and obstructed by necessity, and to return us to life with

11. Thomas Howard, *An Antique Drum* (Philadelphia: J. B. Lippincott Co., 1969). The quotations in the following paragraphs come from pp. 55-56, 59, and 78-79. The book has also been published under the title *Chance of the Dance?*

the awareness that it is packed with glory." The same idea is contained in the title of another of Howard's books, *Splendor in the Ordinary*,[12] a title that would perfectly fit Haydn's collected works. Haydn, good Catholic that he was, no doubt had beliefs in harmony with the old myth. He would have understood and agreed with Father Andrew Greeley who said, "As Catholics, we find our houses and our world haunted by a sense that the objects, events, and persons of daily life are revelations of grace."[13] Haydn's spirituality was thoroughly Christian (catholic with clear Catholic accents), and his music reflects it as it reveals splendor in the ordinary and grace in the common.

Haydn's office as a composer was indeed high, but he carried it out humbly before his Creator in the service of his fellow creatures. Dutch theologian Abraham Kuyper saw art "as a gift of the Holy Ghost and as a consolation in our present life."[14] In that same vein Haydn said, "Consider me a man whom God has granted talent" (Griesinger, p. 55), and he strove to make his art "a source from which the care-worn, or the man burdened with affairs, can derive a few moments' rest and refreshment" (Landon 5, p. 233). His music gives rest and refreshment not as an escape from reality or as a drug that deadens our senses. Quite the contrary. His music awakens our senses to a deeper reality than the confusion, ugliness, and troubles that we see and experience on the surface of our daily lives. Hoffmann's idyllic characterization of Haydn's music was meant to represent an immature spiritual level. Rosen says that although Hoffmann's view that listening to Haydn is "like taking a walk in the country" is "a sentiment destined to make anyone smile today, yet it seizes on an essential aspect of Haydn," namely its "pastoral tone" with its "combination of sophisticated irony and surface innocence."[15] I would take that a step further. By leading us "into vast green woodlands, into a merry, gaily colored throng of happy mortals," Haydn's music is fulfilling art's "mystical task of reminding us of the beautiful that was lost and anticipating its perfect coming luster."[16]

One of Haydn's greatest works is the *Missa in angustiis (Mass in Trou-*

---

12. Thomas Howard, *Splendor in the Ordinary* (Wheaton, Ill.: Tyndale House Publishers, Inc., 1976).

13. Andrew Greeley, *The Catholic Imagination* (Berkeley: University of California Press, 2000), p. 1.

14. Abraham Kuyper, *Lectures on Calvinism* (Grand Rapids: William B. Eerdmans Publishing Co., 1961), p. 155.

15. Rosen, p. 162.

16. Kuyper, p. 155.

bled Times). His music as a whole is *musica in angustiis*. Listening to it gives us cause to rejoice because it is a revelation of grace, a case in point of the way things really are. It should prompt us to sing what Haydn regularly penned at the end of his scores:

LAUS DEO! — PRAISE TO GOD!

Outline of Haydn's Creation

Part I: Days One through Four

The First Day: Light

1. Einleitung/Introduction: orchestra   [The representation of chaos]

   Recitative: Raphael (bass)   [Gen. 1:1-4]
   Im Anfange schuf Gott Himmel und Erde
   In the beginning God created the Heaven and the Earth

2. Aria: Uriel (tenor) with chorus [Ref. to Gen. 1:5; then describes Satan's defeat]
   Nun schwanden vor dem heiligen Strahle
   Now vanished before the holy beams

The Second Day: Firmament and Division of Waters

3. Recitative: Raphael (bass)   [Gen. 1:6-7 + description]
   Und Gott machte das Firmament
   And God made the firmament

4. Chorus with Solo: Gabriel (soprano)   [The angelic choir hymns God's praise]
   Mit Staunen sieht das Wunderwerk
   The marv'lous work beholds amazed

The Third Day: Seas and Dry Land

5. Recitative: Raphael (bass)   [Gen. 1:9-10]
   Und Gott sprach: Es sammle sich das Wasser
   And God said: Let the waters

6. Aria: Raphael (bass)   [Description]
   Rollend in schäumenden Wellen
   Rolling in foaming billows

7. Recitative: Gabriel (soprano)   [Gen. 1:11]
   Und Gott sprach: Es bringe die Erde Gras hervor
   And God said: Let all the earth bring forth grass

8. Aria: Gabriel (soprano)   [Description; related to Gen. 1:12]
   Nun beut die Flur das frische Grün
   With verdure clad

9. Recitative: Uriel (tenor)   [Introduction of angel chorus; trope on Gen. 1:13]
   Und die himmlischen Heerscharen verkündigten
   And the Heavenly host proclaimed the third day

10. Chorus: [The angelic choir hymns God's praise]
    Stimmt an die Saiten
    Awake the harp

The Fourth Day: Sun, Moon, and Stars

11. Recitative: Uriel (tenor)   [Portions of Gen. 1:14-16]
    Und Gott sprach: Es sei'n Lichter an der Feste des Himmels
    And God said: Let there be lights in the firmament of heaven

12. Recitative: Uriel (tenor)   [Description; related to Gen. 1:16-19 (after Ps. 19:5)]
    In vollem Glanze steiget jetzt die Sonne
    In splendour bright is rising now the sun

13. Chorus with trio   [The angelic choir hymns God's praise (after Ps. 19:1-4)]
    Die Himmel erzählen die Ehre Gottes
    The heavens are telling the glory of God

Part II: Days Five and Six

The Fifth Day: Fish and Birds

14. Recitative: Gabriel (soprano)   [Gen. 1:20]
    Und Gott sprach: Es bringe das Wasser in der Fülle hervor
    And God said: Let the waters bring forth abundantly

15. Aria: Gabriel (soprano)   [Description]
    Auf starkem Fittige schwinget sich der Adler stolz
    On mighty pens uplifted soars the eagle aloft

16. **Recitative [and arioso]: Raphael (bass)**   [Gen. 1:21a and 22 elaborated]
    Und Gott schuf große Walfische
    And God created great whales

17. **Recitative: Raphael (bass)**   [Introduction to the angelic trio and chorus]
    Und die Engel rührten ihr' unsterblichen Harpfen
    And the angels struck their immortal harps

18. **Trio**   [Angelic trio contemplates the beautiful and manifold works of God]
    In holder Anmut stehn'n
    Most beautiful appear

19. **Chorus with trio**   [The angelic choir hymns God's praise]
    Der Herr ist groß in seiner Macht
    The Lord is great, and great his might

The Sixth Day: Animals and Man

20. **Recitative: Raphael (bass)**   [Gen. 1:24]
    Und Gott sprach: Es bringe die Erde hervor lebende Geschöpfe
    And God said: Let earth bring forth the living creature

21. **Recitative: Raphael (bass)**   [Description; related to Gen. 1:25]
    Gleich öffnet sich der Erde Schoß
    Straight opening her fertile womb

22. **Aria: Raphael (bass)**   [Description — but "the work was not complete"]
    Nun scheint in vollem Glanze der Himmel
    Now heav'n in fullest glory shone

23. **Recitative: Uriel (tenor)**   [Gen. 1:27 and 2:7]
    Und Gott schuf den Menschen
    And God created man

24. **Aria: Uriel (tenor)**   [Description]
    Mit Würd' und Hoheit angetan
    In native worth and honor clad

25. **Recitative: Raphael (bass)**   [Gen. 1:31]
    Und Gott sah jedes Ding
    And God saw ev'ry thing

26. **Chorus:**   [The angelic choir hymns God's praise]
    Vollendet ist das große Werk
    Achieved is the glorious work

27. Trio: [Meditation on the power and mercy of God; quotes Ps. 104:27-30]
    Zu dir, o Herr, blickt alles auf
    On thee each living soul awaits

28. Chorus: [The angelic choir hymns God's praise]
    Vollendet ist das große Werk
    Achieved is the glorious work

Part III: Adam and Eve in Eden

29. Recitative: Uriel (tenor)   [Depicts "morning young and fair" in Eden]
    Aus Rosenwolken bricht
    In rosy mantle appears

30. Duet: Adam (bass) and Eve (soprano) and chorus: [Adam, Eve, and the angelic
    Von deiner Güt', o Herr und Gott   choir praise God]
    By thee with bliss, o bounteous Lord

31. Recitative: Adam (bass) and Eve (soprano)   [Introduction to love duet]
    Nun ist die erste Pflicht erfüllt
    Our duty we performèd now

32. Duet: Adam (bass) and Eve (soprano)   [Love duet]
    Holde Gattin! dir zur Seite
    Graceful consort! At thy side

33. Recitative: Uriel (tenor) [Eternal happiness unless "false conceit" leads to fall]
    O glücklich Paar, und glücklich immerfort
    O happy pair, and always happy yet

34. Chorus with soloists: [Hymn of thanksgiving and praise]
    Singt dem Herren alle Stimmen!
    Sing the Lord, ye voices all!

Glossary

Antecedent: (See **Phrase**.)

Aria: A piece for solo voice accompanied by instruments, usually part of a larger work (e.g., opera, oratorio), and typically in a lyrical or virtuosic style with much repetition of words and phrases. It is often preceded by a **recitative**.

Arioso: (See **Recitative**.)

Arpeggio: A "broken" **chord**; that is, a chord in which the notes are sounded in succession rather than all together.

Binary form: A two-part form, both parts usually repeated. Binary form is essentially the **antecedent-consequent** principle at a higher structural level than the phrase. Fundamental to binary form is that its first section (A) is open (**antecedent**) and its second section (B) is closed (**consequent**). It can be diagramed ‖: A :‖: B :‖.

In some binary forms, the second section ends with a return to the first section which is then varied to have a closed ending. It is called **rounded binary** because the return of the first section "rounds out" the form. It can be diagramed ‖: A :‖: B A′ :‖. It is a binary form, not a **ternary form** because its first section is open.

Cadence (adj. **cadential**): The moment of resolution at the end of a musical phrase, usually achieved by standard melodic and/or harmonic formulas. Cadences are analogous to punctuation marks. Like them cadences have varying degrees of finality.

Canon: A type of **counterpoint** in which the parts enter successively and imitate the leading part exactly or with very minor changes.

Chord: Three or more notes sounding simultaneously. In traditional harmony, chords are built out of notes a third apart (e.g. C-E-G) and have well-defined functional relationships to each other, which give a series of chords a sense of progression towards a goal.

Chromatic: (See **Diatonic**.)

Coda, codetta: A section at the end of a piece after the regular sections of a standard form have been completed. The coda serves to solidify the conclusion. A codetta is an internal coda at the end of a section of the form.

Consequent: (See **Phrase**.)

Consonance (adj. **consonant**): A relative term that describes a stable, well-blended, sweet-sounding relationship between tones. (See **Dissonance**.)

Counterpoint (adj. **contrapuntal**): A musical **texture** in which two or more parts have essential melodic material simultaneously. (See **Homophony**.)

Development: The expansion of smaller musical units into longer spans by various means of repetition and transformation. Also the label given to a large section of **sonata form**.

Diatonic: Music that melodically and/or harmonically employs the normal, unaltered notes of the scale (or **key**) on which it is based (e.g., C-D-E-F-G-A-B). **Chromatic** music employs many or all of the altered notes as well (e.g., C♯, E♭, G♯, etc.). Increased chromaticism makes music more unstable and intense.

Dissonance (adj. **dissonant**): A relative term that describes an unstable, clashing, harsh-sounding relationship between tones. (See **Consonance**.)

Dotted rhythm: A jerky rhythm consisting of a long note followed by a short note (or group of notes). The long one is at least three times the length of the short one. At a slow to moderate tempo, dotted rhythms give music a stately, ceremonial character associated with the pomp and ceremony of a royal procession.

Exposition: (See **Sonata** [form].)

Fugue (adj. **fugal**): A type of composition based on a theme (called the subject). It typically begins with an exposition in which the subject is first presented alone and then enters in succession in the other parts. Throughout the piece the subject appears periodically in different parts, sometimes with overlapping entrances called **stretto**.

Homophony (adj. **homophonic**): A musical **texture** consisting of a melody with accompaniment, as opposed, for example, to a texture in which all the parts are more or less equal in melodic and rhythmic importance. (See **Counterpoint**.)

Key: (See **Tonality**.)

Ländler: A dance of Austria and southern Germany in three-four meter. Closely related to the **minuet** and later superseded by the waltz.

Minuet and Trio: The minuet was the most common dance of the late eighteenth century. It is in three-four meter and its tempo ranges from moderate to moderately fast. It became one of the standard movements (either second or third) in symphonies and string quartets. Often it was also a movement in keyboard sonatas and trios and other chamber music. When used in these genres it is typically coupled with another minuet called a **trio**. After the trio, the first minuet is repeated making simple **ternary** form:

‖ A (minuet) ‖ B (trio) ‖ A (minuet) ‖

Typically both the minuet and trio are either ternary or **rounded binary** in form.

Modulation: A change of **key**. (See **Tonality**.)

Motive: The smallest building block of a musical structure. It can be as small as two notes and is rarely larger than about six notes. It has a well-defined rhythmic and melodic identity that it retains even as it goes through various transformations.

Phrase: A musical unit that moves to a point of rest (see **Cadence**), analogous to a phrase, clause, or simple sentence in language. An **antecedent** phrase is open; it lacks a feeling of final closure. Typically what makes an antecedent phrase open is that it ends on a chord other than the **tonic** chord. (See **Tonality**.) A **consequent** phrase is closed; it feels complete. A consequent phrase gives the feeling of final closure by ending on the tonic chord.

Recapitulation: (See **Sonata** [form].)

Recitative — **secco, accompanied, arioso**: A piece for solo voice within a larger composition such as an opera or oratorio. The style is declamatory — recitation-like. Words are not usually repeated, there is usually just one note per syllable, and the rhythms and melodic inflections are close to those of oratorical speaking. Some, called **secco recitatives**, have only a bass and keyboard accompaniment. Others, called **accompanied recitatives**, include additional orchestral instruments. Some accompanied recitatives, called **ariosos**, tend toward **arias** in style by virtue of having some repeated words and phrases as well as a more lyrical style.

Rondo: Rondo form expands **ternary form**. Unlike **sonata form** which expands **rounded binary** form from within, rondo form expands ternary form by extension. Ternary form becomes rondo form when one or more contrasting sections (often called episodes) are added, each time followed by a return of the first section (often called the rondo theme) — for example, R - ep. 1 - R - ep. 2 - R.

Rounded binary form: (See **Binary form**.)

Scotch snap: Reversed **dotted rhythm**. The short note comes on the beat and the long note comes after the beat.

Sequence: Successive repetitions of a melodic motive or phrase at regularly higher or lower pitch levels.

Sonata (form): Sonata form, not to be confused with sonata as a genre (see below), is an expanded **rounded binary form**. It is expanded from within. That is, each of the main parts of a sonata form is considerably larger and more fully developed than the corresponding parts of a rounded binary form. In a sonata form the main parts have names that correspond to the parts of a rounded binary form as follows:

$\|$: A = exposition : $\|$: B = development $|$ A$'$ = recapitulation : $\|$

Sonata form is often described in terms of the number and order of the themes in the **exposition** and **recapitulation**. But neither number nor order of themes determines the form. The number of themes especially can vary considerably from one sonata form to another. What is determinant of the form is the **key** structure. The **exposition** (A) is always open ended (in this case it ends in a different key). The **development** (B) always brings the music back to the tonic ("home") key, either directly or, more often, by a longer, more circuitous route through many keys. The **recapitulation** (A$'$) begins and ends back "home" although there may be tonal digressions within it.

Sonata (genre): A multi-movement piece for solo instrument (e.g. keyboard sonata) or solo instrument with keyboard accompaniment (e.g. violin sonata). Not to be confused with sonata form. (See above.)

Stretto: (See **Fugue**.)

Syncopation: Accentuation off the beat or contradictory to the meter.

Ternary form: A three-part form. At its most basic it is simply diagramed A B A. Fundamental to ternary form (as to **binary form**) is the ending of its first section (A). In a ternary form, in distinction from binary form, the first section is closed. Therefore when it returns after the second section (B), it does not need to be changed because its ending is already closed.

In some ternary forms sections are repeated as they are in a rounded binary form: $\| \|$: A : $\| \|$: B A : $\| \|$. But although diagrams are almost identical, this ternary form differs from rounded binary in two ways. First, its first section has a closed ending. Second, the return of the first section is literal because its ending does not need to be altered in order to be closed.

Texture: By analogy with textiles, texture in music refers to the "weave" of the different musical "threads." The most basic aspects of musical texture are the number of parts and how they are related to each other in range, rhythmic activity, melodic shape, and function. (See **Counterpoint** and **Homophony**.)

Tonality: The pull or gravitation of musical sounds toward a central (or "home") pitch called the **tonic**. That pull enables tonal music to create a strong sense of departure and return ("coming home"). **Key** can be used as a synonym for tonality (e.g., the key of D = the tonality of D).

Tonic: (See **Tonality**.)

Trio: (See **Minuet and Trio**.)

Vamp: A simple accompaniment figure that can be repeated indefinitely until the melody comes in.

Works Cited

Abrams, M. H. *The Mirror and the Lamp.* Oxford: Oxford University Press, 1976.

Adams, John. *Diary and Autobiography of John Adams,* vol. 2. Ed. by L. H. Butterfield. Cambridge, Mass.: Harvard University Press, 1961.

Augustine, Saint. *Expositions of the Psalms,* vol. 3. Trans. by Maria Boulding, O.S.B. Hyde Park, N.Y.: New City Press, 2001.

Badley, Allan. "Hofmann, Leopold." In *Oxford Composer Companions: Haydn,* ed. by David Wyn Jones, pp. 156-57. Oxford: Oxford University Press, 2009.

Bartha, Dénes. "Haydn's Italian Opera Repertory at Eszterháza Palace." In *New Looks at Italian Opera: Essays in Honor of Donald J. Grout,* ed. by William W. Austin, pp. 172-219. Ithaca, N.Y.: Cornell University Press, 1968.

Begbie, Jeremy. *Music in God's Purposes.* Edinburgh: The Handsel Press, 1989.

Bernstein, Leonard. "Brahms: Symphony 4 in E Minor." In *The Infinite Variety of Music,* pp. 229-62. New York: Simon and Schuster, 1966.

Breuning, Gerhard von. *Memories of Beethoven: From the House of the Black-Robed Spaniards.* Trans. by Henry Mins and Maynard Solomon. Cambridge: Cambridge University Press, 1992.

Britten, Benjamin. *On Receiving the First Aspen Award.* London: Faber Music in association with Faber and Faber, 1978.

Brodbeck, David Lee. *Brahms: Symphony No. 1.* Cambridge: Cambridge University Press, 1997.

Brook, Barry S. "*Sturm und Drang* and the Romantic Period in Music." *Studies in Romanticism* 9 (1970): 269-84.

Brown, A. Peter. *Joseph Haydn's Keyboard Music.* Bloomington, Ind.: Indiana University Press, 1986.

————. "Musical Settings of Anne Hunter's Poetry." *Journal of the American Musicological Society* 47 (1994): 39-89.

————. "Notes on Haydn's Lieder and Canzonettas." In *For the Love of Music: Fest-schrift in Honor of Theodore Front on His 90th Birthday,* ed. by Darwin F. Scott, pp. 77-103. Lucca, Italy: Lim Antiqua, 2002.

————. "Song." In *Oxford Composer Companions: Haydn,* ed. by David Wyn Jones, pp. 366-71. Oxford: Oxford University Press, 2009.

————. *The Symphonic Repertoire.* Vol. 2, *The First Golden Age of the Viennese Symphony.* Bloomington, Ind.: Indiana University Press, 2002.

Brown, Marshall. "The Poetry of Haydn's Songs: Sexuality, Repetition, Whimsy." In *Haydn and the Performance of Rhetoric,* ed. by Tom Beghin and Sancer M. Goldberg, pp. 229-50. Chicago: University of Chicago Press, 2007.

Chua, Daniel K. L. *Absolute Music and the Construction of Meaning.* Cambridge: Cambridge University Press, 1999.

Clark, Caryl. "Haydn in the Theater: The Operas." In *The Cambridge Companion to Haydn,* ed. by Caryl Clark, pp. 176-99. Cambridge: Cambridge University Press, 2005.

The Collected Correspondence and London Notebooks of Joseph Haydn. Ed., trans., and annotated by H. C. Robbins Landon. Fair Lawn, N. J.: Essential Books, 1959.

Cooper, Barry. "Beethoven, Ludwig van." In *Oxford Composer Companions: Haydn,* ed. by David Wyn Jones, pp. 17-20. Oxford: Oxford University Press, 2009.

Dack, James. "Sacred Music." In *The Cambridge Companion to Haydn,* ed. by Caryl Clark, pp. 138-49. Cambridge: Cambridge University Press, 2005.

Dahlhaus, Carl. *The Idea of Absolute Music.* Trans. by Roger Lustig. Chicago: The University of Chicago Press, 1989.

Dies, A. C. *Biographische Nachrichten von Joseph Haydn.* Vienna, 1810. Trans. by Vernon Gotwals in *Haydn: Two Contemporary Portraits.* Madison, Wisc.: The University of Wisconsin Press, 1968.

Dittersdorf, Karl Ditters von. *The Autobiography of Karl von Dittersdorf Dictated to His Son.* Trans. by A. D. Coleridge. London: Richard Bentley and Son, 1896.

Donakowski, Conrad L. *A Muse for the Masses.* Chicago: The University of Chicago Press, 1977.

Edwall, Harry R. "Ferdinand IV and Haydn's Concertos for the 'Lira Organiz-zata.'" *The Musical Quarterly* 48, no. 2 (April, 1962): 190-203.

Fillion, Michelle. "Intimate Expression for a Widening Public: The Keyboard So-natas and Trios." In *The Cambridge Companion to Haydn,* ed. by Caryl Clark, pp. 126-37. Cambridge: Cambridge University Press, 2005.

Fux, Johann Joseph. *"Gradus ad Parnassum."* In *The Study of Counterpoint,* trans. and ed. by Alfred Mann. New York: W. W. Norton and Co., 1965.

Geiringer, Karl. *Haydn: A Creative Life in Music.* 3rd rev. and enlarged ed. Berkeley: University of California Press, 1982.

Goals of the International Opera Foundation Eszterháza. http://www.eszterhaza opera.com/index.php?p=2

Godt, Irving. "Marianna in Vienna: A Martines Chronology." *The Journal of Musicology* 16, no. 1 (Winter, 1998): 136-58.

Goethe, Johann Wolfgang von. *The Sorrows of Young Werther,* trans. by R. D. Boylan. Boston: Francis A. Niccolls and Co., 1902.

Greeley, Andrew. *The Catholic Imagination.* Berkeley: University of California Press, 2000.

Green, Rebecca. "A Letter from the Wilderness: Revisiting Haydn's Esterházy Environments." In *The Cambridge Companion to Haydn,* ed. by Caryl Clark, pp. 17-29. Cambridge: Cambridge University Press, 2005.

Griesinger, G. A. *Biographische Notizen über Joseph Haydn.* Trans. by Vernon Gotwals in *Haydn: Two Contemporary Portraits.* Madison, Wisc.: The University of Wisconsin Press, 1968.

Grout, Donald J. *A Short History of Opera.* New York: Columbia University Press, 1965.

Halbreich, Henry. CD Notes for *Joseph Haydn, Les sept dernières paroles de notre Rédempteur sur la Croix. Le Concert des Nations,* Jordi Savall, cond., Astrée ES 9935.

Harrison, Bernard. *Haydn: The 'Paris' Symphonies.* Cambridge: Cambridge University Press, 1998.

Heartz, Daniel. *Haydn, Mozart, and the Viennese School: 1740-1780.* New York: W. W. Norton and Co., 1995.

Hoffmann, E. T. A. "Beethoven's Instrumental Music." In *Strunk's Source Readings in Music History.* Rev. ed. Leo Treitler, gen. ed. Vol. 6, *The Nineteenth Century.* Ed. by Ruth A. Solie. New York: W. W. Norton and Co., 1998.

Holmes, E. "The Rev. Christian Ignatius Latrobe." *The Musical Times, and Singing Class Circular* 4/88 (September 1, 1851): 249-56.

Howard, Thomas. *An Antique Drum.* Philadelphia: J. B. Lippincott Co., 1969.

———. *Splendor in the Ordinary.* Wheaton, Ill.: Tyndale House Publishers, Inc., 1976.

Hsu, John. CD notes for *Haydn Divertimenti.* The Haydn Baryton Trio. DOR-90233.

Hughes, Rosemary. *Haydn.* The Master Musician Series, ed. by Stanley Sadie. London: J. M. Dent and Sons, Ltd., 1978.

———. *Haydn String Quartets.* Seattle: University of Washington Press, 1969.

Jones, David Wyn. "Eszterháza." In *Oxford Composer Companions: Haydn,* ed. by David Wyn Jones, pp. 93-95. Oxford: Oxford University Press, 2009.

———. "Freemasonry." In *Oxford Composer Companions: Haydn,* ed. by David Wyn Jones, pp. 106-107. Oxford: Oxford University Press, 2009.

Works Cited

————. *The Life of Haydn.* Cambridge: Cambridge University Press, 2009.

————. "*Missa in tempore belli.*" In *Oxford Composer Companions: Haydn,* ed. by David Wyn Jones, pp. 240-41. Oxford: Oxford University Press, 2009.

————. "Reception." In *Oxford Composer Companions: Haydn,* ed. by David Wyn Jones, pp. 323-25. Oxford: Oxford University Press, 2009.

————. "*Seven Last Words of Our Saviour on the Cross.*" In *Oxford Composer Companions: Haydn,* ed. by David Wyn Jones, pp. 359-61. Oxford: Oxford University Press, 2009.

Kelly, Michael. *Reminiscences.* Vol. 1. London: Henry Colburn, 1826.

Kuyper, Abraham. *Lectures on Calvinism.* Grand Rapids: William B. Eerdmans Publishing Co., 1961.

Landon, H. C. Robbins. *Haydn: Chronicle and Works.* 5 vols. Bloomington, Ind.: Indiana University Press, 1976-80.

————. "Haydn and Eighteenth-Century Patronage in Austria and Hungary." Presented at the Tanner Lectures on Human Values, Clare Hall, Cambridge University, February 25, 1983. http://www.tannerlectures.utah.edu/lectures/documents/Landon84.pdf.

————. *Haydn Symphonies.* Seattle: University of Washington Press, 1969.

———— and David Wyn Jones. *Haydn: His Life and Music.* Bloomington, Ind.: Indiana University Press, 1988.

The Letters of Mozart and His Family. Trans. by Emily Anderson. New York: Macmillan, 1962.

Levy, Kenneth. *Music: A Listener's Introduction.* New York: Harper and Row, 1983.

Lewis, C. S. *The Abolition of Man.* New York: The Macmillan Co., 1985.

————. *The Allegory of Love.* New York: Oxford University Press, 1958.

————, ed. *Essays Presented to Charles Williams.* Grand Rapids: William B. Eerdmans Publishing Co., 1966.

————. *Studies in Words.* Cambridge: Cambridge University Press, 1967.

Loesser, Arthur. *Men, Women, and Pianos.* New York: Simon and Schuster, 1954.

MacPherson, James. *Fragments of Ancient Poetry.* Facsimile of the 1st edition of 1760. Los Angeles: William Andrews Clark Memorial Library, University of California, 1966.

Marshall, Robert. *Mozart Speaks: Views on Music, Musicians, and the World.* New York: Schirmer Books, 1991.

McVeigh, Simon. "Quartet." In *Oxford Composer Companions: Haydn,* ed. by David Wyn Jones, pp. 293-315. Oxford: Oxford University Press, 2009.

————. "Symphony." In *Oxford Composer Companions: Haydn,* ed. by David Wyn Jones, pp. 398-414. Oxford: Oxford University Press, 2009.

Mongrédien, Jean. "Paris: The End of the Ancien Régime." In *Man and Music: The Classical Era,* ed. by Neal Zaslaw, pp. 61-98. Englewood Cliffs, N.J.: Prentice Hall, 1989.

Morrow, Mary Sue. *German Music Criticism in the Late Eighteenth Century.* Cambridge: Cambridge University Press, 1997.

Mraz, Gerda. "Eisenstadt." In *Oxford Composer Companions: Haydn,* ed. by David Wyn Jones, pp. 75-78. Oxford: Oxford University Press, 2009.

———. "Esterházy, Prince Nicolaus I." In *Oxford Composer Companions: Haydn,* ed. by David Wyn Jones, pp. 87-89. Oxford: Oxford University Press, 2009.

Niemetschek, Franz Xaver. *Leben des K. K. Kapellmeisters Wolfgang Gottlieb Mozart.* Trans. by Helen Mautner. In *Mozart: The First Biography.* New York: Berghahn Books, 2007.

Ratner, Leonard G. *Classic Music: Expression, Form, and Style.* New York: Schirmer Books, 1980.

Rice, John A. *"L'isola disabitata."* In *Oxford Composer Companions: Haydn,* ed. by David Wyn Jones, p. 213. Oxford: Oxford University Press, 2009.

Roscoe, Christopher. "Haydn and London in the 1780s," *Music and Letters* 49, no. 3 (1968): 203-12.

Rosen, Charles. *The Classical Style: Haydn, Mozart, Beethoven.* New York: W. W. Norton and Co., 1972.

Sisman, Elaine. "Haydn, Shakespeare, and the Rules of Originality." In *Haydn and His World,* ed. by Elaine Sisman. Princeton: Princeton University Press, 1997.

———. "Haydn's Theater Symphonies." *Journal of the American Musicological Society* 43, no. 2 (Summer, 1990): 292-352.

———. "Variation." In *Oxford Composer Companions: Haydn,* ed. by David Wyn Jones, pp. 422-25. Oxford: Oxford University Press, 2009.

Sutcliffe, W. Dean. *Haydn: String Quartets, Op. 50.* Cambridge: Cambridge University Press, 1992.

Taruskin, Richard. *The Oxford History of Western Music.* Vol. 2, *Music of the Seventeenth and Eighteenth Centuries.* Oxford: Oxford University Press, 2005.

Teachout, Terry. "The Smiling Genius: Emmanuel Chabrier, Music's Master of Good Cheer." *Wall Street Journal,* July 24, 2010.

Thielicke, Helmut. *How the World Began: Man in the First Chapters of the Bible.* Philadelphia: Fortress Press, 1961.

Till, Nicholas. *Mozart and the Enlightenment.* New York: W. W. Norton and Co., 1993.

Tolley, Thomas. *Painting the Cannon's Roar.* Burlington, Vt.: Ashgate Publishing Co., 2001.

Tovey, Donald Francis. *Essays in Musical Analysis.* Vol. 1, *Symphonies.* London: Oxford University Press, 1965.

————. *Essays in Musical Analysis.* Vol. 5, *Vocal Music.* London: Oxford University Press, 1968.

————. "Haydn's Chamber Music." In *The Mainstream of Music and Other Essays,* pp. 1-64. Cleveland: The World Publishing Co., 1959.

Traherne, Thomas. *Centuries.* Wilton, Conn.: Morehouse Publishing, 1985.

Vignal, Marc. "Paris." In *Oxford Composer Companions: Haydn,* ed. by David Wyn Jones, pp. 266-67. Oxford: Oxford University Press, 2009.

Waldorff, Jessica. "Sentiment and Sensibility in *La vera costanza.*" In *Haydn Studies,* ed. by W. Dean Sufcliffe, pp. 70-119. Cambridge: Cambridge University Press, 1998.

Webster, James. "The Falling Out of Haydn and Beethoven: The Evidence of the Sources." In *Beethoven Essays: Studies in Honor of Elliot Forbes,* ed. by Lewis Lockwood and Phyllis Benjamin, pp. 3-29. Cambridge, Mass.: Harvard University Department of Music, 1984.

————. *Haydn's "Farewell" Symphony and the Idea of Classical Style.* Cambridge: Cambridge University Press, 1991.

Weiss, Piero, and Richard Taruskin, eds. *Music in the Western World: A History in Documents.* New York: Schirmer Books, 1984.

Wheelock, Gretchen A. *Haydn's Ingenious Jesting with Art.* New York: Schirmer Books, 1992.

Will, Richard. "When God Met the Sinner, and Other Dramatic Confrontations in Eighteenth-Century Instrumental Music." *Music and Letters* 78, no. 2 (May 1997): 175-209.

Wordsworth, Dorothy. *Recollections of a Tour Made in Scotland A.D. 1803.* 3rd ed. Edinburgh: David Douglas, 1844.

Youngren, William H. "The Operas of Haydn." *Atlantic* 252 (September, 1983): 110-15.

Index of Names, Places, and Terms

Abel, Carl Friedrich, 167-68
Abrams, M. H., 86-87, 268
Accademia Filarmonica (Bologna), 22
Adams, John, 175, 268
Albrechtsberger, Anton, 31
Albrechtsberger, Johann Georg, 31
Allegri, Gregorio, 13
Amadeus (film), 88
Amateur Concerts, Vienna, 248
Amateurs, 135, 136, 142, 158, 173, 175, 178, 220
Anfossi, Pasquale, 116
Archbishop of Salzburg, 83
Artaria (publisher), 138, 141, 148, 149, 156, 158, 160, 161, 162, 174, 176
Ascot, 205
Ashe, Andrew, 226
Auenbrugger, Katharine and Marianna von, 138, 141
Augustine, Saint, 51-52, 268
Augustinerkirche (Vienna), 73

Bach, Carl Philipp Emanuel, 20-21, 103, 155, 229, 245
Bach, Johann Christian, 167, 169
Bach, Johann Sebastian, 152, 167, 178, 238
Badley, Allan, 268
Bareikis, Robert, 85
Baroque, 35, 40, 41, 45, 51, 72, 88, 100, 104, 125-26, 137, 193
Barrault, Emile, 254

Bartha, Dénes, 112, 268
Barthelemon, Caecilia Maria, 221
Barthelemon, François Hippolyte, 237
Baryton, 54, 56, 65-68, 84, 100, 113, 230
Bath, 222
Battle of Aboukir Bay, 236
Battle of Kolin, 54
Battle of Lodi, 235
Battle of the Nile, 236
Battle of Vienna, 2, 234
Beck, Franz, 88
Beethoven, Ludwig van, 4, 5, 51, 52, 56, 84, 97, 109, 132, 142-43, 149-50, 163, 186, 206-7, 208, 230, 235, 245, 246, 248, 252-53, 255
Begbie, Jeremy, x
Bennett, Arnold, 255
Berlin, 124-25, 135, 155, 199, 246
Bernstein, Leonard, 224
Bertie, Willoughby, 167
Binary form, 36, 153, 202
Blair, Hugh, 86
Bland, John, 162
Boccherini, Luigi, 88, 126
Bonn, 186, 206
Boyé & Le Menu (publisher), 176
Boyer (publisher), 167, 168-69. *See also* Boyé & Le Menu
Brahms, Johannes, 34, 105, 144, 163, 178, 183, 224, 254
Brassey, Nathaniel, 188

Breuning, Gerhard von, 4
Bristol, 222
Britten, Benjamin, 101
Broadwood, John, 226
Brodbeck, David Lee, 34
Broderip. *See* Longman & Broderip
Brook, Barry, 87
Brown, A. Peter, 57, 60, 128, 132, 133, 157, 173, 200, 220-21
Brown, Marshall, 157-58
Burgtheater, 28, 122
Burke, Kenneth, 117
Burney, Charles, 11, 100, 137, 189, 218, 231
Burns, Robert, 246

Calais, 186-87, 229
Caldara, Antonio, 13
Campioni, Carlo Antonio, 125
Cannabich, Johann Christian, 125
Canon (canonic), 95, 104
Carpani, Giuseppe, 39-40, 194, 248-49, 252
Castrato, 16, 23
Charles VI (Emperor), 10, 11
Charlotte (Queen of England), 228
Cherubini, Luigi, 247
Chua, Daniel, 125-26, 253
Church of Saints Philip and James (Hainburg), 7
Cimarosa, Domenico, 116
Clark, Caryl, 120
Clavichord, xiv, 102
Clementi, Muzio, 226, 247
Coleridge, Samuel Taylor, xii, xiii
Concert de la Loge Olympique (Paris), 174-75, 176
Concert des Amateurs (Paris), 173-75, 247
Concert of Ancient Music (London), 189
Concert Spirituel (Paris), 174, 183
Cone, Edward T., 154
Cooper, Barry, 207

Dack, James, 29, 72-73
Dahlhaus, Carl, 253-54
Diderot, Denis, 119
Dies, A. C., xiv, 4, 5, 6, 7, 14-15, 16, 18-20,

21, 24, 27, 28, 33, 44, 82, 114-15, 186, 191, 197, 208, 210, 223, 228, 229, 237, 248
Dittersdorf, Ditters von, 24, 88, 125, 147
Divertimento, 38, 56, 57, 68, 99-100, 103, 106-7, 160, 181
D'Ogny, Claude-François-Marie Rigoley (Count), 175, 178
Donakowski, Conrad L., 269
Doni, G. G., 66
Dramma giocoso per musica, 113, 116-17, 119, 120
Dussek, Johann Ladislaus, 192-93

Edwall, Harry R., 179-80
Eisenstadt, 40-41, 42, 54, 74, 90, 122, 160, 185, 208, 236
Elssler, Johann, 249
Enlightenment, 88, 100, 119-20, 178
Erdödy, Joseph, 231
Erdödy, Ladislaus, 160-61
Esterházy, Anton (Prince), 121-22, 185, 196, 205, 206, 211
Esterházy, Joseph (Prince), 41
Esterházy, Maria Elizabeth (Princess), 184
Esterházy, Maria Octavia (Princess), 20
Esterházy, Marie Hermenegild (Princess), 233-34, 246
Esterházy, Michael (Prince), 41
Esterházy, Nicolaus I (Count), 40, 41
Esterházy, Nicolaus I (Prince), 53-56, 65-68, 69-70, 71, 72, 111, 112
Esterházy, Nicolaus II (Prince), 53, 233
Esterházy, Paul (Prince), 40-41
Esterházy, Paul Anton (Prince), 39-40, 41-42, 44-45, 49, 53, 54, 56, 65, 112-13, 114, 116, 119-20, 121, 136, 140, 156, 161, 164, 183, 184, 185, 186
Esterházy Palace (Eisenstadt), 40-41
Esterházy Palace (Vienna), 40
Eszterháza, xx, 54, 69-71, 82-83, 90, 111-13, 114, 120-22, 135, 183-85, 206

Farinelli, 23
Ferdinand IV (King of Naples), 179-80
Fertöd. *See* Süttör
Fillion, Michelle, 136, 139, 163-64, 226-27
Filz, Anton, 155

Forster, William, 149, 160-61, 169, 176
Fortepiano, xiv, 22, 23, 102, 103, 138-39, 158, 160, 162, 166, 185, 190, 192-93, 198, 199, 211, 223, 226, 245
Francis I (Holy Roman Emperor), 10
Francis (Franz) II (Holy Roman Emperor), 206, 232, 248, 249
Franck, Mathias, 6-8
Frankfurt, 205, 206
Frederick the Great (King of Prussia), 10, 54, 148
Freemasonry, 146-47, 166, 174-75
French Revolution, 82, 185, 208, 218
Friedrich Wilhelm II (King of Prussia), 148, 150
Fugue, 57, 72, 73, 79, 95, 108-9, 133, 135, 152, 170, 240
Fürnburg, Carl Joseph, 31-32, 160
Fuseli, Henry, 85
Fux, Johann Joseph, 11, 13, 14, 21

Galant, 32, 34, 50, 88-89, 100-101, 102, 136-37, 162
Gallini, John, 188, 192
Geiringer, Carl, 5, 12-13, 27, 81
Gellert, Christian Fürchtegot, 245
Genzinger, Maria Anna von, 183-84, 187, 191, 196, 199, 200
George III (King of England), 228
Gleim, J. W. L., 245
Gluck, Christoph Willibald, 24, 52, 87, 88, 192
Godt, Irving, 22
Goethe, Johann Wolfgang von, 85, 86-87, 107, 112, 130, 255
Goldoni, Carlo, 113
Grassalkovics, Anton (Prince), 186
Greeley, Andrew, 257
Green, Rebecca, 10, 41
Gregorian chant, 57, 64, 89
Griesinger, G. A., xiv, 6, 7, 8, 9, 13-15, 16, 19-21, 23, 24, 28, 31-34, 39, 43, 44, 82-83, 90, 114, 143, 164-65, 185, 208, 210, 225, 236, 242, 244-45, 248, 249, 257
Grotius, Hugo, 41
Grout, Donald J., 11
Gumpendorf, 229, 247-48

Habsburg, 2, 9, 15, 40-42, 115, 122
Hainburg, 2, 3, 6-8, 10, 15
Halbreich, Henry, 166
Hamburg, 229
Handel, George Frideric, 23, 108, 126, 170, 194, 237
Hanover Square Rooms (London), 168, 181, 192, 201, 211, 223
Harpsichord, xiv, 7, 13, 41, 102-3, 138, 160, 162, 193
Harrach, Carl Anton (Count), 4-5, 31
Hasse, Johann Adolph, 73-75
Haydn, Anna Maria Koller (mother), 3-6, 43, 83, 168, 206
Haydn, Caspar (great-grandfather), 3
Haydn, Catharina (grandmother), 3
Haydn, Elisabeth (great-grandmother), 3
Haydn, Franziska (sister), 19, 247
Haydn, Franz Joseph
    character, ix, 1, 5, 15, 16, 19, 20, 22, 24, 27, 31, 32, 33, 40, 71, 82, 83, 114, 128, 156, 199, 210-11, 222, 225, 242, 247, 256
    "Papa," ix, 90, 186, 207, 221, 249-50, 252
    religion, x, 5, 7, 15, 18, 31, 52, 83, 109-10, 159, 165-66, 168, 190, 218, 223, 225, 237, 241, 243, 245, 248, 257
Haydn, Johann Evangelist (brother), 6
Haydn, Maria Anna Keller (wife), 28, 33, 83-84, 168, 206, 229
Haydn, Mathias (father), 3-6, 16, 31, 43
Haydn, Michael (brother), 1, 6, 15, 83, 247, 250
Haydn, Thomas (grandfather), 3
Heartz, Daniel, 23-24, 32, 51, 64, 109
Herder, Johann Gottfried, 85
Herschel, William, 205
Hiller, Adam, 125
Hoboken, Anthony van, xiii, 103
Hoffmann, E. T. A., 252-53, 255, 257
Hofmann, Leopold, 156-57
Holcroft, Thomas, 188
Holmes, E., 189
Holy Roman Empire, 9, 10, 40, 205, 248
Hotel de Bouillon (Paris), 175
Howard, Thomas, 256-57
Howe, Richard, 222

Index of Names, Places, and Terms

Hsu, John, 66
Hughes, Rosemary, 105-6, 108
Hummel (publisher), 135
Hummel, Johann Nepomuk, 247
Hungary, 2-3, 10, 54, 69-71
Hunter, Anne, 220-21, 226, 228
Hunter, John, 208

Imbault (publisher), 176
Innocent XI (Pope), 3
Isle of Wight, 222

James I (King of England), 66
Jansen, Therese, 226, 227, 230
Jones, David Wyn, 67, 73, 119-20, 122, 147, 165-66, 219, 233, 235
Jones, William, 126
Joseph II (Holy Roman Emperor), 146, 155, 179, 208

Kalkbrenner, Friedrich, 246
Kant, Immanuel, 100
Kärntnerthor, 28, 44, 122
Keller, Georg, 28
Keller, Johann, 28
Keller, Maria Anna. *See* Haydn, Maria Anna Keller
Keller, Therese, 28-29
Kelly, Michael, 22, 147
Kenner und Liebhaber, 136, 139, 178
Kittsee, 54
Klinger, Friedrich von, 85
Kodaly, Zoltan, 131
Koller, Lorenz (maternal grandfather), 3
Kollonicz, Sigismund von (Cardinal), 12
Kozeluch (Kozeluck), Leopold, 152, 193
Kraus, Joseph Martin, 150
Kurzböck, Joseph, 157
Kuyper, Abraham, 257

Landon, H. C. Robbins, xiv, 7, 29, 34, 37, 49, 51, 57, 97, 131, 133, 173, 176, 178, 182-83, 188
Latrobe, Christian Ignatius, 83, 189-91
Lavater, Johann Caspar, 141
Le Gros, Joseph, 174
Le Menu. *See* Boyé & Le Menu

Lessing, Gotthold Ephraim, 112, 119
Levy, Kenneth, 225
Lewis, C. S., ix, xii, 108, 151
Liebhaber. See *Kenner und Liebhaber*
Lira arganizzata, 180, 192
Liszt, Franz, 51, 254
Lobkowitz, Franz Joseph (Prince), 231
Loesser, Arthur, 142
London, 23, 122, 132, 147, 149, 161, 162, 166, 167-69, 176, 178, 181, 186-89, 191-92, 194, 197-99, 205-6, 208-9, 210-11, 218-20, 223, 226-27, 228-29, 230-31, 246
Longman & Broderip (publisher), 149, 161, 176, 227
Louis XVI (King of France), 180, 218

MacPherson, James, 86
Mara, Madam, 188, 226
Maria Carolina (Queen of Naples), 179
Maria Theresa (Empress), 10, 12, 15, 22, 42, 54, 73, 82, 114, 179
Mariazell, 18-19, 41, 73, 164
Marie Antoinette (Queen of France), 218
Martinez, Marianna von, 22
Mary, Blessed Virgin, 3, 30, 41, 72-73, 74-81, 109-10, 234
Mattheson, Johann, 13-14, 21
Maximillian Francis (Elector of Cologne), 186
McVeigh, Simon, 106, 200
Metastasio, Pietro, 21-23, 24, 120
Milton, John, 238
Minuet, 24, 26, 32, 35, 36, 49-50, 56, 57, 63, 92-93, 95, 97, 101, 107, 109, 143, 153, 171
Molière, 112
Mongrédien, Jean, 173, 175
Morzin, Count von, 32-35, 38
Mozart, Leopold, 44, 138, 147-48
Mozart, Wolfgang Amadeus, 22, 32, 52, 56, 64, 88, 97-98, 100, 104, 116-17, 119, 122, 126, 142-43, 144-46, 147-48, 150, 169, 170, 184, 185, 186, 201, 206, 209, 250, 252, 253, 255
Mraz, Gerda, 41, 71
Music publishing, 31, 32, 41, 45, 55, 107, 121, 135, 136, 138, 140-41, 148, 149, 152, 156, 158, 160-63, 166, 167, 168-69, 173,

176, 183, 197-98, 220, 226, 227, 228, 230,
231, 237, 244, 245, 246

Napier, William, 197-98
Napoleon, 82, 235, 236, 247-48, 249
Napoleonic Wars, 82, 235, 236, 247-48, 249
Nelson, Lord Horatio, 234, 236
Neukomm, Sigismund, 1, 246
Neusiedler Sea, 54, 70
Newton, John, 232
Niemetschek, Franz Xaver, 145

Oedenburg, 185
Oettingen-Wallerstein, 185
Ossian, 86-87
Ovid, 115
Owen, John, 130
Oxford University, 179, 188, 194, 197

Palais des Tuileries (Paris), 175
Palestrina, 13
Paris, 32, 152, 166, 167, 169, 173-76, 178,
183, 185, 247
Pascha, Kara Mustafa, 2
Pasiello, Giovanni, 116
Passer, Franz, 112
Percy, Thomas, 85
Pergolesi, Giovanni Battista, 174
Pezzl, Johann, 10
Pianoforte. *See* Fortepiano
Piccini, Niccolo, 116
Pleyel, Ignaz, 55, 160-61, 199-200
Ployer, Barbara von, 209
Polzelli, Luigia, 206
Polzelli, Pietro, 206
Porpora, Nicola, 22-25, 29
Portsmouth, 222
Pressburg, 54, 98, 115, 127, 129, 186, 248
Preston & Son (publisher), 227
Professional Concert (London), 189, 199,
211
Pugnani, Gaetano, 125

Quintilian, 177

Rákóczy, Francis II (Prince), 3
Regnard, Jean-François, 112, 127

Reicha, Anton, 247
Reichardt, Johann Friedrich, 31
Reign of Terror, 218
Reutter, Georg von, 8, 12-16, 26
Rice, John A., 120
Richardson, Samuel, 116
Riesbeck, Baron von, 70
Rohrau, 1, 3, 4-5, 6, 7, 10, 18, 31, 41, 229
Romantic, 85, 88-89, 118, 126, 157, 226, 253
Roscoe, Christopher, 168
Rosen, Charles, 49, 88, 105, 142-43, 150-51,
154, 163, 217, 236, 252, 257
Rosetti, Francesco Antonio, 192
Rousseau, Jean-Jacques, 85
Royal Castle at Hampton Court, 222

St. Apollonia Chapel (Eisenstadt), 41
Saint-Georges, Joseph Bologne, Chevalier
de, 175-76
St. Marx Hospital, 246, 247
St. Michael's Church (Vienna), 22, 26
St. Paul's Church (London), 187
St. Stephen's Cathedral (Vienna), 8, 9-16,
17, 18, 21, 26, 156
St. Vitus's Church (Rohrau), 1
Salieri, Antonio, 88, 116, 248
Salomon, Johann Peter, 185-86, 187, 188,
191-94, 197, 199, 200-201, 205, 208, 211,
218, 219, 223, 229, 237
Sarti, Giuseppe, 116
Scarlatti, Alessandro, 13
Scherzo, 109, 143
Schiller, Friedrich, 85
Schottenkirche (Vienna), 250
Schroeter, John Samuel, 191
Schroeter, Rebecca, 188, 191, 211, 227, 230
Schumann, Robert, 254
Scott, Sir Walter, 246
Seilerstätte, 31
Seven Years' War, 31, 42, 54
Shakespeare, William, 112, 129, 130, 167-
68, 193-94
Sieber, Jean-Georges, 152
Silesian Wars, 10
Sisman, Elaine, 129-30, 193
Slough, 205
Sobieski, Jan, 2, 3

Sonata (form), 93, 133-34, 177, 224-25, 232, 238
Sonata (genre), xiii, 20, 31, 35, 38, 56, 63, 84, 88, 99, 102-3, 104, 105-6, 124, 136-37, 138-39, 141, 143, 160, 161-63, 176, 190, 226-27, 230-31
Sondheimer, Robert, 144
Spangler, Johann Michael, 17-18, 19, 26
Spenser, Edmund, ix
Stockhausen, Johann Christoph, 125
Storace, Nancy, 147, 192
Storace, Stephen, 147
Straits of Dover, 229
Strauss, Johann, II, 10
Sturm und Drang, 85-89, 90-91, 93, 95, 97, 118, 126-27, 135, 169, 170-72, 221, 253
Sutcliffe, W. Dean, 149-50
Süttör, 54, 69
Swieten, Baron van, 125, 166, 194, 210, 237, 241-43

Taruskin, Richard, 100
Tasso, Torquato, 121
Teachout, Terry, 255-56
Ternary form, 36, 133-34, 212
Thielicke, Helmut, 241
Thomson, George, 246
Thomson, James, 45, 242
Thun, Countess, 31
Tieck, Ludwig, 254
Till, Nicolas, 118-19
Toeschin, Joseph, 155
Tolley, Thomas, 66, 121
Tomaschek, Johann Wenzel, 247
Tomasini, Luigi, 44, 50, 68, 93, 107
Torricella, Christoph, 169
Tost, Johann, 152, 178
Tovey, Donald, 108, 110, 143, 152, 178, 232, 238, 240, 243
Traherne, Thomas, x
Treaty of Pressburg, 248
Twining, Thomas, 189

University Hall (Vienna), 248

Vanhal, Johann Baptist, 147

Variation form, 13, 57, 63, 103, 104, 132, 137, 176-77, 204-5, 209, 232
Vernet, Claude-Joseph, 85
Versailles, 69-70
Vienna, 2, 4, 8, 9-13, 15, 16, 18, 19, 22, 23, 25, 28, 31, 40, 41, 44, 54, 73, 113, 122, 145, 146-47, 152, 164, 166, 168-69, 176, 184-85, 187, 191, 194, 205, 206, 208-9, 211, 226, 228, 229, 230, 235, 237, 246, 247, 248, 249, 252
Vienna Tonkünstler Societät, 252
Vignal, Marc, 175
Vivaldi, Antonio, 11, 45, 50
Voltaire, 112

Wagenseil, Georg Christoph, 24, 99
Wahr, Karl, 112, 127, 129-30
Waldorf, Jessica, 118
Waldstein, Ferdinand Ernst von, 206
Wales, Prince Georg Augustus Frederick of, 188, 199
Walpole, Horace, 85
War of the Austrian Succession, 42, 54
Waverley Abbey, 222-23
Weber, Carl Maria von, 247
Webster, James, 51, 93, 152, 154, 207
Weigl, Joseph, 44, 68, 122, 230
Weinzierl Castle, 31
Werner, Gregor, 42, 45, 54-55, 56, 65, 66, 71, 74
Westminster Abbey, 194
Wheelock, Gretchen, 125, 128-29, 151
Whyte, William, 246
Will, Richard, 52
Windsor Castle, 205
Wolf, Hugo, 224
Wordsworth, Dorothy, xii

York, Duchess of, 188
York, Duke Frederick of, 188
Young, Edward, 86
Youngren, William, 117

Zelter, Carl Friedrich, 242, 246
Zwettl, 72

Index of Haydn's Works

Andante and Variations in F Minor, 209

Baryton Trios, 67-68, 84, 100, 113

Canzonettas. *See* Songs, English
Concertos, 230
   baryton, 56
   Cello Concerto in C Major (Hob.
     VIIb:1), 230
   Cello Concerto in D Major (Hob.
     VIIb:2), 230
   Double Concerto for Organ, Violin,
     and Orchestra, 29
   lira organizzata, 180-81
   Organ Concerto in C (Hob. XVIII:1),
     29
   Sinfonia Concertante, 200, 201
   Trumpet Concerto, 230

Folksong Arrangements, 68, 197-98

Gott erhalte Franz der Kaiser, 232, 249

Keyboard Sonatas, 31, 38, 56, 84, 99, 102-6,
   136-39, 226-27
   No. 2, 103
   No. 6, 103
   No. 9, 103
   No. 14, 162
   Nos. 18-20, 103
   No. 20, 105-6, 139
   Nos. 21-26, 136

No. 23, 136
Nos. 27-32, 136-37
No. 27, 137
No. 31, 137
No. 32, 137
No. 33, 136, 137
No. 34, 136, 137
Nos. 35-39, 136, 138, 139
No. 35, 139
No. 36, 139
No. 37, 137, 139
No. 38, 137, 139
No. 39, 139
Nos. 44-47, 103
No. 46, 103-5
Nos. 50-52, 226
No. 50, 230
No. 52, 230
Keyboard Trios, 160-64, 227, 230-31
   No. 2, 161
   Nos. 3-5, 160
   Nos. 6-8, 161
   Nos. 9-10, 161
   Nos. 11-13, 162
   Nos. 15-17, 162
   Nos. 18-20, 227, 230
   Nos. 21-23, 227, 230
   Nos. 24-26, 227, 230
   Nos. 27-29, 230
   No. 30, 230

Masses, 15, 72-73, 164, 233-37

Harmoniemesse, 3, 234, 245
Missa Brevis in F, 15
Missa Cellensis (Mariazeller Mass), 164
Missa Cellensis in Honorem BMV, 72-73
Missa in angustiis, 234, 235-36, 257
Missa in tempori belli, 234, 235, 236
Missa Sancti Bernardi, 234
Schöpfungmesse, 234
Theresienmesse, 234
Motteto di Sancta Thecla, 55

Notturni for two *lira organizzate* and
    ensemble, 181, 182, 192
    Notturno in G Major (Hob. II:27), 182

Operas, 28, 55, 87, 112-21, 192
Acide, 55, 112
Armida, 121, 160
Der krumme Teufel, 28
Der neue krumme Teufel, 28
Dido, 113
La canterina, 55, 87, 112
La fedeltà premiata, 116
La marchese nespola, 55
L'anima del filosofo, 192
La vera costanza, 116-20
Le pescatrici, 87, 113
L'incontro improvviso, 113
L'infedelta delusa, 113, 114
L'isola disabitata, 120
Lo speziale, 112-13
Orlando paladino, 121, 160
Philemon und Baucis, 113, 115
Oratorios, 237-43
The Creation, ix, 21, 46, 127, 206, 207,
    234, 237-41, 242, 248, 249, 259-62
Il ritorno di Tobia, 18, 113, 124, 146, 169
The Seasons, 14, 207, 241-43, 244

Salve regina in E Major, 29-30, 37
Salve regina in G Minor, 72, 83
"Seitenstetten" minuets, 26
Seven Last Words of Christ, ix, 164-66, 189,
    243, 246
Songs, English (Canzonettas), 220-21, 226
    "Despair," 221
    "Fidelity," 221

"The Mermaid's Song," 221
"O Tuneful Voice," 228
"A Pastoral Song," 221
"Pleasing Pain," 221
"Recollection," 220, 221
"To a Friend on New Year's Day," 220
"To My Daughter on Being Separated
    from Her on Marriage," 220
"To My Son at School," 220
"The Wanderer," 226
"William and Nancy," 220
Songs, German (Lieder), 155-59
    "Auf mein Vaters Grab," 159
    "Das strickende Mädchen," 158-59
    "Der Gleichsinn," 159
    "Die Verlassene," 159
    "Geistliche Lied," 159
    "Lob der Faulheit," 159
    "Mein Leben ist ein Traum," 159
    "Zufriedenheit," 159
Songs, German (Partsongs), 245-46
    "Abendlied zu Gott," 245
    "Aus dem Danklied zu Gott," 245, 246
    "Betrachtung des Todes," 245
    "Der Greis," 231, 232, 245
    "Wider den Übermut," 245
Songs, Scottish and Welsh (Folksong
    Settings), 168, 197-98
Stabat mater, ix, 72, 73-80, 83, 88, 174, 183,
    190
String Quartets, 30-31, 99-100, 106-10, 113,
    124-25, 141-44, 148-49, 152-54, 231-32,
    245
Opus 1, 32, 107, 167, 173
    No. 1, 32
Opus 2, 107
Opus 9, 107
Opus 17, 107
Opus 20, 100, 107-10, 135, 141, 144, 145,
    232
    No. 2, 108-9
    No. 5, 108, 109, 170
    No. 6, 108, 109
Opus 33, 141-44
Opus 42, 148
Opus 50, 148-52
    No. 1, 150-51

No. 4, 151-52
No. 5, 151
Opus 54, 152-54
  No. 2, 152-54
Opus 55, 152
Opus 64, 152, 192
Opus 71/74, 209, 211, 212
Opus 76, 231-32
  No. 3, 232
Opus 77, 231-32
  No. 2, 232
Opus 103, 231-32, 245
Symphonies
No. 1, 34
No. 3, 35
Nos. 6-8, 44, 57, 131
No. 6 *(Le matin)*, xi, 45-50, 51
No. 7 *(Le midi)*, 50-51, 52
No. 8 *(Le soir)*, 51-52
No. 9, 56
No. 12, 56
No. 13, 56, 61, 63-64
No. 15, 35-37
No. 20, 35
No. 21, 56, 57-60
No. 22 *(Philosopher)*, 56, 57
No. 26 *(Lamentatione)*, 89
No. 30 *(Alleluia)*, 56, 57
No. 31 *(Horn Signal)*, 56, 57, 61-63
No. 32, 35
No. 33, 35
No. 34, 56
No. 37, 34, 35
No. 39, 56, 89
No. 40, 57
No. 43 *(Mercury)*, 97
No. 44 *(Trauer)*, ix, 89, 93-97
No. 45 *(Farewell)*, 89-93, 97, 127, 133, 175
No. 46, 97
No. 47, 97-98, 145
No. 48 *(Maria Therese)*, 97, 114
No. 49 *(La passione)*, 89
No. 50, 131
No. 51, 131, 132
No. 52, 89
No. 54, 131

No. 55 *(Schoolmaster)*, 132
No. 57, 131, 132-33
No. 60 *(Il distratto)*, 127-29, 130, 131
No. 62, 135, 145
No. 63 *(La Roxelane)*, 132, 135
No. 64 *(Tempora mutantur)*, 129-30
No. 65, 131, 132
No. 67, 131, 133
No. 70, 57, 132, 133-35
No. 71, 135
No. 72, 56, 57, 63
No. 73 *(La chasse)*, 132, 135
No. 74, 135
No. 75, 132, 135, 145
Nos. 76-78, 168
No. 78, 169, 170-71
Nos. 79-81, 169
No. 80, 169, 171-72
Nos. 82-87 *(Paris)*, 173
No. 82 *(L'ours)*, 176
No. 83 *(La poule)*, 169, 171-73, 176
No. 84, 176, 177
No. 85 *(Le reine)*, 176, 177
No. 86, 176, 177
No. 87, 176
Nos. 88-92, 178
No. 88, 178
No. 90, 193
No. 92 *(Oxford)*, 178, 193, 194-95
Nos. 93-104 *(London)*, 169
No. 93, 200-201
No. 94 *(Surprise)*, ix, 1, 200, 201-5, 211, 215, 218
No. 95, 192, 200
No. 96, 192, 200
No. 97, 200, 205
No. 98, 200, 201
No. 99, 209, 211-12
No. 100 *(Military)*, 211, 218-19, 223
No. 101 *(Clock)*, 211, 212-18
No. 102, 223
No. 103, 223, 224-26
No. 104, 223

Te Deum (Hob. XXIIIc:1), 55
Te Deum (Hob. XXIIIc:2), 236, 245